T0103572

SEPARATE LIVES

SEPARATE LIVES

Pankaj Bhattacharyya

PARTRIDGE
A Penguin Random House Company

Copyright © 2015 by Pankaj Bhattacharyya.

ISBN: Hardcover   978-1-4828-5100-7
               Softcover   978-1-4828-5099-4
               eBook   978-1-4828-5098-7

All rights reserved. No part of this book may be used or reproduced by any means, graphic, electronic, or mechanical, including photocopying, recording, taping or by any information storage retrieval system without the written permission of the author except in the case of brief quotations embodied in critical articles and reviews.

Because of the dynamic nature of the Internet, any web addresses or links contained in this book may have changed since publication and may no longer be valid. The views expressed in this work are solely those of the author and do not necessarily reflect the views of the publisher, and the publisher hereby disclaims any responsibility for them.

Print information available on the last page.

To order additional copies of this book, contact
Partridge India
000 800 10062 62
orders.india@partridgepublishing.com

www.partridgepublishing.com/india

About the Author

Pankaj Bhattacharyya is a 40 year old practicing ophthalmologist. Born in Shillong, he grew up in Arunachal Pradesh and Delhi, and studied medicine in Guwahati. Further training took him to London for some years. A proud highlander, he learns from the hills, the rains, the grey skies and the general quiet; and of course, loves the guitar, Einstein and steaming pork momos. He lives in Guwahati with his gynaecologist wife and son, and generates loads of respect from both every time he makes it to the gym or puts together a decent grill for dinner! Separate Lives is his first novel.

Acknowledgements

Upamanyu Chatterjee, for being that intangible force to sow in my head, through a process that bizarrely started 25 years ago and he has no reason to know, that every day lives of unspectacular people can become stories worth telling, and unspectacular people living such lives are capable of telling those stories.

Somnath Batabyal, for teaching me word economics and while telling me that I am not Salman Rushdie – well, at least not yet – shoving me towards writing a printable readable story. Som, thanks to you, I shaved 60,000 words off the original 150,000 words 'epic' that I made you suffer over cheap wine!

Anukriti Sharma – at Random House then – for being the first person to read 'Separate Lives' – 'Chronicles of Failure' then – and telling me that the effort was worthwhile, though not in so many words.

Nelson Cortez, Gemma Ramos and Sophia Park at Partridge India for making 'Separate Lives' come together. I salute you for every patient kick you laid on my backside to salvage me from my various distractions!

Tina, for being the rock, punching bag and reckless propellant of every cavalier wind beneath my wings. Hope to grow really old with you and see the world come to an end!

Ma and Baba, for being wonderful and for learning as I learnt.

All my teachers and all the educational institutes I was fortunate to be at, for giving me experiences and memories.

Wikipedia, for filling in the blanks.

Life, for allowing me my time alone.

Paul Simon, for singing the line: 'I'd rather be a forest than a street'.

* * * * *

To experiences and the power of fiction,
and
to Aaditya, best friend and the centre of everything

Smoking and consumption of alcohol are injurious to health

Prologue

Kajal looked at the mirror. The silver-grey tie knotted perfectly under the crisp collars of a new white shirt, he slipped his arms into the black jacket. He was risking being labelled overdressed but that's just how he was – attire was only an extension of his respect for the occasion. It was big. The Opening of his first solo exhibition. At Lisson, the premier art gallery in London's westend. Sid(dhartha) Tharanga, Sri Lankan-Brit and curator of Lisson, had been extravagant with his appreciation of Kajal's work and opined that great press was inevitable, even some commerce. Though neither was anything that Kajal was holding his breath upon. In fact, as a fresh wave of all that got to him just then, he felt his palms moisten and his body tighten with familiar misgivings. He knew he had come a long way but the unyielding darkness of his thoughts left him bemused.

Pulling the door of Armada Bed & Breakfast behind him, he stepped onto the wide side walk, sucked in the cold dark air on Gower Street once and started to walk towards Warren Street underground station. Two construction men, safe within high-visibility partitions, noisily worked a jack-hammer on the pavement across the street. In London, even the garbage is neat.

Pankaj Bhattacharyya

Singapore, Tuesday, 8th January, 2008, Around 11PM

The phone disconnected but Ramalingam's voice lingered in Q's head. Irreplaceable losses have a way of unnerving even when long anticipated. The impersonal hotel room only compounded the void. But Q had ceased being dramatic, educated by experience and age, which are not necessarily synonymous. From her eyes, however, she could not repudiate Dad's face from the last time she'd seen him. Only two days ago.

Q made two calls. First to her travel agent in Coventry. The news was that there was a Qantas flight to London within the next couple of hours and she'd have a place on it. The second call carried her silence to Delhi. Mama's quivering voice betrayed that she already knew, and that she was going through dealing with the same loss a second time. No double jeopardy clause protected her. In fact the second coming was more conclusive. Absolutely conclusive.

Q didn't bother getting dressed in any detail, and quickly stuffed her Samsonite. The Reception clerk was thankfully quick and handed her a couple of envelopes branded The Carlton, along with returning her credit card and smiling a have-a-nice-flight smile. At the bell desk, there was a blue cab ready to take her to the airport.

As the cab pulled away, Q sat back to realize that for once, she wasn't so overwhelmed by her otherwise morbid fear of flying.

Guwahati, Tuesday, 8th January, 2008, Around 9PM

The feeling cropped up suddenly some two hours earlier even as I fixed me yet another strong black coffee. Coffee had served truly well; it was heartening that such incomplex remedies still worked. And with each one of five brimming mugs, my body recovered to exterminate the nefariousness of the previous night a little bit more. Some birthday party it was!

I concede that I sway to the side of cautious double checks when leaving home, but this particular irksome suspicion was unusual. I couldn't stop blankly surveying my own home, restless that I had forgotten to pack something vital. Now, just what was it?

My books? – I couldn't be expected to pack entire wooden shelves. Equipment of my trade and the cartons of 'Physician's Sample' eye medicines? – Sentimental but indubitably unworthy. My guitar and my collection of music? My shoes? Now, I loved my footwear, and my French-cuffed shirts, but the time for such pursuits had left me behind. Then what the hell on earth was it? The business cards with the logo of the hospital I had ceased to belong to? My phone book with a life time of associates? My driving license? My passport? My coffee mugs? My whisky glasses? The leftover sausages in the fridge? The fridge itself?

As far as I could see, the red toilet bag had everything I needed for the trip – the three ampoules, two bottles of Ringer's Lactate, a couple of intravenous sets, disposable syringes and a tourniquet.

I had to eventually let the feeling be, for every minute thereafter threatened my chances of occupying the procured seat on the night bus to Dibrugarh. And anyway, when I was leaving an entire life behind, why on earth was I shitting my brains out over something that I had apparently forgotten to pack?

Mrs. Deka, my next door neighbour, answered the doorbell. The fingers on her right hand were soiled with yellow gravy and few clustered grains of steamed white rice, and she held it up by her face as she stood preventing my entry beyond the door without really meaning to. I knew her as the owner of an excellent heart, but she was given to overlooking minor courtesies. Her face broke into a questioning smile even as she continued to masticate on auto-pilot. I realized I was disturbing the family dinner but I did have to hand her my apartment keys. To her disinterested query about when I was expected to reclaim them, I could only suggest – "Soon."

Waiting for the elevator, I glanced at my varnished front door and the gun metal 5A. Halfway up the wall next to it stood a delineated rectangle within which the whitewash was whiter. The rectangle from where I had removed my wooden name plate.

* * * * *

BOOK ONE

Prelude to a Disease

1

I arrived back earlier this afternoon. London was a six months long hiatus and it took four good hours to sort out my apartment.

Until I drew all the shameful attention on to myself, I thought I was doing absolutely fine on the flight from Heathrow. Skimming the God of Small Things one more time. And my mind had navigated into the familiar incursion. Isn't the History House really Radley Place? The single parents, Ammu and Atticus. Scout's pink Sunday dress and petticoat, and Rahel's Airport frock with matching knickers. Velutha of the Paravan smell and Tom of the black skin. The God of Small Things and the Mockingbird. And I had concluded once again that no single story can ever be told like it is the only one.

But then standing by the galley, drinking extra whisky, I slipped into dissecting notions of success and failure with this equally sodden fellow. Both unrelentingly mulish, the conversation didn't take long to turn ugly. Eventually one of those motherly hostesses that only Air India can offer had to show us back to our seats.

But what did he mean by suggesting that I was living a farce? He doesn't even know me. He's wrong.

I did well in school, studied medicine and have gone on to become an eye doctor. I have a good job with this very posh, private hospital – posh not just on account of the granite floor and central air conditioning but because of the top notch service we tender. I own

1

a pleasant flat and drive a decent car. And I can play the guitar to hold an audience for a while.

I even have a passion – my community cataract surgeries. The whole process of screening entire villages, bringing the blind over to the hospital and performing free-of-cost surgeries on them. This delight defines my success. Now, just how many people can say that about their jobs? I cannot let anyone make me undermine that the entire purpose of London was only to get better at this skill. Yes, third world necessities fulfilled through first world training. But there's no denying that the west does most things better than us.

But I hate to have that guy still somewhere in my head. Had he grasped that I was sick with these misanthropic images gifted by London? But it is the shaking in my left hand which I'm beginning to fear more. I have a disquieting inkling that this whirlpool will eventually drag me into its dark depths, while I succumb like drifting pollen in a wayward breeze.

I am bewildered with what happened in London. And with each passing day, the surprise has vanquished the disease itself. It's amazing – and distressing – to see my world – full of strength and purpose – to see that world rattle and threaten to disintegrate. But I love to think that I have dealt with the worst of this tempest. Yes tempest, that's what I sometimes call it. At other times, though, I hate to accord it any status. I have this pressing need to reduce it to having been just an event. I'm angry when I cannot.

I'm sure this is not some hostile take-over of me. I'm back in Guwahati and sanity can't be too far behind. I have assigned myself a role in the lives of people with no eyes. And London was just a stepping stone. Towards the goal. How can I let anything come in the way? Least of all, my own weakness.

I'm feeling positive about tomorrow. A new beginning.

* * * * *

2

After walking fifteen twenty minutes benumbed by outrage, her mind and body started reclaiming Q. How could she have been drawn to and damaged by the same mirage once again? How could she have not known? When the thoughts came, it was like a dam breaking. Her legs melted with the agonizing heat of her own blood.

Searching desperately, she found her bearings. Soho Square, still bathed in pleasantness, was on her left. It seemed like only moments earlier that she had passed it. Her mind was then full of blissful anticipation. Jazz After Dark, another bit of London that belonged to Steve and her, had seemed the perfect place. The evening, the perfect moment. And the overpowering dreams that she had long been afraid to dream, the inevitable destiny.

Soho Square remained exactly the same. Only her life had changed. Once again.

Q walked on. Above her, the cloudless, starless, clear London night sky was black. She heard her heels resoundingly click the cobblestoned route of her retreat. She smelt urine from the corner by the noisy Spanish pubs with perpetually out-of-order washrooms. "You are impossible!" Steve had waited bemused while she had once released herself behind a postbox and a hoarding on Tottenham Court Road on one of their nights out. Q felt tears brimming over.

Finding herself at the head of Grafton Street, Q realized where her involuntary steps were taking her. Why was she going back to her room on a night like that? The familiar panic rose. But just as abruptly, she knew why. Doctor! Yes, the doctor. She needed me. Only I'd understand. Only I could help.

From her bag, Q pulled out the book. Steve's final gift. Far From the Madding Crowd. She turned the cover. In the light from a street lamp, she read 'Do what you will!' written in black ink on the first page. Steve's handwriting looked like a fossil. How easily he had settled for life with Q with a scribbled note on a book.

She knew where to find me. I never was any place else at ten in the night but my room. Just as she entered the YMCA building, she buried the book in a garbage bin.

————

Q. It's like a retarded candidate to be someone's name. Just that alphabet and that's all. But you couldn't misspell it. Not because it was difficult to misspell. Being just that one alphabet. You just couldn't call her anything else.

"What does it mean? I'm sorry but I have never before met anyone with that name," I had asked her, trying desperately hard to come across as smart and interesting that first evening I'd ever spent with her. "Too bad you don't know. It's an alternate spell and sound for Meera!" she had replied with characteristic flamboyance. Meera, that legendary admirer of Krishna.

I remember clearly the awful night I named her. I had managed to get myself unimaginably drunk and was tired from walking and running through what couldn't have been less than ten kilometers. And I had just killed her ghost! A suddenly-out-of-job preserver of life by profession was caught in an inescapable murder scenario with evidence strewn all over. It was the night when every minor, abstract hiccup was wiped clean by cataclysmic reality.

That night when I gave her the name, she had no voice or eyes or ears. She wasn't even an animal. She was just an object. A motif that defined a clan.

The first time I met Q, it was at her office in Guwahati. We record our surgeries to show at conferences. They need to be edited. To remain within the time allotted for the presentation. Or one may end up showing all the initial antiseptic cleaning while the time runs out before getting an incision in. Also helps the procedure look more professional when you've sawed off the occasional non-expert-like movements. Anyway. Q worked at this place where I took my videos to edit.

I had never interacted with Q. It had always been Prashant for my editing. Fine young man of about twenty five. Crisp, efficient and very professional. I took him out for a drink every time after we finished. And he was a good talk over the beer as well.

I arrived as scheduled. Kind of six on a darkening November evening. The eastern end of the globe had long ago exchanged sunlit evenings and dragged out romantic dusks for half four sunrises that meant absolutely nothing to late risers like me. I thought this really sucked, till I discovered London, the experience of whose winter makes a whole lot of crappy things on this earth seem like a blessing! Guwahati is nearly as east as it could be without losing all claims to being a part of India. That evening I was chasing a deadline: My video needed to reach Mumbai the day after.

The office was on the sixth floor of this commercial building which looked pretty empty at that hour. Most offices had closed for the day. But not the video editing types. They always had deadlines to meet.

I was to find out that Prashant was not in – he had had to rush to this television news channel where they needed urgent subtitling done for some 'Breaking News'.

5

I was kind of disappointed. I generally don't have too many expectations from people but I sometimes look forward to strange things from strange people. And I can even be sensitive in a silly way about it. I felt let down that Prashant was doing something else when he knew it was my appointed time.

But then he hadn't forgotten altogether. The arrangement was Q.

I have nothing against meeting new people. I avoid it while I can but, honestly, have nothing horribly against it. With work, though, I prefer a familiar hand.

As it turned out, I didn't send the video. Running a check the next morning, I realized there was a major inadequacy. Not something that Q did, or didn't, but something that I had overlooked. I couldn't send it like that and there was no time to sit over it again. But somehow I wasn't all that glum. I am usually a whole lot kinder with my own mistakes then I am with those of others'.

That was how I met Q. Quite by chance. Like the way I met her again, half way across the world. Quite by chance.

* * * * *

3

From where Kajal was, the only way was to keep climbing! Without looking back, or down. Or even up. It didn't make him awfully happy. Ma had taught him years ago to be careful with heights. And he had learnt through all the years to be scared of heights.

But it was not the time to stoke fears. Kajal had to keep climbing on that cell phone tower – three serpentine wooden ladders stacked to meet somewhere in the sky at the pinnacle of a pyramid. Every step he took was another moment to live.

People always said he had strong legs. "Genetic, otherwise they are the most difficult muscles to build," a trainer at his gym had commented, pointing to his drumstick-like calves.

He wasn't exactly dying thinking about it, but was irritated with the red cloak he was wearing. He remembered Ma having given it to him. To stay warm. But why would Ma give him something in red? He hated red. And at a time when his life depended on staying hidden, it made him stick out cruelly.

The ticking of his watch was the only sound that remained.

He had risen far above the ambulance sirens, the police sirens, the fire engine sirens. He liked the quiet. From his earliest memories, Kajal loved the quiet. Away from the queer utterances at home that collided with him in somnambulistic flight; from the scary sounds of defeat; from the cacophony of peril that every new term at school proffered; from the macabre tenor of alien celebrations that forced him to surrender. He always liked it quiet – at his dark brown desk, watching its polished top reflect the yellow light from the lamp. And the ticking of the clock by the bed was the only sound then. Like the colour of air, like the taste of water, the ticking heart-sound of the clock by the bed was the sound of quietness.

But why on earth was that watch on his left wrist ticking backward! No, he wasn't making a mistake. Flouting logical control, the hands were ticking gracefully backward.

Suddenly, a wave of horror rose to deliver a load of bilious acid to his mouth. It struck him that he couldn't feel his left hand. It was not there! The gallop of his breathing echoed in distant recesses of his body. His entire self shuddered with every seismic thrust of his heart.

But the ticking sound remained. The hand wasn't there but the watch was!

Kajal's mouth burnt. He longed for a drop of water. His tongue expectantly explored the lips but razor-like scales threatened to make it bleed.

He figured it was from all the climbing. So far from below, he was very cold and drained. And he had lost his left hand. He must have just lost it. Climbing for that long was daunting. He'd heard stories about how arms came off when people hung onto ladders for too long. Or even hung from a door frame at school. "Come and sit in your place. If you keep hanging like that your hands are going to come off your shoulders!" That is what his teacher had said. Kajal remembered clearly. He was five then. He had always wanted to cross-check with doctor Baba. But somehow he never did. His teacher had already told him, so what did he still want to know? Did he not trust his teacher?

Actually he didn't cross-check because he feared being ridiculed. He knew his imprudence was just under the surface – one dumb question would leave him exposed.

For the same reason he didn't chase a lot of other questions. Some of which burned in his head at almost all times. Like his name – he never asked Baba why the womanish label was picked to be his identity. "Your grandfather named you after the lush eyebrows you were born with, like they had been drawn with *Kajal*." Ma had told him. And every time someone jeered him after that day, Kajal would look at his eyebrows in the mirror, unable to fathom how the diminutive tentacles had managed to confiscate his life.

Alarm bells rang all over Kajal once again! He had come to terms with having lost his left hand, but just then he discerned that he wasn't climbing anymore. How could he have just stopped when his life depended on climbing?

Very rapidly, it became a colossal challenge to keep his vision clothed. He was being forced to open his eyes.

In the blue light – the kind you'd believe is copyrighted by horror flicks – silhouetted shadows took form. Morphing into and out of one another for what seemed like a long time. Kajal recognized his travel bag perched on the single cushioned chair in the room. On its arm rested the legless shape of his dark jeans, the steel buckle on the leather belt gleaming dully like a deformed incisor. Out in the corner, were his shoes where he had laid them neatly. Streaks of geometrically aligned light from the corridor outside outlined a door on the left, about ten feet away.

The blue mist that washed the room emanated from the cell phone charger. Kajal had bought it just days before leaving Guwahati. Not from the Nokia Store, but from that shop in Beltola called Little China where everything, from the fluorescent plastic brooms to dinner-sets to television video games, was 'Made in

China'. Including the cell phone charger with the UK pins Kajal would need in London.

In the last few years, even the balloons and cheap toys sold at temporary kiosks at *Durga Puja* venues in Guwahati have become 'Made in China'.

It was in 1962 that China had invaded the northeast of India. Surprised and grossly ill-prepared, the feeble response of the Indian army was easily brushed aside. Chinese troops overran the mountains of Arunachal Pradesh and were knocking at the gates of Assam. Nehru is famous to have said "My heart bleeds for the people of the northeast" or something to that effect while ordering retreat of the Indian army, leaving the citizen to somehow sort it out with the intruder. That one act by the great man remained etched in the hills, rivers, and general backwardness of the northeast for generations to come. It resonated in every drop of crude oil that left the rich drilling earth of Digboi and Duliajan. It was stamped on every bag of Assam tea that became India's proud export.

My grandmother told me years later what it was like to be thrust into backs of trucks to be repeatedly ferried behind ever receding lines of safety while struggling to protect her four children and fearing for my left-behind grandfather – men and luggage were not allowed on those trucks.

Then it all ended. Not thanks to awesome parleys but courtesy the whim of Zhou Enlai. He simply decided that he'd done enough to teach a dreamer with a red rose on a self-named *bandgala* jacket a lesson on where political poetry ended and brute force took over. India's northeast was relinquished by the conqueror and returned to the one who had sacrificed it with a 'bleeding heart'. But when did cracked mirrors ever come undone to innocence?

Thinking about it now, one cannot but pity China for wasting men and resources in 1962. Pilfering its production surplus to take over our markets is after all such a mess-less, drama-proof way of conquest!

Kajal closed his gritty eyes, sat upright and sighed. His heartbeat decelerated to the boring routine pace. He released his left hand from where he had been sleeping on it. It felt nothing when he touched it. However much he hated heights, he was disappointed he hadn't actually been climbing when he thought he was. Once again, he had achieved nothing.

The trip to Liverpool for the Biennale had been academically unfulfilling. It turned out to be a mere social extravaganza. "These Openings are integral to the art world," Liam, his tutor had said. The final straw was the replacement coach for the cancelled train that extended the journey back to London to six physically draining hours.

All else apart, he was nearly two months into the Fine Art course, and still hadn't been able to make himself at home. That same feeling. Was it in his destiny for things to never change? Yes, young though he was, he had increasingly started relying on things like destiny.

I wouldn't have known Kajal. I had no reason to. And as a thought, he was indeed a perplexing affliction. I should have known him more. There was a whole lot more to him, a contumacious voice kept telling me from within. But I failed to convince myself not to be fearful of him. I was afraid he'd grieve me even further. The anger I had grown to feel for him was subtle, but it gave me some comfort. Funny that I should live, and die, with him somewhere in my head even though I met him just that once. In London.

* * * * *

4

Q was twenty-six when I met her.

You wouldn't turn around and look at Q a second time if you saw her on the street but she looked good when she worked towards it. Over five foot half, she was a healthy slim. Her long black hair was most often left open, only sometimes tied to disburse a horse tail onto her back. She parted in the middle, and swollen curves of thick hair decorated her forehead like palatial archways. Her angular face gave her an air of confident intelligence. She had beautiful feet; just a wonderful shape with perfectly shaped toes and perfectly shaped unpainted toe nails. And when she walked, there was this careful sway like she feared tipping over.

These were the easy bits. It was trying to get inside her mind that took a rewinding and forwarding route. And I kept getting specks of her wrong which pushed me into a dangerous fling with reevaluating her and reclassifying her. But I did fail to concede leniency towards what perhaps was her growing up, in circumstances so diverse, with values so disparate and through years so apart from mine. And even when I died, I wasn't fully convinced that I hated her.

"Prashant asked me to take on your work. He's stuck elsewhere."

Q touched me like the sea. Her wave left my legs frothy and wildly excited. When she receded, she took the sand away from beneath my feet.

It's strange sometimes. When you look back at things. I had gone to that office at least thrice a year over four five years. I had settled into Prashant for my work every time. But there were other people in the office. People that I never really noticed. I didn't know what their names were or even how they looked. In that office, not another person registered on me. Except in a very nagging, irritating way, Q. Somehow, I'd always know where she was, what she was doing. And even feel her absence.

And that evening, I was working with her. And I was getting mighty bugged. And I thought I was getting mighty bugged only because she wasn't Prashant.

"Okay, it's seven minutes and forty six seconds. Under your conference cap of eight." Effecting a loud space bar landing with finality, Q sat back.

Despite having my eyes on the monitor and my ears for Q through those two hours or so, I wasn't quite there. I didn't want to take any decisions. I wished I had the time to come back to the job another day.

"Yes, that's fine. Brilliant. This looks a done thing." I looked at my watch. "We actually took less time than I had imagined."

"Well, even if you don't like it, we can't really do a lot now. I understand you have to send it off tomorrow, and I'm not up for losing sleep over it. But I'd say it looks okay to me. The editing, I mean." Handing me a burnt and labeled disc, she added, "The surgery of course can only be as good as the surgeon you are."

What did she know about surgeries? I really get worked up when people talk like that. But in surprising contrast, Q's impoliteness didn't bruise me as much.

Q filled her hands with a couple of things from the table and rose, and as she did, she smiled at me. In a flash I comprehended the secret of the Mona Lisa! It isn't any unique beauty in that smile which captivates the whole world. Through all these centuries, the Mona Lisa smile has actually been screaming in mocking arrogance, 'I know what I'm doing to you – what are you going to do about it?'

Q vanished into her own cubicle. Since my raw stock was already loaded on Prashant's computer, we had worked there.

"Are you going to be a while, Anshu?" Q shouted out to the only other guy in the office. Another one of them that I had seen a million times before.

"Yeah. At least an hour till I've rendered this Kaziranga documentary," Anshu answered.

"I'll get going then. This doctor here wants to take me out for a drink. And ya, don't turn my computer down. I've got some updates running."

Q followed her voice out of her cubicle. "Shall we? Unless you are still looking for something?"

"No, I'm good. Nice of you to come."

Raising her eyebrows slightly, she held the door open. I, suddenly feeling at my clumsiest best, very commendably managed not to stumble all over myself!

So, there I was going for my first drink with Q. She had invited us to it. Q came across as arrogant, proud, sharp, and mischievous. All things that I love and admire in people. More so in women. I remember not wanting that evening to end even as I worked benumbed. And when time offered to stretch itself, an odd reaction nagged me. Fear perhaps. A very strange I-should-be-running-homewards feeling. But I went for that drink. How was I to know that one day my whole life was going to turn on its head around this woman?

* * * * *

5

Kajal couldn't remember the last time he had recorded. Could have been Margaret Wahlang's ballad. Not awfully long ago though, he actually remembered every one of the recording sessions in every detail. But that afternoon – lying in bed after Khadim's wonderful lamb curry meal that he could still smell off his fingers and in every burp that made him regret the over indulgence – the deeper he dug, more smudged the memories returned.

Khadim was the nearest Indian restaurant. Just across the street, it was a clear view from Kajal's fourth floor room at the Indian YMCA Student Hostel.

Arriving in London some months earlier, he had been immediately surprised how difficult it was to miss Indian food. Amjadbhai, Karachi native and proprietor of Khadim, had grown to become a pleasing acquaintance. Kajal also realized quickly that a sizeable number of 'Indian Restaurants' in London were really owned and run by Pakistanis and Bangladeshis! And also that the menus offered only north Indian fare – from the 'heartland' as it were. And that gave him the sly contentment of playing a card game with an ace still up his sleeve even after all four had been played. The exoticism of the Assamese pork curry in bamboo shoot or *lai xaak* remained undiscovered. Like the legend of the elephant and seven blind men, people – Indians included – could only cognize bits of India, never the whole!

Kajal's departure to London was sudden. He had filled out the application form some months earlier, with scarce belief on it coming through. Without much conviction on his decision to apply either. He wasn't sure the Byam Shaw course even figured in the slim list of things that he could possibly want to do in life. All he knew was that he had turned twenty eight and wasn't getting too far as a sessions guitar player in Shillong, the beautiful town in the northeast where the clouds came down to meet the pine and plum garnished hills and which the British, during their time in India, had christened 'Scotland of the East'.

He didn't tell anyone about it. Not even Ma. No one knew that he had applied.

Ardour for secrecy wasn't a recent trait. Starting with his earliest experiences in school, Kajal had built the walls around him through a slow learning process.

He must have been six or seven, and in second standard. It was near the end of the summer term, the time of the year when the arriving Annual Day – that function in the evening where the kids presented skits, songs, dances and all that in an auditorium full of parents and teachers – drowned every other activity on the calendar. An immensely satisfying day for parents whose wards picked up academic, sporting and various other kinds of awards, including ones for attendance, neatness and all that.

Kajal never got any awards. Even though the categories were so greatly expanded with an obvious intent to let every child go home with an honour of some sort. And not earning any decoration in those first couple of years in school led him to reckon that he would never get any awards. He was okay with it. Only he was sure it was killing Ma and Baba. Guilt seized his subconscious and condemned him undoubtedly culpable for being an embarrassment to Ma and Baba.

It's funny how things get contorted so easily. In time, the tiny creepers of childish guilt inside little Kajal grew into massive redwoods, depriving him of the nourishing sunshine of positive attitude, even as Ma and Baba did not mind in the least that their only son never got any award. But they never told him that it did not matter. It made Kajal even sadder that they never frowned or scowled. He knew they were doing him a huge favour.

There were three kinds of students at the Annual Day.

The first kind lived in the green room — most all over the world are painted white and poorly lit, so I don't really know why they are called green — and the wings by the stage in the auditorium because they had a part in every performance at the show. Their parents grinned widely when they came on stage, though in some group dances which involved up to forty students, it was a struggle spotting their wards from the distance. But they were mighty proud because their son was there — well, somewhere there — as long as the sets of parents sitting next to them realized that and did not have their own children in the dance, definitely not in a more clearly visible row in the formation!

The second lot sat between their parents and waited to be called on stage to pick up awards from the Chief Guest.

And finally the 'all-round-stars' who came on stage from the wings dressed in their costumes to pick up awards. Priyanka's mother told her neighbours in the auditorium how she had no clue that Priyanka was in the dance as well, in addition to her role in the play. And a little later, told them how surprised she was that Priyanka was getting an award for English Spelling, because it was impossible to make her study for even ten minutes!

At all Annual Days before the one when he was in second standard, Kajal had belonged to a rare brigade that was not a part of any of these three. And because this group was made up of less than five percent students, it was not representative enough to be a fourth kind in itself. The singular feature of this group was that these children never went up on stage during the evening. Neither to perform nor to grab an award, and definitely not to do both.

Kajal bided his time sitting next to Ma and Baba, wetting the thighs of his cotton shorts with perspiration from his palms, feeling hot in his ears and the back of his neck. And he kept thinking how no performance would have suffered and no award would have gone unclaimed even if he hadn't come.

Kajal hated Annual Days. He was scared of them. Much like his birthday parties that Ma and Baba arranged and he palpitated with fear that none of his friends would turn up.

————

Miss Thapa was Kajal's class teacher in second grade. She was his favourite. She was the one who rebuked most strongly when students mocked his name.

She was also very pretty. With her long hair and glasses. Her dresses and shirts were always black, Kajal's favourite colour. Kajal knew for a fact that if he was any better at getting awards, he could have asked Miss Thapa to marry him and she wouldn't have refused.

But Miss Thapa reached stratosphere when she picked Kajal for a part in her skit for the upcoming Annual Day. There were only eight characters, and Miss Thapa had selected Kajal for one of them. No one had ever picked him for anything before.

A rejuvenating energy seized Kajal. He felt empty behind his little sternum as all the struggle disappeared. Kajal realized how desperately he had always longed for some participation. Suddenly, it seemed very trivial. It wasn't such a big deal after all.

Miss Thapa was an angel. When they drew her pictures they should put a yellow disc around her head. Like the ones around the heads of Gautam Buddha and Swami Vivekananda in his picture books. Baba had explained that the yellow haloes were God's gift to those who did good to others.

Miss Thapa led her chosen cast to the auditorium. And there, she started explaining.

"Aamir, Dilip, Kajal and Imran, I want the four of you to get down on your knees and put your palms on the floor. Keep your heads down"

They did.

"Yes, that's right. Now, get close to each other."

They did. The others giggled.

"Okay. The four of you are the wheels of a car. You have to maintain your positions and move together. Can you do that for me now?"

Sampling what the kids managed, she was disappointed. "No, just keep it simple. I don't want two of you going to the right and two to the left. Let's do it correctly."

And after another attempt: "No, this is not working." Miss Thapa reflected for a moment, left hand on hip and biting the lower lip. "Okay, let's try differently."

Miss Thapa found a piece of chalk and drew out a large, gently wavy circle on the wooden floor.

"Now, I want the four of you to keep looking at that line and crawl along it."

The children did well. She looked satisfied. "That's better. That really is good!"

Miss Thapa was so bright. She always got everything right.

"Rajat come here. You are the driver of this car. You are the main character, the Amitabh Bachchan, okay."

Kajal didn't think much about the nature of the play or his role in it. The plot was that Rajat would be driving his car, of which Kajal was one of the wheels, and along the way, the tires would keep going flat one by one. Rajat would meet the other characters and the play was about how these people help him complete his journey.

The play demanded tough physical coordination from the 'wheels'. They had to crawl on their knees and palms as a group and had to crouch lower on their individual cues to go flat. They were also to discover later that Miss Thapa's route-guide would get lost in a maze of similar chalk lines drawn by other teachers for their own little plots.

All that was fine with Kajal. But on the fourth day of rehearsals, Miss Thapa disclosed that the 'wheels' would also have a sheet of canvas thrown on them to create the look of a real car. Not that it made the job any more challenging than it already was, but it meant none of the 'wheels' would actually be seen by the audience for who they were. In a strange way, Kajal felt betrayed that Miss Thapa had thought of him in the 'wheel' role.

Kajal had one consolation – he was relieved he hadn't yet broken the news to Ma and Baba. He was so glad that he hadn't told them that he was going to be a crawling 'wheel' covered in a sheet of canvas at the Annual Day. Even when Ma rebuked him for being naughty in school and skinning his knees. How ashamed they would be sharing this with the other parents. They perhaps wouldn't tell anyone.

Just over a week remained and the rehearsals were getting better.

————

Miss Thapa rushed into the auditorium, late and a bit unsettled. The 'wheels' were waiting in position.

"Here Kajal, step out. Try these lines," Miss Thapa said, even as she helped Kajal to his feet and gently pulled him by one shoulder towards the centre.

Kajal knew those lines by heart. From having heard Rajat say them through a week of rehearsals. Miss Thapa looked satisfied. She sneaked out briefly to return with a tentative Shankar. She helped Dilip show Shankar how to be a wheel.

Kajal couldn't believe what had just happened. Rajat had fever and his father had come down to tell Principal Mrs. Rehman that it could be the poxes. So Rajat was not going to be in school for a couple of weeks. Angel Miss Thapa picked Kajal to step up to the driver's spot! Kajal was the 'real' hero, not a crawling 'wheel' under a sheet of canvas. And Ma and Baba would see him on stage.

That evening he told Ma and Baba. Ma joked about Kajal's dream coming true because when he was younger, he'd always wanted to be a bus driver. Baba asked him to be sincere and do his part well even if it was only a play. Kajal didn't bother explaining his previous role or the skinned knees. They were a thing of the past and didn't matter anymore.

As he lay in bed that night, he couldn't sleep for a long time.

————

"Okay children. We have some good news, and a slight change in scenario." Turning to Kajal, Miss Thapa said, "Kajal, you were the best 'wheel' we had, and now we can have you back once again. Without you, it just wasn't working."

Talking to the rest of them, she said, "Shankar, we didn't have a role for you but you can stand with Maitri when Rajat comes up to her. Alright then? Shall we do it now?"

Miss Thapa rested her left hand on Rajat's shoulder as she said that. The doctors had confirmed that he didn't have the poxes, and his fever was gone. So three days later, he was back to reclaim his 'Amitabh Bachchan' part. How easily Miss Thapa had announced it.

Kajal felt crushed. As he rehearsed his crawling. What would he tell Ma and Baba now? They would perhaps never believe that he ever had the driver's part. Baba would tell him later that no job was big or small, that there was nothing to be ashamed of in whatever one did as long as one did it well. And that one should never lie.

———

That year, Kajal went up on stage in school for the first time. He crawled under a sheet of canvas, went flat on cue and remained flat thereafter till the end of the play.

Mingling over refreshments at the end of the function, Ma and Baba seemed very pleased. Shankar's father patted Kajal's back. But even Shankar who came in late for a role he never had wasn't covered in canvas!

———

A couple of weeks later, Baba took him to the stadium to watch a local football game. Afterwards, as they were making their way out in the crowd, Kajal spotted Miss Thapa. She was wearing blue jeans and a red top. Nothing black. She had shades on instead of the regular glasses. Walking next to her was a tall, handsome guy with slightly long hair. Wearing blue jeans and a white shirt. They looked good together.

* * * * *

Eleven year old Kajal had moved into the all boys' convent the previous year.

That day, Leonie Miss arrived with a tray full of assorted trinkets and an olive green cloth, the size of a cravat. "No lessons today. We will do a fun exercise," she announced and then proceeded to explain what was on her mind. Students, one at a time, were going to be blindfolded with the cloth and handed an object from the tray. Facing the class, the student then had to describe the object in hand, and, if at all possible, identify it. It wasn't awfully clear what the class had done to earn this time away from Saki's Dusk, but no one complained.

"Okay, who'll come next?" Leonie Miss asked amidst peals of laughter in the classroom. Mayank had just finished describing an oversized plastic ant as a helicopter!

"No, not you Ankur. You put your hand up for everything! Let's get someone who rarely participates." Leonie Miss's eyes searched the class on her equal-opportunities drive and all volunteering hands went down. "Yes Kajal, at the back there. Come on here."

Kajal hated it. His heart started to race and his entails skydived.

"This is our only chance at finding out if girls are better at this than boys!" Shyamal announced to rapturous reception from the rest of the class.

"Behave Shyamal!" Leonie Miss came down sharply. "I'll not tolerate this in my class. Is this what we've been teaching you – to make fun of other peoples' names?"

Leonie Miss tied the blindfold around Kajal's eyes. "How many fingers?" She put three outstretched fingers of her right hand close to Kajal's face. Kajal of course had no clue and kept quiet, satisfying everyone that he had been genuinely 'blinded'. Leonie Miss smiled understandingly. She picked up an item from her tray and placed it in Kajal's hand.

"There you go dear," she flagged Kajal off.

Kajal turned the object over in his hands a couple of times and the moist from his fingers left strings of tiny droplets. As he explored its surfaces and edges, he felt a zesty surge of excitement. He knew what it was! Minu *mahi* had gifted him one. Quickly, he got its spatial arrangement in place and figured out its top and bottom, right and left. He needed one more confirmation. As he ran a finger along the four sides, close to what he knew was its base, he found what he was looking for – a circular hole leading to the conical depression.

"It's a pencil sharpener," Kajal announced triumphantly.

"Phew!" Someone let out a cry.

"What? No no, not like that. Describe it," Leonie Miss was puzzled as Kajal hit bulls eye.

"Miss, it's one of those European houses with slanting roofs and a," Kajal rolled the object to bring an index finger over the small projection from the roof, "chimney. The pencil sharpener is set through its base, and there's also a lid at the bottom to clear out the scrapings."

Kajal was clearly animated, and eager. On a scale of the performances before him, he knew he had done really well. But he ended up doing a whole lot better then he perhaps should have.

"What colour?" someone asked. The look on Leonie Miss's straight face suggested that her mind was already made up about what was going on.

"Okay, I think the roof is green and the rest of the house is red. The chimney is red." In his excitement, Kajal fell for the bait. He thought, as a follow up to his brilliant display with the description, he was being encouraged to do the impossible – obviously, no one expected him to detail the colours blindfolded. He took on the challenge sportingly and rattled off the colours of the similar pencil sharpener Minu *mahi* had gifted him. What he missed in the bucking-up voices was the sarcasm.

The sound of spoken words can so often have amazingly different meanings when the accompanying facial expressions are stripped off. Alexander Graham Bell obviously invented the greatest tool of hypocrisy!

"That's great. You are absolutely right again Kajal. But none of us here can figure out how you could get the colours right. You are, after all, blindfolded." Leonie Miss resolved in her head to work harder with the children.

"It's just that those are the usual colours of these kind of things," Kajal explained, trying to be modest. And without the slightest clue what direction it had all taken.

Leonie Miss took the object from his hand and removed the blindfold. Sighted again, Kajal turned his head up to look at her face.

"It's okay, Kajal. Go back to your place. You are missing the whole purpose." No one had ever heard Leonie Miss speak as curtly.

Slightly confused, Kajal started to walk back to his seat. His eyes met those of the rest of the class – most mocking, the rest disinterested. A pounding rose in his chest and his palms went moist.

Settling back into his seat, his confusion gave way to surprise, shame and helplessness as realization seeped in.

"Kajal, quite without doubt, you were outstanding. But this is not a test of my blindfolding skills. It is definitely not an exercise for you to unfairly outdo each other. The idea was to help you appreciate the world of a blind man, for you to understand how difficult the simplest tasks become when a faculty that we so take for granted is taken away from us." Leonie Miss was deadpan serious. A rare sight. The students nodded their heads, up-and-down in agreement and right-and-left to express disgust at what Kajal had just done. "The least I expected was honesty!"

"You shouldn't have gone for the colours. That was the giveaway." Anand, who sat next to Kajal, whispered into his ears.

Kajal sat there petrified, palms and soles dripping a lake, back of neck burning his shirt collar, and ears like crimson handles on his face of shame. While Leonie Miss and the rest of the class did a couple of more rounds of the exercise with 'honest' results.

Yes, his success was serendipitous, but Kajal couldn't believe what his streak of good luck had just earned him. He was used to his underperformer status, but cheat was a new. But cheat he didn't. He couldn't have. But why was it so difficult for everyone else to understand?

Kajal taught himself a couple of things that day. For one, one was only as honest as the rest of the world thought one to be. And taking off from what Anand had explained, even if he had cheated but had been wily to check his enthusiasm with the colours, he might have easily passed off as honest. Then there was the greater matter of achievements and results. Kajal realized that the world had an accurately titrated ceiling on how much one could and should achieve.

The comfort of the reclusive underachiever's world seemed a thousand times amplified in the harsh arc lights of overachievement.

It doesn't really matter if what Kajal taught himself that day was right or wrong. He was, after all, only eleven! But it did go a long way towards cementing his quiet aloofness.

And he didn't tell anyone when he applied for the grant to do the course in London. Even when he had secured a university offer. Even when he filed for his Student visa. There were just so many stages to the process, and he had the talent and history to fail at any!

* * * * *

6

"Getting a bit nippy, isn't it?" I said as we stepped out of my car.

It was a short walk to the beer place. A chilly breeze caught me even under my warm suit.

"Ya it is," Q spoke. "About time – it's November. I'm sure in ten years' time the whole of winter will get squeezed into a national holiday week in January! You have to be careful with the arriving winter though, especially the evenings. One can actually catch a cold easily because one is never dressed well enough for it. I know you are a doctor and all, but I'm sure an eye doctor knows precious little about fevers. Is there anything like an eye fever?"

Throughout the evening while we worked on my video, she hardly said a word outside of the professional. Suddenly, it was nice to hear her talk a mile for an inch. Yes, there was nothing like an eye fever.

I have to confess here that I love laying out events from the past in my head, and then they go on to become distinct visions, and sounds, and smells, and colours, till I find myself completely re-living them. I do that very often, and I can consciously choose an event to go back to!

But there is something about first time encounters. I'm not sure what it is. Maybe the thing that is intriguing about 'first-times' is the human inability to unknow what it knows, to unlearn what it has learnt; because the mind knows and learns even if it doesn't plan to. The first time with anything is a pure moment that we lived in and can never ever have again, however realistically we attempt a reenactment!

That first moment with Q was something that I kept thinking about forever. And till the time I lost it all, I wanted so much to live through it again. And again. And again. Not to do anything differently, but just to be in that virgin bit of time again.

"I'll get a bottle of white wine," Q told the waiter. And then turned to me, "What would you like?"

"Ya, can I have a Jack Daniel's. Double, straight and no ice please."

"I'm sorry we don't have Jack Daniel's. Would you like to try a Single Malt?"

It was the place's fault that it didn't have the drink I wanted. And more so because I hadn't really asked for some rare Amazonian concoction. But asking for a drink that they did not have made me feel very stupid. In Q's presence. While she kept a limpid gaze on my face like I had asked for candy floss, I somehow couldn't bring my eyes to meet hers'. "Make that a Laphroaig then. Thanks."

I started to relax with the first sip of the whisky. It was past my dinner time, and the spirit left a burning trail en route to my stomach. Q meanwhile waved to someone. She was known around the place, and I sniffed a childish urge in her to show that off to me.

"So, did Prashant tell you about our little sessions at the bar after work? It's become a rule now, and we both quite enjoy it."

I splattered phony confidence on my tentative voice and then laced it with a stupid grin.

"No, he didn't. I'm here because I felt like a drink. And if we're going to do more work together in the future, I'm sorry it may not be like Prashant and you. I hate it when things become rules."

Q rebuffed my first attempt at conversation. With Prashant it used to be the cricket or the political state of the country.

I pulled out my packet of cigarettes and offered her one. I knew she smoked – I had seen her smoke at work, standing in the corridor.

"No thanks, I'm fine. You go ahead. But I really don't think it's awfully bright to be smoking in enclosed public places."

Between the 'you go ahead' and her take on smoking in public places, I found myself momentarily pondering the next move with the cigarette between my fingers. I lit up. It gave me a sense of triumph. I had defied her. The house might as well have given me a standing ovation!

"Tell me about yourself. Are you from Guwahati?" Shifting in my place, I asked her loudly like the friendly non-technical guy on an interview board. I immediately hated myself for hurrying onto the kind of personal queries that I had always regarded as the last resort of the socially challenged. But I was beginning to fear that we'd see the evening off without a word exchanged. She played ball.

"Ya, my family is from here. But I've lived here only the last couple of years, since this editing job. I grew up in Delhi."

"So you trained to be a video editor in Delhi?"

"Not really. I never trained formally. It's more a hobby. Something I like doing."

"Do you see yourself doing this for the rest of your life?" I was intrigued.

"I don't know. I graduated in law. Labour Law is what interests me. Or used to. I joined as a junior at a firm in Delhi. Ratan & Shawney. You may have heard the name. We did the famous Ajanta Cloth Mill case some years ago. But my drive for law just ran dry. There was this urge to break away and do something completely different. That's when Mama suggested that I come here and be with my grandmother for some time. I don't think I want to practice law anymore. I may want to teach though. And also study some more. Abroad perhaps."

"That's good. I haven't come across a lot of young lawyers who want to teach. Everyone seems to be going for the money and fame in practice," I commented cheerfully. She hadn't lost any of her arrogance, but I sensed her warming up. I am also genuinely appreciative of people with academic penchant. "Do you have any concrete plans about studying abroad? Grants, scholarships – it involves serious money, doesn't it?"

"See, I was born in the UK. So I hold a British passport. That makes it cheaper for me. Otherwise as an international student you do end up paying a fortune. And the UK is a great place to be studying in. I have been looking up universities in London. Let's see."

"That's interesting. How did you get to be born in the UK?"

"Well, Dad had business in Coventry. Still does. My parents separated when I was four. Dad stayed on while Mama came back to India, and I was brought along. She started her own business in handicrafts and folk jewellery in Delhi. She runs an emporium in Connaught Place, on Baba Khadak Singh Marg."

"I'm sorry to hear that. Must have been tough for you as a child."

"No don't be." Q's face suddenly filled with resentment, like I'd offended her. "I'm not sorry myself. I think it's a whole world more convenient when parents come one at a time. Then you only have one half to deal with! And don't think I'm all shattered by these bits of my life. I wouldn't be telling you all this if I was."

The sudden change in her demeanor brought awkwardness. I was perhaps guilty of prying but I did feel encouraged. If she had indicated, I'd have been very happy with the evening remaining confined to the Ajanta Cloth Mill case.

"Hey hey, don't be upset. We don't have to talk about anything that you don't want to."

I managed to say that jocularly and I raised my hands in a gesture of surrender. Q loosened her stance and flashed a lovely smile. *Fluctuating snob.*

It became over an hour. We eventually ended up conversing about a whole lot of here and there things. Like how good Prashant was with his work, and we found consensus on that. And the upcoming state elections. And also about who had discovered radio communication – Marconi or Bose. I don't remember how that came up. But we did talk about it. And she surprised me with her insight. It did turn out to be a pleasing evening.

She didn't ask a thing about me.

But she did smoke a cigarette. Indoors. She borrowed one of mine. I thought it juvenile to hold her to her earlier comment when I was lighting up in the 'public place'.

We asked for the bill, and while I paid, she returned from a quick visit to the restroom.

"You can drop me off at the first crossing. I'm seeing a friend. He'll give me a ride to my grandmother's later. I hope I'm not making you drive off your route."

"No that's fine."

I was tempted to find out who or what this friend was. I understood it was a guy. But I didn't ask. The feeling and also that I wanted to find out about the guy was funny in a way. For I usually didn't split too much hair over other people's matters.

"Ya just here," Q indicated after we'd driven for about ten minutes. "Thanks a lot. Good luck with sending the video. See you soon," she smiled across the car door.

I drove back home in silence. It had rained a bit and the yellow of the neon street lights reflected off the wet tarmac in brilliant blotchy patches. I lowered the window. The freshness of the world outside rushed in but somehow could not displace the evening.

* * * * *

The next day, I was in clinic with Mr. Goswami and his son, Shekhar.

Mr. Goswami was the kind of patient who gives doctors the real shits. His pragmatic, soaking-up-the-details approach to the consultation rattled me every time as I told him that his eye wasn't getting any better. I just so wished he'd scream at me instead of accepting the inevitability of his disease.

"But doctor, if there is no way that his vision will improve after the surgery, what is the point in going ahead?" Shekhar needed his answers.

Mr. Goswami was seventy four, and was slowly losing sight to glaucoma in both eyes. Medicines were failing and it was time for surgery. But it was a tough task convincing a patient to go ahead with a major surgical procedure that could only give him a few more years of not being absolutely blind. Well, that is how glaucoma is.

A whole lot of medical science isn't miraculous. And it's a wretched feeling when you have nothing to offer to elderly people who were going blind at a time in life which they had set aside to watch all the television, do all the reading, do all the traveling with their elderly partners and play with their grand children that they had missed through a lifetime of earning a livelihood.

But Shekhar wasn't anxious for his father's sake only. He himself was nearing fifty, and a couple of months ago, I had had to put him on the same eye drops that his father used. Glaucoma runs in families.

The frustration that glaucoma kicked up was thankfully evened out by my 'free' cataract surgeries. Now, cataract surgery is a miracle. Under five minutes per surgery, and in a couple of hours twenty historically, geographically and economically remote blind people became eyed. And the next morning toothless mouths deposited spit-laden kisses on my cheeks, weather beaten hands ran blessings through my hair and enormous grins broke emaciated faces into deep wrinkles. Made everything worthwhile. Made me acknowledge that the power to make a difference, however miniscule, lay somewhere within each one of us.

What's more, the conversations I had with my patients through the surgeries – they were anaesthesized only around the eye, so we could talk – were like portholes and every time, I understood the world a little bit more.

Once. "*Aaita,* how many children do you have?" I asked. "One son," she said softly. I was impressed – all those decades ago the only families getting planned were big ones! "Wow, that is really good *aaita!*" But just then, my assistant spoke up, "How many daughters?" Hesitantly she replied, "Nine." "Nine!" I screamed even as I continued the surgery. She spoke in a weak voice, "The boy is the youngest. You do need at least one boy, don't you?" "How old is the boy now?" I asked her. "Ten." "He's in school?" I supplemented. She sighed lightly and replied, "Their father died when the boy was five. I can't afford school. I have five more daughters to marry off. He works at the village tea stall."

Another time I was operating on this man who kept refusing surgery forever. "Why were you being so difficult? Don't you realise how much you'll benefit, and how your world will change after tomorrow. And isn't it such a simple procedure? See, we're nearly done." I expected him to affirm with fulfillment. But he surprised me, "What will I do with sight when I have no food?" My mind took a step backward. How can the feeble light my surgeries bring dispel the overpowering darkness of these lives?

Then there was a lady who'd been advised surgery a year back but had missed three scheduled dates. "The cataract has become so dense, why did you delay so much?" I enquired. "I couldn't arrange the money," she replied coyly. I was astounded, "What money? This service is entirely free – transport, stay, food, everything?" "I know the operation is free but I had to arrange the thousand Rupees to give the volunteer. He'd said he won't put us on the bus till we paid!" she explained, much to my horror. Volunteer – yes, we did involve enthusiasts from the community to smoothen the logistics.

"The surgery went well, okay. We'll have a look tomorrow and then final check-up in four weeks," I announced even as my assistant bandaged the man's operated eye. "I can't come back in four weeks. It's election time," the man spoke firmly. I asked him cheekily, "Who you voting for?" His answer was prompt, "The same. Last time he gave us blankets even before the election. This time he's promised us Ration Cards if he wins."

Anyway. I was with the Goswamis that day when my phone began to ring. A hot flush promptly ran from the tips of my hair all the way down to my toes. It was the video editing firm's number. I gave in to a pressing need to answer it right then.

"Hi. Sorry about yesterday."

It was Prashant. I thanked him for checking. And assured him that the person that he had arranged for my work did a great job. I felt tongue-tied in uttering Q's name. Like I feared Prashant would find out something I didn't want him to know. I didn't bother mentioning to him that I couldn't send the video after all.

I found it hard to get back to the Goswamis. Or to anyone else through the rest of the day. I knew it was Q. She was the overpowering impulse that had forced me to divorce discipline and take the phone in the middle of a patient. After I hung up, I realized how disappointed I was that it hadn't been Q on the line.

Little did I know that Q was from another planet. And I had just begun my journey to that celestial world without the skimpiest chance of ever making it there or finding my way back home.

* * * * *

7

Kajal arrived in London in the September of 2006. To realize at Heathrow that he was carrying the navy blue cashmere long coat on his arm for no real reason. London was sunny and warm that afternoon.

The Byam Shaw School of Art had offered him a place on the year-long Post Graduate Diploma in Fine Art. Kajal would have been more at ease with the three years' Bachelors but that stood ruled out by his funding which only supported a year. He had zeroed in on the Foundation Degree, which was also a year, but since he already had a graduation and qualified as a 'mature student' on the merit of his age, he was offered the PG Dip.

But his graduation was not in Fine Art. Or anything to do with the arts at all. Rahul had initiated an inclination but all Kajal truly owned was a mere flavour of Art History. So, even while being welcomed by a bright London afternoon, he couldn't lose it from the back of his mind that there had been a mistake somewhere.

Five years earlier, Kajal had graduated in History. On a most unremarkable day.

In senior school, he had studied the science stream. He loved Biology. The perfectness of the human body fascinated him. Just as Modern History did.

After matriculation, he wanted to study Biology and History. Both. But the curriculum did not allow that. Biology would have to come with the rest of the sciences while History belonged to humanities, the academic antonym of the sciences. There was no 'pick-your-own-filling' option. The fillings for the different academic sandwiches had been prescribed by learned men decades ago.

Kajal fell short of convincingly working out why he gave up History.

It did make Ma and Baba happy though. For Baba, a doctor himself, Biology in senior school was the logical route for his son to take towards Medicine. Kajal's apparent penchant for the human science pleased Ma and Baba. Back then.

And by that time, Kajal's desire to please Ma and Baba had touched silent desperation as their doesn't-matter-at-all attitude to his early failures gradually transgressed through a couple of years of there-is-still-hope to what-will-this-boy-do-in-life. He knew it, even though they never voiced it. Letting History pass came smoothly, for personal choices had ceased to matter.

Biology, however, came with an unsettling baggage because it was only a step towards Medicine. Kajal felt the pressure. From its far end, the monumental challenge of getting into medical school stared back. Not because he really wanted to be a doctor. But because Ma and Baba would be delighted if he went on to become one. He lived with the fear of letting them down. Again.

That tryst with science left Kajal bruised and battered. He wandered through those two years of senior school walking a dangerous tight rope with the skin of his teeth.

* * * * *

"So, Group D. I understand you've finished the gluteal region and anterior thigh so far. In the next two weeks we'll be dissecting the sole of the foot. Read your Cunningham's. And strictly no Chaurasia please. The redness of that hideous book awakens the mad bull in me, and I promise to shower all of that lunacy on anyone I catch brandishing it in the Dissection Hall or during my tutorials. I don't care what you've done before today, but with me, it's Cunningham's for dissection and Grey's for theory."

The caterpillar on the ledge outside the Dissection Hall window did a miniature Mexican wave and inched forward slightly. One could only imagine that the advancing end was its head, there didn't seem another way of telling. And that amused Kajal.

"The two hours in the Dissection Hall are not allowance to catch up on the latest gossip. And I can't stand gloves. You can wait to use them till you become the great surgeons that you've all come here to become. For now, get your bare hands in and get a feel. That's how we learnt it, that's how you will learn it."

That was Dr. Kalita, Assistant Professor, Anatomy, letting his voice boom over the silence of the cadavers and mute students like a drill master addressing a fresh crop of trainee cadets. Over the years, he had painstakingly built himself a proud reputation of being stern-with-the-students-for-their-own-long-term-good. His mere entry into the Dissection Hall ushered a cemetery like hush. Dr. Kalita cherished the mayhem he caused.

On rum nights, small groups in the Boys' Hostels understandingly philosophised that Dr. Kalita's terror tactics were merely a means to accepting his career in Anatomy versus a squashed dream of becoming a Neurosurgeon.

"And, what's your name"?

It was always a chime from the gallows when Dr. Kalita did that. Not just for the one in line of his extended index finger but for the entire group. And the remainder of the session expertly slipped into a frightful celebration of Dr. Kalita's opinion on the quality of present day medical students.

"Jayanta Talukdar, sir."

"Doctor Talukdar. So what is it going to be for you? Urology? Cardiology?"

Prognosis was gravest when a rookie was addressed as doctor. The chap was only seconds away from the guillotine crashing down. Seconds, in which Dr. Kalita delivered his sermon of sarcasm.

Jayanta kept quiet. The others fell back an involuntary half step, to ensure that Dr. Kalita didn't forget who had been picked to face the firing squad.

"What are your hobbies, Doctor Talukdar"?

"Chess, sir. And rock climbing," Jayanta replied, feeling encouraged.

"Chess and rock climbing!" Dr. Kalita whistled, and then turned to the rest of the group. "See, Doctor Talukdar here is the brain and brawn type." He declared with a terse smile.

"But Doctor Talukdar, what on earth gives you the guts to stand before me with these long, lady-like locks of yours?" Dr. Kalita abruptly roared with sadistic menace.

"I don't get paid for doing what your mothers and fathers should have years ago. I don't even get paid for doing what my colleagues should have done much earlier. But I don't mind at all. In all these years I have realized someone eventually has to do it. And like they say, better late than never."

Dr. Kalita was unmistakably charged and demonstratively dramatic, his eyes sparkling with sheer delight. His complaint about not getting that extra dough was clearly for effect only – he was damn well collecting his reward even then. A deep breath followed a pause, for effect, and then with a change of tone, Dr. Kalita continued, "It is with great pleasure that I ask you to leave the class right now, and not return for fifteen days."

Jayanta stood there, uncertain of his response. To begin with, he wasn't sure Dr. Kalita was serious about asking him to leave. He didn't believe he deserved that for the length of his hair. And he wasn't really certain that leaving right away without begging around a bit wouldn't offend Dr. Kalita.

"What part of what I just said is unclear, Doctor Talukdar? You are wasting everyone's time here, including your own. Did you know that your friends won't be allowed to proceed with their dissection till you left?" Dr. Kalita spoke like he was reciting William Blake. And then his eyes followed Jayanta as the latter complied and left the class.

Kajal was in Group D. His mind had succumbed to the hairy caterpillar majestically crawling on the ledge outside a window, even as Dr. Kalita went about making med school a whole lot worse than it really was. Dr. Kalita's monologue and flourishing expulsion of Jayanta distracted him in spurts, but he was able to return quickly to the caterpillar. They said even the sight of one that massive could trigger severe rashes.

* * * * *

"I passed out of this Institution in 1968. Some of my batch mates, you will meet here as your professors. Fate has chosen you for God's work. Here there is no substitute for hard work. I feel blessed because a whole lot of doctors don't get to hand down their stethoscopes to their children."

Baba was a retiring king handing out his kingdom to his son – only Kajal wasn't sure what to do with it. He fiercely wished there was a sibling to take on the mantle.

They were waiting at the Bhangagarh crossing to take the right turn. Kajal spied on Baba's hands. They were always the same. While driving or while waiting for traffic lights to change. Rock steady hands of the surgeon that he was.

The beep of the indicator rang out a muffled treble within the car like the staccato of life-support devices. And the blinking lights on the panel in front of Baba filled the inside of the car with on-and-off orange. Small lights that had grown in calibre. Because the sky outside was grey, its blue obscured by thick clouds that had suddenly turned up to undermine the importance of the day – Kajal's first day in med school.

The rain fell on the roof with every individual drop making a succinct statement before merging with the whole. Kajal found its rhythm. A percussion extravaganza, time signatured by the swish-swosh of the windscreen wipers and the beeping indicator lights, and filled in by the marching boots of a million-strong army of rain.

Kajal looked out of the window across Baba. Once they took that right turn, they would start winding up Narakasur hill to the med school building at its top. It was a beautiful view. Gauhati Medical College – the college retained the anglicized spelling even as the city itself reverted back to the Assamese sound of Guwahati – panned the expanse of the entire hill. The bustling hospital at the foot, the academic and administrative buildings elevated to the serene calm of its top, and the student hostels scattered all over like little white matchboxes in a broccoli-like green. A protected haven right in the middle of Guwahati.

Kajal thought about Baba. If there was one person on earth who triggered awe in Kajal, it was Baba. And not at all because he was his father.

Baba came from a very poor family in a village where everyone and everything was poor. Not one from which you'd expect children to come out with either aptitude or desire to go to med school. Poverty ensured that they didn't stand a chance against all those who went to all the right schools and got all the right coaching; and after failed attempts at leveraging childish joys in the first years of life, only the most primal desires remained for the rest of their time on earth. Birth further chose to put Baba in what the great Indian reservation policy had made the most unfortunate circumstance – the super-poor Brahmin household.

But Baba did emerge out of it all. Even as every voice around him screamed that he was wrong to chase a resolve that was drafted into him by his dying mother who couldn't get medical attention as she bled to death after one more child-birth.

But Baba did emerge out of it all. Through being a domestic help so he could find a place to stay and eat a meal. Through offering private tuitions in Biology and Grammar so he could buy his books. Through working in construction during vacations so he could pay fees for the next term. Baba did emerge out of all that. And when he did, he sped off to spend the next ten years serving the deprived tribal communities entrenched in the ruthless geography of neighbouring Arunachal Pradesh. In places so desolate that only Ma could be with him, so Kajal had to come into the world much later.

Baba made much less money than his peers did in the city. Goodwill and respect were the only things he ever earned. Kajal never heard anyone say anything bad about Baba. Even the other doctors in the city who drove flashy cars and lived in bigger houses. They had all arranged a celebratory dinner when Baba was conferred the silver medal by the President of India. Kajal remembered clearly how uncomfortable Baba was with all the attention.

The lights changed. And the hum of the engine, scripted to a unique crescendoing pitch for every gear, added to the percussion. Kajal felt his palms going moist with perspiration where he had laid them out on his thighs.

———

"Okay Kajal. I leave you here. Ma and I are praying for your success."

After Kajal got off, Baba drove around the brick roundabout with the massive Banyan tree in the middle to make his way down the hill. As the car turned, he looked at Kajal rushing through the rain into the building. Kajal had grown up to be a fine looking young man, athletically built and touching six feet. His hair was closely cropped, his face long with chiseled, high cheek bones and a broad forehead. His eyes were sparkling dark brown, eager and inquisitive. His black leather shoes were carefully chosen. Baba noted how nice the white coat looked over his pale blue shirt and grey trousers. Baba felt very proud.

Baba had had to go to great extents to see that day.

Kajal hadn't done well in the twelfth standard, Board exams. And his rank in the med school entry test wasn't good enough for him to even be on the waiting list. But when a friend suggested to Baba that he shouldn't hesitate pulling a few strings, his eagerness to see Kajal in med school, convinced Baba that there was nothing wrong with it. And the strings Baba could pull were more than willing to show the appreciation they had for his work of a lifetime.

Something else unconsciously nudged the balance in Baba's head. It was the matter of Ronen's son going to the south to study medicine. In one of those institutes where you could pay for a place and they wouldn't waste a stare at your grades. Dr. Ronen Borthakur was a leading cardiologist in Guwahati. And he was Baba's mate. Fourth batch, 1968. His son had fared worse than Kajal at both the Board exams and the med school entry test. But he had the money to not have to pull any strings.

But it all seemed worthwhile. As he drove away after dropping Kajal to his first day at med school.

————

The lecture hall was an amphitheatre, the kind Kajal had seen in movies, and could easily seat about two hundred. Three columns of fixed rows of wooden desks and benches stood on steps arranged like a horse-shoe, narrowing downwards to a well with a stage and a stretched blackboard.

A din of hushed voices echoed within the spread of the architecture like the chorus of thousand buzzing bees. Students stood huddled in groups by the doors and along the steps. Those who knew each other from before shared the same long benches, ladies almost entirely in the first three or four rows and the men brought up the rear. All hundred and fifty of them. The smell of their new, slightly bluish white coats mingled with the fragrance of dreams and positive energy.

Kajal found a place to sit – thirteenth row, middle column. There were just these two other guys sitting at the far end of the bench. Guys with poky hair and slanting eyes the rest of the countrymen called Chinkies and associated with an attitude problem and a general lack of purpose in life.

One of the guys was Nikhil. Nikhil Teron. He was to become Kajal's best friend at Med School.

Silence fell with the entry of Dr. Suresh Mitra, Principal and Chief Superintendent. Along with him came the Heads of the three first year departments – Anatomy, Physiology and Biochemistry. In his welcome, Dr. Mitra said much the same things that Baba had in the car. But in contrast to Baba's words steeling Kajal with some sort of resolve, Dr. Mitra made him feel like he didn't belong there. And he feared it wasn't long before it became generally known.

* * * * *

By the end of the first week, Kajal moved to campus. Room 28, Men's Hostel 5. Baba had promoted the idea. He talked about how important it was to live on campus for the evening tutorials and bed side clinics. He talked about all the discussions that students had after dinner; the inspiration that came from peers; how communal 'academic' tea-breaks charged one up for long nights. As his concluding argument – Ma had done her best to resist the notion – Baba declared that hostels made real men out of boys! Kajal thought that sounded cool.

Ma threw in the towel, but not before she had extracted from Kajal the promise to spend every weekend at home.

* * * * *

I went to the same med school as Kajal. A little calculation would have told me that I was finishing my internship as Kajal was getting baptized, being some five years older than him. And we had even shared time in the same hostel. Even though the hostel had over hundred boarders, it was really unusual not to know another guy, however junior or senior, at least by face. Most people actually knew each other in decent detail.

But I had no recollection of Kajal. And when I did meet him in London, he didn't divulge any recall that he might have had.

But I wasn't innocent to the incident. It had become well known. I remembered Nandini being involved. Everyone knew Nandini. What I did not know, even when it had happened, was that Kajal was its other half.

The hostel I – and Kajal – lived in was the largest. It was this four storied structure built in three spreading wings around a central hub, in aerial view like the Greek letter gamma in lower case.

The main entrance in the central hub led to a foyer, and on its right, the foyer opened to the Common Room – a mostly empty large hall with a television and a couple of carrom boards, and rows of wooden benches with backs and arm rests. Along the entire length of the side opposite the entry door, massive French windows looked onto a cemented courtyard.

The carrom boards were used for their real purpose only when the television was used for its real purpose. And that was when any cricket match or a World Cup football game was on air. Television in those days offered only two channels, and one had to be an absolute loser to be watching either at any other time. The TV itself was caged in a wooden box, with a fall-down door that could be locked through two latches on the top. And Shyam, of Room 135, religiously arranged the hanging ends of the latches in various combinations to ensure that Tendulkar dispatched the next delivery to the ropes.

Another sell-out event in the Common Room was when a repeat offender was being grand-juried, the most frequent being the student who managed the kitchen – a rotational basis post – on account of discrepancy in monthly accounts or diminishing size of the chicken pieces. I remember this one time when the mess manager had presented accounts where he had spent more on transportation for grocery shopping then the shopping itself. The occasion ended just short of him getting lynched, but comments and opinions fuelled great creativity – limericks and cartoons depicting him going grocery shopping on an airplane remained pinned on the never-otherwise-used softboards in the foyer for months.

The dark and half occupied Common Room on Saturday nights provided the weekly dose of porn, played out of awfully eroded magnetic tapes regurgitating hallucinating prints at times. Half full, because entry was strictly restricted to the seniors. The top of the hired VCP had no screws so it could be lifted without fuss to scrub the chrome-head with after-shave in an attempt to salvage some recognizable images. This would need to be done after the initial half hour, and every fifteen minutes thereafter. Most of the audience either got consumed by the machinery like activity of the visuals or were too pressed for some privacy by the third presentation but the diehards would stick around to go straight to Sunday breakfast. The whole affair was run through an elaborate organizational frame, with a secretary, again on a rotational basis, whose job it was to collect the ten Rupees from every member, and rent out the VCP and tapes. Selecting the movies – if they can be called so – was a challenge, for even though there was no conceivable human means of telling one from the other, the diehards pointed out the date of an earlier exhibition thirty two weeks ago in the event of a repeat. And that qualified the secretary for impeachment.

The main flight of stairs going up to the floors rose from the centre of the foyer, and also went to the basement which was the dining hall. There were two other sets of stairs at the ends of two of the wings. Fire escapes. Or entries and escapes for another venture. Because getting girlfriends in and out was a clandestine activity in the hostel. Not that it wasn't allowed as a rule or anything like that. It was just that the door to every room had a large wire meshed ventilator above, and the news of someone being in with his girlfriend presented an opportunity in voyeurism for anyone that cared.

The boarding rooms were single or twin shared, and except on the ground floor, each with its own little balcony, the rusty iron railings of which forever hosted a colourful assemblage of socks and underwear in various stages of drying.

We were all very proud of it. That perhaps was what living in a hostel for as long as medical education demanded was all about. Even though the mildew from decades of having gone without a coat of paint seemed like a whitewash in itself – dirty green and grey. Darker to a near sooty black where the columns of RCC stood above the low wall of the terrace, like frail raised humps of some medieval fortress, the ends of 24 mm iron rods exposed like tentacles reaching for the skies. The building had aged way beyond its years.

At the edge of the eastern wing was the great mango tree. About three floors high, with huge spreading arms and a perennial crop of green. Every summer, it swelled with its fruit. The mangoes were green. Even when ripe. The tree was some wild variety, born and bred on its own like most things in Guwahati. It ushered great camaraderie amongst the boarders. We spent those hot and humid summer afternoons sitting around buckets of mangoes with our fruit knives, dressed in shorts and nothing else; a creaking ceiling fan in a room that smelt like a small scale factory manufacturing mango flavoured deodorant; sweat broke into tiny pearls on foreheads and trickled down the sides of faces, and with great dexterity, the backs of our hands arrested the sweat-streams while keeping the pulp smeared palms away.

It was also a shared responsibility to guard the fruit. From the immigrant kids who were better and swifter at climbing, plucking and making a getaway than we were. The kids belonged to the Bangladeshi construction workers who had settled into a slum within the campus. Their fathers and mothers worked in all the construction work that went on forever in one or other part of the campus. The longest such activity was the building of a new

49

auditorium which had started off with a two-year deadline but was eventually inaugurated after thirteen long years. The slum had in the meanwhile grown satellites of mud houses strewn all over med school hill with amenities like running municipality water, electricity and all that, and there was a report in the newspaper some years back that they were fighting for voting rights. And that the Government in the state was considering it positively. Right there in the middle of med school campus.

Through the late seventies and early eighties, Assam was rocked by a major uprising, led primarily by student leaders but eventually garnering the participation of every Assamese irrespective of age and gender. The six-seven year long agitation culminated in two major events – signing of the famous Assam Accord with the Government of India and the coming to power in the state, through a peaceful democratic process, of the political party formed by the same core group of students that had led the agitation. The crucial tenet of the Accord was the deportation of all illegal Bangladeshi immigrants that had seeped into Assam after 1971. Years later, it still remains unfulfilled. Apparently because of the near impossibility of identifying those Bangladeshis. A recent Government communiqué published in the papers put the cost of identifying and deporting a single Bangladeshi at scarily close to my annual wage! But I swear to you, the job of hunting out a Bangladeshi is so damn easy, only someone with a hidden agenda can find it grueling.

The mango tree also mothered a celebrated symbiotic relationship, with immense third party benefits. The shade under its great spread apparently provided the ideal ecosystem for the most famous hostel crop. Marijuana. Born and bred on its own, like the mango tree itself. True to its fashionable alias – weed. Just a small patch of dry, useless looking herb, with a round the year presence. The connoisseurs regarded the crop to be of the highest grade, much better than the stuff the rest of the campus bought at five Rupees a pouch from the Bangladeshi slum.

* * * * *

Alone in the Dissection Hall, Kajal felt the presence of the fourteen moonlight washed dead bodies laid out on the steel dissection tables. Living eyes burnt with the strong formaldehyde fumes but that was something one got used to with time.

The three third year seniors had latched the door and were waiting outside on the corridor. As was planned.

Kajal hadn't been in the Dissection Hall before. That night he was there as part of an established hazing ritual for rookies – to be left alone in the unlit D-Hall with half dissected cadavers in the middle of the night. The hall was on the fourth floor of the academic building on the hilltop – the nearest lives and lights at that hour were at least two kilometers downhill, scantily strewn in the illegal mud houses or clustered in the hostels.

Kajal wasn't scared. He only felt a deep sense of shock. He was a huge fan of the human body. To him, every individual was a work of immense beauty, the appreciation of which came easily to him. And through his readings, he had learnt about the impeccable clockwork of life.

The fact that the cadavers for dissection came from the numerous unclaimed deaths on our streets, presented to Kajal a raw, ugly but real side of life. And death. It came as a rude jolt. At a time when he was not at all prepared.

He found himself surrounded by a cruel antithesis. Emaciated, expressionless, eyeless faces with holes where teeth had been; listless skin like dry wood, ripped apart distastefully by unskilled hands; exposed muscles spraying out like feathers on some Apache headgear. Various parts of their bodies still shredded open. No blood. Just dried guts with pale yellow fat like the inside of a juiceless pomegranate. Kajal couldn't find the slightest trace of anything human in that hall.

One could censure his romantic seasonings for having villainously debased his ability to deal with sap and viscera. But aren't entry exams that test one on the fundamentals of a step-down transformer mere convenient means of exclusion, that haughtily disregard felicity, than a learned process of selecting future doctors? Despite Kajal's other misgivings, on some plane he had counted on his love for the human form to get him home on dry feet. That strength lay shattered that night.

It was nearly an hour later that Raj Bora, one of the seniors, opened the door.

"Hey fresher. Still alive?"

Kajal walked towards the door.

"So. How was it? Horny for the young lady on table four?"

"I'm sure with a name like Kajal, he doesn't feel too much for females," Moinak suggested.

"Shit man, I'm feeling really unsafe now," Samar dramatically squinted his eyes and brought a hand down to cover his behind in mock protection.

The seniors laughed.

Kajal stood quiet. Not responding.

"You okay?"

In a state of trance, Kajal walked past them. Out of the door. Into the dark corridor. The seniors followed. They were still laughing. Their voices were a collective echo that fell on Kajal's eardrums only to bounce right off leaving no dent or stain.

By the time the seniors piled him on to the back of one of their bikes, they were scared something had gone terribly wrong. Kajal nearly spilled off at a bend, and Moinak had to sandwich him from behind for the rest of the downhill ride.

Back in the hostel, the seniors put him to bed, even as he didn't open his eyes or utter a word. They were alarmed; doubt wrecked their vital functions. They hadn't encountered anything like that before.

Third year is a bad time in med school. After all the dead bodies, rats and test tubes, third year marks the advent of 'real' patients, clinics and surgeries. Along with it comes that responsibility to feel and behave like a doctor. One responds with some pretending – without malice, purely under the circumstance. Because attendants enquire about the status of their patients, unsuspecting juniors seek 'Physician's Sample' medicines which the drug company representatives don't actually hand out to third years, and during the weekend home visits, mothers ring out, "Radhika, you know Shankar uncle's mother has been diagnosed with cancer cervix. He's on the phone and wants to have a word with you." To all this one has to become a doctor. Which is not such a big deal.

Once in a while though, one is faced with a real big deal. Like the crisis Kajal put that bunch of seniors in. Because, even as lectures and clinics had pushed them to bite into acute renal failure and neurofibromatosis, they were unlearning some absolute basics. Nothing seemed straight forward any more. From the indisputable event that it had always seemed, death had grown into a diagnosis with its own symptoms. The signs of death – fixed and dilated pupils, absence of a palpable pulse, absence of heartbeat, absence of breathing, etcetera – which needed to be confirmed before declaring someone dead. What happens if a person has some of these but not all? Is the person dead? If yes, then, presence of how many of these findings sufficed? Any two? Or three? Which two? Which three? All five? If he's not fully dead, then is he partially dead? Then, how 'much' dead? Those concepts of brain dead, heart dead, kidney dead, and God knows whatelse dead and yet not fully dead!

At that moment, their half baked knowledge had driven them to desperation over a life and career threatening matter – Was Kajal dead (*I am so screwed!*) or alive (*Please please God, I swear to you I'm done with ragging!*)?

They turned to Dr. Dhiraj Goswami, batch topper and current intern. It was one of those scenarios where the nerds came in handy. Their technical acumen could be trusted and their gossip-free lifestyles guaranteed minimal mileage.

"He's okay," assured Dhiraj. "Just a vaso-vagal. Let him sleep with two pillows under his feet. Leave the door unlocked so you can check on him later."

The incident marked the exit of the D-Hall sessions from the ragging menu. At least for the year. Kajal's popular status in it was that of a weakling martyr's, not a hero's.

By the end of the first month, it became established in the hostel that Kajal was, for lack of a better label, weird. So the seniors didn't haul him up to the terrace for the mass stripping, he wasn't commanded to do any diagrams for them, he wasn't requisitioned for forced alcohol sessions, he didn't have to gyrate like bar-girls at their parties and provide private massages after.

"*Ee kela bom kamoor be. Iyaak baad de.*"

Soon his own batchmates built opinions. Some decided he was 'quiet and aloof', others argued that he was 'just reserved' and still others were adamant that he was 'weird'. To almost all though, he didn't make any difference. While he quietly carried himself through the daily routine.

Two weeks later, Kajal went for his first 'official' dissection class. He had been looking forward to it, hoping to be able to take in the whole experience anew. But even while the asphyxiating visuals were only amplified in the bright daylight, the smell that he had somehow failed to register earlier became an added horror. A disturbing, soft, persistent stench that had no name or definition.

Kajal started waking up every morning weighed down by the ghosts of his nightly thoughts. His sleep cracked long before the set alarm, eyes gritty and stomach churning in that aching hunger that launches the day after a sleepless night. He remained in bed like a robot out of gas, till the alarm beeped. He thought of Ma making breakfast at that moment while Baba finished his *puja*. At home.

As he laid out a fresh shirt and trousers for the day, and gave his shoes a shine, he tried hard to convince himself that the phase was a passing storm. And in the shower, he promised himself to turn things around and be positive.

But the evening returned after another day of oxygen debt and Kreb's cycle, both interesting propositions but the helpless D-Hall cadavers had taken over Kajal's head like squatters, indefatigably pushing him deeper into a gorge of disconnection.

* * * * *

Kajal came home that Sunday. Around eleven. As was routine.

Baba was weeding the garden. Ma was in the kitchen.

The refrigerator hummed. The air pump in the aquarium purred. An open tap dripped gently into a bucket in one of the upstairs bathrooms, accompanied by the brushing of wet clothes – Ma's part-time help was at work. The singing voice of the rag picker passed the house. A pressure cooker whistle blew in the Baruas' kitchen next door. Kajal knew all of those Sunday morning sounds. It was home.

Kajal left his shoes at the shoe-rack – Ma was aggressively particular about no street footwear in the house – and found a pair of slippers. Next to them lay an upturned, dead cockroach.

It was then that the smell hit him. The smell of Ma frying chopped onions for his favourite chicken curry. It was the D-Hall smell. The stench of the cadavers. The reek of med school. And Kajal was suddenly appalled by the thought of it taking over every other fragrance in his life.

"Eat well, Kajal. Look how much weight you've lost. I don't know what food they give you in the hostel," Ma said at lunch, trying to make a point to Baba.

"It's okay. Medical education is tough." Baba said.

Kajal smiled. He couldn't bring himself to eat the chicken.

Kajal forced the food down. For Ma and Baba's sake. And that made him sick. He urgently went up to his room and threw up, easily and noiselessly. Hardly-chewed chunks of meat and rice in a watery vehicle, and finally a couple of rounds of plain bile. Kneeling beside, he kept looking at the pot for a long time. The chicken bits were white and pale pink as if Ma had never cooked them, disintegrating rapidly into slender rod-like fibres. Kajal detected salty fluid trek down his cheeks. With a start he brought himself to his feet and yanked the lever on the cistern. With a roar, a tiny whirlpool consumed the excrements. But his mouth remained pungent.

"You're sure everything's okay with Kajal?" Ma asked Baba downstairs as she retired next to him for the afternoon nap.

"Why, what do you think could be wrong?"

"I don't know. He seems so distant, so quiet, so pre-occupied".

"You're just being a mother. Don't worry he's fine. Relax. He must be missing the comforts of home and adjusting to his independent life. Before we know it, he'll come out a fine doctor."

* * * * *

Kajal had noticed Nikhil as the most jovial and social in the batch. He had grown to become the most popular in class and also the most loved in the hostel. He was bright with conversation, had great wit and was tactically spot-on in dealing with faculty, seniors and batch mates alike.

"Hi, I'm Nikhil," he said as he slipped beside Kajal with his plate at dinner.

Kajal looked up from eating. "Kajal."

"I know. What room?" Nikhil asked.

"Twenty Eight".

"Okay. Ground floor, last room on the corridor. So you have a single as well." Nikhil impressed Kajal with his knowledge of the layout.

Kajal did not respond. As much as he admired them, people like Nikhil made him uncomfortable with their overpowering propinquity.

"I'm in one one five. First floor. We must be the only first years with single rooms...Isn't it amazing that salt is the only thing they put in these curries and they manage to screw even that up...Only mine is better than yours – I have a balcony." Nikhil added with a smile.

Kajal didn't mind it one bit. That Nikhil's room had a balcony. What he did mind was Nikhil's relentless chasing of a conversation.

"You from Guwahati?" Nikhil continued.

"Ya," replied Kajal with a disinterest that didn't seem to get across to Nikhil.

"I'm from Diphu. You know? NC Hills?" Nikhil said without being asked. Kajal said nothing.

Kajal finished his dinner. He noticed Nikhil helping himself to one more round of rice and yellow *dal*. And he scooped out another spoonful from his once-jam-bottle of homemade green chilly pickle, which Kajal had politely refused when offered earlier. Kajal felt overcome by an appreciation of Nikhil's busy fingers as they mixed the food on the plate and lifted handful after handful in rapid succession. To see Nikhil, the 'star', so heartily enjoy a most depressing hostel meal did something strange to Kajal.

By the time Nikhil finished eating, Kajal's fingers were caked with the dried up curry. Nikhil had told him that it was fine if he wanted to leave. But Kajal just sat there. Watching Nikhil.

"What plans now?" Nikhil asked as they washed their hands at the basin.

"Nothing really. Just back to my room," Kajal replied.

"Why don't you come to my room then? You can check out my music".

Kajal didn't want to. He hated it that Nikhil had a taste in music as well.

"Okay. I'll drop in for a while. I hope I'm not bothering you," Kajal didn't know why he ended up saying that instead of making an excuse.

"Fuck you boss! Don't talk like a formal dickhead," Nikhil retorted loudly, and both the language and volume made Kajal uncomfortable. It was established that barely-one-month-old freshers should mind both.

———

Nikhil's room was dark. Just a pale yellow lamp in a corner on the floor, it's light further buried in a lampshade of loose audio and video cassette tapes thrown like a medusa head. As his eyes adjusted, Kajal realized that the room was really clean and meticulously organized. Nikhil had left music playing and at that moment *Shine On You Crazy Diamond* was somewhere in the middle. Kajal loved Pink Floyd.

"I have the brighter light but I like it this way. You okay?" Nikhil rushed across the length of the room to open the door to the balcony. A gush of fresh air stormed in.

"No that's fine. Can I sit down here?" Kajal said pointing to a huge cushion laid in apparent carelessness on the floor.

"Look boss, you have to stop treating me like I'm the Dean or something. Sit wherever you want to. Spread out in bed if you like. Just relax."

Nikhil spoke with obvious annoyance, but it made Kajal feel good.

"I love Pink Floyd. One of my favourite bands," said Kajal.

"Ya? That makes it the two of us. What's your favourite number? I promise to play it to you right now".

That was a huge promise in those days. Music was still essentially played out of cassettes. Audio CDs had just come around, but cost a bomb and would be quite a feat for one to own the entire

Pink Floyd catalogue in the format. Radio had yet to discover Frequency Modulation and Vividh Bharti understandably preferred to cater to the tastes of *sainik-bhais*. Most importantly, this was a time before one could download music, mp3-4s were yet unborn, ipods and zooms were unconceived.

"*Hey You*. And *Post War Dream*. I really can't put a finger on one though. Actually, I just love them all", Kajal replied, increasingly belonging to the conversation.

"Thank God you didn't say *Another Brick in the Wall*! I already like you. Let me see...here it is – *The Final Cut*," Nikhil said as he fished out a pirated, Peacock book cassette with the famous Remembrance Day poppy on *The Final Cut* jacket. He slipped the cassette into the deck and passed the cover to Kajal. He was visibly proud of possessing the album. Kajal turned to the back cover. The famed controversial subtitle – '*A Requiem for the Post War Dream by Roger Waters, performed by Pink Floyd*' – was very much in place. The album had been the first evidence of the great band falling apart.

News of a rock band disbanding always makes me think how many of us persist with prickly-heat like Management in work environments that suck like hell and don't even pay well!

As the song opened with snatches of a radio being tuned across stations overlaid by the string arrangements, Nikhil pulled out a cigarette and lit it where he was standing. As he carelessly flung the used strike out of the balcony, he said, "I'm sorry I didn't offer. You smoke?"

"No I don't." Kajal forced any 'thanks' out, so as to not annoy Nikhil. "But isn't there a diktat on first-years smoking in the hostel? Shouldn't you be careful, especially in your own room? What if a senior comes in?" Kajal was, more than anything else, itchy about being discovered in the same room as a smoking Nikhil and the long drawn out repercussions.

"Aw, don't worry about all that. They don't come around for me. Just like they don't for you. Isn't that correct?"

"I don't know," Kajal couldn't think of anything else to say, as a familiar heat rose in the back of his neck.

"They think you're a whacko. They are intimidated by you. You scared the crap out of that imbecile Moinak when they took you for the D-hall thing. They were fucking scared you had died or something," Nikhil was heartily amused.

Kajal kept quiet. Shifting in his cushion and trying to look away. *Post War Dream* ended. The next number was *Your Possible Pasts*.

Nikhil sensed that he had made Kajal uncomfortable. "But someone needed to show these seniors how stupidly childish their ghost stories are. I really like your attitude. And because you are also a *real* Pink Floyd fan, you just became cooler!"

It was too late. Kajal knew Nikhil was trying to make amends by being extra nice.

Nikhil wasn't. He just wasn't the kind. He was the type that wouldn't call a spade anything else.

Half of Kajal wanted to leave right then. The rest of him wanted to stay on.

"Why don't they come around for you? Are you also a 'whacko'?" Kajal curled both his index fingers around the word.

"No. Unfortunately I'm not that cool," Nikhil laughed. "You know Sarim? Sarim Ingty? Fourth year. Third floor, Room 317? Short, stocky fellow with the olive green Kawasaki 250cc."

"No. I don't think I do."

"I thought so. Anyway, he's this real real big shot in the hostel. No one messes with him. He's my first cousin. So, no one fucks with me either. A family privilege. But I hate to be 'protected' like this. I'd love to be ragged like everyone else, but they're all scared of my big brother. On my first night in hostel, I got drunk with him and some of his friends and that was like my arrival notice. You drink?"

"No I don't."

"So you're this really good boy, yeah? Doesn't smoke, doesn't drink. But since it's you, I think even that's cool," Nikhil continued to be kind.

Kajal looked at his watch.

"Getting late?"

"Ya, I guess we should be sleeping. Morning class tomorrow," Kajal yawned, "I'm sorry but I'm a bit sleepy".

"Ya I know. Can I show you something before you leave?"

"Yes, of course."

Nikhil went across the room to pick up the brown jumbo acoustic guitar. Kajal had noted its presence as soon as he had come into the room. Nikhil sat down on the floor next to Kajal, back against the wall and knees flexed to cradle the guitar.

  Amaj   Dmaj   Emaj   Amaj
Mother do you think they'll drop the bomb
  Amaj   Dmaj   Emaj   Amaj
Mother do you think they'll like this song
  Dmaj   Amaj
Mother do you think they'll try to break, my balls?
  Emaj   Dmaj   A maj
Oohhhhh …… Aahhhhh …… Mother should I build a wall

"Wow! That was awesome. You're really good with that man," Kajal said, pointing to the guitar, at the end of Nikhil's performance. "And your singing's great as well." Kajal spoke excitedly. For the first time at med school, he felt happy.

"Thanks boss," Nikhil smothered a smile of pride.

"How long have you been playing the guitar?"

"Some years now."

"Wow! That's really amazing. I'm so fond of the guitar."

"You play as well?" Nikhil asked, half knowing that Kajal didn't, in the way that celebrities scout for talent in lesser humans.

"No I don't. But you think I could learn?"

"Of course you can." Celebrity-like encouragement.

"Will you teach me?"

"If you want me to. But I'm essentially self taught. So I can only pass on what I know." Celebrity-like modesty.

"That I am sure is more than good enough for me." Kajal could hide none of his enthusiasm. "Will you help me buy a guitar? Tomorrow, after class?"

"With pleasure. But you can use mine till you get your own, if you don't mind." Celebrity-like benevolence.

"You're sure?" and without waiting for Nikhil's reply, "Then can we start tomorrow?"

"Okay boss. I'm hired," Nikhil smiled and put his hand out for a shake.

———

Nikhil latched the door closed after Kajal left.

Walking across to sit at the table, he turned the study lamp on, cleared a little space on the table and put an old foolscap sheet on it. From the top drawer, he removed a small plastic pouch and pinching out a portion of the weed from it, laid it out on his left palm. Hand stretched out, he got rid of some seeds and then started to fine chop it with a pair of beard trimming scissors. Putting the stuff on the sheet, he emptied out a cigarette and expertly made his two-to-one mix of weed and tobacco and packed it back into the cigarette, tapping the butt end of the cigarette on his left thumb to get that perfect tightness.

Satisfied, he relaxed back on the chair. *The Final Cut* was fully rewound and he flicked the 'play' switch. He lit up, and watched the trail of thick smoke, blue within the cone of the study lamp light as little Tyndalised particles of dust performed a Brownian dance. He closed his eyes.

In a little while, a crystal ship full of rattlesnakes and sailors with looking-glass neck ties filled up his head. And the captain said, "*I am the lizard king, I can do anything!*"

Nikhil poured himself a measure of rum and added the warm Thums Up. He flipped through Ganong's chapter on muscle contraction and by the time he hit the sack, he was prepared for next morning's lecture.

* * * * *

"What happened?! Is everything okay? And whose motorcycle is that? You know I don't like you riding motorcycles," Ma was scared stiff as she opened the door, struggling to win back her breath.

"My friend JMD's. And it's not a motorcycle. It's a Kinetic," replied Kajal, and put his arms on Ma's shoulders.

Ma put one hand across her chest, closed her eyes and sighed heavily.

"Just got worried suddenly. They are all the same. These things on two wheels whatever you call them. Okay, how come you're home on a weekday evening? Baba's not here."

"Come on, Ma. Can't I just come home? And I'm here to see you."

"Of course you can. Are you staying the night? Let me make you some yummy dinner."

"Ma, don't get carried away. I'll come Sunday anyway for lunch. Can I come in now?"

"You didn't come last Sunday. Baba says you're busy with your studies. I don't know. You should at least call no." They were at the dining table in the kitchen. It was two weeks since Kajal had last seen Ma, and she suddenly seemed older. But she was perfectly capable of instantaneously aging by thirty years, on a reversible basis, at the sight of her son coming home on one-of-those two wheelers on a weekday evening.

"I know. I'm sorry. I actually was busy. Stayed at hostel the whole day. I came out to call in the evening, but the PCO had such a massive queue, I would have missed dinner. You know all the boarders make those STD calls after eight." Kajal felt sad as he guiltily made up the lie.

"Okay okay, but don't forget us altogether," Ma smiled. "What will you eat? I'll make pancakes?"

"No Ma, just sit. I've come with a..er..request."

"Request?" Ma's forehead creased neatly along the pre-set son-worry lines.

"Do you have some money on you now?"

"What happened? How much do you need? Are you in some trouble?" Ma's questions bumped into each other with motherly appetite.

"Relax Ma. Everything is okay. Would you have, say, two thousand on you now, max three."

"Of course I do. But why do you need it so urgently?"

"I...wanted to buy...a guitar." Kajal couldn't remember the last time he had asked Ma and Baba for something.

"A guitar!" Ma put one hand across her chest, closed her eyes and sighed heavily, relieved that the crisis only involved a wooden belly and neck with copper strung across.

"Ya Ma. I met someone at the hostel who plays really well. Nikhil. He's teaching me. He let me use his guitar all this time but it would be nice to have my own."

"Of course you can buy a guitar. Wow, I can't believe it. I'm really happy. Baba was right about hostels and all that wisdom he gave me. So, that's what you've been up to behind our backs." Ma smiled. Completely at peace, she rushed to start making the rice pancakes. They were usually mildly sweet and dressed with honey.

"Ma, I don't want anything to eat," Kajal screamed.

"Okay, don't get angry. Just have this juice. It's fresh bitter gourd. Very good for your liver, especially with all that God-only-knows-what you eat in the hostel."

She put the steel tumbler with the juice on the table and sat down. Kajal wondered how she always had a ready stock of all the wrong things. He looked at the drink and remembered clearly how it tasted, but also realized he couldn't waste the opportunity to please her.

"But why do you want to take the money now and keep it in the hostel? All three of us can go and get the guitar when you come this Sunday."

"No, Ma. I thought you and I could go and get it now."

"Today? Now? But how? Baba's not even home. There's no car."

"That's why I borrowed the scooter. We won't be more than an hour."

"The scooter! Kajal, you can't be serious about putting me on the back of that!"

Kajal had anticipated that. "Come on Ma. How can you be such a party pooper? You have no idea how excited I have been about the guitar. I've been dreaming about it the whole time. And now you tell me that I can't have it, all because you can't ride a scooter."

"I didn't say you can't have it." Ma's stand softened. Only problem was that where she was concerned, getting on a scooter was genuinely nothing less than being tied to the head of a space shuttle and dispersed skywards. Baba would kill them both when he found out.

"Okay," Ma took a deep breath. "I can't believe what you're making me do. But do I even have a choice? Let me change my *sari*. And how much money did you say?" Ma's voice trailed as she went to the bedroom.

————

At Rhythmscape, Kajal settled for a black jumbo Signature. He'd checked it out earlier with Nikhil. Two thousand six hundred bucks after the for-you-only two hundred Rupees discount. And a set of Karuna Brand nickel strings and two Gibson plectrums thrown in.

As Ma paid, Kajal sifted through the rack of guitar straps. He had noticed one in black leather on his earlier visit.

"Do you want one of these?" Ma asked as she came up to him, the Rhythmscape guy on her heel.

"No it's okay. They are expensive," Kajal replied. The black leather one was eight hundred.

"That's fine. Take it if you want it." Kajal knew Ma would say precisely that.

Encouraged by a mother's enthusiasm, the Rhythmscape guy shifted his salesmanship to top gear. "You will also need a gig bag. We have some nice ones in faux leather. And we also have great guitar stands, all Korean made. Don't worry about the price tags – I'll give you a good deal." By then, he was talking entirely to Ma.

Kajal and Ma finally left with a guitar (Rs.2600), a strap (Rs.800), a gig bag (Rs.1000) and a stand (Rs.850), all for a rounded off 'good deal' price of five thousand.

"I'd said three thousand max," Kajal said apologetically.

"Don't worry. I carried some extra," Ma smiled reassuringly.

As they reached the scooter, Ma had an idea, "Come let's get a quick coffee."

"You sure? Baba will be back and then he'll have to wait outside."

"Oh we have a lot of time till that. And he won't mind if he has to wait. He'll actually be very happy when I tell him we went to get your guitar. As long as he doesn't see us on the motorcycle."

They walked to a nearby coffee shop. Ma asked for a slice of black forest.

"So, how are things? Are you liking the course? Baba has a lot of expectations from you Kajal."

Kajal sipped his coffee. That familiar heat rose in the back of his neck and his palms went moist. "Ma, can we talk about something else? I'm trying to do my best. I'm nicely settled in the hostel. I have a couple of," pointing to the guitar, "very good friends now."

"But be careful. Don't waste all your time on the guitar. Baba tells me medical education is very rigorous."

Kajal slipped into the deep gutter of his ghosts. He felt a sudden unease. Guilt perhaps. Was he cheating Ma and Baba by not letting them know how his mind had revolted against every attempt to make it belong to med school? Was he even making an attempt? Or had he given up and succumbed completely to the cycle of Room 115? Was the music a mere stunt double for the real thing? But how could he say all this to Ma and Baba? He knew what his being in med school meant to them. Even though Baba never told him, he knew the price Baba had had to pay to get him there.

Just then, even the guitar became a responsibility – now that Ma and Baba knew, he felt the pressure to perform.

"Why are you so quiet?"

"Nothing Ma. Just wondering if it isn't getting too late?"

"Ya okay. I've finished."

As Kajal walked to the counter to pay, Ma realized she'd upset him in some way by bringing up med school. But why? Why did Kajal never want to talk at all about anything on the course? Was something wrong? She brushed the thoughts aside quickly – he would have told her if anything was the matter and as far as that evening was concerned, he was obviously excited about the guitar. She shouldn't spoil it for him.

"Do you play Hindi and Assamese songs as well?" They were walking back to the scooter.

"No Ma. You know the music I like."

"Ya I know. Red Floyd, and what's that other one, 'talks' an entire song between two notes? Ya, Dire Straits."

"Pink Ma. Pink Floyd."

"Red or pink, what's the difference? Someone should tell them that a break in between helps the listener find out when one song ends and the other begins."

As they reached the scooter, Ma suggested suddenly, "Wait. If you are not spending the night at home, you don't have to come to drop me. I'll take an auto. I'll anyway feel a thousand times safer on three wheels than two."

"Don't be silly. It'll just take me fifteen extra minutes."

"No, I actually mean it. Doesn't make sense at all for you to come all the way back. You can sling the guitar bag across, can't you?"

"Ya, that I can. But…"

"Now, *you* stop being silly. Here, stop that auto."

Kajal flagged an empty auto down and explained the destination as Ma got in.

"I have a plan. I won't tell Baba about the guitar. Learn that Dolly Ghosh song I keep singing, and we can both surprise him this

Sunday. And I'll tell you what – get your guitarist friend over as well. But you have to let me know in advance if he's coming. I'll make something nice for lunch." Ma's world essentially oscillated between lunch and dinner, and revolved around tending to Baba and worrying about Kajal.

"Ya, will do that."

"Call when you reach. I insist. I'll worry otherwise."

"Okay, will do that. Bye. And thanks Ma."

Ma made a face and said, "You are most welcome." And then her face turned serious, "Just stay happy, Kajal. Nothing else matters."

Nothing Else Matters. Not bad at all for Ma to be mouthing a Metallica line, Kajal thought as the auto left. He loved her.

Kajal didn't come home that Sunday. Ma and Baba were not really holding their breaths, they were beginning to get used to it. But it helped that he called.

"I guess I should just tell Baba about the guitar. Take care Kajal. Come when you have the time. And yes, bring the guitar along." Ma said over the phone, her voice spoilt by disappointment she failed to conceal.

* * * * *

The next couple of months were unlike any couple of months Kajal had ever lived. He traveled in its alacrity at most times. Unworried. Untroubled. Like he had just been born. On rare occasions, he had to jump off. To take a look and watch it speed past. And that left his palms moist and the heat rose behind his neck. He promptly leapt back.

Kajal was a coiled, wound-up package waiting to be discovered by a guitar. He surprised Nikhil with his progress. By the end of the second month, Kajal had got a handle on the major and minor chords and a couple of octaves as well.

His favourite chord was the open E minor. E minor had bright black eyes with a distant gaze, a straight sharp nose and a beautiful set of lips which never said a word. Its face was sad, yet kind. It suffered, and yet didn't resent. Mellow, yet forceful.

Nikhil and Kajal. A wonderful symbiosis. Complimentary. Supplementary. In hostel life. In being men. In playing music. Neither flashing a sleight of skill to outdo the other. Nikhil held rhythm to relish Kajal's small melodies on *Temple of the King*. And Kajal feasted on Nikhil's finger picking on *Sultans of Swing*. Together, they sounded brilliant, adding without competing.

In that little cocoon of the hostel, they remained immersed in music. In Nikhil's room, palely lit, with the door open to let the breeze find a way in and then out through the balcony at the other end. They made a name for themselves. Walkers on the passage outside stopped to gesture with eyes, upped thumbs or index finger and thumb circles. Approaching loud voices or laughter from the faraway end of the corridor hushed as they came closer.

In time, the cocoon cracked at places. And little flames of reputation leapt out to reach the rest of med school. With a wholesome splash of enigma. Because very few had actually heard them 'perform'– they never played at any of the college events despite pressures. In fact, never beyond Room 115. That is how they both wanted it. They played for themselves, and anyone that cared to take the walk.

In Nikhil, Kajal found the role model he had never had in life.

In Nikhil, Kajal found his first friend. And through music, his first set of close friends.

There was JMD, who's only issue with Kajal was, "You're a fucking only child! So you get the entire loot! My Dad loves this halfwit brother of mine more; the idiot's going to get the fucking lion's share of the family property."

Then there were why-don't-you-play-Megadeth Surojit and Nikhil's tomboyish cousin, Aparna who studied Sociology at the university and never got treated anything like a lady.

Surojit wore a single gold earring, thick as a wedding band. A punk allowed in med school? No, his was a decoration of tradition. An old custom where he came from. The first born in the family had expired, and Surojit was a 'precious child'. Back in the days when male members from every household were recruited for wars, the glint of the metal would have earned him exemption. Even earlier, in the days when able men were sacrificially offered to please wrathful deities, the hole in his ear lobe would have made him imperfect and thereby, unworthy of divine consumption. What privileges did it bring in med school? "Suits my rock n' roll," Surojit had cheekily clarified, flashing the devil's horns with both hands.

The four guys met every evening. Mainly music. And conversations around it. Surojit was a Rock n' Roll encyclopedia, and very generous with information.

Aparna came over at least two three evenings a week. And every Sunday afternoon. Most evenings when she was around, dinner was boiled pork curry which she pressure-cooked over two hours on the electric heater in Nikhil's room. They'd ask for plates of rice to be sent up from the hostel kitchen.

In the hostel, those who played music, or played a sport, or held a post in the Students' Union – or even owned a motorbike, had a girlfriend, and tipped the little immigrant boys fifty *paise* when they brought back cigarettes – were given a higher ground. And that translated into personalised house keeping, room-serviced food and additional heavy duty electrical provisions for 'not-allowed-by-rule' gadgets and equipment – all coming together to put forth the divinity of rice and boiled pork curry in a shyly lit room with Pink Floyd playing.

No, Kajal hadn't recovered from the smell of onions being fried or the sight of meat on his plate. Except in Room 115, where smells were different. The sharp edged smells bellowing from the whistling pressure cooker were soothed by the smother of perfectly blended tobacco and grass.

Nikhil smoked up to six seven joints a day. And this left a lingering grass-tobacco-smoke smell on all his possessions – shirts, jeans, socks, jumpers, jackets, books, belts, shoes, binoculars, boxing gloves, and even the posters on the walls.

This became the smell of Kajal's triumphs – over growing up ghosts, over mutilated cadavers, over being discarded by the hostel, over the weight of expectations and his perennial inability to deliver. Kajal took to the joints himself.

On his baptism in Nikhil's room, the first few hesitant puffs suggested that he was a natural – nothing seemed to happen. Encouraged, he made quick work of the rest of the joint. But very rapidly his mouth went dry, his limbs relaxed all tone and he wanted to sleep. But when he closed his eyes, the world became a spinning spiral, sucking him rapidly into its depth while promising a catastrophic climax when he touched ground. He opened his eyes briskly and saved himself.

The only thing that Kajal truly enjoyed when 'under' were the nightly bike rides they took to drop Aparna back to the university at the other end of the city. Aparna pillioned Nikhil's Hero

Honda CD100 while Kajal occupied the back of JMD's geerless Kinetic.

Every night Guwahati took a long shower, brushed its teeth and changed into starched white night clothes, leaving all evidence of the day long insults behind till morning brought back the human maggots to gnaw its bones to dust. And for that while, its air was virgin and fresh; its dangerously open manholes became tiny open mouths of bewildered innocent children; its mountains of garbage hid in the darkness like little secrets that children keep; its tiny droplets of honest hard work returned to dreams of a better tomorrow; all the daytime treacheries, politics and conspiracies in its narrow guts ceased fire in an intoxicated celebration of the night; all its loudspeakers hushed to the whispers of little children planning a coup against green vegetables. A city that busied itself through the day with childlike energy over childlike schemes executed with childlike extravagance, slept in childlike satisfaction.

On the way back, they detoured via Mizo Basti to pick up the quarter bottle of McDowell Rum from Arvind Paanshop. For Nikhil, who needed his time alone with a drink at his table at the end of everything.

Mizo Basti was Guwahati's underbelly. Like in every city – big or small, celebrated or unknown – the underbelly served the vast humanity that could only afford a bootlegged life. Once the façade of make belief elsewhere went to sleep, the underbelly rose, securely scaffolded by the price paid to the powers that be. At the push of a button called 11 PM, Mizo Basti blossomed into Petromax littered shacks selling everything from LPG cylinders to Phensydyl to rethreaded car tires to Government Fair Price Shop sugar to capsicum *pakodas* and deep fried lamb intestines in caramelized onion. And of course, Nikhil's bottle of dark rum. An oasis that sprang up when the rest of the city died, and disappeared without a stain in the morning light.

But at a time in his life when Nikhil and music were icing him with a layer of contentment, Kajal's academic graph sank miserably. And by the time Nandini realized this, only drastic measures could help.

* * * * *

Kajal saw Nandini for the first time on the 1st of December. On the college bus taking them to the academic block to vote in a new Students' Union.

That Kajal hadn't seen her before was understandable. Nandini was third year, two years his senior. The schedules at med school were such that one didn't meet even the whole of one's own class every day, being emulsified into smaller tutorial groups. And the fact that Gauhati Medical College is spread over an entire hill further reduced possibilities of chance encounters to negligible lows. But strangely, he hadn't even heard of her before that moment. Anyone who's lived on a campus would agree that the Nandini types were hard to miss.

That day, all classes and teaching clinics were cancelled on account of the elections and the college buses carried an admixture of all batches up the hill at the same time.

It had never happened to Kajal before. That morning, his eyes froze on that face the minute he climbed the three steps of the bus and his heart needed to be coaxed back to the job of beating. Even as people getting onto the crowded bus behind him groaned but couldn't get him to move away from being in the middle of everyone else's way. Even as people cursed further contributions to his 'weirdo' status and he stood there proving them right. Even as the Ashok Leyland, shifting its inertial state from rest to motion, jolted him backwards and he mechanically found a rail on the ceiling to clutch. Even as his right hand holding the rail began sweating profusely despite the winter, and gravity pulled down a couple of tiny droplets and planted them on the heads of startled neighbours.

She was the most beautiful piece of humanware Kajal had ever seen. With the sun rays trapped within, her black hair was auburn. It was side parted, and the way it disappeared behind her ears suggested a close crop at the nape. The softness of her face seemed to come from being bred in protective warmth. Her eyes sparkled and their focus shifted trajectory like a fleet footed grasshopper, nothing holding attention for long. Her ear lobes were embellished with straight-forwardly crafted, gun metal studs – two in each ear, one larger than the other. Kajal had a view till a little below her chest, the rest was sheathed in the crowd. She wore a white *kameez* with a slightly raised gold adorned neck, and was buttoned all the way up. Her *dupatta*, which she carried over the right shoulder, was an all white handloom kind, liberally swollen. Kajal could tell she was tall, perhaps five seven, but he couldn't be sure how much her footwear contributed to it.

Never before had he felt so paralyzed and captivated that, try as he might, he just could not look away.

She stood in the aisle, holding on with both hands to the rounded edge of the rail on top of the fifth row seat as the crowded bus torqued its way up the hill. The maternal winter sun wafted in from the windows in well defined beams that held shape even through the undulations of the ride. One beam cut Nandini's face obliquely, leaving one eye warm in the shade and the other struggling to get away from irksome photons. Just then, she moved slightly and turned right to talk to someone behind her. Her oversized bag slid off her left shoulder and she unmindfully flexed her forearm to catch it at the elbow. In returning to her earlier position after the brief word, she overshot the null point just that fraction. And that's when her eyes met Kajal's.

Suddenly conscious that he had been discovered, Kajal briskly found another line of sight. But only momentarily. When his eyes drifted back to hers' again, Kajal found her there. Like she had known that he was going to come back, and so had waited. Kajal smiled at her – shy, nervous. She smiled back at him – amused, kind.

The bus finally reached college, in what seemed like a millionfold magnification of the fifteen minutes.

The academic block looked like a festooned tableau basking under the bright sun and the clear blue sky. Posters of the various candidates hung from strings tied between convenient beams; some posters were printed but most were hand painted across old copies of *The Assam Tribune*. One of the candidates, who, by the way, became Gen Sec later that day, dabbled in some last minute wooing by handing out bars of Cadbury's to a group of first year girls, the boys already taken care of with alcohol and chicken furnished to the hostels the last couple of evenings. The first year was vital – a very malleable 150-strong vote bank. College elections – a practice of grassroots level democracy.

From where he stood armoured by inconspicuousness, Kajal waited and his eyes followed Nandini's hundred metre walk into the building. The rest of her details came home – the white *kameez* reached below the knees and under it, she wore a white *chudidar*. On her feet were a pair of flat, fawn-coloured *jooties* embroidered with bits of red, royal blue, green and black with an inlay of small octagonal mirrors. Her white *dupatta* ended in gold tassels, the same gold as that of the work on the neck of her *kameez*.

Never before had a face, a human being, or even an inanimate sight stimulated Kajal to register so much detail.

* * * * *

Kajal didn't see her again after that day. It had been two weeks.

But he saw her everywhere. From a distance, from behind, anyone with short hair froze the middle of his chest. He rushed to one of the large windows in the canteen from where he could see the third years get off the bus at half eleven but she was never there. He chased the end of a white *dupatta* disappearing into a turn in a corridor but it wouldn't be her.

That night, overcoming restricting impulses, Kajal asked Nikhil about her. It was pork night. Aparna sat on the bed, sifting through Nikhil's photo album while waiting for the pressure cooker to whistle, and the usual foursome shared a joint on the balcony.

"That's new! Kajal's talking about a girl. About time, boss. Okay okay, tell us who. Ape, check this out," Nikhil shouted out to Aparna.

Nikhil's loud enthusiasm was uncharacteristic, and took Kajal by surprise.

"I don't really know her." Kajal murmured, suddenly embarrassed like hell. "And please, don't blow this out of shape. I just wanted to find if any of you guys know her."

"As long as it's a girl, you're in the right queue." Surojit assured. His Rock n' Roll encyclopedia had a couple of appendices on the fairer gender: Appendix 1 – College; Appendix 2 – Guwahati; Appendix 3 – India; Appendix 4(a) – Celebs (India); Appendix 4(b) – Celebs (International). "Right, do we have a name?"

Kajal looked back at the waiting faces. It was definitely not what he had in mind. He had only wanted a quiet word with Nikhil.

"No."

A collective sigh resonated on the small balcony. Inside the room, even Aparna had held her breath momentarily.

Surojit let out a stretched, "All right. Can we have a description?"

Kajal felt the eight eyes sectioning him into thin spiral slices. His palms went moist. A vision of Nandini sprang up with every minute detail highlighted in fluorescence. But he couldn't bring his vocal chords to make the relevant sounds. He cursed himself for bringing the whole thing up and suddenly wished Surojit would disappear.

"I'm not really sure," Kajal whispered.

"Wai-wai-wait. What do you mean you are not sure? Just describe her. Just tell us the way you'd describe, say, Nikhil to someone. How dumb are you?" JMD took over.

"As a starting point, please be informed that Madhubala is dead and Demi Moore doesn't quite live on this campus. And for anyone else, you need to plug in some keywords to get results from my database," Surojit was an architect discussing a client's requirements in a design.

"Ya, come on now Kajal. How can we help you otherwise?" Nikhil had spoken in a long time.

Kajal looked at Nikhil. And started describing Nandini. The others kept quite as Kajal finished a most sketchy depiction.

"And you say you saw her Election Day?" Surojit needed confirmation.

"Yes."

"She was wearing white?" Kajal hadn't told them this but Surojit's question was perfectly informed.

"Yes. How did you know that?" Kajal asked with some bafflement.

Nikhil, Surojit and JMD gave each other understanding stares.

"What I also know is that yesterday she was dressed in peacock blue and today it was lilac. With the trademark matching *jootis* I'm sure you've noted. And if you had come with us to the Beat Contest that Saturday, you would have seen her in blue jeans and a white turtle necked." Surojit sounded like he could go on.

"So you guys know who I'm talking about."

Kajal felt disappointed, a little betrayed even. He realized he would have been happier if none of them could zero in. So quickly. So confidently. In so much detail.

"I'll be damned if I didn't know Nandini Bezbaruah," JMD jumped in. "But which world have *you* been living in, Mr. Only Child?"

Kajal wasn't amused. What did become very clear was that Nandini was very far from being *his* discovery.

"Years down the line if you hear that I couldn't make a baby because my juices had run dry, she'll be entirely to blame," Surojit added with a wink, clearly enjoying the moment. "She's injected wanking talents into tables and chairs."

"Shut up, you sick one-trackers," Aparna shot from inside the room with her usual belting prowess.

"Oops, I'm sorry Ape; I forgot how touchy you are about all the male attention you get." Surojit hit back, with good natured sarcasm. Aparna's tomboyish deportment and fiery attitude were such strong fenders that boys usually didn't dare a trip into her zone.

"Well, if girls thought you were Clint Eastwood you wouldn't have been surviving on mentally undressing one half of the world."

"Alright now, you two," Nikhil interjected. And then turned to Kajal. "Nandini Bezbaruah. Third year. Tea planter family from Jorhat. Academically among the top five in the batch. Top notch debater. Took away a chest of trophies for badminton last College Week. That she is quite a looker is not hidden from you. But what you obviously don't know is that the fantasies she fuels bring the medical school to one great ground of equality. By conservative estimates, she is propositioned twice every day. Boss, she's one big time heart break waiting to happen if you mess too seriously."

A sudden shrill whistle filled a corner with a bonsai mushroom cloud of vapour, infused with the perfect blend of aromas. Aparna's count read six, but none of the others seemed to have made any note of the preceding five. The most vital part with the pork was to pressure cook it through six whistles. No species of tapeworm was known to survive that.

"Did anyone ask for the rice to be sent?"

* * * * *

Point Blank was the heart of the campus. Many believed that through complicated tangents and secants, it was equidistant from each of the hostels. It was a complete world – a standing-only cafeteria; a ten table sit-down joint that sold steamed chicken and pork momos, Indianised chowmein, rolls, puri-sabji, toast and masala omelet, rice plates topped with fish or chicken curry, and tea, coffee and Thums Up; a utility store; a stationer; a 24-hour phone booth with five separate lines; a travel corner for train and bus tickets; a video cassette rental store; a 24-hour paanshop which also provided black tea and cup-cakes through the night; a hair-saloon with three barbers, absolutely non-sexist by intention but restricted to a men-only status by demand; a traveling cobbler who set up shop every Sunday morning.

Kajal's heart screeched to a halt. It wasn't his mind playing tricks on him. It was Nandini. Paying for her purchases at the utility store.

It was the 31st of December. A month since Election Day. A couple of weeks since Nikhil and the gang put a name, and some more, on that face. Around half four in the evening as the last bits of daylight leaked out of the year.

Kajal froze in his tracks and retreated to light a cigarette outside the paanshop.

She was alone. He watched her pick up her shopping and leave, leftovers of the smile she handed out to Utpal at the till still on her face. Kajal espied Utpal checking out Nandini's behind as she walked away. Their eyes met. Utpal smiled an okay-you-caught-me-mate smile. *Aparna was right. Sick guy. Must be mentally undressing her.*

As Nandini went past looking straight ahead, some ten metres from where he stood, Kajal felt an irresistible impulse to pursue her. Before he could reconsider, he was walking and catching up real fast. His heart, and legs, defeated his mind, pulling him out of the walls that habitually sprang up at the slightest prospect of socializing.

"Hi. Can I help?" Kajal was by the side of Nandini.

With a start, Nandini stopped and looked back at him, the middle of her forehead furrowed into a question mark.

"With the bags," Kajal explained, his chin gesturing to the two bags in her hands. Through the flimsy polythene, the bright yellow of the Maggi packets showed in one of them.

"Oh! That's very kind but I'm fine really. Thanks." She was no stranger to such situations. Most often though, they were disgusting sighs and groans. Or a comment. Catcalls, very rarely. And she had learned to handle them all without flinching.

"Let me help. You going back to the hostel?" Kajal persisted.

"Yes I am. But honestly, your friends will have a lot to say to you if they see you trudging beside me with these bags."

Nandini tightened her grip on the bags. Kajal concurred and gave up. But continued to walk beside her.

"What? You want to walk with me?"

Much to an embarrassment that would hit him only later, Kajal nodded his head like a little puppy dying to trail a favourite master.

Nandini smiled. *Allowed.*

"I'm Nandini, by the way. And I'm sorry I'm really lousy with conversation." Nandini smiled again.

"I know."

"What do you mean? You know that I'm bad with conversation?"

"No, no. I mean I know you are Nandini. Kajal. First year."

"Very good to meet you, Kajal."

They passed the mouth of the famous seventy two steps that went up to Men's Hostel 2. It was common practice for ladies going up to their hostel further up the hill to take those steps and pass through Hostel 2, and that reduced walking time by sixty percent. Nandini never walked that route for her understandable need to steer away from high testosterone foci. For that moment, it went well with Kajal too – he didn't really want to venture through a men's hostel towed by Nandini. And also, the other route was worth a good half hour.

As they walked in silence, Kajal started wondering if Nandini was aiming to catch the shuttle bus service that went up the hill to all hostels through the day. He glanced at his watch – just after five. She was in time for the quarter past ride. But as they approached the bus stop, Nandini showed no signs of slowing.

"You don't want to take the bus? Will be here in five minutes." The words left Kajal's mouth before he could discipline them.

"I thought you wanted to walk me to the hostel. Why, tired already?"

"No, not at all. I was just thinking," Kajal shot back promptly, reminding himself not to push his luck too far. A thought of repenting in his cold dark lonely horrible room crossed his mind.

The incline turned steeper as the road started to ascend the hill. The air became sharply chilly and fresh as the city suddenly dropped away. Above them, a group of birds flew in formation, the sun and the moon briefly shared two wings of the same sky and starry specks mottled the rapidly darkening blue.

They curved around the Kaali temple. Dedicated to the aggressive and powerful form of Goddess Durga, the temple was built in the initial days of construction of the college, back in the early sixties, to recruit her strength to protect – four workers had been man-eaten in the first fortnight of clearing out the hill. Hard to believe but where Kajal and Nandini walked in the middle of Guwahati some thirty years later, was the roaming ground of tigers, and the rest of the fraternity, at the erstwhile edge of the city.

The five fifteen bus went past. One head appeared at a window and figured Nandini out, looked back for a long time struggling to establish Kajal and then promptly vanished to break the news in the busmosphere.

"So, what plans for the night?" Nandini asked, finally losing the lousiest-with-conversation crown to Kajal. Kajal realized it was indeed the 31st of December; he had been lost to time and space for a while.

"Just being in the hostel. We are cooking dinner," Kajal replied.

"Pork and alcohol, right? But isn't that like any other night in your hostels? How can *that* make you feel like it's New Year's eve?"

"I don't know. Maybe we'll also play guitars and all that," Kajal answered vaguely.

"Do you play?" Nandini's question sounded impressed.

"A bit. My friend is much better," Kajal's answer sounded hesitant.

"Okay, that's really good," Nandini tore a tone out of Ma's book. "I know some of you in those filthy, out-of-control hostels are actually very talented people. Not so much gift in the Ladies' Hostels. You know Nikhil? He plays really well apparently. I haven't heard him, but he and some friend of his have been in the Ladies' Hostel gossip for a while now." Nandini smiled.

"You know Nikhil?" Kajal was genuinely shocked and suddenly felt betrayed. *The bastard didn't tell me!*

"Ya," Nandini's reply rapidly traversed the *so* and *do* notes of the octave. "I mean, I don't like *know-him* know him, we've said hi a couple of times." She clarified. Kajal granted that the association was insubstantial but that still did not justify Nikhil not telling him.

"Nikhil's my best friend. *(And I just realized – quite a jerk)* We play together."

"Really?" Nandini spoke loudly, "So, are you the famous other half?"

"I guess so," replied Kajal, elated at the opportunity to be meaningfully modest. And that too with Nandini. *A Moment in a Million Years.*

"Wow! Ya...Kajal. The name does ring a bell now. Wow! I must announce in my hostel that I shared this walk with the rockstar! You have no clue what big stars you are."

"No, we are just about okay."

"But I've heard you guys are religious about never performing on stage. Why is that?"

"That's part of the game plan to protect the bubble and keep the reputation intact!" Kajal wasn't being entirely cheeky. At some level he believed it was true. It was a fear, an apprehension, the burden of which he had learnt to never leave behind.

They reached the gate at Nandini's hostel. Barriers were extensive at the Ladies' Hostel, even with a security post. Guests needed to register, elaborately with 'in' and 'out' times and purpose of visit, and could only meet boarders in the Visitors' Room. Couples preferred the solitude of the little clearing outside the gate. That evening there were three motorbikes standing, with a resident couple each, exchanging vows for the New Year in warm whispers, the male halves unable to resist sly peeks at Nandini. *Aparna would have said – "Men!"*

"What are you doing for tonight?" Kajal asked.

"I have family here, I'm going over. Where are you from?"

"Here only, Guwahati."

"How come you are not going home? Or is it unmanly to be doing that?"

"No, nothing like that at all. Just that we made these plans in the hostel."

Kajal suddenly realized that it hadn't even occurred to him that he could have, perhaps should have, gone home. Both Surojit and JMD, who were also 'locals', had left for home after lunch, even as Kajal decided to remain in the hostel with Nikhil. Aparna had her own plans and wasn't coming. With the next day being a holiday, boarders from nearby towns had also packed up. The hostel in fact was going to be pretty empty.

"Okay then Kajal, I've got to be going. Have fun. And in advance, have a great year ahead."

"Thanks a lot. You too."

They smiled. "Will be nice to bump into you again," Nandini chuckled.

Kajal waited to see her walk through the gate.

On way to her room, Nandini couldn't steer her mind away from Kajal. He remained somewhere. Like he had done earlier. When she had first seen him in that bus. In the days since then he had easily gotten replaced by other pressing claimants to brain space. But the half hour that evening restored him from the recycle bin.

She entered her neat, uncluttered room and put the shopping away. Turning the lamp on, she stood in front of the mirror. She knew she was pretty. She knew she was the focus of a whirlwind of desires – not that she spent her days and nights giving that too much thought. But the way Kajal looked at her somehow made her want to look at herself. What was it that he saw? It wasn't what the rest of the world seemed to see. What was it in his eyes that made her quake gently, and left her incapable of looking back at him in the eye?

And then it dawned on her – she had wanted the walk just as much. She smiled at her reflection, and suddenly conscious, lifted a hand and wiped herself off the mirror.

* * * * *

"Give me ten minutes," Kajal said suddenly, putting the guitar down on the floor. The thought came to him in a flash, and rapidly blossomed into something that he needed to do right then.

"Why boss, what happened?" Nikhil asked with surprise.

"Need to make a phone call. I'll be right back."

"You mean you're going to the Point?"

"I'll be back real quick." Kajal pulled on Nikhil's jacket, readying to leave.

"You are not going to be back anything like real quick. It's eleven thirty on 31st night, the phone booth's going to be like some food distribution centre in Somalia." Nikhil removed the lid of the pressure cooker, and began stirring to reduce the curry.

"I just have to make this call."

"Okay boss. But food will be ready in fifteen."

"I'll be back before that."

Kajal was in the middle of having the best 31st night of his life. It had been only Nikhil and him in Room 115 with the usual music, cooking and joints. But the evening earlier had taken every happiness centre within him to eagle and vulture territory. That half hour spent with Nandini was like a drug whose aura resiliently weathered time and triggered an urge to do the right things, and to do them right.

Arriving at Point, Kajal realized how correct Nikhil was – he had never seen Point Blank so heaving. And the phone booth promised a waiting time that would give reasonable chase to a Government office. He joined the queue. He simply had to make the call.

As luck would have it – and add Bollywood-like convenient coincidences – the clocks struck twelve, firecrackers lit up the distant sky, people in Point Blank greeted each other and the new year rolled in as Kajal stepped into the booth.

The phone rang five times before it was received.

"Hello." The sleepy voice sounded tired.

"Hello Baba, happy new year."

"Kajal!" The voice woke up fully. "Happy new year son. Happy new year."

"Sorry, I'm calling this late. Ma's asleep?"

"No, no. Here, talk to her."

"Kajal, happy new year! What are you doing outside this late? Go back to the hostel quickly. Is someone with you or are you alone? Be careful, there will be all those drunkards everywhere." Ma hadn't had a chance to do this in a long time. Kajal hadn't called in three weeks.

"It's okay Ma. Don't worry, I'm with friends. Happy new year Ma. I wish I had come home."

"Come tomorrow. I'll make lunch."

"Ya, I'll do that. Make something yummy. I'll bring Nikhil along. Good night Ma. Say bye to Baba."

"Yes I will. You get back safe. And right now. Otherwise I'll get worried."

———

By two in the morning both Kajal and Nikhil were tripped like never before. Jim Morrison was belting out *Hello, I Love You* for the nth time and they both blasted along, sitting across each other on the floor, backs against the wall, heads thrown back and eyes shut.

"She speaks with the tongue of an angel. The streets were orange and the lights purple. I think we shouldn't have taken the bus." Kajal murmured as the song ended and neither of them had the drive left to rewind one more time.

Reminders of something about lunch next day yo-yoed between Nikhil's sulci and gyri, but the picture wasn't clear enough to reveal Kajal inviting him. "Kajal boss, I'm lunching with Gary Linekar, Che Guevera, Syd Barrett and Stephen Hawkins tomorrow. Strictly by invite – what say, boss, I sneak you in?"

* * * * *

With as many as twelve different dishes vying for every pin-head of space on the teak dining table, Ma had obviously had a busy opening day to the year. And Baba and her aggressive hosting required the boys to respond with loosened waist-belts and unbuttoned jeans.

"Why don't you go up to Kajal's room and take a nap? Leave after tea in the evening." Ma suggested after the meal. With the state of their brimming tummies, the notion of tea, even with the intervening two three hours, was nightmarish. But the thought of a warm duvet on a cold winter afternoon was like a divine magnet, especially with their hung-over heads gravely accentuated by the gluttony.

In Kajal's room, Nikhil inspected Kajal's music tapes as the latter pulled out a second duvet for Nikhil.

"Boss, this is really not on. *The Very Best of Modern Talking*?" Nikhil stumbled all over a laugh he didn't pretend to stifle as he picked out the single 'out-of-taste' and generally 'non-macho' element in Kajal's collection of music.

Kajal looked up. "Baba's gift," he replied.

Kajal remembered the day. He was about twelve. Baba had returned from a trip to Delhi and the cassette was in recognition of Kajal's then new found ear for western music. And even though he shared every micro-ounce of the suffering Bob Dylan's *Street Legal* and Scorpions' *Love at First Sting* went through at having to flank *Cherie Cherie Lady* on the shelf, he couldn't bring himself to displace it. Baba had grown up listening to Assamese folk songs with an occult talent for music that he never had an opportunity to nourish but wanted to encourage Kajal to traverse every trail in life that he himself couldn't. Through all the years, far from losing the cassette, Kajal had in fact had it playing in the house periodically, just because he felt it would make Baba happy. Baba never understood Kajal's taste in music because Kajal never told him.

Nikhil kept quiet. In Kajal's household, a mysterious resident cloud that seemed to shroud human interactions had struck him from the earliest instance that afternoon. The relationships bordered on the formal, like it was foremost on everyone's agenda to be careful. Something told him that a fragment of the same cloud protected *The Very Best of Modern Talking*.

It was dark when Kajal woke Nikhil up from the extended catnap. By the time they got downstairs, Baba had kicked up a small fire in the backyard and Ma was laying out her set for tea, much pruner than the lunch spread. Defying all premonitions, the boys actually found it fondly inviting.

"Had a good nap? Do you want to join Baba by the fire?" Ma stood beaming. It had been quite a while since Kajal had been in the house for that long.

"Wow, that will be perfect," Nikhil exclaimed.

"You go ahead, I'll bring you a plate," offered Kajal. He put a warm veg puff, some crisps and a splash of ketchup each in two plates.

"Will Baba eat?" Kajal asked Ma.

"No, I think he'll just have tea. He's been going on about having overeaten at lunch. You know how he's got a tummy tinier than a rabbit's. You run along, I'll bring the tea over," replied Ma.

The fire burnt with a distinctive smell. And coughed a frequent sputter. Baba needed to keep poking the wood around with a stick and fanning in fresh oxygen now and then.

"Evening sir."

"Hey Nikhil, got up? Come come, sit."

Nikhil felt a tingling as the fire smartly edged the cold out of his body. He sat down and extended his pronated palms to face the fire.

"The wood is moist, that's why the excessive fumes," Baba explained. Nikhil nodded.

Kajal soon came with the plates, shortly followed by Ma who carried a cane tray with cups and a pot of tea.

"Only tea for you, isn't it?" Ma asked Baba as she handed Nikhil his cup. The aroma was brilliant, and that was one thing that Kajal was proud of about home – thanks to Ma's brother Nitu *mama*, they always got vacuum packed, garden-fresh stock from Tetelibari Tea Estate.

"Are we out of *narikol laru*?" The super sweet, little white cannon balls of grated coconut were Baba's famous Achilles' heel, and back in the days when some in Ma's family had a well-meaning opinion against his cavalier philanthropic distribution of professional skill in Arunachal Pradesh, withholding their supply had come up for consideration as the single infallible means of luring him back to Assam, and was discarded only on grounds of inhuman cruelty.

"You should cut down. You are not getting any younger," Ma retorted as she started walking back to the kitchen.

Baba winked at the boys and whispered, "I don't have diabetes and she thinks restricting sweet will guarantee that I never do."

"You guys want as well?"

"No thanks auntie. But can I have another patty?"

"Of course."

Baba and Nikhil resumed their pre-lunch conversation about the latter's father's work. Baba was very impressed to know that Dr. Teron was a researcher with the Centre for Promotion of Indigenous Farming. In Delhi.

And then Ma returned. "Can we have the music now?

"Oh auntie, I'm so sorry. Nearly forgot." As Nikhil got up with a start to get the guitars, Kajal felt a little extra hot behind the neck and his palms went moist. His first time in front of Ma and Baba, and he felt a real pressure-to-perform.

"I'll just make a phone call and come back," Baba said.

"Do that later no," Ma screamed.

"It won't be long. Let the boys get ready." Baba walked indoors.

Nikhil and Kajal tuned up even as Ma's face broke into a smile looking at her son holding the guitar.

"*Holiday?*" Nikhil looked at Kajal.

Kajal nodded and started finger picking on D minor with the C and B flat notes falling off on the fifth string before the cycle ended with a full A major on the fourth bar. Nikhil came in with the intro solo and then brought in the vocals.

"Fantastic! You sing really well, Nikhil. Come on now, Kajal sing us a song," Ma crisply came to her pick on the menu.

"Ma! I don't sing."

"Of course you do. Nikhil, don't tell me you haven't heard him sing," Ma was insistent.

"Never. What's this boss, keeping secrets with friends?"

"I don't sing, you know it Nikhil." Kajal sounded stern in begging for rescue.

"He sings really well. But that's just the way he is – he'll never tell you anything till you find out. Enough now Kajal. Sing. It's just us anyway," Ma wasn't going to give up.

"Okay, but only a couple of lines." Even through his attempt at slithering out, he had fished himself a song. A song to Ma's liking. Not for Paul Simon's poetry but for the pleasing melody.

"Now, that was a discovery! So you do have a singing voice, boss." Nikhil spoke out loudly when Kajal finished. His pretentious enthusiasm was obvious to Kajal – Kajal would have given himself a five on ten, but Nikhil would surely have been much less generous with the performance. But such technicalities meant nothing to Ma. All the hard work of a lifetime of child nurturing had just returned its first fruits, by the fire that was struggling to stay alive in Baba's prolonged absentia.

Meanwhile, Baba had found convenience in the dark bedroom, by one of its windows that opened into the backyard. Even with the panes closed and blinds drawn, the music carried unhindered from outside.

Baba realised it was strange. That he couldn't sit facing Kajal when the latter performed. Because he felt that his presence would inhibit Kajal's stride. Not just that evening, but even when Kajal was six and recited a poem. When he was twelve and rehearsed his elocution piece at dinner. But Baba never missed a thing, always finding a vantage point from where to watch with paternal fulfillment over a son's flourish. But what Baba never construed was how Kajal was completely aware of this curious state of affairs. And at that moment, with his singing done, Kajal knew Baba would soon make his return.

"Can I sing one?" Ma asked innocently. "Will you guys play with me?"

"Ma, just sing like that no. We don't know your kind of songs."

"No, we'll play. What song is it, auntie?"

"Nikhil, Ma will sing Assamese."

"That's brilliant. Which one, auntie?"

Kajal resigned to his lack of influence over the matter.

"Do you know *Du Haatote*? Dolly Ghosh." Ma addressed Nikhil. Kajal had known that was going to be the song.

"Ya ya, auntie. Lovely song. Sing sing." Nikhil sounded excited, as he searched for a scale. He turned to Kajal, "Let's take it from D minor."

Just then Baba came out to join them. "Tchh tchh, the fire's almost gone."

"Ya, just like you. What took you so long? You missed everything." Extraordinary that Ma never saw the pattern in his vanishing acts.

"I'm sorry, just got stuck. That Dr. Bagchi is one solid example of post-retirement joblessness. My mistake entirely to have called him now. But I did hear the singing. Very good, Very good." Baba applauded no one in particular; the only care he seemed to be taking was to keep his eyes firmly on the fire, lest they wandered to meet Kajal's.

"Okay okay. Be quiet now. They are forcing me to sing as well." Ma retorted curtly and cleared her throat.

Nikhil warmly supported Ma's singing. As he landed understated cue notes and fillers between muted rhythm strokes, Kajal discovered the soft beauty of helping a mother sing Dolly Ghosh by the fire even if your guitar God was Malmstein.

Later, they declined Ma's offer for dinner. They were filled good to go without food for a couple of nights. Nikhil always thought it was cruel to place before hostellers a spread larger than appetites could accommodate – why couldn't they come on installment basis, one dish a day?

"Let's go and drop them off," Ma suggested to Baba. They had all moved indoors.

"Yes yes, of course."

"No uncle, please don't bother. We'll be fine."

"Ya Baba, there's no need at all."

"But then you must take an auto. Don't try the bus. Leave quickly, before it becomes too late." And then she added, "Just hang on a minute, Kajal." Ma rushed to her bedroom.

Nikhil understood it was one of those family moments, and moved away towards the drawing room. Baba understood it was one of those mother and son moments, and promptly followed Nikhil.

"What's this Ma?" Kajal exclaimed as Ma returned and slipped a cylinder of paper the size of a cigar into his hand. Kajal spread out his palm to stare at the roll of hundred Rupee notes. Eight or nine perhaps – Ma wasn't a sucker for perfection, she wouldn't have bothered rounding it off to a thousand.

"Just keep it. Buy something." Ma whispered, and she pushed his fingers back so the currency returned to hiding. "Don't tell Baba, he has his dumb ideas about youngsters getting more money than needed." She winked.

Kajal and Nikhil said final goodbyes at the gate. Baba invited Nikhil over for *Uruka* and *Magh Bihu*, which were a fortnight away, and the latter promised to come again soon.

A little pool building in the corner of Ma's eye made Kajal uncomfortable, and he looked away. Ma was given to hyperlacrimation, and the lower end of her triggers included songs from tragic flicks on the radio. That particular moment was much greater in intensity – the final act of half an earth day well spent, but the climactic parting after a maternal geological era – and she deserved to shed some.

"See if you can make the weekend. But you must call anyhow, Okay?" Baba came close as he spoke. For a moment, Kajal thought Baba was going to shake his hand – he couldn't remember if they had ever done that before. But Baba's hand went past his to deposit something in Kajal's jacket pocket. Kajal retrieved it as soon they had walked away a bit, and in the fading light of the gate lamps, recognized the five hundred Rupee note – crisp, neat and folded across the middle.

Nikhil noticed it from the corner of his eye. "You should make it a point to come home every Sunday. They must miss you, boss."

* * * * *

After managing to live half a year in med school like a Parisian without a clue what the Eiffel Tower was, Kajal's strike rate at bumping into Nandini soared.

Once. "Hi. How's it going, Kajal?" She came up to his table in the college canteen. "Oh, hi. Good, good. Everything fine with you?" He survived a heart attack, stood up and stuttered. She nodded, smiled and went back to her friends, and bought a *samosa* at the counter.

Another time. It was the 26th of January, Republic Day, and for everyone in Assam, nothing more than just another holiday. Thanks to the guarantee of major public acts of terror offered by the 'true' sons of the land who regard education, agriculture, industry and tourism as unthinkably boring means of progress. People stay in, and homes have mute televisions tuned to the live stream of the main parade in New Delhi while children finish school work, ladies go about the daily routine and men tend to domestic chores that had been long awaiting masculine attention. Politicians and bureaucrats rise to the annual challenge of organizing a 'celebration' within a security safety net which leaves the 'common' man cordoned off. Not that the 'common' man cares too much either – sixty odd years have done a great job of ensuring that any sense of nationalism is entirely restricted to cricket.

Well, that 26th Jan, Kajal was playing tennis-ball cricket with friends just outside the hostel. Nandini walked past, with a companion. Kajal saw her, survived a heart attack and urgently looked away. Giving in to an irresistible impulse to look again, he plummeted into an eye-lock with Nandini's why-can't-you-just-relax eyes. She smiled widely, and waved her hand. Some twenty other hands, completely unaware of the real source of their collective good luck, joined Kajal in waving back, the cricket momentarily renounced to oblige Nandini's passage. The flutter of limbs created ripples in the air which enlarged, converged and traveled as a giant wave to strike the face of the four floors of the hostel. More hands spilled out onto the balconies and waved back.

Yet another time. Aparna had typhoid and was admitted in Medicine Unit IV. Kajal came one morning carrying her breakfast from the hostel. Nandini was there at the Nurses' Station, waiting with her tutorial group for the morning clinic. She smiled at him and shrugged her shoulders to ask what he was doing there. Kajal survived a heart attack and explanatorily raised the Milton case he was carrying.

And then finally. "Hey Kajal boss, can you run down and get our man a block of ice-cream for lunch?" JMD had undergone a tonsillectomy, perhaps the only surgery on earth where the post-op diet, or its popular interpretation, was something to look forward to. At Milky Way, down on the main street, Kajal realized he hadn't been advised on the flavour so he made his own choice. "Vanilla."

"So our hard-rocking guitarman likes vanilla." Nandini was ten feet away to his right at the long counter, inspecting a dark chocolate cake with *Happy 20ᵗʰ, Anchita* scrawled across.

Kajal survived a heart attack and rediscovered his voice, "It's for my friend JMD. He's had a tonsillectomy."

"Hi Kajal." Another head craned out from behind Nandini, giggling that excitement of being party to a good friend's secret. Nandini, smiling, reined her in with a discreet nudge to the side of her ribs. "You know my friend Vandana?" Nandini put a question mark on the introduction.

"Hi Vandana." Kajal glued his eyes to an imaginary spot on the counter top till the ice cream arrived. Washed with relief, he prepared to deliver a farewell word, only to realize that the ladies had also finished.

"You headed back?" Nandini asked.

"Ya. They'll be waiting." Kajal still couldn't look into her eyes. Vandana remained fixated on grinning stupidly. He hated her already, much like he hated his own friends where Nandini was concerned.

"Okay then. We've got some more things to pick up. See you again Kajal." Nandini discharged him. And then she took a step towards him and said in a low voice, "I'm coming to the Point later in the evening." Stunned, Kajal looked at her. She looked back and showed him how she was capable of producing her own version of Vandana's stupid grin.

Coming to the Point later in the evening. Kajal suspected that he was getting into his first date. At Point Blank? Where the whole world came every evening like it was everybody's home. Yes, the established, century-old couples who had started seeing the scary side of solitude did bring a sprinkling of romance. But for a first date? And that too with Nandini's Eiffel Tower like stature on campus.

It was near the end of February and dusks had pleasantly lengthened. People left Point Blank only after getting severely mauled by the mosquitoes – during my time, a good friend actually went deaf while slapping a mosquito to its death against his right ear at Point Blank – and even then, some stayed put, fruitlessly using their lit cigarettes like finger-held weapons of anopheles annihilation.

Point Blank was a horrible choice of location for a date.

Between four and half five that evening, Kajal smoked seven cigarettes at the Point.

A gentle tap on the shoulder from behind and a "Hi". That's how she arrived. Kajal turned around, survived a heart attack and smiled into her eyes. Nandini survived a tiny heart attack of her own.

"What? Are you just going to keep sitting here growing blisters on your lungs?"

Kajal threw the only-just-lit fag away. "I was waiting for you," Kajal explained, unsure what else he was expected to do in those one and half hours.

"Shall we walk?" Saccharine poured again.

"I thought you had some work here?"

"How can you be so dull?" Nandini's strident exclamation surprised Kajal, and he urgently took off with her, even as he nervously scanned the Point Blank horizon for RADARs and SONARs.

———

Some thirty metres away, Kabindra was the first to recover in the group. "Now, who the fuck was that?" They had just watched Nandini touchdown and scoop up a most unlikely candidate.

"It's that Hostel 5 weirdo," Daniel replied.

"Holy crap, will someone tell me what on earth he's got that I haven't? Or does Madam Nandini have a thing for toy boys with girlie names?" Shyamanta laughed with that agitation of male jealousy. Aggrieved further by what couldn't be denied – Kajal's sensibly clothed athletic frame walking in perfect agreement with Nandini's tall and dainty form was straight out of the Heavenly Matches advert.

————

The young assistant blew the conch-shell in long pulses, his face purple with congestion, cheeks billowing alternately like sails of a face-shaped ship and the great vessels of the neck swollen like overfed leeches; while the priest rhythmically clanked a hand-held brass bell in his left hand and offered *aarti* with the right, muttering *shlokas* with expert incomprehensibility that validated his years on the job. Incense sticks were generous with smoke, and burning camphor painted the thick air in the Kaali temple an iridescent yellow. And everywhere, that Hindu temple smell – incense, Annapurna *Ghee*, sandalwood paste, camphor, milk and marigold, topped by a bizarrely pleasing stench of cow and goat excreta.

The priest's right foot twitched as a smoldering splinter from his plate of *aarti* dived to its sizzling demise amidst the perspiration on his bare belly. He absent mindedly rubbed the spot with the stem of the brass bell. Other grain sized, hazy brown evidences of twenty years of evening *aarti* adorned his tummy, approving its summit around the navel which broke nearly all flaming flights.

From where Nandini had guided them to from the Point that evening, Kajal and she had no means of being a spectator to any of that. Only the med school hill stretched out all the way down from the rock they sat on. In the sea of darkness, lights shimmered like stationary fireflies, hidden and found as breeze after breeze bustled through the dense foliage of tall *Segun* trees. Though much smaller than the hostels and the loaf-shaped members of the hospital complex at the bottom of the hill, the Kaali temple was the brightest.

While the rock kept away every harsh staccato of man and machine, the sounds of the temple – the conch and the brass bell – seemed proximate.

"Isn't this like heaven?" Nandini dared to be only a bit louder than a whisper, lest she break the fragile calm. "I come here once in a while. There's never been another I could think of sharing this spot with."

Kajal didn't reply immediately. Suddenly, the heart attack was more visceral. He noted that the bell from the temple missed a beat. That's when gravity singed the priest's tummy with a burning splinter. Kajal was only bothered that a congenial rhythm had been broken.

"Ya, really. Great place to play guitar perhaps," was all that Kajal could suggest.

"I know music's wonderful. But there are some places even it shouldn't touch." Nandini closed her eyes and took a deep breath. Kajal worried he had let her down with a casual comment.

Nandini got up with a start and dusted the back of her jeans. "We'll miss dinner. And I completely forgot Anchita's birthday. Isn't it amazing how you lose count of time here?"

It had been three hours of nearly absolute silence. Kajal wished it could go on forever.

———

When Kajal reached 115, he was pleased to find only Nikhil.

"Hey Kajal boss, where have you been? JMD's mum was here. Shall we go down for dinner?"

"Ya Nikhil. Do you want to come back and play for a while?"

"Test's in three weeks boss. I think we should put in some time." Nikhil brought home a hard fact.

The third and final semester exam was round the corner. Traditionally, it was referred to as the 'Test' before the first Prof, after which most of the batch would go ahead into the third year clinics – technically inaccurate, but, yes, after first Prof you were in third year even though you had only done one and a half years in college – while some would fail and be relegated to the 'irregular' batch, and re-take the Prof six months later. Failing first Prof was a big deal.

The months had rushed by while Kajal haggled for more time to settle in. His fears and discomforts, like foreign invaders, made secure homes on his territory and banished him to find shelter in 115, music, cushioning friends and increasingly, Nandini. After fifteen moons, his backlog was immense.

They parted ways after dinner. The first time in a long time.

"Ten now. Let's meet at twelve for tea. My room." Nikhil took his voice up the steps.

As he entered his room, Kajal felt empty. With the lamp on, his room was colder, like the visibility of his isolation had induced a thermal plunge. On the shelf to his right, Chourasia's Human

Anatomy volumes resided in snug disuse. Langman's Medical Embryology had had leisure to auto-translate to Greek. Baba's gift from two weekends before, Harper's Illustrated Biochemistry was actually advanced fodder, and amongst only a handful of copies in the hostel, had only just returned from its second borrowing.

A while later, when Kajal checked his watch, he had long missed Nikhil's call for tea. It was nearly one.

Leaving his room, he walked up the corridor and stepped out on to the clearing just by the foyer. Taking a long drag from his cigarette, he stared into the cold dark sky. It was the time of the year when spring had claimed the days but the nights were still wintry.

Somewhere on the second floor a door slammed and hurried chappals echoed.

"Feeling really sleepy, man. Will you wake me up at four?" A voice, on the first floor.

"I tell you, Tendulkar plays only for himself. Look how Steve Waugh wins matches batting around tailenders." The debate raged on as a group on the third floor took a tea break. Black tea with coarsely crushed pepper corns worked wonders for unaffordable sleep and stiff backs.

Hostel 5, and every other on the campus, didn't sleep that night. And wouldn't for the next couple of weeks till the 'Test'.

Back in his room, Kajal sat on the bed and picked up the guitar. He stared at the sheet of paper. The result of his efforts over the preceding hours – Three verses without the obligatory chorus, called Stories in Black and White, set in the E minor key.

If lives were like train tracks
Who'd need so many colours
Every story would be black or white

On the rock the lovers sat cautious and anonymous
Protected in a speechless shell
And "Don't bring me your rock n' roll" was all she said

But you should come and see where I live
A raging storm threatens my spider's web
Smudged the two become, black and white

He sang it one more time. Softly. The result pleased him. He knew Nikhil would inject perfect arrangements into it. "Let's get those three notes on flute," he'd say. Kajal's first song. Written the first time he had ever played the guitar without Nikhil.

* * * * *

From the moment he woke up the next morning, an unfamiliar drive inspired him to put in two weeks of undiluted, frenzied hard work. He buried himself amidst all the print that he had forever run away from. And the experience left him invigorated with positive energy.

Tormenting lectures from ten months earlier started making sense and six month old practical sessions became lucid. As the first week unfolded to the baton of his cogent scheduling, he finally seemed to triumph over the ghosts.

He went up to 115 for breaks, and over tea and a cigarette, efficiently participated in discussions with Surojit and sometimes even contributed to dispel some of JMD's grey areas. He knew it was uphill, but for the first time began to trust that it was doable.

But even as Kajal was beginning to get his act in some order, his start was an entire Olympic too late, and the call was for him to run a marathon at the sustained speed of a hundred metres dash. There was no way he was going to cover all bases. And soon his head recognized it.

One week from the exam, he took it up to Nikhil. Nearly two in the morning.

"Tea? Do you want to make it yourself?" Kajal's was not a scheduled pit-stop.

"Could I get a joint?"

"Of course boss. But you'll have to fix it. And one for me as well, if you don't mind." As Kajal took the stuff from Nikhil's famous top drawer, he glanced at the latter drawing a diagram of the arterial Circle of Willis. A massive pang of anxiousness hit him – the job on hand was mightier than even he had conceded.

Kajal sat on the bed and rolled two joints in silence, and distractedly lit one.

"How's it going boss?" Nikhil eased the unlit joint out of Kajal's hand to find one end soggy with perspiration. "You studying well?" Nikhil asked with that ability to instantly put a finger on the reason for the other's joy or bother that is resident in good friendships.

"I'm not going to make it Nikhil."

"Oh, come on boss. We have time." Nikhil feigned cheerfulness. He suspected Kajal was right.

"Not enough. I'm only about twenty percent home in Anatomy and Physiology, and yet to get off the blocks in Biochem."

"Okay boss. Maybe you don't have time for everything. I'd suggest you stick to probable questions."

Kajal's expression betrayed his bafflement – while he was a complete stranger to the concept of probable questions, it suddenly did show some hope after all.

"Don't tell me you haven't been checking out previous years' papers." Nikhil once again read his mind.

Nikhil came to his desk and pulled out a sheaf of about ten stapled sheets. Handing them to Kajal, he declared, "Don't even look elsewhere. I have sorted these out from the last ten years' question papers."

Kajal looked through the sheets he held. Split into three sections by the subjects and further categorized as long essays and short notes, were a total of seventy eight entries.

"I'm sure ninety percent of our papers will be from amongst these. Don't pass them around boss, it's taken some effort," Nikhil added with a wink. "And don't worry too hard. Do what you can. It's only the 'Test'. Don't kill yourself over it. We'll have a month after it to get ship-shape for the Prof."

Kajal spent that final week before the 'Test' rummaging through the question bank. Nikhil checked on him periodically. But at the end of it all, Kajal fell way short – both in the number of topics he'd covered and also how much energy he'd put into each.

Kajal returned devastating grades in the 'Test'. In summary, he scraped through Physiology, marginally missed the bar in Anatomy but majorly flunked Biochemistry. Two out of three going kaput was nearly as bad as not having taken the exam at all. In a batch of 150, his performance landed him a spot amongst a rare five percent. Just like at the Annual Days in school. And Nikhil was right – ninety percent of the questions were from his bank.

"It's okay boss. At least you now have a game plan. And the Prof's still a month away." Nikhil said on the day the last of the marks returned.

* * * * *

The month between Test and the Prof offered a barren college routine. Just a couple of lectures now and then, and the odd tutorial or 'specially arranged' sessions here and there. It was essentially a time to prepare for the Prof. People struck studious modes and hit panic buttons in an epidemic wave that left every 'fun' switch forgotten.

Hostels stood taciturn. Hostellers were caught in sleepless eddies of anxious deadlines and shared only apprehensions. Point Blank adjusted to the six-monthly ordained increase in through-the-night, for-a-quick-bite visitors and soaring cigarette sales, more the cheaper stock as budgets forced compromise from king size to filterless and even *bidis* to accommodate the quantity.

Home-tied locals grew roots amidst hot mugs of Horlicks, bowls of grapes and pomegranate, and twice-daily doses of Memory Plus capsules, and fleetingly visited campus to pick up insider pulse on probable questions.

Kajal pushed his gears. Like the rest. The tea breaks became increasingly academic. Aparna came over on Sundays and made the boys her pork curry for lunch. But she convinced them that her drop-back rides were a luxury they couldn't afford for the while.

Kajal didn't come home but he did call up regularly, keeping Baba posted on progress and confirming adherence to Ma's diet and adequate sleep routine. "Pray every day. And don't forget to shave and shower. Don't start looking like a scientist," and thus remained Ma's parting lines at the end of every call.

Two hours, or a little longer, every Saturday evening was, however, an irresistible immoderation Kajal allowed himself. In the entire batch, he should have been most parsimonious with time but it was irresistible. It was Nandini time.

Yes, the two had blossomed. They had found a pleasant cadence. It remained unsaid but clearly understood that Nandini would be at the Point around five on Saturday evenings, and Kajal would be waiting.

And they had moved on from the rock and med school hill. There was coffee at CBee's, noodles at The Oriental and momos at Momo Ghar, all followed by long walks back to her hostel.

But apart from the food and very general conversation, they mostly shared silence.

Kajal, dazed and mowed within the academic pressure cooker, found a safety valve in these excursions and itemizing her and him in any other light could wait a thousand years.

With the year-and-a-halfly schedule of the Profs in med school those days, Nandini's batch wasn't taking a Prof then. Devoid of any other pressing demands, wizened by being two years older and generally not being a live-in-the-moment person, Nandini did think beyond. But she was happy to see off Kajal's Prof before bringing things to the table.

They were getting noticed on campus. But it was the time of the year when gossip wasn't quite the priority with most.

One Saturday as Kajal returned straight into a tea break at 115, Surojit asked, "How was it man?" "How was what?" Kajal retorted, half irritated and half self-conscious, completely aware of what the probe implied. "Don't tell me you don't do anything," Surojit was generally hard to bring unstuck from such matters.

Kajal responded with a puzzled look that sought support from Nikhil's direction.

"Such a waste, I don't believe it. Why? Does madam keep you at one arm, or does your joystick not work?" Surojit persisted. Kajal again looked at Nikhil, who stood there letting him down with a sheepish smile. *Et tu.*

And for once something snapped inside Kajal, "Why don't you just go fuck yourself, Surojit?"

Surojit backed off, surprised by Kajal's reaction.

Nikhil realized it had gone beyond friendly banter, and that, more than anything else, irritated him. "Okay ladies, can we not lose focus for these couple of weeks?"

* * * * *

Half way through the month, doubts and worries crept right back into Kajal. There was something about the stuff. While they were all appealing concepts with the textbooks in front of him, it left him terrified that he remembered nothing. As he subjected his innocent brain to rapid information overload, the blood supply of the liver started feeling more at home in the knee joint and certain intermediaries of carbohydrate metabolism found slots in the scheme of protein synthesis.

Kajal withdrew. He was not meant for it. It was only him. JMD, Nikhil, Surojit, everyone else, they were all at ease, even enjoying the hard work. He was not meant for it. But what could he do? Ma and Baba?

"I'm doing a few daily, but also reading some text," he'd reply to Nikhil's efforts to keep him confined to the question bank.

* * * * *

"So are you all set? Can't wait to go?"

And for the first time Nandini asked Kajal about the exam, over coffee at Pinto's. That last Saturday before the Prof began on Thursday next.

Strangely, despite the exam irrefutably overpowering everything else at the time, they had never before gotten down to talking about it. Entirely because Nandini couldn't imagine anything being the matter with it. For her it was plain and simple – one got into a course, had lectures and turorials, had fun and friends, had an exam to take at the end of a semester or year or whenever, worked for the exam, sailed through it and went to the next level. There was absolutely no room for anything extraordinary within this inelastic frame.

It was raining and the street outside had formed a steadily widening 'aquatic lane' where it met the sidewalk. Looking out the glass door of Pinto's, all Kajal could see was raindrops. Kajal thought of how divergent their ends were – some vaulted with flippant lust within the 'aquatic lane', others disappeared on adjacent tarmac, some were unceremoniously ricocheted by windscreen wipers, some ran off perimeters of umbrellas like the leaves of weeping willows, still others majestically fell off the edge of Pinto's' roof in a steady parade.

"What? Can you not be so distracted? At least when you're with me." Kajal's lack of response annoyed Nandini.

"Be careful Kajal! Don't go out in the rain."

A high pitched shout suddenly filled the small café, drawing no heed from most but startling Kajal and Nandini. As their heads turned to its direction, they saw a mother scurrying towards her three four year old boy.

A quaint warmth filled Kajal. Kajal was finally victorious against a world that had forever made him feel shamefully unique. But sadly the whole world wasn't around to witness his triumph. Only Nandini. How could she comprehend in so little time what wardens of his entire twenty odd years of existence didn't?

But when he looked, her eyes were alive with understanding.

She tenderly touched his fingers. "It's okay. It was never a big deal anyway." The honesty of her words dissolved the walls around Kajal. A lump in the throat embarrassed him and he forced a weak smile.

"I'm really bad. I don't think I'm going to come through."

"Really bad with what?" Kajal's sudden disclaimer puzzled Nandini.

"With the Prof."

"Why? What's going on?" Nandini asked in surprise.

"I'm just way behind with the preparations." Kajal suddenly found himself trusting that Nandini was capable of making it all alright. "Biochemistry is like almost untouched."

"What do you mean?" Nandini was horrified with disbelief.

Kajal said nothing.

"What have you been doing? What do you mean by saying that you haven't even touched Biochem? When are you planning to do it?" Kajal led her to simultaneous seething anger and numbing worry. "How could you waste a full year? And you go about wasting even more time with me like nothing matters." A few heads turned as Nandini's voice reached them. "Are you by any chance trying to be funny with me?" And she fervently hoped Kajal would laugh out and affirm.

Kajal said nothing.

"How were the 'Test' marks?" Nandini hadn't asked before. Kajal told her.

Kajal waited as Nandini kept quiet for five minutes or so that lasted forever. At long she took a deep breath, and then abruptly gathering her things, said, "Come on, let's go."

"It's pouring outside," Kajal's resistance was weak.

"It doesn't matter, okay" Nandini screamed straight into his face. "You've anyway lived long enough being outrageously kind to yourself. Who do you think will do your share of work? You think the entire world is queuing up to sympathize with you because someone gave you a girlish name, because you have these palms that sweat at all times, because you can think of playing your guitar everywhere but can't get yourself up on a stage to perform, because the whole college thinks you are weird, because Mister-tender-touch-me-not will get soaked if he steps out in the rain right now!" And she turned and stormed out.

Leaving the café, Kajal felt eyes following them and he feared they couldn't come back to Pinto's for a while without being recognized.

Once outside, it took less than a minute for them to get drenched as they waited for a means of transport. The rain flattened Nandini's hair and ran down her forehead and face – you had to give it to Kajal that he had no way of telling her tears from the stringy rivulets of rain.

Then, as if seized by a moment of indiscretion, Nandini reached out and put her left hand on Kajal's nape, and pulling him towards her, kissed him. Their first kiss – on the sidewalk outside Pinto's in the middle of the helter-skelter rain, under a sky bloodied a grey red by the sun setting behind an envelope of dark clouds. Feeling nothing, he kissed her back.

Falling back, she clutched the hair on the back of his head. "We'll make it, okay. I'll sort it out."

And Nandini took over. At that moment though she didn't exactly know how she was going to sort it out. But for all the love she felt, she wouldn't have made the mistake she was about to.

————

By the time she reached her room, physical and emotional bankruptcy inundated Nandini. Changing out of her wets, she passed out within minutes of lying in bed.

When she looked at her bedside clock after what seemed like only a couple of minutes, it was three in the morning.

The room light threw a most harsh brightness. The downpour had ceased only to be replaced by the famously violent *bor-doi-chila* winds. Woodwind harmonies and creaking appendages of giant trees reverberated in med school hill, while in her room, the thick olive green curtains on the balcony door bawled in threatening full-stretch excursions.

Nandini sprang up to latch the balcony door. Her stomach croaked in hunger. She broke a cake of Maggi into boiling water and ended up with an over-boiled, over-watered bowl of the 2-minute noodles.

She couldn't get back to sleeping, and with a pre-occupied mind watched the twisting trees outside her window. In time the winds calmed and just as the birds noisily flocked out to their day jobs with the first rays of light, it occurred to Nandini. She knew what was going to work.

It was wrong. It was risqué, but she knew people had pulled it off time and again with nonchalant aplomb. It was the only way Kajal would pass.

* * * * *

Next day. Sunday. Around nine in the morning.

When Nandini knocked a second time, she realized the door was open. A tentative peek confirmed the non-occupancy. She scanned the room – neatly made bed; the open window let in the crisp morning, rinsed by the overnight rains and drying in the tender sun; tidy study table with only the table lamp and a packet of cigarettes; unflustered book shelf. There could be only two explanations – the resident was nowhere in the vicinity of an exam or had hit that final patch of relaxed confidence where one used the last Sunday before the exam to tidy up and go to church. Nandini knew Kajal was far from both. But she was sure she hadn't made a mistake with the room number. She let herself in, left the door ajar and sat on the chair at the table.

Kajal walked in after a little while. Their eyes met, and momentarily froze his arrival. In silence, he put his toothbrush away. Nandini noticed that he was still wearing the blue jeans and tee from the evening before, dried by body heat.

"Hi."

"Hi Kajal. Did you sleep well?" Nandini felt an inescapable urge to be nice to him. Guilt enveloped her as if it was entirely her fault that Kajal was feeling the way she thought he was.

Kajal kept quiet.

"Say good morning at least," Nandini tried to be playful.

"Good morning Nandini. Great to see you here." If she had had an unslept night, her appearance didn't betray it in the least. She looked pretty as ever.

"Come, sit."

Kajal sat down on the bed, surveying his own room.

"Say something, Kajal." Nandini was worried.

"I wrote a song the other day. Can I play it?"

Moron. Absolute idiot. Will someone plug this blockhead onto a reality socket? Nandini didn't bother answering him. "Tell me again. How bad is it?" Nandini came to the point.

Kajal realized she had come with a mission. And he started laying the answer out. Even as his palms found convenience in dripping away and the familiar heat rose in the back of the neck.

"Like I told you. Anatomy and Physiology – I'm about halfway home. Biochem – I'm still sorting out." Kajal prayed that she'd stop pinning him down with those uncomfortable questions. And yet in some way take him under her aegis.

"Okay Kajal, this is what we'll do. We'll get you the four long questions on the Anatomy and Physiology papers. They are worth eighty percent and with minimum justice to them you'll score the fifty you need to pass. And then we'll fix you up in good hands for safe Practicals."

"What do you mean we'll get the questions?"

"Leave that to me. We'll go see Rajbongshida right away." Nandini replied, much to the befuddlement of Kajal.

"Biochem is the issue. Arati ma'am brings the question papers herself from the University, so we can rule out getting a prior hand on them." Dr. Arati Das was Head of Biochemistry. "But the fill-in-the-blanks are our chance there. They are worth fifty percent and you can get them all correct – so that regardless of what you do with the rest of the paper, you'll be home." Nandini went on. She truly felt like every inch of the misadventure was an essential part of her. "And for that, we'll get Narayanda on our team."

Kajal realised what was being suggested. Rajbongshida was a senior clerk in the Principal's Office, and apart from admission procedures, hostel allotments and all that, took care of logistics during the Profs. Narayanda was a bearer in the Biochemistry department but more importantly, Dr. Arati Das's Man Friday.

"Do you want to get some footwear on?" Nandini said impatiently.

"No, hang on a minute. What are we trying to do?"

"I'll explain on the way. Right now we need to catch Rajbongshida at home before he takes his daughter to art school at ten." Nandini had hatched these intricacies from snatches of conversations in her hostel. She had never actively participated, assured that she would never have to find recourse in these means. Right then however she was happy that at least half her ears had taken the hints on board.

Kajal obliged, and watched by Nandini, quietly put on his shoes.

———

By the time they were eating lunch at Point, the clogs were in place, and the machinery had been rolled. It would have cost them dearly, quite literally, but Nandini's charm was an acceptable substitute at all stations.

Rajbonsgshida would hand over his 'package' as soon as office opened the next morning. Narayanda assured concurrence, but he belonged to a climax that would need to be played out to perfection by him, Kajal and Nandini in tandem on the day.

"Why are you so quiet, Kajal?"

"You do know that what we are doing is wrong," Kajal spoke thoughtfully.

"Yes Kajal. And don't think it's easy for me. I know as well as you do, perhaps even better, that you don't deserve to pass. But you know what – you fail, and you carry your first Prof around for the rest of your life. For anything you do later, even a residency, you will be marked 'irregular' and your certificates will be mementoes screaming that you didn't get through first Prof at first attempt. We pull off this little trick of ours, life treats you a whole world differently.

"You have to understand that you are only as good as the exams you pass and what your transcripts say. The world only judges you by what you have, and it gives stuff-all about whether you deserve to have what you have or not.

"Trust me, years down the line when you become the great doctor that I know you will, even you and I will find it hard to relate to this present mess and these means that we are resorting to. It will be like retrograde convincing – your success in the long run will make the whole world, including you and me, firmly believe that you always were worth every bit of it.

"It's wrong, and don't doubt for a moment that I'm not aware of it. It's just that the way I see it, the first Prof is simply not worth failing."

And then she added with a smile, "Once we get out of this, just see what I do to you for the rest of your time in med school. I don't care what labels your friends stick on you but you are going to do exactly what I tell you to. I never imagined someone could be this spoilt."

Kajal smiled back.

* * * * *

Wednesday. Around four on a bright afternoon. Kajal's room. Prof started the next day – Anatomy theory, Papers 1 & 2.

"I have a strong feeling Pancreas will be one of the long questions, boss," Nikhil advised innocently. "It's not been repeated in three years." Nikhil's probability theories were splendid, but Kajal knew he was wrong. Pancreas was not on. And that secure information came from Rajbongshida's 'package' that Kajal possessed. Kajal wished he could share this with Nikhil – he owed it to him. But he couldn't. Nikhil would never approve of the means. Further and bigger – Nandini's role would stand compromised.

"I don't know but I have a hunch they have planned a surprise, maybe something like Superior Vena Cava." The course of the Superior Vena Cava was the second long question on Paper 1. Kajal couldn't resist dropping the hint but feared he wouldn't get taken seriously.

There was a tap on the door, and then it was pushed open. Nandini.

"Hello Nikhil," Nandini's greeting broke the momentary discomfort in the Boxer-shorted air.

"Hey. How you doing?"

"Very good, Nikhil. How's it going?"

"You know how it is. Never smooth. But we should be fine." Even caught in his Boxers, Nikhil oozed the confidence of a James Bond. "But I must add Kajal's come around really strongly. One has absolutely nothing to worry about." A Bollywoodian James Bond with a sensitive heart that read perfectly the true reason behind Nandini's visit.

"I know," Nandini confirmed, and her smile filled the entire room. She turned to Kajal, "Shall we go?"

Kajal wasn't aware they had planned to go anyplace.

"Okay kids, but don't make it too long," Nikhil winked and excused himself. Nandini wished him best.

Alone, Kajal looked at Nandini questioningly.

"We are going to the *Mazaar*." Nandini informed.

Peer Baba's *Mazaar*. Kajal had heard of the place. The burial memorial of a Muslim preacher that had grown into a popular place of worship for all, regardless of religion. A place where dreams came true and requests were granted, almost on demand.

A fifteen minute ride on JMD's bike brought them to *Mazaar*. Five steps below street level, the tabernacle was much smaller than Kajal had pictured. The grave stood in the middle, clothed in layers of embroidered green and red *chaddars* that came as offerings. The stained glass on the ventilators threw coloured wedges of light on the white ceiling and mosaic floor.

Nandini covered her head with her *dupatta*, and as they descended the last of the steps, she pointed to her right. About ten skull caps hung from a wooden stand. Kajal picked one in white crochete, and placed it on his head. Nandini smiled at him and gently touched his cheek.

"*Sallallah. Aamin.*" The Maulvi suddenly rang out loud and clear in the small space. More frequent visitors knew these intermittent chants as routine practice, but Kajal saw it as a deliberate intervention to keep Nandini and him from getting carried away.

Nandini led Kajal in walking around the grave once, before they knelt for *dua*, heads bowed to touch the edge of the grave.

*"...... gharon mein, dilon mein khush-haali de
Har kaam mein barqat de
Imtehanon mein kaamyaabi de ......"*

The Maulvi recited.

Still kneeling, hands on thighs and back straight, Nandini looked at Kajal. "Ask what you want." And she closed her eyes and reverted to the grave to requisition her own wish.

God, thanks for everything. Please take care. Kajal didn't need to say anything else. The God he believed in must already know what he was there for.

"Just pass, okay Kajal?" Their eyes locked for a minute, till they were startled again – *"Sallallah. Aamin."*

* * * * *

Saturday. Day three of the Prof. Last of the theory papers. Biochemistry. Around 9:15 in the morning.

Days one and two hadn't swayed an inch off the procured course. There couldn't be a doubt – Kajal had passed the Anatomy and Physiology theory papers.

Dr. Arati Das walked in at the head of her entourage. Bisecting the columns of a hundred fifty students seated on single desks and chairs, she reached the rostrum at the front of the imposing Examination Hall.

A slight anxiety gripped Kajal. Shifting slightly in his chair, he pulled out his handkerchief and held it between both flooded palms. For once, he didn't know what was on the slips of paper in the manila envelope that Dr. Arati Das held. Kajal searched for an assuring glance from Narayanda but the latter calmly avoided his line of sight as he went about handing out the question papers.

Half past nine, and 150 pens touched answer sheets for one last squabble that Prof.

One long question and a couple of fill-in-the-blanks were what Kajal could attempt on his own – not enough to pass but handy to keep himself occupied.

He didn't notice Narayanda quietly slip out of the Examination Hall. At 9:50 AM.

It was the sixth, and topmost, floor of the academic building. The staircase – and the two elevators – opened onto a foyer, to the left of which was the large Central Library. The way to the Examination Hall was through a corridor to the right, just off the inside of the library entrance. The corridor led past the smaller reading rooms, and ended with a turn to the left, where there was another corridor with the men's and ladies' washrooms on either side. This then opened into an ante area where students left their books and belongings, and the indocile nerds wallowed in nervous last minute revisions. The massive wooden doors of the Examination Hall were at the only end of this space.

Nandini was in the library a little past half nine. Save for a librarian, it was empty. The high ceiling and large windows lent an airy freshness, but that didn't counter the mustiness of the overwrought woodwork and the monstrous collection of books.

At 10:00 AM she made her way to the wooden chest which housed the card catalogue. The fifty odd drawers had lavish brass handles and were marked with an alphabet. With her heart thundering, Nandini pulled the drawer marked 'N'. 'N' for Nandini. 'N' for Narayanda. Or should it have been 'K' for Kajal? Flipping through the cards it held, Nandini found the folded question paper immediately. A quick glance confirmed its validity and Nandini stuffed it into the pocket of her white coat. Narayanda had delivered. Pushing the drawer back, she left the library.

In another five minutes, Nandini was in the vacant fourth floor seminar room. From the bag she had left there earlier, she pulled out the two books and proceeded to answer the fill-in-the-blanks. Twenty five fill-in-the-blanks worth fifty marks. And that was all Kajal needed to pass Biochemistry.

———

Dr. Suresh Mitra, Principal and Chief Superintendant, was never religious but since that day two years ago when his wife, Dr. Sulochona Mitra, Head of Obs & Gynae, and he returned as the only survivors of that horrific car crash in the hills of Mizoram, he had turned a believer. Three other senior faculty members had perished.

Sulochana might have to endure bouts of severe pain for the rest of her life because of the cervical cord compression, but every morning, looking at the black and white photograph in the photo frame on his desk, he had learnt to count his blessings. The picture was from their honeymoon in Simla. Sulochana had dressed in *Pahadi* attire – a *rahide* and a *thapada* long jacket, complete with chunky metal jewelry. She was younger, but the smile was the same. Their childlessness had never come in the way of their happiness, and the event of two years ago had only cemented them stronger. Thirty married years and the preceding seven years of courtship from the very first year in med school. And the 11 o' clock coffee had stayed a ritual. His promotion to

Principal's office did put the distance of med school hill between him and Sulochana's department in the Hospital building, but that was only a minor hindrance. Since the accident, Suresh had barred Sulochana from taking the ride up the hill, so every morning he drove down to her office.

As he looked at his watch that morning, it was still only about half past ten. But with nothing else to do, he decided to catch Sulochana a wee bit early.

And at 10:35 AM he was waiting for the elevator on the third floor.

————

Nandini hurriedly put the books back in her satchel. Depositing the question paper with the answers to the fill-in-the-blanks scribbled on it in her coat pocket, she checked the time. 10:20 AM.

She left the seminar room and made for the staircase. They had fixed on 10:30 AM. That would give Kajal an hour till the end of the two hour exam.

————

Liftman Ramakant stood up from the wooden stool with a start as the elevator doors opened on third floor.

"Good morning sir."

"Morning Ramakant," Dr. Mitra replied in his tranquil voice. "Ground floor."

"Yes sir." Ramakant knew. He even knew that that morning the good doctor was ten minutes too early for the routine ground floor trip.

On the final flight of stairs, Nandini slowed down. She paused to regain composure and her breathing returned to near normal. Buildings from the sixties have such high steps on their staircases. It was still a couple of minutes to 10:30. Three students were waiting for the elevator, and just as Nandini walked into the library, she overheard one of them saying, "Let's take the stairs, the lift is taking ages."

She made her way to the rendezvous point – the men's washroom outside the Examination Hall. Nandini had loads of other options to stage the handover but Kajal couldn't get further than that.

At 10:25 AM Kajal raised his hand and asked to use the washroom. The nearest member of the invigilation team allowed him with a nod. Little did Kajal suspect that he wasn't going to come back to the hall. Ever again.

As the elevator started moving, they realized it was headed up, instead of downwards.

"Someone must have pressed on one of the higher floors," Ramakant explained apologetically.

"It's okay." Dr. Mitra was in no rush that morning.

When the elevator came to a halt and the doors opened, it was on the sixth floor. No one was in the vicinage. Whoever had pressed for it didn't care to wait.

"Sixth, isn't it?" Dr. Mitra asked.

"Yes sir." And Ramakant vigorously pushed the 'close doors' button.

"Hang on a minute," Dr. Mitra said as he calmly stepped out. It was the last day of the theory papers. Dr. Mitra decided to pay a quick visit to the Examination Hall.

———

When Nandini entered the men's washroom, Kajal was already there.

"I was worried something had gone wrong."

"Shshsh...just keep quiet." Nandini pulled him into one of the cubicles. "Here." She pulled the paper out of her pocket and put it in his hand. "I'll wait in the other cubicle while you put the answers into your head."

About five minutes later, on Kajal's cue, they both stepped out.

"Thanks Nandini. The rest of the paper is actually okay. I can get something out of the long questions as well," Kajal beamed excitedly. He unmindfully returned the paper to Nandini and turned to leave. To get back to answering the Biochemistry paper.

"Keep the paper with you. Just in case."

Kajal turned to take the paper back. As he looked at Nandini, his back was to the door of the washroom. Nandini looked back at him, and smiled. *It had been done. Kajal was going to pass.*

"I love you Nandini."

Kajal caught her by surprise. Despite the stress, she nearly broke into a laugh. "Okay Kajal Baba, just one more hour and then you can tell me all about it. Just get back now." *I love you too.*

And I don't believe what I've just done for you. Nandini smiled and pushed him even as he continued to look at her with a mischief that was entirely new.

And then the smile on her face vanished, confiscated by a locust wind of horror that moved in rapidly.

Standing at the washroom door behind Kajal was Dr. Mitra.

Kajal turned with a start to find Dr. Mitra's emotionless face of authority. And slowly turned back to Nandini.

The last time they looked at each other was in that men's washroom – his eyes scared and unsure, her praying and hoping. He was twenty then, and she twenty two – definitely age to fall in love and dream of having children, but perhaps not to nurture an uncelebrated love that one didn't fall out of for the rest of one's life. Well, Kajal didn't. Nandini – I never knew much about.

Nandini and Kajal were slapped one year rustications. Nandini returned to become a doctor. Some years earlier she popped up in a conversation, and a friend had informed me that she'd joined a prominent, super-specialty, cardiology hospital in Delhi as a consultant with a budding professional reputation.

Kajal never went back to med school.

* * * * *

"Why don't you have a word with him?"

Ma and Baba were eating dinner.

A week had passed since Kajal had returned home with a bag of clothes, a few books and the guitar that Ma had gifted him. When Ma opened the door that day, she didn't know how to welcome him, and he walked past her in silence up to his room. And since then, he and Baba lived like watchful strangers. Both pushed off facing each other till they had learnt not to run into each other's paths. Kajal came down for breakfast after Baba left for work, spent the day in his room playing the guitar and listening to turned-down music and came down to eat a quick dinner when Baba took his evening shower. Ma understood. And as much as she wanted circumstances to change, she complied with their need to live separate lives through skilful home-making. In the surreal calm of the house, Ma, more than anyone else, pretended that all was well.

"I don't know. Something's just gone. I don't find the drive anymore, for anything." Baba didn't look up from his plate.

"How can you break down like this? He needs your support right now. Why are you reacting like it's the end of everything? Everyone makes mistakes. It's only a matter of time. Soon everyone will forget."

"I won't. You won't. And he won't." Baba had been hurt. Deeply. And that shattered a man who had lived an entire life with his head held high.

"Our lives have been lived. But he's only beginning. He's only twenty Goddammit," and suddenly Ma's voice raised itself against nature and she pushed her plate away. The relationship she and Baba shared gave her ample opportunity to assume the dominant partner's role but only over issues they both knew were paltry. Seldom did she make a vociferous expression of her position in matters that were undeniably consequential. Tears welled up, and brimmed over to run down either side of a rapidly reddening nose.

Taken aback, Baba felt jostled. Ma had just splashed a bucket of ice cold water on his slumber.

"Does he know what he wants to do now?" Baba recovered.

"He doesn't want to go back," answered Ma, wiping her eyes and sniffing noisily, while keeping her stare away from Baba's.

"I don't want him to either." And after a brief silence, Baba asked again, "Then what does he want to do?"

"Why don't you ask him yourself?" Ma was an incurable optimist. Despite the hopelessness of the situation, she fondly visualized Baba and Kajal having a heart-to-heart, man-to-man. That would bring her world to complete rest.

But Baba only replied with silence. And when the stalemate lasted long enough to dispel any sense of having a foot in the door that Ma might have entertained, she responded, "He wants to study History."

Baba turned the information over in his head. The rest of the dinner was devoid of conversation. As Ma cleared the table and Baba finished his nightly round of checking that all doors and windows were locked, he finally said, "Ask him to start checking with the colleges."

Why don't you tell him yourself? Ma was tempted to but refrained from suggesting it.

* * * * *

Some years earlier, Kajal had made a choice between his two favourite subjects – Biology and History. As he saw it then, he could pursue only one from that point on. But through a route lengthened by providence, Kajal found himself at the gates of the second after being ostracized by the first.

There was no hostel this time. But there was once again a friend. People who made few friends perhaps only made ones that touched their lives deeply.

Rahul Agarwal was on the BSc course, majoring in Physics. A prolific reader, his interests traversed cook-books and film magazines to religion and philosophy. But it was with Physics that his repertoire was not limited by the requirements of his course. To the discourses that the two frequently had, Kajal brought a flavour of Modern History.

"The Nuremberg trials eventually led to the Nuremberg Code that still holds in medical research." Kajal concluded. The holocaust was a favourite subject with Kajal.

"But did you know that it is impossible to get a true account of History?" Rahul suggested, pulling on the straw in a bottle of cola in the canteen.

"Why do you say that?" Kajal queried.

"If we consider Heisenberg's Uncertainty Principle."

Kajal knew the great principle of quantum mechanics summarily, but it wasn't immediately obvious to him how it could come into History.

"You see, observing a phenomenon requires that the observer be in the environment where the event is taking place. And by his very presence, he ends up altering the event. This implies that what we read is the historian's interpretation of an event and not necessarily the truth." Rahul explained.

"That sounds interesting."

"It is actually. You remember Schroedinger's Cat? Quantum mechanics is incomplete because fundamental to it is that there is no phenomenon till it is observed and no outcome till it is measured. And in a way similar to this, our knowledge of History is also far from complete. Just as every episode need not have happened the way it is described, events that have not been chronicled need not actually have not happened."

"Phew!" Kajal was impressed.

"Einstein himself felt that failure to see reality as something independent of what is experimentally established was a risky game. One could say the same about documented History." Rahul carried on.

"No absolute truth, no certainty...hunh!" said Kajal. "Are you suggesting that the greatest scientist of the planet was actually post-modernist?"

"The thing about all these great men is our inability to straight jacket them," Rahul replied unmindfully, shuffling through his papers. Kajal caught a fleeting glimpse of one with colourful symmetric forms printed across x, y and z coordinates.

"Hey, that looks like a piece of art," Kajal suggested cheerfully. "The famous Butterfly Effect, right?"

"The Butterfly Effect in the Lorenz Extractor," Rahul elaborated. "I don't know what you think of it, but I find the whole concept most intriguing. How small differences in the initial condition of a dynamic system get amplified over time to produce large variations in its long term behavior. The flapping of a butterfly's wings in Brazil setting off a tornado in Texas. Only there was no predictability. It is the essence of chaos. One could argue that it applies to human behaviour."

Kajal kept quiet. Rahul was clearly animated. He went on.

"Lorenz was a meteorologist working on a mathematical model for weather forecasts when he stumbled upon the Butterfly Effect. He realized that long term weather forecast was impossible with any degree of certainty – weather is non-linear and fell into chaotic behavior with time. Non linear entities cannot be predicted.

"I love to think that someday we would build a mathematical model for something that we all know and experience – how differences in environment can influence long term changes in human behavior and also perhaps how the same factor can produce altogether different changes in two individuals. Imagine that there existed an equation that mathematised the past, present and future of this conversation!"

"I must say that would be scarily dehumanizing!" Kajal responded.

"Accepted. That's one way of looking at it. But you have to admit that it's an awesome thought."

"For the moment though I'd thank God for giving us 'chaos' and killing Laplace's Demon. 'Chaos breeds life' – You know who said that?"

"Henry Adams."

"An assembly line can only provide order, not life. It is the uncertainty of life that makes it live," Kajal said. "And didn't you just mention that it was Einstein himself who'd said that reality needed to be seen as different from what experiments explained?"

"I'm not debating that. But don't you wish that with every new turn in your life, with every new person that you met, you knew precisely what will follow?"

They both fell quiet for a moment. Then as a passing thought, Rahul added, "Great that you noted the Fine Art element in it. Did you know that critics believe that the works of the most prominent abstract expressionist painter, Jackson Pollock, had at some level been influenced by an understanding of the Chaos Theory, even though the theory itself came much after Pollock?"

And thus Rahul introduced Kajal to the world of Fine Art. Though neither had so much as ever held a paint brush, their discussions started oscillating around art. Kajal took to reading, and discovered Cubism and Dadaism; Dali, van Gough, Duchamp, Warhold, Liechstintein and Bourgeois. Jackson Pollock's paintings, which some felt were no better than brainless wall papers, led Kajal into an exploration. In a couple of months, he realized that Fine Art was a whole lot more than paint on canvas.

Egged on by Rahul, Kajal also joined a band. An established band was looking for a guitar player to fill a vacancy. Kajal auditioned, and was hired as rhythm and second lead. But the band was a motley ensemble of thirty plus musicians who were learning to assign a secondary status to octaval passions in the face of failing business propositions and children that needed to start school. They arrived at rehearsals with their nerves frayed by worldly compulsions and performed on shows with a vengeful competitiveness in the only battle they all vied to win. Kajal quit the band after two shows. The band itself lasted four more. There was no formal shutdown, everyone just stopped coming to rehearsals.

Kajal did get noticed. A small scale music producer got in touch with him backstage after the second show and offered him an opportunity to record the guitar tracks on an Assamese album by an upcoming singer. Kajal accepted.

Kajal immediately fell in love with the recording studio. And how it worked – time lines spread across three monitors, headphones bringing him the drum and bass tracks, the avenue to raise a hand and correct a mistake, and the suspense of how the singer would finally sing on top of it all. His head brought back lingering details of the soft yellow lighting, glass walled cubicles, the warm-sweet smell and the whisper of footfalls on the padded floor.

Kajal planned to buy Ma a *mekhela sador* with his remuneration. But the money when it came was too less and was exhausted after a night out with Rahul.

* * * * *

That day was close to the exams. The third year final exams for the Bachelors degree. Rahul and Kajal were sitting in the canteen.

"You know, after graduating, you could take up Art History for a Masters. My older cousin went to Central St. Martin in London and did the same. He now teaches at the Sotheby's Institute in New York."

Kajal tucked Rahul's suggestion deep into a recess of his brain. Studying abroad wasn't something he could arise to consider. Definitely not Art History. Some years earlier, Baba used to prophesise that Kajal would go abroad, get an FRCS or something and return to serve the poor in India. But the medical dream was long over.

At the end of the three years, Kajal graduated in History. On a day that brought no real joy to anyone. In terms of realistically influencing his life, he finished his time on the course with three things – a BA degree, an appreciation and appetite for fine art, and a recording studio resume.

* * * * *

After BA, Kajal spent nearly a year in Guwahati. Masters? Mass Communication? Journalism? Law? All came up for consideration. Brought over by Ma, endorsed by Baba who had had to reorient.

By then, Baba and Kajal were communicating entirely through the medium of Ma. Not due to any outstanding anger, the culprit was guilt – Kajal for his failures and Baba for his inability to accept that despite everything, his son was not going to be a doctor.

With every suggestion, Ma felt like she was offering an undeniable ace that Kajal would lap up. Only that didn't quite happen. When all efforts failed to make an impression with Kajal and generate any response, she learned to give up.

Within six months, Kajal was on his own – unmentored, untutored and unshepherded. The guitar led to more recordings. No bands, no live shows, only studio work where he recorded his pieces in the isolation that technology provided. His readings continued. Art and Art History; History in general and the holocaust in particular.

When he had saved some from his small recording income he bought an easel, a couple of mounted canvasses, some brushes, turpentine and a box of paints. A corner in his room became his studio and he took to painting. When one was done, he placed it facing the wall, and went onto the next.

A perfect fireball in the geometric centre of a black canvas, titled 'Night Sky'. That was one of his paintings.

Ma couldn't resist sneaking up to his room when he was not in, eager to explore the son's latest venture and relay the positive to Baba. But she was disappointed with the produce. No landscapes, no portraits.

Ma lifted one for a puzzled inspection. This one was a matrix of squares in black-green-ochre gridlines, filled with livid colours;

one square blank – or white – some bleeding colour onto the adjacent. In the bottom right corner, where the artiste's signature should have been, was scribbled 'Separate Lives'. What was Kajal thinking? Its dark deep sadness despite the overwhelming brightness hassled Ma.

While Kajal continued to ply the paints neither encouraged nor discouraged, much like his paintings he himself became abstract. And Ma and Baba ceased to belong within the boundaries of the same world.

When Kajal turned twenty five, he started feeling like the dog who'd let the master down by letting the cat steal fish from the kitchen. He still didn't pay the electricity bills, the newspaper bills, still didn't do the weekly grocery shopping. He had become a guest in his own home, without a departure date or any concrete plans for the future. He wanted to run away. No longer could he bear to live suffocated by unfulfilled responsibilities.

"I'm going to Shillong." Kajal told Ma at breakfast that day.

"When?"

"This afternoon."

"For how long?" Ma put one more *aaloo paratha* on Kajal's plate and gingerly sat down across him.

"I have an offer from a studio. They'll pay me a wage for being a resident guitarist."

Ma didn't quite understand what a resident guitarist was, but it didn't matter. "Where will you stay?"

"They're giving me a place now. I'll sort something out for the long term."

And then it struck Ma. Was this the conclusion? Was this Kajal's destiny? And with him, theirs'? To be known as the parents of a resident guitarist in a Shillong recording studio. But despite a fervent desire to deny fate this turn, Ma felt washed by a sense of odd relief, like she could finally let down a guard that had been gnawing her insides for ages. She was ameliorated that Kajal had come to some decision. Not anymore would Ma have to play custodian of an unreal peace that threatened to burst in her face every moment.

"Baba won't be back by afternoon."

"Please say bye to him for me."

* * * * *

And in Shillong, Kajal embarked on his first career. Resident sessions guitarist at The Nest. William, the sound engineer who owned the studio, introduced him to Tom Anthony, and by day three Kajal had moved into the Anthony household, paying fifty percent of his studio salary for room and three meals.

Kajal acquired a cell phone. Call charges were high, more when landlines were called and even incoming was charged. His calls to Ma were military wireless messages – location update, headcount, ammo status and 'over-and-out' – delivered within the safe hours when Baba was at work.

"Hello." And once Baba answered the phone.

Kajal kept quiet. How was Baba home at eleven on a Wednesday morning? Was he unwell or something? Or was it something with Ma? Kajal kept quite.

"Hello." Baba said again. He was louder this time but his voice sounded weak and old. Something was wrong. But who would tell him?

"Who is it?" Kajal heard Ma's voice faintly echo from far, kitchen perhaps. Kajal visualised her and Baba's positions in the house.

"Won't say." Baba replied, away from the phone. And then back to it, "Hello!". Louder.

Kajal kept quiet.

Baba put the phone down.

After two restless hours, Kajal called again. Ma answered and Kajal felt comfortably home. He shot off his routine reporting and Ma asked him to eat well and bathe regularly despite the Shillong cold. But why was Baba home? Was something the matter?

"Are you planning to come?" Ma asked.

"Not now, Ma. A bit busy. Maybe soon."

"Okay, take care. We miss you."

"Miss you too, Ma."

But it was a 'miss you' that one had accepted as inevitable, and even found beneficial. The only way to keep a family from entirely disintegrating over a showdown of frustrated hopes was to put distance between one another.

* * * * *

Rahul had moved to Delhi University for his Masters in Physics. It was his mail that came with the attachment. Kajal reluctantly opened it. The Ministry of Culture, Government of India was offering two scholarships – covering travel, course fees and living expenses for a year – exclusively for eligible students from the northeast of India. For a course in Fine Art in London.

Some force within that was absolutely unknown to him made Kajal pursue the link. And before he knew it, he had filled out the forms, written out the two thousand word essay on renascence art, and had an offer letter. And one chilly Shillong night, he applied for a Visa with the British Deputy High Commission in Kolkata through a travel agent. The process took four months that flew by on him and he kept from Ma. And Baba.

He was surprised at his selection. Perhaps no one else heard about it. And applied. It wasn't entirely untrue. These inconsequential feelgood measures that the Central Government chose time and again to put down in its dossiers as its we-care-for-the-northeast efforts, usually went unadvertised and unsought. After all, what else could be expected of people that had had to respond with over hundred 'terrorist' organisations over unresolved matters that occupied a little bit more space in their lives than a Fine Art course in London.

The only other 'eligible' application that did come in, and was promptly approved, was that of the daughter of a top Indian Police Service official who had served in the northeast for all of a cumulative two years during a career that otherwise furnished top notch security to Union Ministers in Delhi over thirty years. In all fairness, the daughter herself had always found pictures of perennial clouds covering the green, blue and grey hills surrounding Shillong outrageously attractive but her Dad never thought it safe for her to travel to that insurgency afflicted part of the country.

* * * * *

The only place in Guwahati that offered cashmere long coats those days was Sumangal in the heart of busy Fancy Bazaar.

"It's very cold in London." Ma said.

And Kajal selected one in navy blue.

"Great with both jeans and formals," the *Marwadi* owner opined. "So, is it studies or job that's taking you to London?"

"Studies."

"Very good. And what will you be studying?"

"Fine Art."

"Fine Art?" The salesman hunched forward and brought his face closer to Kajal across the counter top, his squinting eyes looked back from below a berating frown on his forehead. "You mean," he raised his right hand, and bringing the thumb and forefinger together to hold an implied pen, vigorously painted the air, "art? I wouldn't have thought one needed to learn that anywhere other than primary school." And then he looked at Ma, "The world is changing, Maaji."

Ma suddenly felt mortified like a damning family secret had been leaked. She realised only then that the feeling had perhaps been inside her. The whole act of procuring a length of well stitched cashmere to protect a son from the London cold seemed such a sham, now that the world had found out that it was only Fine Art that was taking the son there.

"But there's good money. My brother in Delhi took me to a gallery and there was this hardly one foot by one foot splash of colours that cost some fifty thousand bucks. Even the frame was very ordinary." Selling his suits by length, he of course considered cinema posters and life size cutouts of politicians better value for money.

* * * * *

It was after a long time that they were eating together. Baba, Ma and Kajal. Kajal was leaving for Kolkata the next afternoon and from there, at six the following morning, taking the British Airways flight to London.

It had seemed a good idea. Ma somehow thought the family could pull it off. On his way out to clinic earlier in the evening, "I'll bring some chicken," Baba had told Ma. And she had read it as encouragement to put together a parting dinner.

"Did you pack that bag of socks?" Ma this to Kajal, like reminded abruptly of an urgent task. What she did remember clearly was having put the bag of socks in Kajal's suitcase herself.

Baba ate quietly.

There were ants, laboriously marching a straight line from the jar of sugar to disappear over the edge of the table. Two armies, one from each end, and when they collided head-on, they stopped briefly to say hi. Yes, each one of them.

"If you can find the weighing machine, Kajal could check his suitcase. I believe all these international flights are very strict." Ma again, this time to Baba.

Baba helped himself to chicken from the bowl.

Ma's chicken that evening was unusually unctuous. Where the oil reached the surface, it was like blotches of amoebae reflecting the spectrum. The excursion of the serving spoon fissured them polynarily, but they came together again after the momentary hindrance, with pseudopodia reoriented.

"Be careful with your passport." Ma, back to Kajal.

Baba washed his hands in the basin.

From one of the corners where the legs met the dining table top, the machinery-like grating sound came loud and pompous. Usually it worked in silence, unnoticed. The insect, whatever

143

it was called, gorged on wood that it preferred crushed. Some said it was merely to keep their teeth perfectly edged to gorge on other things. No one however knew if the insect had any teeth at all. By morning, there would be a small heap of wood-dust on the floor beneath, like a brown talcum powder hillock. Ma would dab the spot on the furniture with a cloth dipped in a mix of phenyl and kerosene. But the insect would return, or perhaps never even leave. To nibble silently, and become audible when the environment sank into a deep silence.

"Oh, I nearly forgot – there's dessert." Ma hadn't really forgotten. The jar of sugar which had resident ants, black and yet hidden in the white like illegal immigrants, was on the dining table because she liked her *paayas* sweeter then the men.

———————

Baba stood quietly at the door to Kajal's room. Kajal, his back to the door, was tying a red ribbon on the handle of his suitcase so he'd know it on the carousal at Heathrow.

"Here Kajal, keep this somewhere handy."

Kajal turned around with a start. Standing briskly, he took the pocket sized, black rexin bound address book from Baba's outstretched hand.

"Hiren Barua is my friend from med school. He's settled in the UK. I spoke with him earlier this evening. He won't be able to pick you up from the airport, but he's sure you'll have no trouble at all. He has asked you to take the tube train. He knows the YMCA Hostel." Pointing to the address book, "I have written out his address, phone number, everything there. Give him a call once you arrive and he has insisted that should you have any problem, you must get in touch with him without thinking twice."

Kajal turned to the page. A shiver ran through him at the sight of Baba's handwriting. The Manhattan skyline – bold, proud and confident. Airy along the luxury of the left indent, but suffocated and cramped with the unanticipated arrival of the right. It was the most personal side of Baba he'd seen in a long long time.

While Baba stealthily surveyed Kajal's room like it had ceased to belong to the same house, Kajal read on. Dr. Hiren Barua, Baba's hand had written, followed by the attractive foreign address, ending with a post code that seemed cooler than the Indian PIN. The phone number – long, pausing and with a lenient splash of zeroes. There was no London though. Nor any of the other UK places Kajal knew from the Premier League or County cricket. Dr. Barua lived in Truro.

Judging that Kajal had reached the bottom of the address by then, Baba explained. "He's not in London. He said his place was a little away. But don't worry, he'll be most helpful."

Later, once in the UK, Kajal would realize that Truro is in Wales, and a good five six hours and a couple of hundred Pounds on a train from London. He'd also gather, not exactly from Dr. Hiren Barua but generally, that 'happily permanently settled' people in the UK that far away, faced with the daily job of sorting their own lives out, didn't really go out of their ways to cater to sons of long lost friends from back home.

"Take care Kajal. Be careful with money. The scholarship's all there is. Get a phone so Ma can call you. I've got the ISD line on the home phone now. I've made an e-mail account. I'll check it every evening at the café, so you can use it for urgent messages as well."

Baba pulled out a brown envelope from his pocket and handed it to Kajal. "There are some Pounds in there. Put it safely. There's also a picture of *Maa Kamakhya*. Keep it in your wallet. She'll protect you".

And Baba walked away, leaving Kajal under the wings of an over-burdened Goddess. Preparations for London had thus far been mechanical, with neither excitement nor sadness, but Kajal suddenly felt forsaken as he watched Baba leave the room. His palms went moist. The ears became warm. He felt alone.

Kajal turned to the next page on the address book and found himself staring at his own home address and phone number. Did Baba fear that Kajal would forget that? Even that?

Kajal brusquely wished that he wasn't going anywhere. But the way he saw it, he needed to get away. Not as far as London, but get away.

* * * * *

8

It was after seven months that I met Q again. My life had gone on. In the meanwhile. The routine clinic, patients, conferences, lectures. Enormous glaucoma battles and small cataract victories. I was happy and content. But I actually didn't have much of a life. Then again, who does anyway? Not many a thirty something professional sucked deep into the job of being a thirty something professional goes sky diving or wild life photographing every weekend.

I was successful. My career, that is. It's so much easier with careers – for the most part, they are tangible.

But life had somehow become stuck on Q. Or Q had stuck to it. Like a tattoo that one no longer related to and also didn't know what to do with. I couldn't explain how someone that I had spent so little time with and knew so little about could linger for so long.

Q had called. "Hi doctor, remember me?"

I knew that voice like I'd been waiting forever to hear it.

"Of course. Long time. How are you?"

"I'm fine, thank you. All well with you?"

"Ya, thanks."

"I was wondering if you were free for a drink this Saturday evening. Let's meet at SixtyNine. Seven good for you?"

Nothing had changed. She had already decided the place and time. I craved to make an excuse. Not by any means to pull out of the evening completely – I was frigging delighted I was going to meet her, and no event already in place in my diary could come in the way. But I so wished I could tweak the place or the time.

"I'd love that. Saturday's perfect. I'm traveling with work on Sunday."

The Sunday bit was a lie. I just wanted to sound like I had other things going on with me.

"Cool. I'll see you at seven then. Bye, take care."

She still made me feel like I was insufferably dumb. Even across a telephone.

It was June, when Guwahati perhaps looks its worst. Everything in shades of orange and brown – the colours of dust. Even the green of the leaves and the not-so-far-away hills around this once lovely city that has suddenly been forced to embrace its status as the hub of the northeast of India. While waiting for the monsoons to arrive and cleanse it.

Guwahati is a thirteen, fourteen year old school boy at the end of a day in summer. He is lanky and thin with a massively prominent Adam's apple; he badly needs a haircut; the full day at school and in the sun has left his skin lifeless, parched and tanned; hormones have erupted as unruly facial hair. The white of his school shirt is dulled to a pale yellow, even as the day's activities have propelled it out of being tucked into the trousers, which themselves are unhemmed and yet a couple of inches short.

And through all this, you know that in a couple of years he'll be a different man. Only Guwahati seems captured in a perpetual pubescence that one never grows out of.

Assam – of beautiful hills; of tea gardens; of mild, soft spoken people; of non-pretentious homes with a circumference of tall coconut and betel nut trees, a backyard shrubbed with star-fruit and *paaleng,* and the signature pond providing the afternoon catch of *poothi*; of lovely weather even if a touch rainy for some likings; of a society uncorrupted by dowry and where caste is just a surname – felt like such a distant cry from what Guwahati seemed to have become. One understood and waited patiently for the city to finish its obligatory growing up. But one got tired, and lost hope.

SixtyNine was a half hour drive from my hospital. Not wanting to wrestle the rush hour traffic, I was on the road just past six. The evening was warm and humid. I intended to spend some time at the bookstore near SixtyNine and be with Q only by about quarter past seven. And then apologise for being a little late and blame it on my secretary scheduling a late patient. No, that wasn't a habit. Only with Q. I somehow felt the need to shield my eagerness.

Ten minutes into the drive and I realized something was wrong. I had my windows up and the music on, and with my mind entirely captured by the evening ahead, it took me a while to note that.

The whole street on the side I was driving on was an arrested chain of vehicles. Traffic on the opposite side was very sparse, only an occasional car or an empty city bus zipping by.

There were more than the usual people on the sidewalks. Men and women walked briskly, talking on their cell phones with fear and anxiety on their faces. Shops and offices by the street on both sides were mostly closed; the rare open ones were hurriedly bringing their shutters down.

I lowered the windows. And the first sounds of the evening wafted in. It was the sound of sirens and fire engine bells. I couldn't say where they were coming from. But they were not very far away.

And then I picked it on the car radio. There had been bomb blasts.

Three of them. The first, at forty seven minutes past five in the evening, outside the Sessions Court; the second five minutes later in a fruit stall at the new Inter State Bus Terminus; and the third, at three minutes past six, in a parking lot under the flyover in a busy retail area. The third spot was a fifteen minute drive from my hospital, and halfway on the way to SixtyNine. I looked at my watch. It was six forty – a mere half hour since the nearest blast.

Massive casualties were evenly spread out at all three sites. None of Assam's twenty odd terrorist organizations had yet claimed responsibility, like they usually did within minutes of having added one more feather of success to their mindless caps. Success being defined as transposing their nuisance value into an announcement of existence – even though completely stripped of any real direction and usually remote controlled from some friendly foreign soil – through infliction of insurmountable miseries on the very people whose liberation, for whatever that means, they had set out to fight for.

As an Assamese, I completely identify with the northern star these Fronts set themselves upon when they were born. But just like most of my brethren, I honestly have no clue what these guys are still sticking around for today. And while gradually disappearing altogether from the goings-on in every sphere of life, they keep coming back as outright irritating flashes in the pan that have no fathomable purpose, even as the people want a move-on to catch up with the rest of the world that has long left this land far behind. What I'd rather die to see is them coming forward to set up primary schools with teachers whose salaries they pay from their outrageous coffers, set up primary health centres and deal with all the corruption in whatever way they fancy, instead of blasting the lives out of innocent people.

If a significant chunk of world population is going to make a career in terrorism, there may be a strong case for our universities to offer courses in the discipline. The ultimate objective being to ensure that two hundred years down the line, the Gandhis and the Mandelas do not end up sharing the same space in history as some zealot suicide bombing the world for his seventy two virgins.

As the string of cars crawled delicately, restlessness got me. My views on meaningless human suffering had little to do with it. I was jittery for other reasons.

For one, I knew I wasn't going to be able to make it by seven, as planned.

I wasn't sure I would be able to take the regular route, with one of the blasts having taken place on it.

I wasn't sure SixtyNine would be open after what had happened.

Then, I wasn't sure Q was going to be able to make it.

Most of all, I had no means of communicating with Q. She had my number, I didn't have hers'. Of course I could call up Prashant or whoever, and get Q's number and all that, but I didn't want to. So, as I saw it then, unless Q called me, I couldn't get in touch with her.

The street ended in a T-junction. I usually turned left at that time of the day. To get home. That evening however, I needed to take the right. To meet Q. But I soon realized all traffic was being diverted leftward. With the third blast having taken place only mere kilometers away, the zone had been cordoned off. Police officers tried hard to stay in control, while answering anxious queries in non-confirming, staccato monosyllables. There was some haggling, but eventually no one disobeyed.

Faced with a situation, my thoughts raced and I suddenly came alive. Having taken that left turn, there was no easy way to get to SixtyNine. I could drive through a maze of narrow inside lanes, but I wasn't sure they hadn't become altogether inaccessible by then. I couldn't see any other option.

Except one.

I needed to get rid of my car. I couldn't just leave it by the street. That is perfectly acceptable practice in Guwahati, but not that evening. The freshest crop of blasts would have invigorated the cops and they were sure to remove, scrutinize and destroy every suspicious item at least for the coming week.

Creeping forward in that chain of cars, I saw Asha Residency a little ahead, and an idea presented itself. My good friend Jatin had his flat in Asha Residency. After several failed attempts to reach his cell, I got through on his home number.

"Hey, what's up? Such horrible things have happened. Sick people. Just horribly mad people. I'm so worried I can't get through to Jatin. The network's completely jammed," said Riya, Jatin's wife.

"Don't worry, I'm sure he's fine. It's all haywire right now. He must be trying hard to get to you on the phone as well," I assured her.

"I know. The whole situation just sucks so bad. Where are you?"

"I'm right next to your apartment. I have this really important meeting I just can't pull out of. I'm already late, but I had a word with them and they are happy to wait."

I obviously guarded against letting Riya know that I was going to meet Q – not that she knew anything about Q – or even anyone else for a mere socializing drink on an evening like that.

"You must be mad. You should be going home. More than anything else, how can we be sure three are all those bastards planned?"

"You're right. But I just can't give this one a miss. And I won't make it there before midnight if I attempt driving. What I had in mind was to leave my car at your apartment. You think I could do that?"

"No problem, I'll tell the security. But are sure you'll find a cab or an auto this evening?"

"I don't really know. It's not awfully far. I can just walk. But thanks for the parking. You don't come down now. If it's not too late, I'll drop in on my way back. And give me a buzz when you hear from Jatin."

It was half past seven as I walked out of Asha Court. Humidity got to me immediately and I started sweating profusely. Darkness had duly fallen. The world was a frightful montage of mopish head lamps and tail lights with a deathly machinery hum; a sea of desperate humanity frantically strived to reach somewhere while trying to make sense of it all.

As I crossed the street, melting through six lanes of automobiles, I identified a route.

I planned to take the narrow lane behind the row of Officers' bungalows, cross the wooden bridge and enter the Government

Colony through its rear. Bisecting the Colony and emerging out of its front entrance, I would be on the main street, GS Road. I roughly knew the area, but had never actually traversed it. The good thing about the route – apart from it being the shortest – was that it was entirely inside the Government Colony and I wasn't likely to encounter any police.

I took to the course. I figured I'd reach GS Road in about twenty minutes. Then, I needed to once again turn left and keep walking up GS Road, past the flyover, and in another half hour max, I would be at SixtyNine. I was looking at almost an hour of walking but I wasn't disconcerted in the least by that. There was the other issue. The third blast had occurred under the flyover on GS Road and I had no means of bypassing it.

I walked briskly, and thankfully, uneventfully, between the Government quarters. Almost every soul in the colony was out on its narrow, criss-crossing pathways. Cursing the insanity, blaming the Government. The media blared loudly out of each of those one-bedroom, Assam-type households which stood united by shock and uncertainty. Somewhere a phone rang. "Hello… hello, *aapuni niki?* Hello…*kot aase? Xuna paisene?*" If it was her husband, she didn't find out in that brief while before the service disconnected. She spoke softly to the woman standing with her, "*Aakou koribo niki?*" But the phone didn't ring again. At least not in the time that I was in earshot.

At the other end of the Officers' Colony, good fortune awaited me. I realized I didn't have to turn out on to GS Road just yet. There was a service lane along the edge of the colony, running parallel to GS Road, separated from the latter by ill-maintained horticulture and a wire fence. The colony itself, and with it that service lane, spanned the entire length of the flyover and beyond. At the end of the lane, a gate opened on to GS Road, past the site of the blast.

Walking on the service lane, I couldn't keep my eyes from witnessing the destructive power and the fragility that lay scattered simultaneously to my right. Closer to that flyover, an unbelievable din of voices and screams took over. It wasn't like anything I had known before.

The smell in the air was distinct. Without a doubt, it was the smell of burnt human flesh. A smell that retained the pain of every tiny hair that singed before the skin scalded into the melting muscles and sooting bones. How the body must have twisted; how the eyes stayed open in disbelief; and how dreams got sucked out of the mind. And eventually after unending minutes of numbing pain, nothing remained.

The normally super busy area was eerily dark. The shops were all shut. Some blown away. The only light came from the huge glow sign of Prerna Sweets, the fifty year old icon of that part of Guwahati. The glow sign, ironically bright and colourful that evening, was all that remained of it. Under it, human forms shone on the side walk and street. A crowd of, I figured, over two hundred. Stunned, agitated, concerned, searching, helping, participating, talking, shouting, crying. Or just being there. And those on the ground, strewn out like leftovers of a monster meal. Obviously dead, and beyond recognition perhaps, for the 'merely' injured would have been removed for treatment by then.

The underside of the flyover was coated a grimy black, visible even in the darkness. The mangled remains of the city bus that had taken the entire impact stood slightly to one side like a carefully positioned installation. I would find out the next morning that thirty six passengers had died.

An ambulance with the signage of the largest private hospital in the city stood torched – the mob had found a vent to its impatient helplessness in the first instrument of help to arrive, even as it had taken a further half hour for the Government medical machinery to make an appearance. That same knee jerk also fuelled the manhandling of a State Police van with a sprinkling of manpower that had turned up to control the situation.

But all the chaos was before the energies had found a baton wielder. At that moment, despite the darkness and the distance, there was no missing the portly frame of the famous leader of the opposition in all her valor. Her voice was loud and clear, as she marshaled the available humanity to an end of her own.

Mrs. Vijayanti Kashyap orchestrated the mother of all protests that evening. She inspired the mob to pile up the charred bodies onto hand carts and personally led a march of about hundred, with the hand carts, to the State Assembly, to present right then to the Chief Minister in general, and the people in particular, one more evidence of the failing incumbent.

The distasteful inhumanity of the act would have earned it top billing on the 'Never To Be Done' list of the roguest scoundrel, but to her it was obviously nothing less than political *hara kiri* to not bite deep into and suck hard upon the sheer meat and juice of the opportunity. I hoped that when the rest of the world came to know of it, it appreciated that she was a standalone mutant, and no one with half a brain and a quarter of a heart did anything like that even in my part of the world.

I reached the other end of the flyover. In front of me, I saw the gate that would take me out of the Government Colony. It was a whole lot quieter on this side.

My mind relaxed a bit. A sense of the worst being over and a renewed focus on Q brought calm.

It was just then that my right foot struck something. I stopped, and looked down. The sinking sensation started in the middle of the chest and rapidly became a powerful squeeze that threatened my control over all sphincters. My whole body ached.

The sock was dark. Brown perhaps. I couldn't say too well in the little light. The shoe was black. Brogues. Very similar to mine. Laces tied. The skin was fair over the calf, with no hair at all. It looked very neat. No dirt, no blood, no ripped tissue. Only a couple of tendons, and perhaps a bit of the medial cruciate ligament stood out like loose circuitry at the end of a robotic limb. Where the leg had gotten severed at the knee. The shoe suggested that it possibly was the left.

––––––––

It was exactly half past nine when I reached Sherwood Manor, the star property where SixtyNine was the lounge bar. Two and a half hours behind. Felt strange stepping into the driveway with all the tall pine trees, flying satin of different colours upon the white flag poles and the tall, bearded usher dressed like Indian royalty at the entrance.

I had been there earlier, but the lobby felt like another planet that evening. The chandeliers were bright and a far cry from the darkness of the streets I had just traversed. The floor was polished black granite, and squeaky clean. The large water body in the middle with hundreds of floating red rose petals filled the space with a strong fragrance, completely divorced from the truth I had experienced over the preceding two hours.

I found out at the front desk that SixtyNine was open. The scheduled performance by the Dkhar Boys Band was however understandably cancelled.

Inside SixtyNine, I scanned the tables – I was more expecting to hear 'Doctor!' called out in Q's voice. It took me whole of five minutes to grasp that Q wasn't there. There were two men at a table, another one at the bar, and a young couple at another table by the corner. And that was all. No Q.

Maybe she never came. Maybe she couldn't make it. And decided that I wouldn't either. Maybe she waited and left. But then she could have called. She should have called. Or was it the network?

I chose a spot and slumped in. Disappointed? Yes, definitely. But the actualities of the evening hit me harder. Why was I there, going through all that I had, to meet someone I hardly even knew? I somehow wasn't worried at all about her being safe – I seemed to know that she was. Even as my own worries about having to repeat my whole walk, retrieve my car and then get home started to bother me.

I got myself a whisky. They had Jack Daniel's.

My senses settled into an acceptance of Q's absence. I decided to take a while finishing the drink, and head off. Meanwhile, one of my favourite Springsteens played.

Is a dream a lie if it don't come true
Or is it something worse

The song seemed like a playback moment in a Bollywood flick, sitting brilliantly on my own state of play, where 'Intermission' appears over a still of the drunk hero in an empty bar with the outro of the song, camera craning out to capture a long shot.

Consumed by morose musings, I didn't notice the door open and someone step in.

"I'm so sorry for this. When did you get here? Have you been waiting long?"

I looked up. Standing next to my table was a smiling Q. Looking fresh and lovely. She seemed different from the picture I'd had in my mind for all the time since I'd last seen her.

With hindsight, I'd rather have 'Intermission' at this point. On a still of Q, harbinger of every tectonic shift in this tale.

"Well, hello. Now, this is a real surprise. I thought we were meeting tomorrow."

I tried hard with my opening line. As always, Q's presence robbed me of my most basic skills. There were other things as well. Like how I didn't want to let her know all that I had gone through to be there that evening; didn't want her to know how disappointed I was with not finding her earlier; didn't want her to know how thrilled I was to finally see her.

"It's okay. You don't have to be mean," Q said, pulling a chair. "I hope you don't mind me joining you."

"Let me explain." Q offered as soon as she was seated.

"That can wait. It's alright anyway. I myself got here only a little while ago. What can I get you?"

"Just a glass of the house white. Thanks."

I returned with her drink.

"I did get here at seven sharp. I swear. I was here till about quarter past," Q said. "But you have no clue what happened after that," Q's eyes lit up.

"I'm sure I shouldn't even attempt a guess."

I was half sure she was going to talk about the blasts. I had no inclination to return to that subject, but I was happy to just watch her talk.

"Don't. It's been such a day. It's left me completely dazed."

I could understand. I loved it that she was a conscientious citizen.

"Let me begin with the beginning, this morning that is. I wake up, make myself a coffee and start checking mail." She paused, for effect and also a sip of the wine, before continuing, "And sitting in my inbox is this mail from Vishesh. I send him a reply. And even before I'm signed out, he replies. I hadn't been half as happy in a long time."

From the minute I saw her that evening, and increasingly so by the time she was telling me all that, I knew something was different. Q was bubbling like a child with a permanent twinkle drafted in her eyes. I loved it that she seemed so eager to tell me. Like she had no one else to tell.

"What? You don't want to know who Vishesh is? How can you be so dull?" She was someone else that evening.

"Ya Ya. I was thinking about that. Good friend?" I felt a slight awkwardness. I wasn't sure if I wanted to hear her tell me about her guy friends or if I felt jealous and possessive.

"Vishesh Sahejwani and I were like Siamese. Joined everywhere. We were together at the law firm in Delhi. I hadn't heard from him in two years."

"How come?"

"I don't know. Just stopped staying in touch, I guess." Her eyes looked into the distance. And just for a split, I sensed a touch of sadness.

"It's not over yet. There's more," Q said like she'd briskly finished brushing off an inelegant moment. "You know Rani, my boss at the editing office?"

"Ya I do. She'd brought her mother to the clinic sometime back."

"Okay. Rani called me a couple of days back and asked me over at office this afternoon. So I got down there, and what did I find – they'd arranged lunch for me. A surprise."

I asked for one more round of drinks. We both lit cigarettes.

"Such yummy Chinese!" she continued. "Anyway, I had a really busy afternoon after that. I had to redo my tickets and also pick up things from the dry cleaner. I sorted everything and reached home by about five. And by the time I showered and all that, I swear, I was really looking forward to the evening with you. Just wanted to unwind and relax with a doctor. My only available option is one who only knows the eye. Think of it, how much of the body would the eyes be? Five %? So, you're like a 5% doctor." I loved that old mischief.

"Have you heard about the blasts? Horrible isn't it?" Q spoke like it was the traffic, without any hint of emotion.

What blasts? Q had already made everything other than herself disappear for me.

"Ya I know. Such a mess. Had a bit of a problem getting here. How was it for you?" I asked distractedly.

I didn't want to talk about the blasts. And I also realized how little they perhaps meant to Q. For her, life hadn't only gone on, she was quite untouched. But I didn't mind it at all. Strangely. Because I generally detested people who were so full of their own water-tight insulated lives.

"No, I was fine. Took an auto. Anyway. I got here on time. And fifteen minutes later, Rohan, who I'd gone to school with in Delhi, lands at my table. We were together at SPV from sixth to twelfth standard. And we hadn't seen each other since. Isn't it incredibly spooky?" Q clearly felt it was.

"Yes, of course it is. Two knockings from the past – one right from the depths of amnesia – on the same day. Can't remember something like that happen to me ever," I seconded her opinion.

"I still can't believe it. He's with Airtel in Kolkata and is here for a meeting, which got cancelled because of the blasts. He's staying at the hotel. He literally pulled me up to his room."

"All right. So between then and now, you were with him. And completely forgot about me." I tried to sound offended. I was worse, actually. Inappropriately.

"Stop whining! He'd arranged for the bar to call up his room as soon as you arrived. Rohan's always been such a gentleman. Obviously, you didn't ask for me. But it was really nice. Talking about old times. We had some wine and didn't even realize how late it had become."

"I can understand," I wasn't sure how I was feeling with all the information. "I completely acknowledge it – incredible day for you. Vishesh, then the lunch, and now Rohan. On a day where I was perhaps slated to be the only starring act," I added playfully.

"Don't worry, doctor, you still are the one and only star."

"Thanks. That is really helpful. But you should have asked Rohan to join us".

Much as I was feeling strange, I did feel an urge to meet Rohan. Just to know what Q's men friends were like.

"No way. This is my time with you. Exclusively," said Q. Funny how people can say massive things so casually.

"But what is this thing about being invited for a surprise lunch to your own office?" I asked.

"Oh, oh. I'm sorry I didn't tell you. In fact that's why I wanted to see you. It's not my office anymore. It's been a couple of months now. I'm going to London. I have been accepted for a Masters."

"Congrats. That's great news. I'm really happy for you. So you did go ahead and get it."

It would be a lie to say that I wasn't glad. I was. But would also be a lie to say that delighted was all I was. I had perhaps come to terms with Q being just a thought – undefined, simultaneously pleasing and disturbing. The evening made her real again. And she telling me that she was off to London didn't help at all.

"Thanks. Ya, I've been happy."

"So, how long do we have you here in my city? Doesn't the academic calendar in the UK start in September or thereabouts? A month?" I asked, half hoping, I don't know why, that she'd tell me she was joking about the whole London thing.

"Much less than that actually. I'm leaving day after. I redid the tickets today. Well, there's nothing much I'm doing here. Mama's happy that I'm spending time with her in Delhi. And then I'll also catch up with Vishesh."

"Wow, good for you," said I.

"Then I'm off to Coventry, to my Dad. We need to sort out my accommodation, bank account and all that in London before the course starts in September."

"That's nice. None of my business, but it's nice that you're in touch with your Dad."

"But I've always been. Very honestly, I was way too small when my parents separated. And I've always considered it a coincidence that I grew up with Mama. I'm not judgmental about them at all, about who was right or wrong. Even they themselves are not.

You see, they married when both were students in London, only to realize that love wasn't really enough to burnish cracks of incompatibility that made a 24-hour joint venture more painful then pleasurable. They took time away and grew to like that view from a distance. But they never divorced. Neither did they find others. I've actually become increasingly proud that they neither settled for a squabbling companionship both despised every living moment nor forced themselves into other relationships just to show the world that they'd moved on."

Q suddenly looked me straight in the eye. Unlike she'd ever done before. Her eyes were tender, filled with feelings that I had never seen in them.

"You know doctor, Dad's not been well. I'm happy I'll be seeing him soon."

"I'm sorry. What happened?"

"I guess he's just growing old." And for the second time that evening Q seemed to be forcefully committed to keeping me out of her space. Like she was obliged to portray a strength that wasn't real, but one that she was very proud of.

"It's very strange but the first person that came to my mind when I learnt of Dad's illness was you. Maybe because you are the only doctor friend I have." Q smiled weakly.

Q was making a habit of dropping huge comments with a carelessness that disregarded what they did to me. I was her only doctor friend. To my mind it sounded like I was her only friend.

"And I also had to tell you that I was leaving."

My eyes lowered as I smiled. I feared my ears had probably turned red. I hated what this woman did to me!

As if to confirm that she read my thoughts, Q added, "Don't worry, I'm not in love with you."

I hadn't thought of that. I couldn't imagine Q being in love with anyone. More than anything else, I was sure she'd scare the crap out of the average, everyday, ordinary guy. But just then, my mind did throw up an image of Q being in someone's arms and looking tenderly into his eyes. Unthinkable!

Q and I were the only people left.

Q excused herself. And returned, like only she could after last calls at the bar, with a glass of her wine and a JD for me. It was the first time she was buying me a drink.

"This one's for London and great surgery videos."

That was the end of the evening. Q was going to London and we had met to say goodbye. And I didn't know if I was ever going to see her again.

"I'm really sorry once again to have kept you waiting. Thanks for making the time," Q said as we readied to leave.

"Don't bother being formal. I had a really good time myself. All the very best, and my regards to your mum and Dad," I replied, and slipping my arm around her waist, gave her a squeeze. Q didn't pull away. For a moment I actually thought Q wanted to hug me. But maybe that was just me. I really hate whisky sometimes!

"Are you going to drive me home or what?" Q asked, a smile on her face declared that she knew I was going to drop her home.

"I'm sorry, I don't have my car. Left it at a friend's on my way here. But let me arrange for a hotel vehicle to drop you."

I really was sorry I didn't have my car. Maybe I should have just driven up anyway earlier in the evening.

"No, don't bother," said Q. She held on to her smile, but now it seemed to suggest that even if I had the car and offered her a ride, she would have declined.

We walked together in silence till the entrance of the hotel. Past the smile at the reception desk. Past the water body with the rose petals. And then Q suddenly stopped where the long flight of steps started descending. I stopped and turned to her.

"All okay?" I asked.

"Ya, ya. Thanks again. You take care. And miss me, okay," Q surprised me.

"Are you not leaving?" My face hid little of my confusion.

"I just remembered something."

Q stood there as I walked down. From about the tenth step, I looked back without really stopping. Q was still there. She had worn a pair of dark blue, boot-cut jeans and a tucked-in, white shirt with the sleeves rolled up and three buttons open at the neck. Her feet in those dark boots were together. I knew immediately that that was the image my mental and emotional database would conjure up every time I thought of her for the rest of my life.

There was a gentle breeze outside. I looked skywards and saw dark clouds gathered. The quiet was broken by distant flashes and claps of thunder. It was going to rain. The monsoons had arrived.

As much as I didn't want to get soaked, I longed for that smell of the first rains kissing the hot, baked earth. I walked fast. But the thoughts raced faster.

Q was physically attractive and perfectly desirable. But she didn't send my hormones into a tizzy. She could be intellectually purging over a talk. But that didn't make her unique. I was her friend. But she seemed to guard so severely against letting me in. She could hurt. And yet fleetingly become a child demanding to be protected.

Q opened up new facets that ridiculed my ability to gauge people.

Most of all, why was I killing myself trying to understand her? Why was I succumbing to this need to know her?

Was I in love with her?

Love for me was a deal as mighty as they came. I had spent thirty three years of my life without actually finding that feeling. Not that I lugged around a set-in-stone definition. But I knew I hadn't felt it. And I also didn't subscribe to what I had heard someone say – you fall in love many times, but you find the right one only once. For me, one fell in love only once. And that was the right one.

Was what I was feeling for Q that once-in-a-lifetime thing called love?

What also teased me was that at some level, I actually celebrated the fact that I had never been in love. Sacred though love was, I disapproved my life to spin around it. And that is how I was convinced love should be – just one of several occupations of the mind, not the only one. I perhaps feared Q as capable of wrecking that alignment.

It was nearly two when I reached Jatin's apartment. I didn't intend to wake them up. I was happy the security guy didn't make a fuss over me collecting my car.

"Did you notice what time Jatin *saab* got back?" I asked him.

"I don't know sir. Riya madam's brother was here and she left with him a while ago," he answered.

I thanked him and called Jatin up as I drove. There was no answer.

I flicked the wipers on. It had started raining, and turned heavy by the time I reached home.

It suddenly occurred to me that I once again had no means to communicate with Q. No phone number, no mail id, no postal address. I didn't even know where she lived in Guwahati, even though, every time I had thought about it earlier, my mind suggested that her grandmother owned one of those old Assam-type houses with front gardens that had survived the apartment onslaught on Zoo Road. Much like the persona, the person was once again beyond me.

* * * * *

It was a little past half five. Earlier that evening. Jatin was getting out of his car outside the Sessions Court. He had booked a meeting with Advocate Choudhury over the matter of Jadav Kurmi, the Accounts Manager his company had recently sacked. Kurmi had moved the Labour Court on grounds of caste discrimination. The matter had reached Bangalore, and a fresh round of 'we-should-have-never-taken-shop-to-the-northeast' was abuzz.

Jatin was in time for his six o'clock appointment. He hadn't forgotten that on his way back home, he had to pick up the swimsuit that Anushka, Riya and his three year old daughter, needed for her 'Day in the Pool' at playschool next day.

The blast went off at five forty seven. Strange time for a sophisticated, timer controlled device.

Jatin's body was never found. It came to popular light some months later that the Police had dumped several bodies through that night into the Brahmaputra river, which flowed right behind the Court, to restrict the death count to a more presentable number.

From a distance it looks sinister. Like foreign cricketers fear a trip to the whole of India for some time after such an incident, within India, Indians learn to stay away from her troubled parts. But life goes on everywhere. Even if it leaves you dazed for a while.

* * * * *

9

My Diary: Khonsa, Wednesday, 9th January 2008, PM

Got here earlier this evening. Was very hungry but I slept off. Just woke up. I can't remember the last time I had slept so well.

Jagat said he'll bring some food. Poured myself a drink in the meanwhile. The feeling is alien, even drolly, the more I think about it. My last whisky, my last dinner, my last black coffee, my last cigarette. The last time I slip under the covers and sleep a night. Tomorrow morning – my last morning tea, my last pee, my last crap, my last shave, my last shower.

The Guest House is old, wooden floored and warm. The bed is creaky but the linen and duvet are a pleasing commix of homely detergent and dry clean.

I enjoyed the four hour drive from Dibrugarh. Absolutely uninhabited hills. Just the meandering road, with the mountains climbing steeply on one side, and falling off deeply on the other.

It was raining even as our bus left Dibrugarh, and it stayed with us all the way to Khonsa.

While inviting me to visit him, my friend had mentioned that March was the best time, otherwise Khonsa was too cold. This is January. I've arrived without information and of course, I'm not planning on seeing him. But I still love this sleepy little mountain town where everything is a comfortable monochrome of dark grey – the sky, the greenery, the clouds, and if the cold and the rain had colour, I'm sure even they would be dark grey here.

The cold here reminds me of the winter in London. But I am unharmed. For I have finally understood. Qs are only windows to the real world. It is absolutely no fault of the window when it is the view outside that is killing me. I had completely forgotten this feeling of not having a blizzard within. Running away to cling on to an apparently invaluable life can be tough, but I have run only to find a decent enough spot to stand still.

It's nearly eleven in the night now. A couple of hours earlier last night, I was in Guwahati, leaving the keys to my apartment with Mrs. Deka. Never to take them back.

I hope the sun shines tomorrow. Would be a shame if I have to leave without seeing more of Khonsa. But I don't have a lot of time. I don't want to give myself a lot of time. Time makes one weak. And teaches one to find hope.

* * * * *

BOOK TWO

Nam-myoho-renge-kyo

10

She sits on a plush velvet throne, both hands on the armrests in deliberate firmness and her feet on an ornate footboard. Her long robe is stiff silk embellished with overflowing gold. She is fat, like an expensive pink cake coated in elaborate marzipan. And she is old with a grandmotherly face. But her forehead is creased in stoic vigilance. She'll let you breathe under her clear blue sky, walk her cobble stone alleys and live in her manor. But you would be criminally foolish to take even a moment for granted. She'll be the distant espial while you prosper unhindered; she will lend you a nonchalant hand when you fall; she'll ostracize you in ways you can never fathom If you hurt her.

She is London. The city that lingers, however little one experiences of it. And I reckon, even a thousand years later she won't be just another city.

I play around with the sequence and fall for this seemingly irresistible urge to suspensize a rather straightforward narration. Maybe I want to ensure that when I finish, I leave you thinking about me. A small privilege. For I do know I'm not the rightest person in this tale.

Within a couple of weeks of meeting Q – SixtyNine on the evening of the blasts – I was offered a sabbatical in London. Six months at the UCL Institute of Ophthalmology and with it an opportunity to be a part of that Mecca of eye doctors, Moorfields Eye Hospital. The Institute has been one of the pioneers in research in eye care worldwide, including my poor-people approach.

My decision to take up the offer had nothing to do with Q. She was gone and I wasn't going to be found chasing her. I believed that I had banished her conclusively from every mainframe. But as I attended to the logistics of making the trip, she crept right back to reclaim my thoughts. I couldn't unknow that she was in London. The distance and apparent inaccessibility had made me commodious, but my own trip conspired to make such conveniences vanish. I hated the way fate propositioned to put us in each other's trajectories.

As the day of my departure came closer, I became increasingly fidgety, until all resistance thawed. I had to find out where Q was in London. I had to see her just that once.

* * * * *

"Hey doc, great news." Prashant, my friend from Q's video editing firm, walked in where I was waiting for him.

"Thanks for making it. I was beginning to worry I'd have to leave without saying goodbye to you."

"I'm sorry. Have just been unfairly busy since I've joined this FM Channel. Honestly, sometimes I feel like I'm the *chowkidar* – first to arrive and the last to leave."

I suddenly felt cheap that I hadn't actually insisted on the evening entirely to say goodbye to him, and that I had brought an agenda.

"I can understand. I know how that kind of backstage work can be. Beer?" I asked.

"Vodka perhaps," Prashant replied.

I signaled a service guy. "Okay, make it a 60, add a dash of fresh lime, half Sprite and half soda. Put lots of ice and drop a lemon peel," Prashant explained elaborately. When it came, there was a bonus of a cocktail stirrer with an 'umbrella' and a red cherry which seemed awfully uncomfortable, like it didn't really belong to the cocktail, whatever it was called.

"So, how long will you be gone?" Satisfied and settled, Prashant directed his attention me-wards.

"Six months."

"But don't stay back okay. We keep hearing about bright doctors that never came back!" Prashant winked.

"No fears, I'm not bright enough for London to want to latch on to me."

Through my restlessness to arrive at the crux, and through the spirit getting to Prashant uncharacteristically quickly, we patiently talked about the rigors of his new job. "After all the programming we techies do, I swear doc, it's cruel the blabbering RJ's with their fake accents become the stars!"

And then finally, I brought the gavel down. "So who's left at the old video editing firm?"

"I know. So many have left. But I guess in life you have to move on."

Prashant had overdone his vodka and all my queries faced the threat of being answered philosophically. I had to bring it up directly – I asked him about Q.

"Oh she. She left as well. They all do," Prashant answered vaguely. And then abruptly put his drink down in the middle of a sip, "Hey! She's in London as well!" Prashant brightened up like a long sputtering tube light finally getting it right, and promptly celebrated the million-dollar information he'd just given me by polishing off his drink. I wasn't going to buy him another. Not for a while.

"Really? What's she doing there?" I feigned innocence.

"I don't really know. Maybe she went to get married or something like that. No no, I don't know. She didn't marry Rishabh. Poor him!"

Rishabh?

Optimism gradually left me. But I persisted. "Would you have a number or an address? You know, I could say hi to her when I'm there."

"Sorry doc. When she left, she just left."

When she left, she just left – Pray tell me something I don't know!

Despite the effort proving futile, there was a strange joy. A relief that my sleuthing had returned nothing on Q. Distant stars were protecting me.

* * * * *

The September of 2006 brought me to London. And I failed to overcome sensing that Q was there somewhere in the same city. In odd moments, the city seemed so frighteningly small, every next step conspired to bump me into her. At other times, the reasonably non-existent probability of such an encounter comforted me. That's right – comforted me. Because Q was essentially a tormenting thought that I feared, as much as I sometimes thought I loved.

By the end of October, I was decently settled. The Institute and my little work-group took me in pleasantly. While Moorfields Eye Hospital is the top referral centre for eye care in the UK, the

Institute of Ophthalmology is an academic and research unit. Together, they are best described as neighbours in the same trade, with varying degrees of shared physical space and overlapping manpower, while enjoying financial and administrative autonomy.

"If you like to hit the ground running, there's this project on hand that could do with some data. You can of course find it uninspiring and say no. In which case, you and I will have to build you a fresh proposal."

That was Walter Connery, my assigned mentor. Walter was about fifty, over six foot and the bulletin board above his office desk proudly displayed two sepia tinted pictures from a time when his pate was lush. After introductions, accustomed with the Indian way, I had addressed him as 'Connery sir'. "The knighthood's still on its way, mate!" was his reply, "Let's stick to Walter till then."

I liked him right away. He was a well travelled man – which is not such a big deal for a European. But he understood the world. He understood India better than to climax over the sight of bone-thin women dressed in orange and yellow, trudging miles with water filled earthen pots under the harshest sun on earth against the backdrop of Rajasthan's desert that most Sunday visitors can't resist earmarking as the highlight of their 'Palace-on-Wheels' experience. He comprehended reality unhindered by colourful romance.

"Coffee, people?"

As Walter ground his favourite roasted beans and mixed a brew for his 'Team', I browsed through the proposal he had handed me. The 'Team' that afternoon comprised Heidi and Andrew, Walter's final year PhD students.

There were a couple of others on the 'Team' but elsewhere that afternoon.

Iris was a Greek optometrist who'd started a part-time PhD under Walter the previous year. "When you wake up with a second name like mine, you know you should have gotten married yesterday!" Her opinion on Greek surnames was only the tip of the iceberg where her copious quotes were concerned.

Then there was Xian, ophthalmologist from China. "You Indians actually do really well with your English," Heidi had commented in reference to Xian. "Xian's a wonderful chap and I'm sure he's great at his work, but his English is such a handicap, he honestly can't get a lot done outside his country." I took what Heidi said as a compliment and felt encouraged to put forth an insight into India's English medium education system. Heidi was wide-eyed and all ears. "Really!"

But I often wonder. It cannot be disregarded as mere coincidence that fifteen of the G20 economies have non-English mother tongues as official language. Of the five that do function in English, it is the mother tongue for three. Then, all G7 countries work in their mother tongues, which is not English for four of them. Even amongst BRIC, we are the only nation operating in a foreign language.

Even though in India, I religiously detest the idiots that get loads of pride out of announcing 'Shit dude, my Hindi's so bad', it did feel good to have impressed Heidi in London!

Finally there was Greg. At forty five, he was nearly Walter's age. Greg had started off being a banker with Barclays Capital. This he gave up after five bonus-laden years during the time when every soap bubble he and his clan created sailed high and strong. No, he wasn't laid off – long before the bubbles went kaput and only the bonuses survived, he had taken off on his own accord. "The meaninglessness of a life spent entirely on advising ridiculously rich obnoxious buggers how best to get richer made me want to go to the Himalayas." Himalayas he didn't go to, but joined the British Army, and served in Gulf War: Season 2. "That was one helluva meaningful job helping America fuck an arrogant rogue who refused to sing Uncle Sam's tune!" Greg declared with a twinkle in his eye. Somewhere in the middle of that oily war he discovered his true calling – medicine. Greg was a Specialty Grade Registrar on rotation under Walter when I met him. Hard core clinician he was, but the association with Walter was bearing some research sprouts, an effect of Walter's trademark 'welcome to research' speech: "It's a real shame when people with brains the size of the planet are content with merely pulling out cataracts!"

I myself was ten days old that afternoon, but wasn't sure if I was 'Team' yet, or for that matter, will ever be.

"Milk? Sugar?"

"Black, and no sugar please." I answered with hesitation. I was awkward with Walter, boss of the unit, serving us – me – a beverage. Heidi's mannerism made it plain that there was nothing remarkable about it, but it was going to take me some getting used to.

"What do you think?" Walter asked about the proposal, handing me a mug and settling down on his chair.

"Good. Interesting in fact," I replied.

"It is actually a tight little project and we can write up a couple of quick papers. Let's go through it once and plug any gaps waiting to bring us down. And then we'll run across and find a place on one of the wards for you to interview the patients. We should be good to count numbers from Monday."

The dependable British efficiency placed me in Victoria Ward on Monday morning, ready to commence data collection for my hospital-based research project. I was required to carry out two projects in the six months, the second one set in a 'rural' community on the outskirts of London.

Positioned in my booth, I spent a good hour gawping at the surroundings. I was after all at Moorfields Eye Hospital. The informed consent protocol required me to introduce myself to prospective participants in the study as: "I am one of the eye doctors here. While you're waiting for the surgery, I'd like to quickly take a picture of your eye and have a little chat – if that's okay with you. This is for a research we are carrying out." *One of the eye doctors here!* Merely rehearsing the opening line over in my head gave me some kind of a kick.

I was finally jolted back to my senses by Grace, sister-in-charge of Victoria ward. "Walter will know how well you use your time here!" Hands on her hips but she seemed kind.

I sifted through the patient records laid on the Nurses' Station counter. For my first recruit, I decided on the safety of a 'colonial cousin' – an Indian gentleman from Southall who was getting his cataract removed. When I approached him, he declined to partake – citing that his head was too full of the cataract surgery to consider anything else. Fair enough.

The rest of the day wasn't all that bad as I managed to draw in ten participants.

* * * * *

The bus I took at the end of my day was the number 205 to Paddington. It was a Mercedes. The famous red London Routemaster had fallen. When you come from a country which is unarguably many rungs below in so many ways despite its panache for wearing Versace over undergarments ridden with holes, it is perhaps unavoidable that you see these as wishful evidence of decay in the top seeds, and that brings some cheap thrill.

Through my immense pride at finding a spot on the Moorfields staff roster, I suspected that stumbling across some small aspect of its service that my hospital back home was better at would leave me ecstatic. The gentleman from Southall came to my mind. I wondered which flag he waved when he went to an India-England cricket match at Lords.

Climate control kept me warm in the bus, but scarves and jackets were suddenly rampant on the streets outside. Almost all black, the odd one bright red. The brisk takeover of the pleasant day by chilly blackness bewildered me.

"You must miss the sun," Heidi had spoken thoughtfully. And I had stood up bravely, "It's a thousand times better than what I had come prepared for." "Don't let this welcome package fool you. By November we will have tweaked our clocks and yet it will be dark by four In the afternoon," Heidi had appeared offended by me belittling the prowess of the English winter.

The streets were narrow. Much narrower than what I had pictured any first world street would be or even what one was used to in the bigger Indian cities – that despite the width, our streets are an altogether different bedlam is another tale.

On my second day, the traffic at King's Cross turned briefly higgledy-piggledy, triggering a sadistic delight in me. But sooner than that, authorities leapt in to intervene like it was a shameful national crisis.

The bus glided noiselessly, strictly within the 'bus lane', along the route which for me had become a trail of familiar stops by then.

Angel – Caledonian Road – King's Cross – British Library went by. My mind was essentially blank as I shiftily surveyed my co-passengers. Visually scavenging other people's faces in moments they considered private is perhaps a matter of habit with me! In fact, I'm not awfully convinced anyone is entitled to any privacy at all on public transport. I don't ever mean any harm, and neither am I particularly nosy. And it's only always when I have nothing else better to do – like on the upper deck of a city bus that moved with such gentle monotony so as to become entirely devoid of any personality.

Around me, there were seven people surviving on headphones of varying consruction, another five had found conversations on their phones, twelve momentarily lived lives of celebrity heiresses and Premier League stars in free copies of *LondonLite*, and two others read paperbacks.

The city was an assembly line of individuals who dressed in the same black, who stuffed their ears with the same headphones and whose eyes had the same I-need-to-be-someplace-else-but-I'm-not-in-a-hurry look!

"Aar kou, Murad baalaa aase? Taare bejaan miss *kori re bai."* Pause. *"Suti pawa to muskil. Dekhi* Christmas*e."* Longer pause. *"Baalaa thako te. Kaati aar."* He was in the seat in front of me. In the safety of language, he didn't bother checking his volume. He was of course unaware that behind him I easily followed every bit of his Bangla. Not that he had the next move in a coup to offer – only sweet family talk, as he explained to his wife back home how much he missed Murad, perhaps their son, and how difficult it was to get leave from work. He then added, overcoming immediate self-consciousness in pursuit of brownie points a thousand miles away, "I love you," and broke into peals of laughter. *"Ei* London *re bai, keu kaaro maate kaan dei naa!"* More laughter.

Yes, it was London and like he said, no one cared to tune in on other people's conversations.

I thought about his country. It is perhaps the only country on earth whose single export is people! Okay okay, PJ and I know I'm not great at being witty. But there honestly must be more Bangladeshis in other countries than at home. And it must be a matter of celestial design – those born with Jupiter and Sun in the seventh house, or whatever is the best combination of these elements, found check-out jobs at supermarkets in London and those born under awful signs illegally crossed the border into my Assam!

I felt my eyelids putting on irresistible weight and gradually dozed off. In ten minutes or thereabouts, the bus took a sharp turn and I was stirred out of my reverie. A quick look outside showed the purple of the PC World store. It was my stop. I pressed the bell while rushing down the steps and arrived at the door just as it was opening.

The wind outside was strong and cold. But it was only a short walk – just about five minutes, past the two pubs and Khadim – to the Indian YMCA Student Hostel. That's right, that's where I had reserved to lodge my time in London.

* * * * *

11

Q sneaked in just as the elevator doors were closing. Her bag got caught and the doors responded by opening again.

"Sorry sorry," she smiled an apology.

Kajal was the only other passenger. The elevator started up again, quiet and still, like it wasn't moving at all.

"Those hands look fancy. What have you been up to?" Q asked.

Kajal looked at his hands. He hadn't realized his fingers still carried bits of the white acrylic paint he had been working with. There was also white on the knees of his jeans and a fine spray on his left shoe. He stuffed his hands into his pockets and smiled at her, not bothering to answer her.

"Are you studying here?" Q rephrased her question.

"Fine Art. At Byam Shaw." Kajal knew she won't comprehend but hoped she wouldn't force him into an explanation that he couldn't escape from without seeming boorish.

"Wow, that's a whole different world! I study Law at SOAS."

Kajal offered a brief smile in acknowledgement and returned his gaze to the orange numbers changing above the elevator door till it reached the fourth floor.

They collided as they tried to step out. Q halted and suggested, "After you." Kajal took the offer, eager to lose her. As he walked away to the left, she called out, "I'm on the fourth floor as well. Ladies wing, of course." She stood smiling. Kajal turned back, baffled why she was telling him. "Four-o-five," he told her his room number, and again took a step away.

"It's Friday night. What plans?" She wasn't giving up.

"I'm seeing some friends from school after dinner." Kajal lied.

"Okay, see you at dinner." And Q finally let him go.

————

It was a quarter past eight when Kajal walked into the cafeteria. Dinner at the YMCA closed at half eight. He filled his plate at the counter and took his tray to an empty table.

Most tables were unoccupied that evening. It was Friday night and only October in the academic year. Boarders in the hostel – mostly Indian students on a first visit to London – had still not progressed beyond the Leicester Square and Piccadilly Circus stage of knowing the city. There was rush to cover as much ground as possible over the weekends before the winter and course-work wiped out such pleasures.

Q wasn't there. It was only when the relief of not finding her in the cafeteria hit Kajal did he realize that she'd actually been on his mind.

He quietly ploughed through his *rajma-chawal* and finished with a coffee. Stepping outside, he walked to his usual spot by the corner and lit a cigarette. London had brought back his smoking, something he hadn't done since the Nikhil days.

"Hey Kajal. It's DJ night at the ISH Bar. Want to join us?" Prateek shouted on his way out of the hostel with a group of friends. Prateek was on a Masters at AA and was amongst only a couple of people that Kajal was on talking terms with after a month in the hostel.

"I'm meeting friends from school. You guys carry on." Kajal stuck to the lie he had invented for Q.

Back in his room, he pulled out the DVD he had borrowed from the college library – 'Pollock', the Ed Harris movie on the life of Jackson Pollock. Selecting the 'full screen' mode on his laptop, he plugged on his noise-cancellation headphones – high-end Bose, parting gift from William, owner of the recording studio in Shillong.

* * * * *

Nearly a week later, Kajal returned to YMCA exhausted from college one evening. He got himself a coffee from the dispenser and took it to the television room. There was no one else. He sank into one of the cosy chairs and settled into a BBC cook show. While the host demonstrated the intricacies of the Shepherd's Pie, Kajal dozed off.

Nandini and he were sharing a macaroni-cheese at Pinto's and she was telling him about her home in the tea garden.

"Hey, painter boy!"

Nandini was on the phone. Incessant rains had trapped her. She was going to miss her flight to London.

"Hello!"

The phone line was dying. They were both screaming, trying desperately to hang on to the communication.

"Wake up painter boy."

Kajal woke up with a start. As he lifted his head, a thick strand of saliva stretched between the corner of his mouth and the cloth of the sofa; the strand thinned, then thinnered and finally snapped. Kajal wiped his mouth with the back of his hand. His body felt limp and was strangely twisted. It was a miracle that he had managed to find comfort in that position. He looked up.

Q was standing next to him, her face over him. Smiling.

"I just passed out," Kajal pulled himself up.

"Tired?" Q spoke with kindness.

"What time is it?"

She grabbed Kajal's left arm and brought his watch to his face. "Just past nine."

"Shit, I missed dinner." Kajal stood up and picked up his backpack from the floor.

"Join my team. Dinner's horrible anyway," she declared. "Want to grab a bite?"

Kajal didn't want to spend money, neither was he interested in company. "I think I'll just sleep."

"Come on, how can you be so dull? We'll just get a Subway."

Kajal realized it would be impolite to still stand his ground. A Sub wasn't economically taxing, and also didn't present the threat of a sit-down conversation.

"I'll need to clean up and change." Kajal said.

"And so will I. Lobby in fifteen?"

"Okay."

———

Walking back with their sandwiches, Q suggested that they ate at one of the benches by Fitzroy Square outside the hostel.

"So where are you from in India?" Q asked him.

"Assam, northeast." Kajal replied. He had gotten used to qualifying Assam with the northeast suffix. No one ever seemed to know where Assam was. "Isn't that where the tea comes from, or is that Darjeeling?" "The land of bombs." "Aren't you guys famous for the hippopotamus?" These were some of the better informed comments he had encountered.

"Assam!" She screamed, startling Kajal with a novel dimension to public response to his origin. *"Axomot kor pora?* Guwahati?" And then she surprised him more with her Assamese, even though spoken with a slight struggle and a heavy accent. A fat piece of bacon along with a rich accompaniment of chili sauce found release from her sandwich and fell 'plop' on Kajal's thigh.

"Shit, sorry." She rushed to clean up.

"Don't bother, it's okay," Kajal stiffened up.

"But are you from Guwahati? Are you Assamese?" She persisted with the cleaning even as she asked.

"Yes I'm from Guwahati. Been there?"

"I'm half Assamese – my mum. And I've lived in Guwahati these last two years before coming to London. God, I don't believe this."

Unexpectedly stumbling across someone from one's own city, especially if it's something like Guwahati, in a foreign land perhaps sends even a sloth into a jig. "You went to the Law College?" Kajal enquired. The Guwahati Law College was next door to where Kajal had studied History.

"No." And she followed up with a brisk report – Law School and Law firm in Delhi, video editing in Guwahati and then studying in London. *She had nothing to hide.* "And you?" she asked.

Kajal was faced with the job of laying out his life for scrutiny. The tissue holding the footlong sandwich in his hand quickly became soggy with perspiration. "Well, I've been a bit of a rolling stone. The last thing I did was work in a recording studio in Shillong." Kajal obviously didn't realize that he could have easily said something like "I went to Med School – didn't like it – graduated in History – took up a guitaring job – and here I am in London studying Fine Art." And Q might have even responded with a "Wow, that is so effing cool!" Kajal only knew what Nandini would have said – "There's absolutely nothing cool about being a pathological compulsive drifter."

"Work in a studio – do you play an instrument?"

"Guitar."

"I love musicians! Do you know Steve in the hostel?"

Kajal shook his head.

"Tall blonde, bearded, British," Q elaborated with a hint of disappointment in her voice. *How could anyone not know Steve?* "He's in the hostel only on Mondays and Tuesdays – he's from Liverpool. You guys must meet. He's brilliant with the guitar. I'll give you a shout the next time he's here."

The guitar and thoughts of jamming somehow didn't excite Kajal.

"Shall we go in? I'm a bit cold." Q rubbed her hands and placed them on her nose.

Stepping out of the elevator that brought them back to the fourth floor, she said, "We've talked about everything except the most basic."

Kajal looked at her nonplussed.

"I don't even know your name," she explained. "So dumb, isn't it?"

"I'm Kajal."

"Kajal! I'll tell you what, I actually know another guy who shares your name. Till I'd met him, the only Kajal I'd known was the Bollywood actress. And he'd hit the roof every time I told him that. I must let him know that there's at least one other guy to substantiate his claim that there's nothing ladies-only about the name." Q was innocent to any raw nerves getting stroked.

"The Bollywood actress is Kajol, with an 'o'," Kajal defended. But he knew victories with vowels offered little respite in the real world.

"I didn't know that." She replied like it didn't matter.

And then Q introduced herself. As she walked away, Q said, "One of these days, I must see what art you've been up to."

Kajal smiled back.

* * * * *

Kajal met Q at a time when seeds of uncertainty were bursting forth once again. Fine Art granted no easy foothold, and the structure of the course tendered miserly help.

He had an allotted space on the third floor of Elthorne Studios, across the street from the Byam Shaw building. He had access to the library and other resources. Then there were Francis in the sculpture yard and Mel in woodworks to help execute his ideas.

And of course there was Liam, his tutor who spent a full hour with him every fortnight. "I sense some sparks. I get a hang of your ideas but you need to build on them. It's time we started seeing some real work." That's the pattern the tutorials were falling into.

But classroom lectures titled 'Introduction to Modern Sculpture', 'Twentieth Century Installations' and 'The Great Art Movements', and escorted tours of museums and galleries, those were the kind of things Kajal had come expecting. Instead of a mere 'Welcome to Byam Shaw – We have a long history – This is your studio space'.

He searched for similar discomfort in others. But everyone had calmly settled into the job of making art. Kajal had found out even during the welcome bull session that almost everyone else had brought some background in fine art, even university degrees. Absolutely no one had drifted in with merely a taste and superfluous reading of art history.

"Interesting! The growing appeal is most heartening. I'm very happy you made the distance. Enjoy your time on the course." Dr. Helen Luthert, Director of Byam Shaw had commented after Kajal's introduction.

Ed – Edward – occupied the next space in the studio. He was a couple of years older and held a BA from Goldsmiths. Before coming into the PG Dip, he had followed that up with an internship at the South London Gallery and a couple of months of working for Damien Hirst. "Damien's a Goldsmiths alumnus himself, did you know that?" Kajal was vaguely familiar with the 'blockbuster' artist.

Ed was from a small town near Portsmouth, down by the southern coast of England. "It's all industrial down there."

One day, Kajal sneaked upon Ed's work. Until Ed proffered some insight, his art was hard to pick from the general disarray in his studio space. "Destruction. Things fall apart and I'm trying to capture the moment of the disintegration. It's mostly sculpture and photography as you can see, but I don't know, I fear a performance creeping up at some point." A breaking chair. A soap bubble bursting. A bullet tearing into tissue. A glass vase shattering.

When he talked about his work, Ed became a different person.

At all other times, with his dreadlocked long hair, waxing-and-waning beard and awfully soiled black overall, he was a dope-smoking hippie in dire need of a shower. If Ma saw a picture declaring Ed as Kajal's closest friend in London, she wouldn't waste a minute in pulling Kajal out of the course!

"You like Dream Theater mate?"

A small, five or ten watt CD player played music in Ed's space. Kajal loved its sound – like a radio playing in a kitchen.

"They're okay." Kajal disappointed Ed with his opinion. The band had individual brilliance but Kajal found the frequent time signature and melody changes overdone. They were like fine artists who wouldn't paint a simple landscape even if they were burning to just because of an inescapable need to be different.

"Do you guys listen to any music from the west in India?"

"Yes yes. A lot. All these bands are truly international and there's nothing western about them." Kajal explained. Questions of this nature always triggered a defensive streak in him, and it became a religious responsibility to educate the world. "Where I come from, even our folk music is so much like western country music." But before the year ran out, Kajal would realize that stereotype was among the most unbreakable things man ever created.

The space adjacent to Kajal's on the other side was Sophie's. She worked in sculpture – human forms, and that had excited Kajal when he first learnt about it. As she researched volumes of Anatomy textbooks and atlases, her passion was above anything that Kajal had come across in med school, even among the most dedicated. Her work dealt in the grotesque and her sculptures aimed to shock. There was a female head and torso with rows of mammaries arranged linearly like a mouse's. That sculpture was complete, in wiremesh, thermocol and wax and painted in garish nude tones. Her work-in-progress was a massive male face endowed with members and ball-bags all over.

"Hi. These textures are immaculate. They could almost be breathing." Kajal had drifted across to her space. She looked up to smile at Kajal and quickly returned to her work.

"I'm Kajal. Your neighbour."

"Hi." Sophie made a distracted sound.

"I'm from India."

She exploded on that cue. "Big deal dude! More than half this country seems to be from India. And I swear all of you are equally nosy. Do you mind staying away from my face while I'm trying to work?"

Kajal struggled to refrain from classifying her unexpected outburst as racist. What he felt about the Bangladeshis back home wasn't racist. Because racist after all, is a bad word. But Sophie's comments did make him feel like a Bangladeshi in Assam. Kajal stayed away from her.

But some weeks later, he found himself face to face with her in the library. She smiled and surprised him by asking most pleasantly, "How's it going?" If Sophie was indeed racist, it wasn't a permanent manner of thought.

Kajal did notice that after work, Sophie and Ed often shared a drink at The Mother, the large pub five minutes down Holloway Road, which was like the in-house drinking hole for all Byam Shaw students and most staff.

It was at The Mother that the seniors had hosted an ice-breaking event for the new entrants. The welcome cocktail was a prodigious blend of fruit and spice and from there on, the mood was wanton, way beyond the proverbial wayfaring of arty folk.

Ice broke rapidly, but to achieve any lasting effect wasn't anybody's purpose. Kajal acquired the label 'Posh Indian' for drinking whisky – everyone else drank beer.

By next morning though, he was back to being one whose name people had trouble saying right on account of it being exotic Sanskrit. "What does it mean?" they asked him after reciting Kay-jul. "Born in the thirteenth month," Kajal replied; finally he could lie and not tell them that it actually meant 'eyeliner'.

'Languages' was one of several party games that evening. On his pink bit of paper, Kajal listed out English, Hindi, Assamese and Bengali as the languages he was adept at. And then the results were declared, "Aaron aces the 'Languages' round with three – English, Spanish and Portugese." Kajal realized that was one less than his four. But perhaps his languages did not qualify for not coming from different countries.

"Oh Sophie's a complete darling," Ed declared.

Kajal narrated his own experience with Sophie.

"Come on mate, you must have really stirred the shit in her. You have to stop being juvenile. Everyone here can whip themselves into quite a trance with work." After a pause, Ed added, "And if you must know, she's actually going through quite a patch right now. Her partner Nicola's just been diagnosed with HIV."

"You mean Nicola with the long hair?" Same-sex relationships were one of those things that belonged to others and you read about in magazines. Kajal had never thought he'd actually come to know anyone involved in one.

"Right. They are together. I know them from Goldsmiths. It's real sad."

* * * * *

Even while struggling to make any work to write home about, Kajal's thoughts laid tiny questions in nooks and corners of his mind. The longevity of an artwork. Was there anything permanent about what he may paint or create? If it was transient, how long would it last? What domain of time and space would his work occupy? And would that domain be entirely his?

And what about nature itself? For God, the Creator is really nature and nature itself is energy. Undoubtedly, it is nature that makes the monumental creations. Everything that man makes is but an attempt. Some are good, some better, but all merely attempts to create a Platonic world of ideas in the imperfect world of sensations.

Could he get nature to make his artwork?

And the questions gave his work a vague shape – an intangible form that wasn't immediately obvious, even to him.

Kajal bought a mounted canvas and some white acrylic emulsion from Thomas Brothers. Putting the canvas on the floor, he placed it standing against one of the walls in his studio. With his hands he picked up dollops of white paint and slapped them on the canvas, close to the top edge. And then he let nature take over – time and gravity dripped the paint down, etching their marks on his canvas. Some stopped early. Some carried on. Still others met other drip lines, coalesced and dripped on. Or stopped.

He tried the same with blue paint. Then with both blue and white. Dripping lines of blue, white and blue-white. Paint that gravity pulled down till it dried. And left the trace of nature's rendezvous with time on a canvas.

"Like I said, I get the hang but there's incompleteness. Do you see what I mean? It's not quite a home run yet," Liam opined at the next tutorial. "But I suspect I'm beginning to like this!"

* * * * *

"Hey Kajal. How's it going?" Walking back from the bus stop, Kajal bumped into Q as she stepped out of the Tesco store near the YMCA.

"Not too bad." Kajal replied half-heartedly. They walked on towards the hostel.

"You have something against asking others how they've been?"

"No no, not at all." Kajal responded, a little surprised.

"So."

"So?"

"Ask me dumbo."

"Ya okay." Kajal felt perfectly stupid slipping into Q's script and delivering his line, "How have you been?" while she looked at his face waiting.

"Listen then. It's just been one of the lousiest days of my whole God damned life. I had an assignment to hand in which kept me up the whole fucking night. You'd think that was the end of the hard work. But this morning when I got to the school library to get the stuff printed – my dumb password won't work. So I rushed to Kinko's and shelled out nine Pounds for the print. Can you bloody imagine I paid seven fucking hundred Rupees to print some ten pages of nonsense? And then this stupid woman at Admin made me lick her massive ass just because I brought in the assignment half an hour late."

"Hmmm...that's a lot of anger." Kajal couldn't help feeling a bit amused. That she was also going through some inclemency on her course, for the moment, was sufficient ground for bonding.

"Wait." Q screamed. "Then, I had this lecture in the afternoon. And I could have easily not gone for it. I actually shouldn't have. But I took myself over and was handed a mock case to present. And the whole time, this dimwit Hispanic tutor who really needs English diction classes has a problem with every single one of my arguments, till she really thulped me with that final sum up."

"Thulped?"

"Ya thulped."

Kajal looked quizilly at her.

"Thulped is somewhere between being tickled to death and getting shot through a nostril," Q explained. "In Mylese."

"Mylese?"

"Mylese. My language!" Q explained again, and added, "I must say you are horribly unimaginative for an artist."

Silence marked their arrival at the hostel and Kajal unthinkingly followed her to a sofa in the lobby, and that's when he noticed Alex, the receptionist, eyeing Q.

Kajal scrutinised Q coyly as she replied to a text on her phone. Her hair was unkempt and oily, screaming for a wash. Her face looked worn out. The ends of her jeans were soiled. And that was something Kajal despised – grubby hems and pockets of jeans. The winter-wear only saddened matters – her oversized black pullover had a hole just below the neck.

Kajal looked back at Alex – the blacks of his eyeballs were still hanging around the corners, picking the direction of Q. *Very strange, where was there anything to stare at about Q?*

But that hole in her sweater bothered him more; perhaps she wasn't aware and needed to be told before she embarrassed herself elsewhere.

"Your sweater..," Kajal didn't know how to say it.

"Nice no?" Q ran a hand down the front of it, as Kajal's enquiry efficiently disentangled her from her foul mood. "Guess how much?" She didn't wait for Kajal to guess. "Five Quid. That's all I paid for it. Guess where?" She again did not wait for an answer. "There's this Oxfam Charity Store just down on Charlotte Street. You should check it out, you might find something for yourself." Her joy was real. "It's got this tiny hole you won't even notice," and she pointed at it with a finger. "But then why else would they be selling this quality at such price."

The question of the hole stood resolved.

"Care for coffee?" Q asked.

"I'm not exactly a fan of the coffee machine stuff."

"Neither am I. I'm offering you the divinest cappuccino on earth." Q pulled out a box of Nescafe sachets from her Tesco shopping bag.

"I guess I'll give that a miss. A bit tired, just want to lie down for a while."

More than wanting to lie down, Kajal wanted a coffee. But his response had nothing to do with Q; it was just his generally swarthy attitude towards people.

"Why don't you just say that you are scared to come to the Ladies' Wing?"

Kajal kept quiet.

"Has anyone heard of chivalry?" Q went on. "I've just told you about the awful day I've had and all you can tell me is that you are tired yourself and want to lie down."

Kajal, nonplussed, looked back at her apologetically.

"Okay don't worry, I'm not going to kill you for that."

Kajal felt a strange relief; the fleeting fear of terminal action had seemed genuine.

"What's your day like tomorrow?" Q stood up and gathered her bags.

"Day's off."

"Brilliant. I'm without a schedule myself. Let's plan something." Q's eyes sparkled suddenly, "Take me for an arty loaf."

"Arty loaf?"

"God! Are you like deliberately doing this to impress me? You'd be absolutely foolish to think that girls find dumb guys cute!"

Why were they even talking to each other? For an instant, that's what Kajal found himself pondering. In short bursts, Q seemed to find him lethally prosaic.

If he had asked me, I'd have let him know that it was just Q being herself. Now, not everything that Q ever said was awfully smart, but it was more the gruff sharpness that usually made her next, slightly less haughty comment seem like a demonstration of ideal polite talk. She enjoyed doing this to people, that's what I thought. Or was it a shield she wore to protect herself?

"Arty as in art and loaf as in loaf-about." Q explained fractiously; half smiling with the sadistic pleasure she extracted from Kajal like he was some ludicrous comic act. "They say London has an art gallery in every street corner. We'll go somewhere you haven't been, so you don't find it so much a waste of time."

They quickly decided on the Tate Modern. There wasn't too much of a debate – it was the first name Kajal suggested and Q accepted saying, "You are the boss," once again with a snicker. That made him uncomfortable. He couldn't tell her that he himself was yet to experience any of London's art avenues, and that suddenly seemed like a terrible shame.

"Isn't Tate Modern that electricity power house thing?" Q asked as they were parting.

"No, it's an art gallery – I believe the largest in London." Kajal clarified innocently.

"There you go again. I know it's an art gallery. I was talking about its history."

Kajal looked perplexed. If the Tate Modern did have any history, he should have been better versed with it than a Law student.

"Nine? Let's get breakfast together and leave right after. That'll give us loads of sun." Q said.

"That's a plan." Kajal tried hard to look and sound excited.

* * * * *

Yes, the premises of the Tate Modern had indeed been the Bankside Power Station at one time. In fact, it was only in 1981 that the station closed and the building was converted into Britain's national museum of international modern art.

That and some more enlightenment was the result of an exhaustive hour that Kajal spent on the internet after dinner that evening. At the YMCA Library. He had a subscription for the recently installed wifi service in the hostel, but its efficiency in his room, as in a couple of others, had remained a sham. And Kajal had let that become the singular deterrent to getting some much needed learning. He had been obscenely inert in taking up the matter with the hostel management and wholly uninitiated to regularly bring himself down to the Library, where broadband cables were available. He hadn't even visited the Byam Shaw intranet for nearly a week.

Q didn't seem like a pushover. She was going to challenge him intellectually and not spare a hit below the belt. She threatened to be well informed and wouldn't tolerate Kajal being a sulking piece of furniture beside her. Kajal was beginning to be scared of her.

He brushed aside a brief thought of Nandini that stirred in his head.

The first few minutes of search returned several links and Kajal rapidly immersed in a sea of windows. The wealth of information bewildered him, and also showed him how hopelessly out of tune he had managed to make himself. He was studying art out of his own accord, and in London, the city that had so much to offer in the field. And yet he had tested no water in all that time.

When he left the library that night, he was not only armed for a knowledgeable visit to the Tate, he had also saved material for an essay he needed to hand in the week after.

* * * * *

Kajal finally walked up to the counter and got his breakfast tray. *Let's get breakfast together and leave right after* – that's what Q had said. But nearly half an hour over the decided time, she was nowhere in the cafeteria.

Two girls joined Kajal at the table, continuing their conversation, "Some woman that one is! It's the same story every night. Guitar and singing and noise. Something's horribly screwed in her head. I'm going to take it up to Mr. Abraham if it doesn't stop." The other shook her head in assertion. "Isn't that white guy a whole lot older than her? I'm sure he's married."

A slight awkwardness ruffled Kajal. They were talking about Q.

Kajal finished the fried egg and excused himself. He had no choice but to wait for Q. Stepping out of the cafeteria, Kajal picked up a travel brochure and sat on a sofa in the lobby. Before the year was through, he wanted to make a trip to Paris.

And just then Q appeared.

"Hey dude, ready? Breakfast?"

"I finished."

"Great. I thought we're on a date."

Kajal kept quiet, and blankly stared at her. He had managed to badger her yet again. But between her arriving late and his going ahead with breakfast, which was the greater offence? Of course it didn't matter.

"It's okay. You don't have to be cute now. Let me get a bite." And she walked into the cafeteria. Kajal realized she still looked the exact same way that he had left her the evening before. Same clothes, same hair – the precise tramp.

Kajal wasn't sure if he was supposed to follow her into the cafeteria. He remained on his sofa. He put the brochure back in its place and proceeded to revisit the Tate-information in his mind.

The elevator in the lobby opened and Ashwin, who had a room on Kajal's floor, came out with his parents. They had arrived the previous evening from India. His mother wore a lovely indigo and gold silk sari and walked with a slight waddle on brand new white Campus sneakers. His father tentatively pulled out a packet of Four Square. "Baba ... ... indoors ... ... five minutes," Ashwin shot back in Marathi. Baba gingerly put the packet of cigarettes back in his pocket. Ashwin went up to the Reception guy and Kajal heard him say Madame Tussauds. "Just jump on the 18 and get off at Baker Street," the receptionist explained. "They're here for just a week," Ashwin thanked him.

Ashwin's mother caught Kajal staring at them and responded with a smile and a slight bow. Feeling awkward, Kajal smiled back but really wanted to tell her – No I'm not British, please don't bow; I am your regular Indian and unlike your son, who I'm sure is doing brilliantly well, am living through a nightmare of a course!

Ashwin led them briskly out of the hostel – very happy in private to have given his folks the vacation but perhaps embarrassed in public with them innocently threatening to smoke indoors and their clumsy walks.

Kajal thought about Ma and Baba. He'd called home the previous weekend. "Hello…oh Kajal," Baba had promptly handed the phone to Ma. But Kajal knew Baba was sitting right beside Ma while she talked. "It's Bublu's wedding on the 24th; they were asking about you. We're sad you'll miss it." And she finished with, "Eat well, whatever you get, don't be choosy. Stay warm. How's the winter?" No enquiries about the course. It didn't matter anymore.

"Stop ogling at them!" Q arrived on the scene and her words, forced through clenched teeth, jolted Kajal. "Give me ten minutes for a quick shower." As she breezed past him, she shouted, "Meanwhile, do you want to sort out how best to get to Tate?"

A good half hour elapsed before Q reappeared. And when she did, Kajal missed a beat like he hadn't since his eyes had become stuck on a certain Nandini years ago.

Q's charcoal grey, pencil skirt ended just at the knee. She wore a black shirt and a toffee-brown, short formal jacket on top. On her feet were a pair of excellently cut dark tan suede boots that went up to below the knees, leaving just that slight hint of skin between them and the skirt hemline. As she walked towards him with a smile, her long hair bounced with every step. As she came closer, Kajal stood up in super slow-mo with that proverbial dropped jaw!

Q looked ravishing when she worked towards it.

"Don't you think the backpack's killing everything?" Q held on to a mischievous smile, relishing the effect she was having on

Kajal, as she brought attention to the backpack flung across one of her shoulders.

"Ya, I think so," Kajal stuttered, still behaving like he'd taken a hit between the eyes.

"Then take it from me no, dumbo."

"Yes yes, of course." And the backpack changed hands.

"How are we going?" Q asked as they stepped outdoors. In the gratifying early November morning sun, her face shone like a baby's bum. The heart notes of her perfume caught Kajal.

"Be Delicious." Q told a still-coping Kajal. She was a fortune teller. Kajal's mind was a crystal ball. Kajal looked back questioningly, "My perfume," Q explained. "Okay, give me the plan. How are we going?"

Kajal recovered to answer. "There's nothing direct to Tate. Thirty minutes on the tube and forty five on the bus, both with one change each. Shall we just cab it?"

Q stopped walking and looked at him scornfully. "How spoilt are you? You know what's in the backpack? Me-made sandwiches, orange juice and a thermos of coffee. Just so we don't waste twenty fucking Pounds on lunch. And you want to take a cab!"

Kajal kept quite. Q obviously cared for the money. The Subway sandwich, the rage at having to spend for printing her assignment at Kinko's, the Charity Shop sweater. Maybe she was limited by a scholarship just like him.

He didn't know what kind of a background she came from. But what Q had just said made him very happy. Also that she'd had the thought to pack lunch even while keeping him waiting.

"We'll take the bus." Q declared. "It's a beautiful day. There's so much of London we can see from a bus."

* * * * *

"I can't believe this was your first time," Q exclaimed one more time as they exited the Tate.

They sat by the Thames, finishing the sandwiches. Close to three in the afternoon, the blooming melancholy of the sky was in stark contrast to the sun earlier in the day.

It was cold, even with a disagreeable breeze on that bench by the river. But there is something bizarrely affable about the south bank of the Thames. Like a powerful enticement, the Thames lures the entire city – joggers and lovers, students and city-workers, whites and black-brown-yellows – to its south bank. If one traverses its length, it is a motley tableau of London's childhood, adolescence and youth, all the way up to its present.

The vicinity of the Tate Modern holds unique charm. The futuristic, suspended steel of the Millenium Bridge blends seamlessly, and somewhat illogically, with the backdrop of St. Paul's Cathedral across the Thames. A slight walk away is the bucolic charisma of Burrough Market. Along the riverfront, rows of small eateries and street cafes nest next to upmarket chains in cutting-edge architectural showpieces. The HMS Belfast and the legendary Shakespeare's Globe, where one still carried cushions for a floor seat, lend a strong touch of history.

When I'd first seen the Thames, it was in an evening low tide. It was astoundingly bereft of volume, too narrow and dismally mucky – its somniferous saunter was singularly underwhelming. But by the time I left London, it had truly grown into the majestic civilization-bearing umbilicus that it is. For the rest of my life, a bit of it remained somewhere in my eyes.

Q and Kajal discarded the juice for becoming uncomfortably cold, but the coffee was pleasant.

They were both quiet. In between staring out riverward, Q engaged in what appeared a matter of constitution with her – texting on her phone. There always was someone at the other end willing to reply promptly and then continue swapping the rest of the conversation. *Was it always the same person? Or did she have a list to recruit from? Did she have even a single woman friend or were there only men?* It wasn't yet my time to be bothered by these questions.

Beside her, Kajal munched, but was really still floundering with the exultation of Tate.

At the Tate that day – in the middle of God-only-knows how many thousand daily visitors from all over the world – Kajal felt a victory surge and completely drown him in those four hours. As they coursed through floor after floor, the entire cannon of art was laid out for him. The works of all the great names – from the pole-bearers of the great art movements to the contemporaries and the lesser known who bestowed individual nuances – acquired an inspiring human physicality.

On the second floor, Q and Kajal sat through a documentary that packaged the history of modern art into an engaging half hour. Kajal turned to Q at its end. "I can't believe this is your first time here!" Q said.

The exhibit in the famous Turbine Hall was Test Site, an installation by Carsten Holler consisting of a series of five metal slides completely covered with fibreglass, two starting on the second floor and one on each floor up to the fifth. Visitors could slide down the slides, and interact with the installation.

"Isn't it amazing how the canvas of the artist has broadened?" Q said, looking up towards the summit of the installation while a bunch of kids slid down noisily.

"Really is," affirmed Kajal. "You remember the Urinal?"

"How can I not? Fountain is like the strongest image I'll leave this place with. Duchamp, right? I love the guts of that man. That he didn't even bother signing his own name is so cool."

"But there's more to Duchamp's 'readymades' then mere rebellion. Duchamp was already a part of Dadaism and that offered enough opportunity to be insurgent. With Fountain he wanted to shift the focus of art from physical craft to intellectual interpretation. It's unbelievable what an epic moment this one piece of work represents. It was the beginning of conceptual art. And the signature – R Mutt, 1917 – has so many sides to it, from the German for poverty *armut* to the comic strip characters Mutt and Jeff. It is the kind of stuff that make solid PhDs." Kajal had done his reading. The discussion itself was déjà vu from the sessions with Rahul. His own mind however was still tottering from the effect of actually being face-to-face with it.

"Wow Professor!" exclaimed Q. "But let me just enjoy its machismo. I'm sure Duchamp would have appreciated this interpretation." Then after a bit of a thought, she added, "I don't know, but it's a bit disturbing as well. The question is – who decides what is art and what is not? I mean, at some level, isn't it insulting that I come down here and Duchamp thinks that an upside down urinal is all my sensibilities and intellect deserve?"

"Well, Duchamp did answer that question. It's the artist's choice. He is documented to have said that the artist chooses what is art," replied Kajal. He himself wasn't all that convinced with that answer. At least, not till then.

"But then if all it takes is just another everyday object, how about me signing a tube light Osama and placing it at say, forty eight degrees inside a wooden box. The world can spend the rest of its spinning finding metaphysical explanations for the forty eight degrees. And if I sign it with my real name, I'm sure there'll be a school of thought believing that this was my way of getting back at Duchamp! But does that qualify as artwork? And does that, then, make me an artist?" The lawyer in Q suddenly seemed excited.

Kajal did not know the answers, not well enough to explain them to Q. But he did know that it was a negative for both. The tube light would not qualify as artwork nor would Q become an artist. Ma had excellent remedies for the headaches Kajal suffered as a child, but that didn't make Ma a doctor. Nor did her remedies qualify as standard treatment protocols. But there again, medical science and art were entirely different. Kajal didn't have the answers.

"Maybe it's not entirely black and white. Because while what you just said does make the artist seem annoyingly arrogant, it was Duchamp himself who was at the helm of anti-art. He strived to bring art down from an unreal pedestal, to dismiss the notion that art must appeal aesthetically. For him, the audience was integral to art, with no wall between the audience and the performer," Kajal replied, after a good while. "I don't know."

"It's okay, I'm not going to scream at you. You don't have to be cute!" Q replied with another one of her mischievous smiles. She had at least ten subtly different smiles all of which were mischievous.

They walked in silence up the slight incline of the passage from the Turbine Hall which took them out of the Tate. And on that bench by the Thames they finished Q's sandwiches.

"Shall we go, painter boy?" Q asked, her eyes attentively following her right hand flicking bread crumbs from her jacket. Kajal nodded and picked up Q's backpack.

"I really loved it. Let's make it our weekly date. Every Sunday? You plan where we go. *Moi pise pise aahim!*" Q's smile made up for her effort-laden Assamese.

Kajal smiled. And then he suddenly remembered, "Not next weekend. I have a show to prepare for."

"A show! Wow! When were you going to tell me about it?"

"No no, it's not like a *show* show. It's just in school. We have a gallery space called the Concourse where students put up stuff from time to time. Concourse is actually just a little passageway and a lobby. Thursday the week after is the PG Dip show, that's my class."

"Can I come?"

"You want to?"

"Of course I want to. Are visitors allowed?"

"Yes. In the evening. But there's really nothing great about it."

"I want to come – You have a problem with that? Don't worry, I won't embarrass you – I'll dress yummily!" Q smiled another variant of her mischievous smile.

"But my participation is neither guaranteed nor compulsory. It doesn't even count for my grades. I may actually drop out."

"You try that and see what I do to you," said Q sternly. "I'm coming and you better have something to show me, painter boy. And I'll treat you to a beer and dinner after."

A Subway sandwich and a supermarket beer on a park bench!

* * * * *

12

I had dreaded that it could happen. But somehow I trusted it won't. Not with the surgeries.

The shaking appeared briefly during the fifth surgery. I swear I wasn't thinking things or seeing images. I was completely focused. The operating room music was good old Jagjit Singh. Yes, the conversation with Tridip had died for a little while, but that isn't unusual. I survived that bout, but was left perspiring and gooseflesh engulfed me like blitzkrieg.

But two surgeries later, my left hand shook again. And this time it was like a fierce polar wind rattling a lonesome scarecrow. I had to stop. I prayed for it to pass. Tridip is too intelligent a man to not notice. Thankfully he didn't ask me about it. I will however assume that he made no note of my left leg joining the shaking as well.

I did complete the remaining surgeries uneventfully. Tridip – and I imagine he did it deliberately – kept me engaged in loose talk and that really helped.

The shakes were there alright. The only physical attribute of the little twist in my head. Always the left side – mostly the hand, seldom the leg. But they had only ever taken me when a gust of perilous thoughts had seduced my spent mind at the end of a day. Never ever during

213

the day. Never at work. Jayesh has explained that I am somatising. The mood stabilizers and tranquilisers that he's put me on, along with his inspiring counseling sessions have been helpful.

But everything changes after today.

I know Tridip won't talk. But how long before I'm hit when I'm with other assistants? How long before I have to stop and SOS a colleague to take over the rest of my surgeries?

Most of all, am I being fair to the innocent souls who place themselves in my hands with dreams of seeing the world the next day?

I hate this dilemma.

Who do I take this to? Jayesh? He suddenly seems fragile and incapable. My Director? His understanding support is assured. But I'm scared. For I know him far too well.

My surgeries mean everything to me. I can't lose them at any cost. I'm so scared. And tonight, the fright is choking me from every side.

Is this really happening to me? There's got to be something I can do about it.

* * * * *

13

The Mahatma Gandhi Hall is in the basement of the YMCA Hostel. It has a two-floors high ceiling, with a horse-shoe shaped balcony going like a collaret at level one, on three sides except over the stage. A flight of steps descends down one of its stage-ends. The stage is nearly theatre sized, with a convenient backstage area with its own entrance. At full capacity, MG Hall can seat up to hundred and fifty. It is entirely wooden floored and has pleasant acoustics.

It is a busy venue. It gets booked for get-togethers and cultural occurrences of different associations from all over London; dinners, meetings, evangelistic assemblies – everything takes place through the week.

During my time, there were a couple of fixed reservations. And to the attraction of one of them, I gave-in dedicatedly. Every Sunday evening a chamber orchestra used it for practice. Apart from the space, MG Hall offered a permanently positioned grand piano and a conductor's high chair.

Now, I'm no more learned in western classical music than knowing a major scale from a minor and a famous Vivaldi from a famous Mozart. But as far as I was concerned, those guys sounded great. Every Sunday evening, I took position on a balcony chair to savour the exercise. I wasn't sure if I was welcome, or even whether my presence was a hindrance. But encouraged by never being rebuffed, I continued.

It was sometime in November. I returned later than usual one evening. I had finished my first project and Walter had taken the available 'team' for a celebratory glass of wine after work.

I stopped at the reception to check for posts in my pigeon hole. That's when I heard the piano from MG Hall. It was uncharacteristic but you could tell a Chopin – Fantaisie-Imprompto overpowered the quiet winter evening. I had never heard it played before at the hostel. It suddenly occurred to me that it was Tuesday – it couldn't be the orchestra.

"Must be one of the residents. I have only just come into my shift." The Reception guy answered my query.

I found myself on the steps leading down to the hall and soon I was at my spot on the balcony.

She sat at the piano, her back to me. All I could comprehend was the long hair. Only pale fragments of the stage lights reached her. The rest of the hall was dark and empty, and with the chairs stacked along the perimeter, looked like the crater on top of a burning candle. The piano notes were clear and resonated freely in the volume of the space.

I settled down quietly. The music did not stop. My presence was either disregarded or not sensed.

Another Chopin followed. One of the famous Nocturnes.

When she finished, she brought the cover down on the keys with a clap. And then a resonant click as she locked it.

I stood up and clapped four times. "Sorry I sneaked in. You are really good."

She looked up at me across the distance. Her face was backlit and I deciphered a pleasing shape.

I picked up my bag and turned to leave.

"Doctor!"

There was no mistaking that voice even in a scream, and it turned the air around me into lead.

I turned back to see her get up from the piano and hurry towards me. The paucity of light remained, but there was no doubt anymore. It was Q. Her footfalls echoed emphatically as she made her way up the steps to where I stood rooted.

"I didn't know you were this good with the piano," I told her as she reached me.

"Don't you think that's an awfully dull thing to say right now? What the hell are you doing in London?" And then her face straightened with mischief, "I never thought you'd carry stalking me this far!"

I realized my reaction had been inappropriate. But why? I should have been ecstatic, and nothing else. It was quaint that Q should appear a frightful proposition with bad prognosis written all over.

I started explaining the intent that had brought me to London. She interjected halfway, "God, you're so lousy with telling stories."

I stopped.

She returned the piano keys at the Reception. While she put in '9-something PM' under the 'returned at' column in the register and put her signature, – everything at the YMCA was documented – the Reception guy eyed her, and then me, curiously. Q seemed oblivious to it.

"What are you doing now?" She asked me.

"Nothing really."

"Good. Come with me then." Q ordered.

"Where? My bag?"

"Stop being a sissy, just carry it along. You're not going to die!" She had always been impelling.

I followed her out of the hostel. And I could tell behind our backs, the Reception guy's eyes followed us.

Out on the street, Q stopped to ask, "Doctor, do you have some cash on you? I'm broke."

"Kind of. But not a lot." I didn't know what was on her mind.

We walked into the nearby 24-hour shop. From the 'Ready Meals' shelf, she picked up two large sausage rolls and walked to the till, where she asked for a small bottle of Jack Daniel's. "That's the brand, isn't it?" She smiled at me as we waited to be handed the bottle. *Q remembered.* "They don't take cards," she said as I collected the change, in way of explaining why she couldn't pay.

We were out on Tottenham Court Road. "Fuck, I hate this place," Q said as a sharp chilly breeze hit us.

"Where are we going?" I was chafed. To be honest, I'm not impulsive in the least, and am timidly uncomfortable when caught in an unprepared situation. But I forced an amused laugh as I asked her then.

"Fuck, I can't believe you're here. I've been so restless the whole day, and just look who comes over to calm me. There's so much I have to tell you." Q spoke excitedly to the air in front of her as we walked urgently towards Oxford Street. She ignored my question about our destination. I kept quiet, waiting for her to launch into the 'so much' that she had to tell me. She didn't. And after ten minutes of walking in silence, we were at Charring Cross.

"You've been to Covent Garden, haven't you?"

"Actually no. I've heard much but somehow have never been there." I replied.

"Oh you'll love it! Street musicians, food, knick-knack shops. And the people. The whole mood is just so cultural. There's even free open air opera on Thursdays."

"Is that where we are going?"

"I thought I told you."

We walked for another ten minutes.

An elderly gentleman played the saxophone on the cobblestone street leading to the piazza at Covent Garden. As we walked past him and turned a corner, his sound died abruptly to be taken over by the reggae of three dreadlocked black guys. I was taken by the ease of the transition, without overlap or interference. They played, okay, Bob Marley, but I swear to you the drummer had worked up a beat that was to die for, and I dare say, better than the original. They were surrounded by a youthful congregation.

We walked on and settled on a bench in the piazza, and once again the acoustics of the whole place left me bewildered – you couldn't hear the reggae anymore from where we sat.

Performing in front of us were two young ladies, singing folk accompanied by the guitars they played. There wasn't a stage or anything like that. Les Sorority, a flex behind them proclaimed. The crowd was much thinner here, just a couple and another middle aged man who seemed to know the ladies. I wasn't sure why we hadn't picked the livelier reggae.

"Are you carrying cigarettes doctor?"

We smoked in silence, only clapping our hands when a number ended.

"How's your Masters coming along?" I asked Q. The silence was making me uneasy.

"Not great, not too bad either." Q replied with disinterest, and turned to the shopping bag. "Let's eat," and she handed me a sausage roll.

Les Sorority finished their set as Q took a swig from the bottle of JD and passed it to me. We were left alone, watching the band pack up.

"How's your father?" There I thought was a subject that could get us talking.

"Oh, he's okay. Now that you are here, we can go down and see him on a weekend." *Did she offer that to everyone?*

"Yes of course."

"Now's the best part." It took me a while to realize that she had commandeered the conversation onto another theme. "It's Phil now. He's awesome. You'll love him."

"Phil?"

"Ya Phil. His singing is just out of the world."

Okay, so Phil was the next performer. Q obviously was a regular.

"Have you met my friend Steve at the Y?" Q turned to me suddenly and her eyes lit up.

"No I haven't. Why?"

"Steve is an amazing musician himself. Phil is his friend. That's how I know him." Q explained, a note of disappointment in her voice. *How could anyone not know Steve?*

"Is Steve Indian?" I asked. Not that I cared. But suddenly that evening at SixtyNine came back to me. Vishesh, Rohan, Steve, Phil. *There always was so much she had to tell me.*

"No!" Q sounded like I had insulted her by suggesting that Steve could be Indian. "He is British. He's in the hostel only on Mondays and Tuesdays. He lives in Liverpool and runs an NGO that works with education in Africa."

All that was fine, but it was Tuesday that day. Was he caught up elsewhere? *Why had she been restless the whole day?* I quickly rebuked myself for reading more than there was in it.

"I remember you telling me your Dad wasn't keeping well. How's he doing now?" I asked more deliberately. I liked her to tell me once more that we could go and see him. Perhaps I was being invasive. Perhaps she didn't want to talk about his illness. Or even him – her family was after all estranged and I didn't know what the current status of communication was.

"He's okay really." Q was disinterested, and forceful. *End of discussion.*

And just then a tall man appeared behind the performing end of the piazza, pushing a wheel barrow loaded with gear. As he moved into more light, a fine-looking man with sandy hair took form. In his forties, I guessed. I figured he was Phil. Very strangely, I found myself urgently hating the thought of his impressive frame getting an additional touch with him holding a guitar. Q's part in it was everything – I swear to you that I had never been given to such thoughts before that occasion. In fact, I surprised myself with that sudden emotion.

Looking back now, that instance perhaps marked the beginning of a new me shrouded in insecurities and jealousies, and a lot more. And like in the case of the absolutely inconsequential Phil, as the trait secured itself further, it started defeating reason.

"Hey Phil!" Q rang out loud.

Phil looked up from laying out his amplifier and effect pedals. "Hiya," he responded. "Where's the man?" *Asking about Steve?*

"Well, *he* is the man this evening," Q answered wrapping her hands around my right arm. I felt small. What did she mean by 'the man this evening'? "He's a friend from India and, he's a doctor." Q added with a hint of childish pride. I was dignified again.

"Hey doctor."

"Hello Phil." He was a good man. Very often you can tell that within the first couple of minutes of seeing someone.

A sizeable audience gathered by the time Phil was onto his third offering or so. He really was very good. A wonderful singing voice and amazing guitar picking skills. But Q's lavish praise made me uncomfortable. "Didn't I tell you he can bring the dead alive." *Oh, come on Q, you don't have to sell him.* And after another song, "You have no idea what it means to perform in Covent Garden. You can't just bring your kit up and start singing here. You have to apply with the council and then it takes years to get an audition. Only when you make it past all that, you are allotted a spot." *Okay Q, that makes Phil the first musician ever to perform inside an aquarium.*

In a while, it was time for him to wind up and people started leaving, but Q requested an encore, "Not without Romeo and Juliet, Phil." "Steve does that one better than me," Phil shouted back. But he did sing the song. And once again it was commendable.

We walked up to him as he was packing his stuff, and shook hands. He asked me things like how long I was going to be in London and all that. Closer quarters confirmed my earlier feeling that Phil was a nice human being. It's always in the eyes. But my mind was already committed – *So Q thinks he is Mark Knopfler.*

Q offered him the bottle of whisky. *It was my bottle!* "JD eh," Phil commented and took a swig. "It's the doctor's brand," Q said with a smile and again held my arm. Trying to belong to the bonhomie, I offered Phil a cigarette. Before he could say anything, Q intervened, "He doesn't smoke. Singing voice that he needs to take care of," she said with a chuckle. *Like my lungs were some maintenance-free, Made-in-China contraption.*

Phil rolled his eyes up slightly and I even saw a hint of annoyance which made me happy – I wanted him to abhor Q – "Nothing like that. Just that the wife never took kindly to it and over the years I've learnt to live without," he explained to me. I of course didn't care the least about his smoking but his being married came as a relief. I looked at Q to make sure she'd registered that bit of information. I couldn't tell from her eyes if it mattered.

Q and I walked alongside as Phil navigated the wheel barrow full of his equipment back to his car. Once there, we gave him a hand at loading the stuff. And then goodbyes with a quick round from the bottle. But not before Phil enquired, "What's up with Stevie?"

"I texted him. He's in London but stuck down with work," Q answered somberly.

It was past twelve when we were back on Tottenham Court Road. "Hungry?" Q had spoken in a long time. Q always came across as preoccupied whenever with me. Like a ship that would rather sail a different sea. And then when she spoke, it was as if alien words had taken form out of the air.

We bought hotdogs at a roadside cart.

"Hey, there's something else I have to tell you," Q said excitedly. "There's this other guy from Guwahati in the hostel. Kajal. I'm sure you didn't know that."

I didn't know that. Neither was I too happy to know. Steve, Phil, Kajal. To add to Vishesh and Rohan. And a certain Rishabh that Prashant had mentioned.

Q tended to soak up the mind to leave it bloodless and dehydrated. I needed to sleep urgently.

* * * * *

14

Q called Kajal once more when she reached Byam Shaw. His cell was switched off. She was beginning to get perplexed. A student gave her directions to the Concourse Gallery.

Leaving the hostel earlier, she was excited. She had devoted attention to her dressing, like she'd promised Kajal. And that was when she had called him the first time. No reply. Choosing not to waste time, she had left anyway. She made one more fruitless call to him from the bus.

Q realized that Kajal had been right. It wasn't at all like an art exhibition. The Concourse Gallery was indeed a poorly lit cramped corridor and a tiny foyer. Paintings, sculptures and videos were on display. Students and visitors hung around in noisy or thoughtful groups. Everyone seemed to have gone the extra mile to turn up unkempt and shabby. There were some bottles of Red Stripe and red and white wine on a table in one corner. The glasses were disposable plastic.

Searching through the faces, it became apparent that Kajal wasn't there. The thought that Kajal had stood her up perturbed Q. She didn't know what to do. She seemed to be the only one who didn't know anyone else and no one bothered about her. Q proceeded to inspect some of the exhibits but failed to find focus. She scrutinized the labels next to the works to find Kajal's, but more than half were unmarked.

At the drinks table, the wine bottles were empty just as the first three beer bottles that she picked up were.

The Gallery opened onto a large cemented courtyard. Q noticed that there were some people out on it. Stepping out, she was immediately hit by the smell of marijuana. A few disinterested heads turned in her direction. Moving beyond the clutches of the smell, Q gulped in some fresh air and scanned the scene.

Just then she spotted Kajal! He was seated on the floor of the courtyard next to an overfilled skip from which immense pieces of packaging thermocol stuck out and spilled over, fluorescing brightly in the dark. Kajal and the two guys with him were using them as cushions.

"What the fuck is wrong with you?" Walking up to him, she startled him from behind.

"Hey," Kajal acknowledged, seeming flabbergasted.

"Why didn't you pick up your phone?"

"It just died." Sounding slightly inebriated, Kajal scampered to his feet.

"God, I can't believe it. This is just not done man!" Q was louder this time, making Kajal suddenly conscious of a scene building up.

"My friends Ed and Marvin," Kajal lunged for a safety net.

Q became aware of their presence and calmed down. "Hey." Still sprawled out on the thermocol and resting on their elbows, they waved back at her.

"She's from my dorm." Kajal went on. "She's studying law."

Ed looked Q up in an exaggerated sweep and said, "You might as well have said that she was a talent scout from one of those posh galleries." He broke into a laugh and Marvin joined in.

Not knowing how to react, Kajal smiled. Q looked at him. She suddenly felt a whole lot worse than she had when she was alone minutes earlier. In a maroon satin dress, black long coat and stilettos, even if one forgot the makeup and hair, she did stick out like a long necked crane in a chicken coop.

"Shall we go see your work?" Q spoke to Kajal, eager to get away.

"Private viewing, eh? You never told us you put anything up, mate." Ed shifted focus on to Kajal.

"I'll see you guys later." And Kajal started to walk away, taking Q lightly by the elbow.

"See you around guys." Q spoke over her shoulder. She usually wouldn't have had any parting words to say to those guys. At that moment though she had a much greater score to settle with Kajal – and if she was being civil with him, she could definitely behave with rank outsiders.

"You take it easy with our man, ma'am." Ed chuckled, unrelenting in his quest to be a real pain that evening.

"They're both a little high." Kajal explained as they retreated back into the gallery.

———

Sitting on the bench, Q and Kajal shared a heavy silence that didn't seem to bother either right away. Sometimes when the minds are full, conversations fail to trickle.

Just then, the roar startled them simultaneously with inappropriate suddenness. It was deafening within the concrete tube, some hundred feet inside the earth. Metal sparked off metal as the train screeched to a halt. After a stand-off lasting a couple of seconds, the train let out a hiss and all carriage doors opened. Travelers were exchanged.

Within the next minute, that omnipresent mechanical voice of London – 'This train is ready to leave. Please stand clear of the closing doors.'

Sealed safely, the train contemplated for a second before snaking its way through the earth; its rumble, a pleasant muffled rhythm, stayed in the air a while after its black rear had vanished.

The platform in Archway underground station fell quiet again, and Q and Kajal were left alone.

Kajal looked up at the information display. Their train was six minutes away. Next to him, Ben Stiller shined a bright flashlight from a poster of A Night at the Museum.

Invigorated by the sudden flurry of activity, Q turned to Kajal. "Why didn't you put up any work?" she asked sedately.

Kajal pulled out of his many distractions and returned to the moment. He kept quiet.

Q was anyway not waiting for an answer. A whole lot more than her self-defining pride had been hurt. "Why didn't you let me know? Did you forget I was coming?"

Kajal kept quiet. Their train was still four long minutes away.

"Forget it. Why am I even asking you?" Q cinched her coat tighter around her. "Stupid me. I didn't even meet you after Tate but it's just that I fucking remembered your dumb exhibition."

The faint strains of a distant rumble wafted in. Kajal looked up at the information display. It was their train.

The Northern Line train thundered in and screeched to a halt.

Kajal got up and walked towards the nearest carriage door. It was only when he lifted a leg to board the train that he realized that Q was still seated on the bench. He looked back at her.

"You go on, I'll get the next," Q answered from the bench, her voice bouncing about in the still of the platform. She hated being melodramatic but she needed to see Kajal react and own up his unacceptable conduct.

Kajal knew he had wronged her. He had deliberately not answered her calls, believing that it would discourage her from coming for the show. Every day after Tate, he remembered that she had suggested coming for his show. And as the day drew nearer, it had started to feel more and more like a threat. But he didn't know how to tell her not to. And that he wasn't going to be displaying any work. Kajal knew it was his fault all the way – he was even going to be mad at Ed at the next opportunity – but saying sorry was such a dramatic proposition.

Kajal stepped into the train.

'This train is ready to leave. Please stand clear of the closing doors.'

Kajal stole a look at the information display. Q's wait for the next Northern Line train was going to be at least seventeen minutes. He felt bad for her.

———

It would seem entirely by some queer design but it was true that every time Kajal walked into the Television Room at the YMCA, a cookery show played to an empty house.

Two chefs were wrestling each other out to cobble together a three course dinner within the time. It took Kajal surprisingly little effort to find interest and sail into the programme.

The cookery show was therapeutic. It's competence in mollifying him in every maligning thought was phenomenal. Like that evening, when two images had become stuck obstinately – one, Ed making those smartass cracks at Q and two, Q's face on that bench telling him that she'll take the next train. The only thing that mattered was which of the chefs would win.

Q'd been mad at people before, but Kajal made her blood boil. But she wasn't so sure smack him across the face was what she wanted to do. Despite it all, she needed to see him. And once the resolve had been arrived at, Q knew she'd find him in the Television Room.

It was only after she had walked around him and was seated on the same sofa at one-man distance, that Kajal noticed Q. Q looked at the television – it was hard to comprehend that the show had so completely captured him.

"Oh, you're back." *I was expecting you to return much later. Did you have a good time?* Kajal even thought a fake smile of surprise wouldn't be out of place.

Q had nothing to say. Kajal had nothing else to ask.

A timer counted down the last minute of the chefs' allotments. The host was leading the audience into an appropriate frenzy. Someone was soon going to win a battle, the kind that people win on television and we love to watch.

"Can we watch something else?"

But it's the climax. I want to see who wins! Kajal handed her the remote.

Q shuffled through the six channels with brief stoppages; they were all at war to be the most humdrum. The YMCA did not waste money on the Sky kind of packages.

When she'd restlessly gone through the programmes a third time over, Kajal broke the silence. "I had nothing ready for the exhibition."

A wave of comfort flowed through Q. Kajal had said sorry. She hadn't realized till that moment what strange relief the fall of the wall would bring. In a flash, the evening was wiped clean, ready to begin afresh.

But she kept quiet. Enjoying it. *My turn.* She was happy. And it was a lot of hard work to kill a smile that would shatter her pride. *Not so soon, not so easily.*

"I gave it a lot of thought. I looked at everything. But the fact is that I haven't made any decent work at all."

"Who said so?"

"No one did. But no one's ever had anything nice to say either."

"Who said it's bad?" The situation was waking Q's prosecution skills.

"No one did."

"Did you have any reasonable ground to think that people wouldn't appreciate your work? And how does it matter so much anyway? It was, like you said, only an in-house show. I went through a fair bit of it. I didn't think there was anything extraordinary."

Kajal kept quite. He wasn't quite certain what Q was trying to bring home.

"What do you think? About your own work."

"I think it's all just crap." Kajal replied dismissively.

"You're sure that's what you think?"

By then Q was fully focused on the conversation. Kajal intrigued her. Increasingly.

"I don't really know," Kajal spoke after a prolonged silence that peeved Q – *He's drifted again.* "My tutor tells me all my pieces seem incomplete, like they don't convey anything. Ed thinks I'm not stunning enough. I don't impact the senses in any way for one to take notice."

"That doesn't answer my question, does it? I asked about your own opinion."

"Frankly, I don't have much of one." Kajal was prompt. An unsuspecting Q was taken aback by the suddenness of his response. *How could anyone worth his twenty five thirty years on earth not have an opinion about his own work?*

"You can stop me if you find me intruding. But the way I see it, doesn't that make it immensely hard to find inspiration to carry on, to remain motivated?"

But motivation was such an alien feeling for Kajal even otherwise, insight into such exotic delicacies as what kept one motivated and all that was non-existent. *When did one need inspiration to emerge out of the other end of a course in college anyway?* Kajal said nothing.

"I can understand it's different with artists. And I'm sure you'll one day be hit by that proverbial irradiance and produce your Sistine Chapel. But till then, don't you need something to give you a direction, just to go through every day? Some kind of day-to-day, short term goals?"

Kajal suddenly sniffed the air. Then a couple of more times. And his back stiffened as he sat up attentively. "Do you smell something burning?"

"No, there's nothing burning," speaking firmly, Q glared at him. "And," pointing at a smoke detector on the ceiling, "we have all these fancy devices just for the rare occasion – don't deny them the limelight." *Why am I mothering this moron?*

Kajal turned an elegiac face at her. One of his frequent nightmares involved being trapped in a chimney while trying to escape out of a cottage on fire; the brick red cottage albeit tremendously picturesque amidst a snow covered valley.

"Okay Kajal, this is going all over the place. Let us just assume that you are indeed clear in your head why you've come all this distance to study art. And that somewhere on a not very obvious plane, you are motivated."

The intercourse had become increasingly arduous for Kajal. Demons that he carried around like cancer cells in a phantom part of his body but kept concealed by a cultivated expertise at befooling himself that they did not exist were getting resuscitated back to active life. He wasn't unmindful but he felt protected by a belief that things will sort themselves out in time, on their own. What if they didn't? – That was a pernicious incertitude that he stayed away from.

"How many people have seen your work?" Q wasn't giving up.

"My tutor Liam, Ed and a couple of other guys."

"You don't get what I'm trying to say, do you? I don't know how better to come across to you." Q took a deep breath. "You are going to be an artist. And that's what you'll do for the rest of your life. You've got to break out of this lack of confidence. You have to let more people – all the people – see your work. I don't know a lot, but I really do think there's nothing like good art and bad art as an absolute; there's just art. I'm sure there were people who didn't think much about even the most celebrated pieces. Imagine if those artists had only met the detractors and decided to shelve the work – the world would have never known those masterpieces.

"I have no clue how your work is. I don't even know what it's about. But what I do know is that you are not doing justice to it. You have no right to label it as all rubbish. Just give yourself that push."

When Q didn't say anything for a while, Kajal concluded that she had finished. She must have realized the futility of the exercise.

"Can we step outside for a smoke?"

Q turned to him and ruffled his hair. And then said with a soothing smile, "Heavy talk, yeah? I'm sorry. Come I'll take you for a drink."

The sudden softening surprised Kajal. "You sure?"

"You may have ditched me but I haven't forgotten. Remember, I promised beer and dinner after the show?"

"It's late."

"It's never too late." Q felt immediately conscious as the cheesy words left her. Kajal looked away. Dramatic quotes straight out of the movies embarrassed him.

———

Q froze in her tracks. She and Kajal had only just left the hostel on their way to the pub around the corner.

A tall blonde man with a thick beard, dressed in a dark blue business suit with a pink shirt and pink tie stood in their way.

"Surprise, surprise!" the man's face lit up at the sight of Q.

"Stevie, you didn't tell me!" Q exclaimed.

"Long story. I had a meeting in the afternoon. I didn't bother telling you since I'd planned to drive back. But it dragged on till it became this late. So, here I am," he stood with his arms spread wide. Q rushed in to give him a hug and they both kissed the air on either side of Q's cheeks and his beard. Mooah, mooah.

Kajal felt like a wraith in distress with more silver screen stuff unfolding.

"Someone's dressed," Steve commented, inspecting Q at an arm's length. Q hadn't changed out of her dress from earlier in the evening.

"For you!" Q replied playfully. Steve smiled back.

"Have you eaten?"

"No," Q replied.

"I'm starving. Let's go get something. Eggs Benedict?"

"You know what works, don't you? But if you are famished like you say, we could eat at Khadim's?"

"I won't die before we get to Soho. We'll take a cab."

It was only then that Kajal reclaimed Q's attention. "Oh, by the way, this is Kajal. He's at the hostel."

"Hi Kay-jul. I'm Steve. And I'm *sometimes* at the hostel!" He was a cheerful man. There was something mirthful about him, like his very next statement would leave you in splits. His eyes were alive with intelligence. They shook hands.

"Sorry Kajal, but the drink will have to wait." Q said. Kajal realized that he was being ejected out of the scenario.

"That's fine."

"Were you going out for a drink?" Steve said, suddenly mindful that he had barged in on their plan. "Sorry mate, you guys go ahead. Or maybe I can come along?"

"No, it's okay. Kajal and I can catch up anytime." Q dismissed the suggestion. "He isn't exactly a comet, Stevie," and offering Steve the freshest version of her mischievous smile, this one supported by an appropriate twinkle in the eyes, she added cheekily, "Unlike some other people I know! But seriously, it wasn't anything, we were only talking." And then turning to Kajal, she added, "And don't you think I've finished, I'll chase you down with more *gyan*."

Tidying up is efficient when it leaves minimal mess and causes zero collateral damage. Q was good at tidying up. Situations. People. Men.

———

After they parted, Kajal bought two cans of Foster's and took them to Khadim. The place didn't have a permit but there was a small inside room where people who were known could sneak in a drink.

As he entered, Amjadbhai greeted him, "Welcome, welcome, Sanjay Dutt!"

That was the Bollywood name Amjadbhai had settled on for Kajal. There was something cheerfully childish about the greeting coming from the oversized man. On a number of occasions, like when walking alone on a sidewalk, it sailed back to occupy Kajal's head and left him grinning warmly to himself.

Well, as a nation, Pakistan has undoubtedly been up to...a whole lot more...monkey business than decency and America should have ever allowed. As a child, Kajal knew the country as one whose cricket players were a million times better looking than their Indian counterparts; that had actually made it difficult for little Kajal to support India whole heartedly – he couldn't really plot and cheer the fall of such good-looking men with Mughal emperor names. By the Bombay blasts and Kargil, Kajal was single minded in his undiluted despise for the country. But before Amjadbhai, he had never met a Pakistani.

Kajal lifted up the beer cans in way of seeking permission. *"Jaao jaao, andar jao. Peeoge nahin to jeeoge kaise?"* Amjadbhai reminded Kajal of the Air India Maharaja. Kajal ordered his favourite lamb curry and rice.

* * * * *

15

Steve had turned a new leaf. It had been merely over two months, for Q had only come to know him at the YMCA Hostel. But with him, her dreams were hostile.

Steve was much older. He was married with two children.

But he could make Q laugh. They conversed about philosophy, human rights in the third world, the Middle East conflict. There was much to learn from him. And then of course, his music. His brilliant slide guitar playing. He opened the doors of jazz on her, and had gifted her a sizeable collection of CDs. Q's rapidly acquired taste for Dizzy Gillespie was more an effort to appeal to him, her own orientation was David Gray and Coldplay.

She had lost her power to resist. The Steve Mondays and Tuesdays became the most important part of her existence. And in that short span, they had traversed all roads in mind and body that a man and woman could. She had fallen in love again. This time with the wrongest man.

Q thought of Mama and Dad. She thought about herself. The only way that her forbidding dreams about Steve could come true was by breaking his home. She had only seen pictures of Steve's children on his Mac. She could tell that he loved them. Was she guilty of inflicting upon them what she herself had had to grow up without? But life didn't stop when a home got ripped, she told herself.

She turned over and pulled the sheets closer to try and sleep. It wasn't her fault – *I'm in love and there can never be anything wrong with that. I can't help it if this how it has to be. I'm not the only one to blame.*

She knew people at the hostel were talking. London it was, but the YMCA Hostel was like a like a little piece of India that someone had laid in it. And for all the devil-may-care that she surrounded herself with, it did matter. She felt eyes following her every movement from behind her back. *What did they think of her?* Except the love, everything else seemed wrong.

Steve brought her gifts when he returned from Africa – a set of wooden masks, a male and a female, which prompted Q to declare, "I think I'll start collecting masks for the home." *Which home? The one she hoped to build with Steve someday?* But he had procured another set of the same masks for his home in Liverpool.

He did care for Q. In a way that he himself perhaps couldn't define. *I'll give it to him that he, just like Q, had lost the power to resist. And I refrain from labeling him as of flaccid character, for a turmoil may have resided in his soul too.*

But Steve stopped nothing. And for this I hated him. In my lucid intervals. At all other times, I loved to believe that in this whole big fat world, I had the least reason, if any at all, to be kind to Q. I wish I was stronger. Then maybe I could have been fair to her.

* * * * *

16

Well, if men were not allowed in the Ladies' Wing at the YMCA Hostel, Q had two already in her room that evening. I was the third. And when I got there in response to Q's "I have a surprise you don't want to miss!" call, Kajal and Steve had already sunk into some serious jamming.

"It's open." A British male voice answered my knock on the door. The light inside was distinctly weaker than the corridor and I took a while adjusting. I stepped in and after the ambience itself, the two men on the rug on the floor with guitars in their laps struck me.

The room was tastefully done. That one could do so many things to that little space was a revelation. All rooms had the same basic furniture which left precious little scope for personal touch. But Q had redone the arrangement to find room for a rug on the floor with fashionably carelessly strewn pillows. On one of the walls hung a brightly coloured runner that you knew straightaway as a Fab India. The lighting was courtesy a string of tiny blue lights across the top of another wall and a lamp that burnt yellow in one corner. I was reminded of my own room in med school from fifteen years before. It occurred to me just then how many years had gone by.

"You must be the doctor. I'm Steve."

"Oh, hi Steve. I've heard about you."

"I'm sure they've told you that my hair and beard are both green, making me some kind of an eco-friendly Jesus Christ!" Steve had an immediate wit. He did look like a blonde Jesus Christ – though he was seated and the lighting was dim, I could tell that he was tall, lean and of course, bearded and long haired. I felt a pressing sympathy for what he must do to women. "This is Kay-jul," he said, gesturing towards Kajal.

"Hi, Kajal," Kajal said his name again, the way it was supposed to be pronounced, and produced a hand for a shake.

"Axomiya?" I asked Kajal.

"Aw!" I had surprised him.

"I've heard about you as well. Guwahati?"

"Aw aw, Guwahati. *Aapuni?"*

Three months in a land where age was no bar to being on first-name terms, and *Aapuni* had become a forgotten respectful address. I introduced myself. "I'm with Netrajyoti Eye Care. I'm here on a research programme."

"Netrajyoti!" Kajal exclaimed. And then turning to Steve, added with pride, "The eye hospital he works in is perhaps the only thing in Guwahati that can be said to be truly world class."

"I'm sure," Steve said dispassionately. I was sure he didn't believe it.

"Tumi Londonot ki kori aasa?" I asked Kajal what had brought him to London. He explained about his course and all that.

In return, Kajal asked me, "Did you go to med school in Guwahati?" Without thinking anything about it, I answered and also his supplement on the year of my graduation. He told me nothing about his own time, which he obviously realized overlapped mine, in the same college.

"And Kay-jul's a mean guitar player," Steve brightened up. My conversation with Kajal in Assamese had momentarily relegated Steve to audience status but he hadn't missed the overall mood of the intercourse.

"Do you play anything?" Kajal asked me. "You know Steve, almost everyone in the northeast of India plays a musical instrument. In Shillong, cab drivers have a guitar stowed in the boot which they pull out between trips." He was excited. He wasn't painting an entirely untrue picture, though I wasn't convinced about his generalization of Shillong cab drivers.

"I play the guitar a bit." I hadn't touched one in years.

"Great, so that validates what Kay-jul just said," Steve said. "We'll need another guitar then. Know anyone who could lend us one?" He asked Kajal.

Kajal shook his head even as he extended the guitar he was playing towards me, "But you can play this one."

"No, no. It's okay. Why don't you guys carry on? I'm more than happy to listen."

"Come on mate. We can do with fresh fingers," Steve encouraged me. I took the offered guitar. Kajal had been waving it too close to my face to refuse anyway.

"We really do need a third guitar," Steve spoke. "Maybe the lady can help when she gets back."

It was only then that Q's absence struck me. "She ran out saying she'd be back in a jiffy," Steve proffered when I asked the both of them where she was.

"Here doctor." Steve passed me a can of Budweiser. I opened it clumsily, and with a huge hiss it bundled out with champagne-like flourish. "Oops," Steve was concerned about the rug on Q's floor. Embarrassed, I sucked at the can's rim and wiped my hands on my jeans.

"So," Steve said loudly, "what's your music, doctor?

"Country." I answered tentatively. I still don't know why I said that. I enjoyed country music but it was far from being *my* music.

"Okay." Steve said with a sneer. "Not quite my cup of tea. You've got to lead. I'll come in on the guitar. E, A, B major isn't it?" and then turning to Kajal, "That's all the chords they ever wrote country on!" He smiled. Kajal smiled back. I realized neither of them thought very highly of it. I sensed Kajal conclude that a third guitar wouldn't be worth the effort.

And then the song. The only one immediately available in my head was Big Wheels in the Moonlight. Steve joined in. I was glad it had a C sharp minor as well.

When Q pushed the door open, bathed in a cone of the harsh corridor light, I was in the middle of the song, increasingly wishing that I was singing something else or not singing at all. All of us looked up but didn't stop. Q settled quietly in a corner of the room.

Blood rushed into every frontier of my body. I felt warm behind the sternum. I looked at Q again. She smiled back at me. She was someone I connected with from another life.

"Wow doctor!" Q rushed to give me a little hug – she standing, I seated, the guitar between us – when I finished. "Amazing, wasn't it?" she sought approval from the others.

"Best in the price range," was Steve's opinion.

243

"*Biraat bhaal hoise de*," Kajal was courteous.

"You took a while," Steve spoke to Q, putting the guitar down to one side.

"Sure did," Q said with a hint of sarcasm. "Just look at all you men being nice and cozy while I do all the hard work in the fucking cold!" Q turned to me and seeing the can in my hand, "What's that? Beer?" She reached out and removed the can. And pulling out a bottle of Jack Daniel's from within her long coat, she put it in my hands. I felt her icy fingers brush against mine.

"Did you go out to get that?" Steve quipped, eyeing the bottle of whisky. "You could have asked me."

"I like taking care of my guests." Q replied back. I hated what I saw in her eyes as she looked at Steve. But in my hand I held the bottle of JD which had she had bothered about only for me.

"All right, all apart, we have a situation. We need another guitar." Steve said bluntly.

"There's this guy on your floor who plays. I think he's in four-o-eight," Q spoke to Kajal.

Kajal shook his head.

"Okay, let me go and try." Q said and rose to leave.

"Just don't bring the man along," Steve winked. Something in his tone suggested that he was dying to get rid of Kajal and me as well.

I hated Q for knowing yet another guy in the hostel. The bottle of JD and her freezing fingers were easily forgotten as the pounding rose in my chest. They say jealousy is a beautiful attribute of love. But how does one draw a line between it and insecurity? And then stop insecurity from leading one down a disastrous trail?

Steve was a horse with peacock's feathers. And Kajal was a turtle with a most adorable head. I was scared of them both. That was the only time I ever met them.

* * * * *

Just give yourself that push.

Q's words had lodged somewhere within and kept returning like a flashing glow-sign on a dark highway.

In his studio, Kajal sat on the floor, face to face with another canvas that stood against the wall across, and watched the paint flow southward in silent canter. Like a cautious army marking virgin enemy territory. A painting occurring like an unchoreographed event.

He had slapped the paint on with a degree of violence. Bubbles of various sizes had formed and were now bursting – the small ones quietly, bleeding tiny driblets; the large ones with deadened thuds and spitting out a rain. There was one particularly large, like a water-balloon sagging with the weight of its own contents and yet resisting being rent. Kajal surveyed it with watchful intent. It did not move down, it did not seem like exploding, just stood its ground in pompous invulnerability. *Can it hold on till the paint dried? Then it will never have to burst.*

"Think of scale." Liam had said at the last tutorial. "Your work is about its concept, not about technically challenging artistry. Scale will be a wonderful compliment. Think of massive canvases." And then like awakening to a new realization, his eyes had brightened, "For the degree show, this can be a performance – art forming itself while you supply the paint." Kneading his chin between his thumb and two fingers, he had added, "I'm beginning to like this. The artist is a mere supplier of material – versus the found object bringing the artist inarguable powers to turn knickers into art objects by merely signing them, this is interesting."

And Liam had gone on animatedly. "Are you aware of Fluxus?"

Kajal shook his head.

"Read up. Fluxus, Intermedia and Performance Art." Liam had suggested distractedly. "I don't perceive the incompleteness your work had brought to me earlier. It had always been complete. Just increase the scale. For gravity's deft touch to be evident, you have to amplify its simplicity. The process is the whole work, not so much the product. I have a feeling we'll like the way this ends." And he had slapped Kajal's back, not something that he did often.

Kajal stared at the canvas in front of him. The scale. Larger canvases. He could smear acrylic on the Gherkin. The Big Ben. Gravity and time. Dimensions where the human being was a non-participating audience, artist or not.

The paint dried. Still sticky but immobile. The end point of the work. Did the paint now flout gravity? It had turned that corner in its plasticity beyond which it defied change – what did time matter to the paint now? The overgrown bubble in the middle of the canvas survived.

A loud crash from Ed's space shook Kajal up. Kajal rushed to check.

Ed was sprawled on the floor, head cranked up and one leg in the air. Clicking pictures. In front of him lay a smashed wooden chair.

"Hey mate. Did my flash of devastation sway your paints off their walk in the park?" He stood up slowly, reviewing the pictures on his camera. "I like this one," Ed turned the Nikon

SLR 1146 in his hands so that Kajal could view the screen. Ed had captured the precise moment of the destruction – one leg of the chair breaking off from the seat just as it touched ground; the string which had given way from suspending the chair, remained frozen at a tilt with an undulated limp.

———

Spending time at the YMCA library had become a matter of regularity. After dinner. That night Kajal delved into Liam's suggestions.

The Tate came back to him. The real textbooks of his erudition. Jackson Pollock, even Picasso, Duchamp, Warhol, Lichtenstein. When he had arrived on the course, the absence of a tutored journey through the history and theory behind the practice of art had triggered a disconnect which effectively abashed his lithe piquancy. It was finally at the Tate that it all seemed to come together.

I have no clue how your work is. I don't even know what it's about. No. No, Q was not a mere coincidence. Kajal felt a rapid pining for Q to see his work. He urgently needed her to. He was finally ready.

Feelings of affirmation came upon Kajal like desert rain.

* * * * *

17

I lost my job today.

I have been made an offer. My diagnosis of course won't come in the way of my research work. I can be as mad as I wished and yet carry on functioning as a researcher from some beyond-public corner of the hospital. No such position existed, as far as I know. One has been created for me. For there is no doubt in my head that they all like me. I have grown up in this hospital. The blue eyed boy at one point in time not too far in the past. But there is also no denying that where performing surgeries and treating patients are concerned, a potential disaster no organization can afford or allow is what I have become.

But how can I ever come to terms with walking to my researcher's cubicle past the patients waiting for surgeries, knowing that I was not going to have anything to do with them? With my surgeries taken away, how can I just hang in there?

I've been given time to reconsider.

My Director couldn't look me in the eye but I was more ashamed. I'm guilty of letting him down. I know there will be tons of others, willing and able, drawn like iron filings to a magnet to take my place, and he'll once again start from scratch, invest in any one of them the time and effort that he had in me. His time and effort – the

248

value of that is no joking matter in this skill starved crevice of the world I belong to.

And my seventy year olds. They are such a part of me. I feel like my toothbrush has been taken away. Only I can never buy another one. The trust is gone, including my own.

I wish life could decide which side to place me on. I want to be able to either hate devotedly or not hate at all. For then I can decide if it's me or Q that I should blame. It is tough being on both sides simultaneously.

There is something final about today. I feel sober again. From being drunk with simultaneous hope and disquiet.

* * * * *

18

When I woke up that morning, the whole world was clothed in white. Everywhere I looked. The snowfall had stopped and a remarkably bright sun shone in a clear blue sky – the blue of the European sky is an altogether different pristine hue – leaving behind, for the dilettante, a view as gorgeous as a sun bleached beach to a Siberian. There was snow on rooftops, on the sidewalks, on the road, on the tops of parked cars, on railings and balustrades. A bunch of YMCians frolicked in the street below, indulging in action that had every probability of being once in a lifetime.

Transformed to another world, it was like a sudden grasp when the magnanimity of the day came back to me. I rushed to shower.

————

"I was worried the trains would be cancelled. The snow's heavier outside London." Q said as she returned with the tickets. "There's time, let's get something to eat."

Between bites of a Cornish pasty, Q gave me more information, "It'll be nearly two hours on the train to Laem and from there we have to bus it, roughly forty five minutes. There's a direct train to Coventry from Euston, but that costs twice as much. We'll save some money and," she brightened up like a child and touched my forearm, "you'll see more of the countryside."

"But you should have let me pay. At least for my ticket."

"No way. This is my treat," Q retorted firmly.

Things were fine till then. But as the train pulled out of Marylebone Station, Q logged onto a forlorn vacant patch way beyond her usual absent mindedness.

The spread of the English countryside lay clad in snow melting under the sun to reveal patches of manicured green. As we traversed through landscape that was singularly breathtaking for me, life would have been a whole lot complete if Q hadn't been the way she'd suddenly become.

We reached Laemington Spa more or less without a word exchanged. It was a bit of a walk from the station to the bus stop and that offered me an experience of a smaller English town. The UK of course is about London and the rest of it. Unlike India where at least ten different cities have simultaneously grown into competing stature, the UK story is smeared with historically massive names like Manchester and Liverpool falling into pleasant decay.

Across the street from where we waited for our bus to Coventry, there was a huge church, blackened by time and yet radiating unique glory. On its large front steps was a congregation of men dressed in black suits and women in flowing white gowns. An English wedding. Not overflowing with the colours, loudness and food of an Indian but very disciplined, restrained and I'm sure, punctual.

In time, our bus showed up and we boarded.

"Dad is expecting us by lunch," Q said with a distant gaze.

"You know Steve studied here."

The usual liveliness the name brought to Q's face wasn't there, and that, to my own surprise, somehow saddened me that day.

The bus was taking us through Warwick and the renowned University essentially sprawled the entire town. The buildings were an imposing blend of Victorian architecture and modern structures in steel and glass distributed amidst lavish allotments of lush green open spaces.

'Really? Wow! What was his subject?" No, I didn't say any of that to Q.

———

The legendary unpredictability found the weather as we arrived in Coventry. It was raining. No it was no monsoon, English rain is usually a spray that kind of dews one up. But it did bring to the day gloom to match Q's demeanor.

"Do you want to pick up flowers?" Q asked me as we passed a florist on our way to her home.

"Yes yes, of course."

As far as I could recall, I had never before bought flowers for any one. Feeling conscious and a bit out of place, I selected a smashing looking bunch of red roses. Q had drifted to another end of the longish store. I started making my way to the till, holding the roses very stiffly like a samurai holding his sword.

"Red roses!" Q leapt to my side screaming. "You are quite a man, aren't you? But the flowers are for my Dad, not for me." Q smiled and it seemed like it had broken through a mountain.

Q returned the roses to their place and picked up another bunch instead. This one looked very elegant, like something a man gives another man. Tall green stems ending in yellow and white flattish flowers, perhaps lilies or carnations.

"You okay with this?"

"I like them."

Q smiled broadly, with a natural flow. I was thrilled. If it took my stupidity with flowers to bring her cheer, I was willing to offer more. I stood stuck to my spot and watched her walk past me.

She looked back at me from the till, "Are you going to pay or shall I?" From the way she sounded one would have thought I was quite a leech.

"I guess he still wants those roses for you." The fat middle aged man at the counter, looking more like an overfed American than a disciplined Brit, joined Q in staring back at me.

———

It was a two storied brick house with a slanting slate roof, surrounded by a high unpainted wooden fence. A sky-blue Bentley stood in the small driveway.

"This is home," Q said. A large brass knocker occupied the centre of the polished black front door but Q chose the electric bell on the side, and a chime went out somewhere inside. In a while, it was answered by a beaming, elderly man dressed in a smart grey business suit.

"Uncle!" Q exclaimed and rushed to give him a hug.

"Baby! It's been a while, hasn't it?" He planted a kiss on Q's cheek.

His attention fell on me, still standing in the rain. "He must be the doctor."

"Yes," Q confirmed and turned to me, "and this is Ramalingam uncle."

"I'm sorry, you're getting drenched." Ramalingam smiled generously and offered me his hand. I couldn't take it – I had the flowers in one hand and Q's satchel in the other.

"Mike we need a hand here." Ramalingam shouted into the house. "Come in, come in," he ushered us in.

Young and athletic Mike met us halfway down the passage from the front door. I let him take the bag but held on to the flowers.

"Hey Mikey, how's it going?" Mike seemed roughly the same age as Q.

"Not too bad, Baby."

Maybe it's cheap, but I did feel elated at the sight of a white domestic help in an Indian household in the UK!

"Uncle, will you make doctor comfortable?" And Q started up a flight of stairs to our right. An open door before the stairs allowed me glimpse of a snug reception room with minimalistic mahogany furniture.

"Come in here doctor," Ramalingam led me into a swanky hall at the end of the corridor. The floor was slick white marble – you usually didn't find that in the average UK home. Chic, classily restrained and yet upbeat rugs of different sizes lolled like the welcoming vicinity of a bonfire on a winter night. What immediately caught attention was a massive chandelier in the centre, its many lights glowing yellow, creating an umbra that tore the prematurely descending dark. Wood crackled in a fire place. And above it, framed pictures – most proffered Q recognizable through various stages of growing up, but there was also a huge blow up of a young couple simultaneously cuddling an infant on the deck of a cruise liner. Q's parents – so I figured – made an amazingly good looking set. Against the wall directly ahead of me was an imposing stone Ganesha. Along another, was the bust of a man in plaster.

"Let me take your jacket." Ramalingam pulled my jacket and me out of getting lost amongst the many highlights in the hall. The main seating area was two steps lower and I swished into a liberal leather sofa.

"What can I offer you doctor, a drink or some coffee?"

He brought me the requested whisky.

"You?" I enquired.

"I don't drink doctor. And it's close to lunch anyway."

I nodded and smiled. He smiled back. I took a sip of my drink – expensive Scotch, its feel like buttered leather. He stared at me quietly. I smiled again. "Very good. Single Malt?" *I knew it was; what a dumb question!* He nodded and smiled. We reciprocally eyed each other with caution, avoiding discovery.

From another wall of the hall, large French windows opened on to a carpet grass covered garden; two men busied themselves with some gear in this section.

Ramalingam sensed my gaze, "We'd planned a barbeque in the garden. But the rain spoilt it. We are moving it to the covered backyard."

I nodded. And then some more quiet.

Despite the material stateliness, there was an unnerving loneliness about the house. Like a majestic hall where one wrote an exam. It was as if every brick stood mourning an unbearable loss. *Was Q's mood an unavoidable preparation for this?*

Rescue finally as Q breezed into the room, lighting up the faces of both men.

"Who drinks whisky in the middle of the day?" Q screamed at me like my deed was a capital offence.

"Baby, that's rude." Ramalingam interjected, smiling.

"Drink drink, I'm only worried you won't be able to handle the real stuff – it's not your Bourbon." And then turning to Ramalingam, "You know uncle, he drinks Jack Daniel's!" Q's talent for wry humour wasn't new to me. But I hadn't suspected she thought poorly about my choice of whisky. I had also credited her with knowing that JD is Tennesse, and not Bourbon.

"Baby!" Ramalingam objected again, raising his voice but still smiling.

And the very next blink, she turned serious. "You want to say hi to Dad?"

———

The man had lost at least thirty kilos. No, my reference wasn't that picture from his dashing youth I'd seen downstairs. Sometimes you can tell that even when you are seeing someone for the very first time. His eyes had sunk into deep gorges. The skin held on to the bones like wrinkled cling-wrap. And the sight dived into me, creating ripples of disbelief and distress. I suddenly realized how my reaction to disease had been touched by those three four months away from clinical work.

The melancholy of the house no more seemed out of place, it was only reacting to what was happening to its master.

He occupied an armchair by the neatly made bed. A white woman in a nurse's uniform stood alert next to him. A fire burned quietly in one corner. The room was grand, like the rest of the house. Prim and well-tended. But somehow everything looked like belonging to a meticulously planned set. The way he sat betrayed that he had been planted there temporarily with neither resistance nor participation from his end. He wore his clean shaven face like a masquerade.

"Dad, this is doctor. Remember I'd told you about meeting him in Guwahati? He is my best friend now."

But for once, she had forced an exuberance that reeked of fakeness even she could not mask. And neither did the 'my best friend' have any effect on me.

"Hello." His voice was like crumpled paper, dry and hoarse from the lack of hope. He smiled at me like precious crystal about to shatter.

He offered me his hand. I stood rooted to my spot for what seemed like a long time. And then suddenly aware of the immense physical exhaustion it must cause him, I lunged with a dramatic swish to take it. The tall flowers wriggled close to his face – I had forgotten my right hand still held the bunch.

Without saying a word, I took two steps backward, eager to get away. If I had ever seen a dying man, it was then.

I turned to Q, standing a couple of paces behind me. She looked devoid of any means of turning the situation around. I felt ashamed of my inability to handle the state.

"You people must be hungry," Q's father broke the awkwardness.

And that rejuvenated Q. "Come on doctor, I offer you the best barbeque on earth!" And to her Dad, "we'll see you after lunch."

It was obvious he wasn't going to join us for lunch.

———

The gloom trudged along like valuable excess baggage. The backyard was warm with the smell of meat being grilled.

"Doctor, these sausages are just out of this world. They come from a hundred year old local butcher that uncle has a long relationship with." Q had summoned her upbeat self back on.

A middle aged Indian brought Ramalingam a plate of *chapatis*, *sambar* in a bowl and some curd. Ramalingam looked apologetically at Q, "Sorry baby, I'm still a boring veggie."

"You have no clue what you are missing, uncle." And to me, Q said, "You must try Gopal Anna's *Mysore Paak*," pointing with her chin toward the man who was serving Ramalingam. Gopal Anna paused for a minute to beam at us, and then proceeded to disappear where he had emerged from.

———

Ramalingam had to leave after lunch. I was informed that he lived with his wife a block away. "Siddhant is visiting us," he told Q. "Oh! He must be quite a man now. I haven't seen him in so long," Q spoke excitedly. Looking very pleased, Ramalingam said, "He's fourteen. And a couple of inches taller than me."

Helps cleared the barbeque with assembly-line precision as we walked Ramalingam to the front door. "I'll bring Sid back in the evening. You're staying the night, aren't you?" "No uncle, we'll head back," Q replied.

After Ramalingam left, Q led me into the smaller reception room by the passage. This one was warmly carpeted and had thick curtains which were drawn. The overall tone was beige and the lighting was toned down.

We sat down facing each other across the room. Mike brought us coffee.

"How's she? Is she going to stay?" Q asked him.

"Yeah, Magda's fine. She's from Coventry and has a little son, no husband – so there's a fair chance she'll stick for the money." Mike answered her.

Mike hung around for a minute while we sipped our coffee – Q slurped loudly and was sitting with both legs crossed on the sofa. The coffee was filter and perfectly doused in milk and sugar, like the faultless produce of south Indian homes.

"You know it's such a hassle finding a decent nurse that'll stay even when you're willing to pay a bomb," Q spoke to me.

"Will you need anything else, baby?" Mike was eager to leave us.

"Thanks Mikey, you've been a star," Q grinned luxuriously, before adding, "What's the latest with that Polish woman – you still together?"

"Well, women, they come and go," Mike didn't seem too interested in delving into the matter.

For a long time after Mike left, Q and I didn't seem to have anything to talk about. Q drifted back to her black hole from the morning. And her Dad returned to perturb my mind. I must also confess that I do tend to go into the famous Assamese standby mode in afternoons, especially after a generous meal.

"Ramalingam uncle's son, Mahesh uncle, heads Dad's India office." Q's voice was like an announcement at yesterday's event. "Siddhant is uncle's grandson. He's a complete stud, you know. He's into kick boxing, Salsa and what not. I feel so old next to him."

The day had seen extremes unfold far too briskly for me, especially since we had been in Coventry. The opulence of the Bentley and the imposing finery, and yet every ounce of the air you breathed was heavy with defeat. The black and white blow up of bliss over the fireplace from a dream that never was. The dashing young man in the picture and how he lay crushed by mortality in a room from a theatrical set. I didn't even know what was wrong with him. But even while everything that he controlled hung in indecision, his own fate appeared so conclusively decided. And nurses were perpetually on the lookout for new assignments for they didn't know how long they'll be needed in the current. But then they end up leaving too soon, for the ailment lives longer, and death comes slower.

As I looked at Q sitting across and talking about Ramalingam, I suddenly felt very sad that she should belong in that lugubrious pool.

"Where's the business based in India?"

"Pune. Dad's from Amritsar." Q answered. And then carried on. "Ramalingam uncle was like a son to my grandfather. He was in the UK when Dad came here to study engineering. And since then he has held Dad by the finger and taken him through places. When Dad started the India office, Varun *chacha*, Dad's brother, logically headed it. Till Dad realized some years back that he had been usurping company funds and had even been up to some rather shameful investments. Dad had to get rid of him quite unceremoniously. And since then Mahesh uncle has been doing a great job. Even though the business isn't going through its brightest patch right now. Uncle tells me that the world could be going into a major recession that may even upstage 1929. We are in the automobile sector, engine components."

"Never do business with a brother – you might lose both." I summed up Q's information the best that I could.

"No doctor, that can't be original. It's too bright for a dull, eye mechanic like you." Q's evanescent mind could rise out of Stygian gloom to bubbling elation in a dizzying instant.

I smiled, and turning my head, found myself staring at a most elegant bar. Polished wood stretching floor to ceiling, and a granite topped counter. Richly stacked, it was a connoisseur's delight.

Q caught my stare. And most unpredictably, the heartiness left her face, just as abruptly as it had appeared.

"Dad wasn't much of a drinker himself – just the two drinks once in a while. But he was famous for the parties he hosted. You know, there's even a DJ's console and he used to mix music. He loved his time with people."

"You talk in the past tense."

"Just shut up, doctor!"

Q stunned me. She had never spoken to me like that before, and I wasn't used to people asking me to shut me. A hint of tear I saw in her eyes filled me with unease. "We were going to see your Dad after lunch."

She continued to look away as she replied dismissively, "He's resting. Anyway, he's not much into people anymore." She moved in the chair, tucking her feet further under herself, like a snail fortifying itself. "You know I'd brought Steve home and Dad didn't even meet him."

For a moment I didn't know if I was happy that her Dad had granted me a showing or miserable because Steve had beaten me with the home run.

"Doctor, there's so much here. And everything Dad built from scratch. He still has so many plans for the business. But who's to nurture it now?"

"What do you mean?" I cleaned up the brief visit of shameful jealousy on Steve's account.

Q sighed, and said nothing. Her wretchedness scared me. I brought myself to ask her, "What's the diagnosis?"

"I thought I'd told you. Pancreatic cancer." And then without allowing time for me to take that in she added, "Quite advanced. Inoperable."

Of course I had read about pancreatic cancer from the best of textbooks. Surgery for pancreatic cancer was rare in those days, especially in my med school, but I was fortunate to have observed a Whipple's being performed. I distinctly remembered the couple of patients I'd come across. The physical pain and anguish was of a scale that was impossible to forget. I had sat with them and had so many things to say to them and their families. Hollow, mechanical, rehearsed words that I had then thought made a difference.

But with Q telling me about her Dad, I was entirely voiceless. It wasn't only the years of Ophthalmology, where death was rarer than a poor politician, which had rendered me incapable.

"But there's chemotherapy." I suggested feebly.

"They say chemotherapy is only palliative in his case, it's not going to cure nothing. It's gone way beyond that. I'm sure you understand all that better than me." Q broke down. With a haunting sincerity that could only come from being an equal in the suffering. "You should see him when he's in pain. I know he's a strong man. He's just such a strong man." The tears ran freely.

Large drops hung from the tip of her nose and the prominence of her jaw line like prized pearls.

"Dad is dying. And he's waiting for it. Just waiting."

I knew he was. If it was inoperable and chemotherapy was only palliative, he didn't have more than six months, twelve at best. And I didn't know how many of them he had already spent.

It was Q who had told me in a bar in Guwahati that parents were easier when you had only one half to handle. And since then, it was Q who was always in control. It was Q who always said the last line, not too seldom with stinging causticity that turned your knees to powder. It was life that toed Q's line. It was Q who was invincible.

Suddenly my whole self became consumed by despondent helplessness. Of course there were millions on this earth who lived lives which were a million times gloomier than Q's. But they were not Q. I looked at her. She stared vaguely.

And just then it became as obvious as the night, as clear as the day. I had been scared of it and had tried to run away. I had even found relief in not finding it when I had chased it desperately. But it never gave up. Till it won.

Whatever I had ever felt for Q metamorphosed into love. It was that sacred bliss that touches you only that once in a lifetime.

While I had forever found Q's overpowering individuality incalculably magnetic, I perhaps needed to see the vulnerability that surfaced that afternoon. That she owned such passion as could bring her to tears was a long way from the deeply superficial person Q had possibly been to my mind. It made her complete.

My body stiffened. And my legs offered me the strength to raise myself just that little bit towards her. The slim movement found

Q's attention and she became taut with consciousness. "I'm sorry, I don't usually do this," said Q and brushed away her tears. I sat back.

"What about your mum?"

"She doesn't know. Dad made us promise. He feels that when he left her at a time she perhaps needed him, he lost the right to turn to her shattered and reeling. Ramalingam uncle informed me, without Dad's knowledge. Dad would have gone without either of us knowing. When Dad realized that I was aware, he rejected having me around, nursing him. This rubbish law course is the compromise."

"If you are free, Arun would like to see you." Magda suddenly appeared at the edge of the room.

Pulling herself together, her face contorting with an eruption of worry, Q jumped out of the chair, "Is there anything?"

"No, he's okay. Just wants to see the two of you."

———

"Hope lunch was okay. I'm sorry I'm kind of indisposed." Dad spoke to me.

My second time in the room in a little over a couple of hours and the world seemed to have become a different place. Sometimes being informed can cause unfamiliarity.

Q sensed my trepidation. She rushed to protect her Dad from understanding that I knew. Leaving my side, she walked up to her Dad, still seated like we had left him earlier, and throwing her arms round his neck from behind, she said cheerfully, "Dad, doctor here was going to drown in the food if I hadn't rescued him. You should see how eats like a chicken at the Y otherwise." Her Dad smiled.

Q carried on, turning to me, "You know Dad lived in the YMCA for a while as a student years ago." I smiled back. The way Q melted into her different moulds astonished me.

"This little girl of mine is a wonderful human being. I'm glad she has your mature company." *Was he reading my mind? Did he know that I had conclusively fallen in love with his daughter moments earlier?*

"You have nothing to worry, sir." I finally managed to say something. I thought it was appropriate in the context, even to a dying man.

"Dad!" Q screamed. "You have no idea how dumb he is. I guess he manages his patients okay, but that's about all there's to him." She seemed happy. I offered the both of them a smile again. To which she fondly commented, "Look how dumbly he keeps smiling the whole time."

My smile widened and I shifted my standing leg. Magda occupied her corner of the room impatiently and disinterestedly through the most valuable moment of my life.

Dad forced a weak smile. "I believe you plan to proceed back. I'd suggest you start early. Thanks for making the time, doctor."

———

"We can stay the night if you want." I offered Q as we walked back downstairs.

"No doctor, we have to get back. Kajal's taking me to some art galleries tomorrow."

* * * * *

19

"Will you mind if I suggest a change?"

"Kajal, you know I hate it when you talk like that. Just say."

"No, I was wondering if we could drop the gallery and go to my studio instead."

"I'd love that," Q exclaimed. "You know I've been dying to. But can we get in on a Sunday?"

"Yes yes, no problem with that."

———

For Q, interest in Fine Art was a newly cultivated faculty. And her only reason for delving an insider plane was Kajal.

What had started as mere fuel for her insatiable need for activity, the weekly round of London's art galleries and museums had grown into an unconscious effort to kindle Kajal into his chosen field. Kicking off predictably – Tate Modern, and then traversing the rather touristy route through Tate Britain, National Gallery and National Portrait Gallery on Trafalgar Square, Victoria and Albert Museum in South Kensington and the Haunch of Venison off Saville Row – they discovered Hoxton and Shoreditch with the turn of the new year. For contemporary art in London had truly moved eastward, out of its famous traditional addresses and beyond the big commercial houses around Bond and Regent Streets.

"Today I offer you London's East End," Kajal had announced with uncharacteristic enthusiasm that Sunday. Like a child on a day-out with a secret plan, he pulled out a printed map, with a route marked in green felt.

They started at Old Street Station and a short walk brought them to Hoxton Square. While every square in London owns charisma, and some even history, Hoxton Square radiated a unique individuality, surrounded by art galleries and big and small eateries abounding in connoisseurs of all age and intriguing disposition. One could breathe the culture and touch the bohemian vigour. Hoxton Square was the destination for all new age artists, both established and emerging. And at one edge stood the holiest – The White Cube, the gallery that has housed the brightest names of British contemporary art, including Damien Hirst and Tracey Emin.

After the White Cube, Q and Kajal ate lunch at the Hoxton Bar and Kitchen. Kajal was surprised to find a batch mate, a French girl he didn't know by name but recognized distinctly for the Yoko Ono glasses and hair, waiting their table there. "Part time job, I fund my education," she explained in fractured English. Kajal was immediately impressed with the effort she was putting towards the course and conveyed his appreciation. "*Merci*," she replied without patronising. Kajal introduced Q as a friend and student of law. "So you become a rich lawyer, *formidable*," her face cracked with expression, 'And we become struggling street artists!" she grinned at Kajal. "Enjoy your meal!" she left them. "Very nice girl," Kajal told Q as they ate. "Like you knew her before today. Did you see her face? Such bad skin," Q said balefully. But for once, Q enjoyed a meal that needed to be paid for.

After lunch, they found the Bischoff/Weiss gallery on Rivington Street. It was typical new East End – a small converted ground floor, displaying paintings on a bare wall. Since its opening, it had built a name for supporting upcoming artistes.

Continuing further, they reached the Paul Stolper Gallery on Luke Street, old dilapidated buildings making the scene look straight out of Jack the Ripper.

They crossed Great Eastern Street to emerge on Shoreditch High Street and turned southward onto Bethnal Green Road, where they visited the Andrew Mummery Gallery and the Rocket Gallery, famous for works rich in scale.

By then, it had turned dark and the walking was getting to them. "You okay with a little bit more?" Kajal asked Q. "You bet," she replied energetically.

On the final leg, they walked along Commercial Street to the famous old Spitalfields Market. I was told by not-very-reliable sources that it is London's own *Chor Bazar* – you lose anything from a hair pin to an apartment, you may be able to buy it back at Spitalfields. After a quick round of the home-made food kiosks and clothes and trinkets stalls, Kajal searched out Spitz, a bar, bistro and gallery all in one. They surveyed its walls covered with photojournalism exploring new social trends in the East End. At the terrace bar, they ordered canapés and two glasses of the house white. "They have live music, but not on Sundays," Kajal informed.

"I'm really tired, Kajal."

"I'm sorry," Kajal spoke guiltily.

"Fuck you! Can't I be honest without you making me feel guilty." Q screamed back tersely. "I had a really good time. It's just my legs."

The most exhausting of all the 'arty loafs', but the day had brought a culmination. Q's thin crust of familiarity with art had consolidated into a much rounded sphere. Just as Kajal had blossomed into a confident and knowledgeable student who was beginning to see a place for himself in that world.

———

And that day, two Sundays later, Q was standing in Kajal's studio, face to face with his work. She had suggested it many times earlier, and then had learnt to shelve it. Kajal had been unrelenting, finding masterful and yet obvious means of procrastination.

"There are a few more behind, here." Kajal said, and pulled forth a couple of canvases from behind a stack of paint buckets and boxes.

Q kept quiet. An engulfing pang of disappointment seized her. Kajal's lack of confidence in his work did not seem unfounded any more. His blobs of incoherent paints failed to bring any meaning to her.

"What does your tutor say?" Q asked uncertainly. She wasn't prepared for a technical situation where she feared her word could be of consequence. Kajal failed to pick up the apprehension in the question coming from that one person who had taught him that all that mattered was his own belief.

"Oh, he's really upbeat. You should have seen how he suddenly turned around and said – your work was always complete, only I wasn't seeing it!" Kajal mimicked Liam, complete with kneading the chin. He followed it up with planting a swinging arm on Q's back, "And then he thwacked my back like that."

Kajal was an altogether different person that day. Expressive, demonstrative, there was no mistaking his contentment. But the enthusiasm saddened Q further. For she truly believed that he had miles to go and tons of effort to put in. What was he trying to get at? Who would appreciate it? In her worldly mind, it wasn't just his course – if he was going to make a living out of that kind of work, who was going to buy it?

"I guess he is impressed then," Q spoke vaguely.

"I think so. You know it's quite difficult to get a positive comment out of him. Out of all tutors in general."

"Right then Kajal, you seem set. But don't rest. Work hard and keep bouncing things off people that know. Talk to Ed." Q suddenly wanted to run away. It wasn't in her nature to mince words, to be unnecessarily kind. But Kajal made her weak. She couldn't be honest with him for the fear of grounding him just as he seemed to be finding flight.

"No, I won't. I realize there is so much to be done yet. Liam has handed me down quite an agenda. I can't let him down, for I really think he values my work. You know it's important for the tutors as well how their wards turn out. There's only some months to the degree show, which is like the 'final exam' if you please. We not only get assessed and graded, the show is attended by an entire world beyond the school. Artists, curators, art-collectors sometimes, and also parents and family."

"Wow! So I'll get to meet your parents." Q seized the opportunity to redirect focus.

"I'm not too sure they'll be here," Kajal spoke with a straight face.

But Q was at her sensitive best that day. She didn't miss the hint of soreness that Kajal tried hard to suppress. "What do you mean you're not sure?"

Kajal took a deep breath. "They're not awfully proud of me studying Art. Ma's kind of okay, but Baba really, really wanted me to become a doctor, just like him."

"But you'd be happy if they came for the show?"

"May be they shouldn't. I'm scared of disappointing them again." Kajal recovered quickly, "But anyway, the degree show is the biggest. I owe it to Liam."

Kajal suddenly turned solemn again. "You like my work, don't you?" All along, just that Q had seen his work had seemed enough. Quite abruptly, he realized she hadn't yet offered an opinion.

"No I don't." Q made a jocular face to take honesty away from her reply. She felt restless. "But I'm just an outsider, you are the painter boy. As long as you are satisfied, that's all that counts. And who am I to contest someone like Liam's opinion." She continued to put it across jovially.

Kajal smiled. "What is that supposed to mean? Do you like my work or not?" Just the fact that she was standing there facing his work was confirmation that she approved it. He just needed to hear her say it.

"That means I'm really hungry." Q evaded a direct answer once again. "You didn't even let me eat breakfast."

"I want to take you to the Mother. They do a special lunch menu on Sundays. Do you mind traditional Irish food?"

"Potatoes?"

At Mother Red Cap, they ordered Kajal's selections for the both. "We'll sit in the beer garden," Kajal told the temperamental woman at the bar. "I'll bring the food over. It'll be about twenty minutes," she explained un-invitingly as she handed them the pints of beer. "I'm sure the bitch is PMS-ing!" Q muttered her impression of the bartender as they walked to the small back garden.

The air outside was chilly but the sun was out. The garden was crammed, nearly all its haphazard spots occupied and bursting with conversation. But they did find a table.

"You will come for my degree show, won't you?" Half way through his Corned Beef and Cabbage, Kajal suddenly asked Q.

"Yes I will." Q answered. "And I already have a surprise planned for you," she added cheekily.

"What is it?" Kajal stopped eating.

"It's a surprise. Let it be."

Kajal's eyes filled with Nandini's face the last time he had seen it in that men's lavatory. *Of course, she wasn't going to be there for his show.*

* * * * *

20

It was Monday. Steve Monday. Since Coventry, it had become the hugest thorn in my flesh.

My second research project, set in Ealing on the outskirts of London, was coming to a close. The earlier venture had just been accepted for publication by a major journal.

My imminent departure from London was in the air. Time had flown. People were finding the 'it's a shame you won't be around for the summer' kind of things to say to me. True enough, spring was palpably on its way.

The knocking on my door was feeble. I was out on the balcony, smoking. I wasn't expecting any one.

When I opened the door, Q stood calm. Like she was suspended mid-air on a cobweb. She had dressed. Like she always did on the Mondays and Tuesdays. And after all that time, she still stole a breath away.

Without moving from the door, and with Q still in the corridor, I, most discourteously, looked at my watch. Just after ten. The time belonged to Steve.

"Can I come in?" Q spoke like she'd borrowed someone else's voice.

"Yes….yes, of course." I stepped aside to let her in.

"Are you busy?" Q asked me.

"No, not really." I had grown comfortable with Q being the propellant of our interactions. Her tentative deportment that evening made me immediately uneasy.

Her eyes fell on the laptop. "Do you have the net?" I nodded. "Can I check mail?" I removed a tee shirt from the chair to let her sit at the table.

An awkward stillness took root and rapidly grew into a vine in my room as she surfed the net for about half an hour with apparent lack of purpose, trailing links like she was on a vacation.

I stepped onto the balcony and lit a cigarette – I had just smoked one and wasn't really dying for another but I didn't seem to have anything else to do.

"Give me a drag no, *kanjoos*," Q screamed out.

I walked back and passed her the fag apprehensively. I didn't like people smoking in my room. I didn't do it myself. Q took a long drag, right there sitting at my table and handed the cigarette back to me. "Don't get terrorised doctor, the fire alarm won't go off. You'll need to touch it with fire for that. These are actually thermal sensors and not smoke detectors," Q spoke dismissively, like she was irritated by something.

I started to head back to the balcony.

"Can you sit here and forget your dumb cigarette!" Q gave me a start. She pushed the laptop away – spoiled by the stoppers at its base, it only jerked violently. Her eyes followed me as I obediently stubbed the cigarette in the ashtray and sat down at the edge of the bed. Q turned the chair so we were face to face.

"I just feel so wrecked. I can't believe it." Q spoke up suddenly. I didn't know what she was talking about. "Fuck! I can't believe it." She kicked the nearest table-leg.

I kept quiet.

"Don't you have anything to say?"

I looked at her face. She seemed to have shriveled. Some dreadful privation had soiled her pretty face unsightly. Tears brimmed over in a lush stream. These were different from the tears I had seen her cry at Coventry. "What's going on?" I finally asked her.

"It's Steve."

I had lived my life well. Or so I thought. Concert of providence, education and hard work had given me meaning, purpose and had even put me in a position of resourcefulness to others. But who could have known that everything I ever possessed was to be mislaid that blustery night?

"He just ended it. Just like that, he just let me go. Far from the Madding Crowd!" Her tears flowed freely even as a sentinel draft of alarm ruffled me. "I have never ever questioned him. But what was I supposed to do? How long did he think I could carry on like this?"

I was losing track. Till that evening, I had no inkling of what I was about to hear Q tell me. "What do you mean?" I asked Q.

"You don't know doctor. Steve and I were seeing each other." Q spoke with bitterness. It hit me like a bolt. For a moment, I felt nothing. I hadn't, in the least, suspected anything like that. Yes, there were the jealousies, but they were resident in every other name Q ever told me. What Q had just told me was altogether different.

"But his wife?" My follow-up question came mechanically.

"I know it doesn't even make sense. God, how did I ever get me into this mess?" Q was restless, her face sour.

I lit a cigarette. In my room, sitting on my bed. She carried on.

"He didn't hide anything from me. The very first few occasions, we actually only talked about his wife, his children and his home. I was so happy just to listen. Till everything just grew. He told me that he cared for me. He was there whenever I sought him. But his home was sacred. Something I couldn't touch. And I was happy to keep it that way as long as I had that little bit of him.

"And here at Y, in my room, in the different rooms that he checked into on every visit, we owned each other completely. It never seemed a farce." Q paused, and looked at me.

I was quiet. A new emotion was conquering me like burning acid. I feared it was anger. She had stopped crying. She was composed. She carried on.

"I started believing we were special. We even talked about it. And that's what he told me – special. So many years apart in age, so out of the blue it was that we ever even met. He wasn't unhappy in his life. He wasn't searching for anything. But he found me. We just happened. We even joked about how he'd deal with me going away, me seeing someone else, me getting married to someone else. That had always seemed the inevitable reality and we'd be prepared to cope with it like just another event. And we both concluded that we'd keep ourselves special forever. Hide it away like some stolen treasure that was only for us, not for the world to know. It seemed so simple, so easy, so blessed. And then we'd kiss. And tell each other we'd keep pilfering these moments from our lives for as long as we lived. It really felt like we could. What fools we were."

She took a deep breath. I walked to the cabinet under the sink and poured myself a JD. I didn't offer Q, but brought the bottle to the table, so she could help herself if she liked. Back to my spot on the bed, I lit another cigarette. I picked a slight tremor in my fingers. Q carried on. Telling me seemed to soothe her. By then, her rhetoric was almost without sentiment.

"But the whole situation was making me increasingly edgy. You will understand. I started needing more. I needed to see a more definite end point. The dream wasn't enough. Questions took birth. The arrangement began to shame me. I thought I had accepted that I could go on being just 'special'. But suddenly I couldn't. I was in love. And I needed my man. Without strings. Without rules.

"This evening, we met at Jazz After Dark, and there I asked him. I told him he had to take a call. I had somehow trusted that we had both come to the point where a decision was inevitable, and not too difficult make. It seemed so plain that we both needed each other entirely. But when I heard it, I couldn't believe his answer. I couldn't believe that was all there ever was in it for him. There never was anything special. I feel...I feel so cheap, doctor."

And she looked at me with pleading eyes. I looked away and said, "But you should have known."

Q kept quiet.

"What do you want now?" I asked her flatly. I suddenly didn't know what she was doing in my room.

Q kept quiet.

"It's all yours to deal with. You were there with your eyes wide open." My accusing tone flowed with a natural drive I couldn't inhibit.

"Is that all you have to say to me?" Q demanded. And that was like the moment when the levee broke. Questions inundated me. All equally bad, but I selected the worst. "What about Kajal?"

My inquiry confused her. "What about him?" she asked me.

"No, aren't you like close to him as well, leading him up some God-only-knows-where-it-ends trail?" The bitterness was naked.

Q squared up to me. "Doctor, doesn't what I've just told you mean anything to you?"

I had gone deaf. My mind was full of me. Only my thoughts mattered. I reached for the bottle of JD and took a straight swig. If love could bestow divinity, it could also arouse the beast.

"What about Rohan that you couldn't resist spending a night with in a hotel room on a day when hundreds around you died in bomb blasts?" There was this sadistic thrill in rubbing the bomb blasts in. It didn't matter that I had spent the same evening drinking imported whisky at a posh bar. With her.

"And what about Vishesh from the Law firm in Delhi? What about Rishabh at the video firm in Guwahati? What about them all?" I couldn't believe the vengeance pouring out.

I reached to light another cigarette. I couldn't. My left hand, yes the whole of it, shook. It was no mere twitch. It was shaking. Q slapped it hard and the cigarette flew to the floor. "Can you stop smoking so much?" she screamed.

"God! Doctor, how much do you have bottled up? Since when?" Q spoke loudly, histrionically.

"Can we cut the drama?" I said to her face, eyeball to eyeball, my face full of the ugliness of disgust. And I picked up the cigarette from the carpet and lit it. Unlike musical scores, when conversations find their crescendos, heaven becomes a poisonous cranny.

"What do you want to know?" Q asked me. My outburst had reduced her to sobbing again. Not so much with sadness, more in desperate defenselessness. "And can you stop smoking?" And she slapped my trembling hand again. The cigarette went flying. I hastily retrieved it, scared that the carpet would catch fire, and stubbed it out. I had that much insight.

"Nothing." I answered.

"No, don't fool yourself. You do want to hear it all," Q snapped back, speaking fiercely.

We shouldn't have crossed that line. Postcards from the past are best left buried. Never challenge your strength – you won't know when it gives way.

"Yes, I was seeing Vishesh. Everyone knew us for a couple. It seems so distant now, it's almost like it had never happened. But at that point in time, there was no doubt that we were destined for life. Till I screwed up." She stopped.

She wasn't going to tell me anything more. But I had tasted blood, as it were. I'm not sure if I even wasn't enjoying it at some level. Her face was full of sincerity, clear it was that she relied on me to understand. But in those couple of hours, I had changed as a man. Incapable of kindness. Full of loathing and misanthropy.

"And how did you *screw* up?" I wasn't giving up, and most distastefully emphasized the 'screw'.

She took a deep breath.

"Vishesh had gone to Ahmedabad for a client meeting. Arjun, a colleague, asked me out for a drink. Vishesh, Arjun, me – we were all one big gang and we went out together at least once every week. That night it became very late and we both got very drunk. We were laughing, joking, talking general nonsense. I wasn't guarding against anything. I was relaxed. When Arjun started reaching for me, I still didn't think anything of it. He tried to kiss me a couple of times." She paused. "And then I don't know what came over me but I kissed him back." She took a deep breath. Telling me was like living through it again for Q. "We quickly realized what had happened. A moment of indiscretion." Her shame, her remorse was plain, only I couldn't see it. "This never happened, okay – That's what he said. I agreed." Shifting in her chair she went on, "But I couldn't live like that, holding a secret that Vishesh deserved to know. When Vishesh returned, I confessed, trusting he'd understand. But he couldn't take it. That's it, we're over – I can still hear his voice in my ears. I left the law firm and came to Guwahati."

"And his mail?" Q didn't immediately fathom my question. "The day we met at SixtyNine, just before you left for London," I explained.

"You remember everything, don't you? He had written to me in two years. He told me how he hadn't been able to get over us. He was willing to give us a second chance. I didn't know what to tell him. I mentioned that I was going to be in Delhi shortly and we planned to meet up. I was happy myself. Not because I had started seeing us together again. But the way we split had always troubled me. I hadn't cheated on him. If his mail proffered a second chance, it was at finding a closure to take us to a civil conclusion. We couldn't be together. In those two years, Rishabh had come into my life."

"But you were so thrilled, bubbling like an excited bottle of cola that you were going to be spending time with Vishesh. You even changed your departure from Guwahati." Why was Q submitting herself to my sarcasm? She failed to notice how dwarfed I had become by horror and anger.

"Was I?" she asked innocently, even smiling a bit. "But I met him just that once in Delhi, and that isn't like spending time, is it? My sudden departure had nothing to do with him. Guwahati had become unlivable on a different count."

It was past two in the morning. The bottle of JD was spent. But I still had cigarettes and it didn't matter anymore where I smoked them.

"Rishabh was a very different person. He wasn't just laid back, he was a sloth. Working at a video editing firm and he had already achieved too much at twenty five, there was no other place he could think of being. You could tell right away that success to him was a *samosa* and a cup of hot *chai*. That's all he wanted in life.

"But he grew on you. Quietly. Affably. Till you started looking for him. You must have him around, and you start missing him when he's not. And he was there. When I started needing him. The man of my dreams was intelligent, ambitious and a reasonable achiever, someone I could learn from and respect. The alpha-male, you could say. Rishabh was the exact opposite. But defying all reason, I had fallen in love with him. There could be no doubt. Once again, I was surrounding myself with a cloud of dreams.

"It was the most pleasing time of my life. Vishesh had kept me on my toes, leaving me high strung. I loved it then. But with Rishabh, I was completely relaxed. The entire space around us was only mine. He slowed my life down to a most serene pace. I hadn't realized before him how edgy I had always been. Rishabh was like one of those *Art of Living* sessions – only I had it twenty four seven three six five, and free.

"Then I found out about Dad's illness. Rishabh absolutely broke down. For him, my leaving for London was the equivalent of us breaking up. He failed to realize that my father was dying and everything else simply had to wait. At a time when *I* perhaps needed support, he returned incapable of providing any. I had to be the one talking him out of *his* desolation, day in and day out. Can you imagine? – I'm trying to deal with Ramalingam uncle telling me about Dad, then I'm told that I can't share the load with anyone, then I have to hunt down a good enough reason double quick to be in the UK because Dad wouldn't let me come down to *merely* nurse him. Rishabh was the only one I had told about Dad, but he brought me such drama that I just didn't have the energy for.

"He started turning up at home – late, drunk and a tearful wreck. I felt sad for him. I felt responsible. But how could I help? I asked him to come with me to London, but he wouldn't.

"I left the job. I was anyway going to but Rishabh forced me to hurry up.

"When I came to London, I'd also brought this resolve to stay away from relationships. But when Steve happened, I was once again at a loss for control."

Q stopped. It was three in the morning. I was washing my face in the basin. "You know it all now," Q said, looking at me. I turned the tap closed. For a while the sound of the water still trickling down the plumbing remained as I dried my face on my shirt sleeve. Q kept looking at me. Like she was waiting for my verdict. But I wasn't through examining her.

"Where's Rohan in this tale?"

"Rohan!" Q exclaimed. "There's nothing with Rohan." The name brought her relief. The worst was over.

"Rohan and I are buddies from school. That's all. I swear to you there never was anything more. I was just thrilled to see him after all those years. I was in such high spirits that evening. I don't know why, and I don't know if you will believe it, but I was actually very happy about meeting you." She looked at me with candid eyes. If she wanted to see me pleased, I couldn't give it to her. "He'd gifted me a scarf. I had left it behind when I rushed down to meet you. I only went back to pick it and say goodnight. I wasn't there longer than ten minutes after you left."

The emotion changed again. From fear and anger. For the first time, I didn't believe Q. I suspected that she was lying. And I had no way of confirming. It was just her word. Suddenly, that didn't seem enough.

"And Kajal?"

"What all do you keep thinking doctor?" Her voice was a mix of persuasion and restlessness. "He's just a friend. And I enjoy doing the arty stuff with him. That's all. And anyway, as much as it baffles me now, all this time, I've been in love with Steve. Or are you suggesting that I've been two timing?"

Two timing wasn't on my mind. Not in so many words. But hearing her say it, it didn't seem improbable. What had she become to me?

"What doctor, say something." Q implored.

"Don't you think this whole thing is a man too many. You are what – twenty five, twenty six?"

Q replied calmly, thinking behind every word. "Do you think it's a disease? Is there a name for it? I feel scared and restless when alone. I've always needed people. And it's always been men. I feel protected by their strength.

"I can't sleep. I feel claustrophobic. It's just so necessary for me to have something going on. Then it doesn't even matter what it is that I am doing. What I do is completely decided by who I'm with and what *he* wants to do. I just hang there, ever grateful to him for being there. I must return to my room only when dead sleepy, otherwise, my mind is twitching with fear.

"This then creates a pattern. I end up spending loads of time with that *one* person. And before I know it, I'm completely dependent on him. And I construe that's love.

"Come to think of it, why was I with Arjun in that pub till that late when Vishesh was away? I swear to you I kissed him back for I thought I owed it to him for being with me.

"You remember the time we went for a drink after your video? I remember it so clearly. When we finished work, I was filled with sudden dread. I didn't want to go home. So I led you to the drink. You were willing. And that's another thing – I've always found willing men. But when we finished at the bar, it was still too early for me. Just before we left, I went to the ladies' room. There was no one else there and the thought of being alone hit me in a big way. I called Rishabh and arranged to meet him. After you dropped me, I went to his place and was there till about three in the morning."

She paused. For the first time that evening, she seemed completely at ease.

"You know doctor, I had never put these thoughts together in my mind. I feel so rested talking to you tonight. That's what you've always done for me doctor." She smiled fully. But I was a wall she had lost every footing on. Doubt crept back to her face. "Yes, it does sound like I have shamelessly used men. But I swear to you, to every one of these relationships I've given one hundred percent. I was thrilled that I had finally found it. I had seen children, and my own old age nested in some sacred alcove."

I still had nothing to say.

"Do you think it could have something to do with my upbringing? That my fears, and the security I find with men, stem from the fact that I've grown up without a male presence? I hate to blame either Mama or Dad, but do you think that has a role to play? Not that it matters. I am who I am and I just have to sort out."

When I didn't fill in for a long while, Q took it upon herself. "I'll come around doctor. I'll be strong. I'll make you proud of me." *Why was she telling me that? Who was I?*

And then she said that one thing that should have captured my life completely like nothing else existed.

"I love you, doctor." Q said.

But that night it was like a headlight in dense fog – smudged, bloated and disfigured. It left me confused. All her words from the preceding hours were running amok in my brain, turning it into a treacherous mine field. That night when Q told me that she loved me, it did sound bad.

"I think we need to sleep." That's all I said.

"Can I sleep here?"

I got up from the bed. She stood up from the chair. And just as I was hurriedly removing myself from her immediate vicinity like I was scared of catching her disease, she held me. Sinking into me, she held me tight. Meaning nothing, I sent my arms lightly around her. "Please cure me. I won't let you down." Her whisper was warm in my ears. "Come," I said, and I put her in bed.

She curled up into the foetal position and was asleep in the next instant.

It was five in the morning.

———

I sat on the floor, paralyzed. My back burned against the room heating panel but I did nothing about it. I was a Panini getting grilled on one side. I visualized the dark brown pattern of lines forming on my back. The rest of me was cold. Like oil and water, the heat from my back and the cold of the rest resisted mingling.

I felt a shiver. Was it fever? I touched my forehead with the back of my right hand. It felt hot. But then my hand was frozen. Its reading couldn't be trusted. But it did feel nice. The cold hand. Over my gritty, burning eyes it was a balm. Over my cheeks it was a soothing splash.

I looked at my left hand. It lay in innocent quietness. Tired perhaps. It needed to rest. It baffled me.

What was going on? It had never happened before. For a good half hour, my left hand just shook. Like it was experiencing a localized epileptic attack. My knowledge of medicine deserted me. I couldn't explain it. And it hurts one immensely to not be able to explain a phenomenon. And it was my own body. I could only wait for the shaking to die. It did. In about half an hour.

The noise arrived on the street below. It was the trash-truck. It was six o'clock. The truck was always on time. From my room, still palely lit by the single lamp over the washbasin like it had been the whole night, I knew exactly how the morning looked at that time beyond the thick curtains.

I looked at Q's sleeping face. Serene. Calm. Like a baby that had just had a wet diaper attended.

How easily she slept. Her burden released. But the weight of one's life cannot be destroyed altogether, it can only be shifted. Her life lay scattered in my room for me to pick up, inspect and clear. By the time she woke up, there would be none of it left.

Did I grudge her peace? I shouldn't have. I loved her. She had confessed to me and I should have stormed in to take charge. Maybe issued a couple of harsh words. But then been there for her. At the end of it all. Forever. But at that moment, I resented her undisturbed sleep while I occupied that ghastly floor. The more I thought about it, I seethed with anger. I pictured myself dragging her out of bed and throwing her out of my room.

From the very first few moments, this woman had seemed like the answer to my vision of love. And circumstances had nourished it. Why was it all getting drowned in the discovery of her limitations? Why was my love incapable of conquering? Or was it that I was incapable of loving?

No, I wasn't going to disturb her. I put my face in my palms and brought it between my knees and sobbed.

I left my room, clicking the door gently behind me. I left the hostel. I started walking. First along Fitzroy Street, then on Charlotte Street till I reached Oxford Street. Then I turned back. Past the ISKCON temple and onto Tottenham Court Road.

I sat on a bench by Fitzroy Square, just outside the hostel. Around me, bright springtime revelry blossomed and the world busied itself in the celebration of another day. It was just another day. But its normalcy seemed so worthy of salutation.

* * * * *

BOOK THREE

The Butterfly Rests

21

Q was queerly excited from the moment she woke up that morning. The energy she felt was a curious brew of satisfaction, thrill and anxiousness. She spent the good part of the day at the SOAS library. She was taking her final exam in two weeks and time was precious. When she left the library at length, she feared she was behind schedule.

As she walked into Heathrow Terminal 3, she was relieved that she'd beaten the arrival by quarter of an hour. She bought herself a coffee and eased into the wait. Her suggestion of the reception at airport had been contested but eventually her doggedness had prevailed.

Her eyes were vaguely sifting through the stores at the terminal when it struck her abruptly. She had forgotten. Not that it was important but she wanted to. From Tie Rack she bought a dark blue tie with bold silver stripes.

———

Some hours later that evening, Kajal returned just in time for dinner at the hostel. He ate quickly, by himself in the after-rush-hour calm of the cafeteria. A distinct memory of the last time he had been that nervous brought a sweat to his palms. That was from another life. Yes, Nandini was there on that occasion.

He went straight up to his room. After two cigarettes and a while of fidgeting aimlessly, it finally dawned upon him that he actually had nothing to do. Nothing could be done anyway, from his room.

He changed and went under his duvet. It was ten. Outside, the light was fading. The day lived really long in July London.

Lying in bed, he ran a quick mental checklist. One last time. The canvas was neatly folded in his studio. Quite a heap it had turned into. The chair, with the platform secured around its base, was in place on the terrace. Along with the length of rope. "It'll be quite the thing of the year, mate," Mel, the woodworks assistant, had announced. Mel had been singularly most helpful, but he yet had a greater service to disburse. Kajal's life, and quite literally, depended on his strength. The pails of paint had been procured. Blue, green and magenta. The colours were Liam's. There was the unresolved matter of the second pump but he had Ed's assurance to rest upon. Kajal hated having to rely on Ed's seemingly meager reserve of dependability but he himself had failed to find another means.

"I'm sorry I can't do it. I'm planning on dressing for the show, I won't come within a mile of any paint," Ed had declined Kajal's other request. "But I'm sure you'll find willing hands," he had added. True enough, Jose and Kevin had excitedly confirmed they'd operate the pumps.

Kajal's 'Artist's Statement' was still at the printers but he had time to collect it in the morning. His was a performance, slated for the evening and was to be assessed only then. Not displayed through the day like the works of the other students. His painting could be performed only once.

Kajal fell asleep. That night before his Degree Show. Unaware of what the next day was destined to bring to him. Unaware of Q's secret little sideshow.

———

The all important weather didn't let down as a proud sun announced occupancy of the sky early, even turning a dash hot, with the temperature touching seventeen degrees by noon.

Both the Byam Shaw and Elthorne buildings were a born-again sight. Year after year, they put on that look for the Degree Show. It was more a festival, not so much an exam, even though some hundred students across different courses were to get assessed.

The frontage and common areas were shining faces of neatness. All evidence of incomplete work, all the rubbish and discards generated in the frantic lead up were gone. Not a sniff of sawdust, not a drop of outlying paint, not a strand of loose wiring, not even a stray cigarette butt remained. It was a miracle, but it had been achieved.

Inside, the corridors and studio spaces were straight out of a top end gallery. The walls were dazzling white, the floor proficient grey – both freshly painted by the students themselves.

The exhibits – all from paintings to sculptures to installations to videos – stood skillfully oriented. Innovatively designed visiting cards and 'Artist's Statements' were placed in critically positioned acrylic boxes. The student's eye for such detail in utilizing studio space was important to the assessment.

By three in the afternoon, the carnival came of age. The arrivals – friends, well-wishers and family – a trickle that soon became an overpowering assembly. Within the next hour, it was choc-a-bloc. Students guided tours for family and friends, starting with their own spaces. When they finished, they congressed in the common areas till they all burst out. First, onto the immediate front vicinage of the two buildings. By four in the evening, the hundred metres of street between the Byam Shaw building and Elthorne Studio was a stream of human heads.

The students themselves were a revelation. From the way they carried themselves through the year, one wouldn't have suspected them capable of turning out the way they did. Ladies in gowns and dresses, even flowers in some hair, and the men all neat and smart. Some of them went through minor identity crises – like Ed, who had shaved, had gathered his crazy locks into a tidy ponytail and was wearing a black suit, frilly white tuxedo and a black bow tie like he'd come to collect the Golden Globe or something! No wonder he wanted to have nothing to do with paints that evening. And yes, he did deliver the second pump that Kajal needed.

Kajal himself was in blue jeans, a white shirt and a pair of black boots.

The courtyard in Byam Shaw was the hub – complete with food and beverages stalls. Hotdogs, burgers, salads. And beer and wine. Had to be bought, but were underpriced. Coronas for a quid and smoked salmon for three.

The day had started early for Kajal. After a quick breakfast, he was in his room at the YMCA and readying to leave when Q came by. "All set, painter boy?"

A flash of déjà-vu caught Kajal. It was Nandini asking him. "All set?" Before his first Prof at med school. "I don't know," Kajal replied nervously.

"Still trying to be modest, eh?" Q attempted to lighten the mood. "I have no doubt it will be grand." She wasn't sure at all. But she fervently hoped he'd do well for the surprise she already had in place for him. "When do I come?"

"I'm scheduled at five."

———

At half past four, Kajal was on the terrace. With him, Mel. They put down the immense canvas they were carrying.

Kajal looked over the low wall. Four Elthorne Studio floors below him was the crowd. Cheerful, mingling, celebrating in the afterglow of hard work. Unknown to them, Kajal was about to embark on a defining moment of his life.

Kajal felt dizzy. Heights always did that to him. But Liam had insisted on scale. When Kajal figured how best to bring that element of awe into his otherwise understated paint-work, he could let nothing come in the way. But just then it occurred to him that he had never rehearsed. Suddenly, he wasn't all that sure.

"Let's go mate." Mel helped him recover. As they proceeded, Kajal's mind thankfully blanked out. It's a blessing when you're an unthinking robot.

With the thick ropes that Kajal had passed through at six places, they tied the top end of the canvas to the drilled-in iron pegs on the flat of the half wall of the terrace.

Then they heaved the canvas and let it fall across the front of the building. It unfurled. Bounced and fluttered briefly before finding rest. It reached to metres from the ground. As it cut out the brilliance of the sun, every floor inside the building was reduced to artificial light.

It caught the innocent spectators below completely unawares. A cumulative gasp. And then a fleeting moment when you could have heard a pin drop.

"Showtime!" A rant rang out loud.

Then claps, whistles, murmurs and laughter. Enthusiasm was copious that evening and it spread like an outbreak. An act was unfolding.

Up on the terrace, "All right, let's go," Mel shouted.

The chair was balanced on the parapet wall. Then they passed the thick rope through the pulley. On the platform Kajal had built around the base of the chair, they loaded the buckets. Twenty six of them. One hundred and thirty litres of paint. And much more from the pumps below.

Then, to a second loud gasp from the crowd below, Kajal, by then the point of everyone's resolute attention, climbed the wall and eased himself into the chair. And just before he kicked the building away to suspend himself in air, Mel confirmed, "I'll let you down every two minutes." And then he screamed, "Hang in there mate." Kajal didn't doubt Mel's strong arms. And while Mel controlled the rate of descend, the rope was eventually secured to an iron post on the terrace – so Kajal wasn't exactly going to crash four floors below even if Mel slipped up.

In the silence, there was finality about the pulley turning slowly as Mel lowered him, its grating sound completely filling Kajal's head like an echo in an empty, furniture-less room. The taut rope scraped the edge of the wall, discharging a fine dust.

Mel stopped. It was the first stop. This was it! Kajal closed his eyes and took a deep breath. There just below the top of a midline through the canvas. Time for work.

Reaching for the first bucket, Kajal swung it to his right and deposited its contents on the white canvas. The splash and then the drip. Magenta.

From below, a cheer rang out!

Then a second bucket. The swing wider, cutting a huge arc to his left. Blue.

And then the pumps opened from below. The two of them.

The immediate crowd dispersed to protect itself. *Beware of Wet and Falling Paint!* Even though Kajal's signpost had been neglected, it covered any legal hassles.

In two lush jets, the powerful pumps deposited paint on the canvass. Starting at the top, the trajectories were adjusted so that the paint rapidly marked out the entire extent of the canvas. Then once again. And then once more. The splash and then the drip.

Kajal meanwhile continued. Splashing his buckets. Left and right. While Mel steadily lowered him.

The pumps shifted gears. The jets were thicker. More laden. And when the paint made contact, the blisters formed. Those blisters. Massive blisters. And they exploded. The small ones held shape. Then a few of the bigger ones sagged but did not break.

Mel stopped rolling out from above. It was a stop. And Kajal was caught in the gush from one of the pumps. The jet didn't adjust. Mel didn't shift him. Kajal was obstructing the paint and its force rocked him gently. And on the canvas, a Kajal shaped negative space, complete with the chair, rapidly took form. It wasn't planned. The artist was an undeniable watermark in the painting, not a mere supplier of material!

But then the drip from all the paint above and the spray from the bursting blisters wiped it. The artist had no place in what nature created. He was only a device. Transient. Like the pumps. Like the pulley. Like Mel's strong arms.

The crowd, clapping, whistling and cheering, split into two, to offer Kajal passage after he disembarked from the chair. No one wanted to venture near him – he was a warty green crocodile like some over made-up, slimy silver screen alien.

"What was that, boy? You fucking son of a gun froze my blasted breath!" Ed rushed out of the crowd and gave Kajal a tight hug before lifting him off the ground. They lost balance and fell, Ed on top. He sat on Kajal's chest, screaming, "Confess it was all my idea or I squeeze the life out of you!" They both rolled again once more, laughing. Then they stood up.

"Your suit?" Kajal asked when he got his breath back. Ed's black suit was soiled green.

"You get to buy me another!"

Just then the rest of the crowd fell in. A whole lot of expensive dresses picked up lavish blotches of green. But suddenly, all caution belonged only to the wind. Bottles of Corona ejected beer like champagne. Then it was a salad slinging-fest. Someone emptied a bottle of red wine on Kajal's head. It was a chaotic celebration.

In its midst, Kajal, the artist was born. As much as he was anesthetized to its effect, he felt it slowly rising inside. He looked up at the canvas. The riot of colours, drying but still dripping. The blisters that had survived till then were unlikely to burst. But they'll keep changing and by the next morning, it will all be different. The chair was gone. Further up on the edge of the terrace, no rope, no pulley remained. Mel had cleared up. He could be down somewhere around him. Of course he was – the very next instant Kajal heard him, "Seems like I'm the only one that missed it." "Thank God for Youtube, Mel!" someone replied.

Away from the immediate crowd, Kajal spotted Liam. Standing next to him was Dr. Helen Luthert, Director of Byam Shaw. From the distance, Liam put forth a thumbs-up and mouthed a well done. Kajal tipped his head slightly. Liam smiled. And so did Dr. Luthert.

In time, the frenzy cleared and the party moved elsewhere. Kajal wasn't the only occasion that evening. Things turned sober. And voices fell out from the roar. The comments. The conversations.

"That was one helluva way to paint!"

"What are you trying to convey?"

"It was the element of shock. Without it, the drip of gravity would have gone unnoticed." Someone had got the crux.

"Who's your tutor?" Kajal didn't leave that unanswered.

And some unpleasant ones.

"It's just gimmick. I hate to think what's going on in the name of art these days. Where was the painting?"

"I swear it was such a stunt."

Kajal was in public domain. All the reaction couldn't be positive. Just a few months ago, he would have shuddered from its effect. But not anymore.

––––––––

Against the red brick wall some paces away, Q stood very still.

It fell out of the sky. Q looked up. She watched it shower and drench her. The calm it brought to her was without equal, was nothing like she had ever thought existed. It dribbled from the ends of her long hair, from the tips of her fingers, from the summit of her nose, and streamed down her rarest crevices to grow roots that bound her to the innermost strength of the earth. For the first time in her life, she stood very still.

Watching Kajal walk towards her with reluctant self esteem, she swallowed a lump. It wasn't the breathing, it wasn't the heart. Life needed a reason to go on. The reason didn't need to own you. The reason needn't be yours.

And Q broke free. It was only freedom that she ever needed. And suddenly there was no conflict that weakened her from within. It had all just been a waste of precious time and she couldn't wait another moment to take every contest by its neck. She was bathed. She loved feeling clean.

Kajal smiled at her. When Q smiled back, she captured all the art all around. Kajal held back a tear. *He had redeemed Nandini. Where was she?*

And then Kajal's eyes fell on them. They were right next to Q all the time, but his unsuspecting eyes had failed him. He blinked stupidly. No, it was no vision. Kajal froze, and then recovered just as soon to reach for them. Q and the two of them. The little surprise that Q had promised. She always kept her promises.

Baba was dressed in a black suit. Kajal didn't recognise it from before – it was new. And on his white shirt, he wore a very contemporary looking dark blue tie with bold silver stripes. It was the kind of thing that sons and daughters gifted their fathers.

Ma was wearing a white *Paat* silk *mekhela sador* with work in silver.

Together they looked like they'd stepped out of the framed picture from their wedding on top of the refrigerator back home.

Baba smiled at him. It conveyed satisfaction. Approval. It was no big deal that a doctor couldn't hand over his stethoscope to a son. The son was meant for a different world. And if medical science makes a difference to people, there are other avenues of touching lives.

Kajal was still a couple of steps from them. But Ma couldn't hold back anymore. "That was so risky! You could have fallen any moment. And I thought I was coming to an art exhibition. There surely must be safer ways to paint."

"Ma..."

But before Kajal could complete, he was intercepted. By a slightly funny looking, squirmy man with a disheveled thatch for hair.

"Hi, I'm Sid. I'm with the Lisson Gallery. Great act, Kay-jul."

"Thanks Sid."

"I don't want to stall no celebration. I'll keep this short. On behalf of the gallery, I'd like to offer you a show. A solo exhibition." Sid fished out his card, and laying it on Kajal's hand said, "Give me a call Monday, and we'll chalk out some preliminary details. I'd say we're looking at sometime next January." Kajal didn't have a place to stow the card – there wasn't a clean bit on him. Q came forward and took it. "Enjoy the evening," Sid disappeared.

It was a minor history of sorts. Never before had a Byam Shaw student been offered a solo exhibition, let alone by a prestigious gallery, based on a Degree Show performance!

Kajal looked at Q.

* * * * *

22

"Come Baby, let me show you the new cabin."

Ramalingam escorted Q down the carpeted corridor to her room at its end.

"Uncle, you can't be calling me Baby here in office!" Q complained.

"Allow me a learning curve on that." And then he quickly added, "I promise to clear that hurdle the minute you call me Mr. Ramalingam." Q made a face.

He opened the door and looked at Q, "There. Do you like it?" He remained at the door as Q stepped in.

The curtains were apart and a late August sun tenderly filled the room. Q stepped in and with her eyes closed shut, took a deep breath. Audibly. The air was fresh, cold and had that familiar scent. It was the air her Dad had breathed for the twenty years that he had operated out of that chair which stood vacant and ready for the new occupant.

After Mama and she left – it wasn't apparent to little Q at that time why they were leaving and what it meant to be leaving – she'd return to spend a part of school holidays in Coventry. That very room was where she spent most of her time. Dad never asked to be left alone. Important meetings took place while she drew with her crayons in one corner. She had grown up simultaneously – in Delhi with Mama, in that room in Coventry with her Dad.

When she was older, she came to prefer the variety of London over the small-industrial-town monotony of Coventry. Dad took time off, and for three four days, it was just Q and him. First London; the next year Scotland; then Warsaw and Prague, Paris and Amsterdam; Istanbul and the fiords in Norway; then they turned inward and discovered the charm of small English villages.

From the time she was fifteen sixteen, Dad insisted that she came to office. And when they finished, he'd take her out to meet people. What she was being groomed for she didn't understand. For never ever was she going to have anything to do with that Coventry office.

"This room is like completely new. It's great. Thanks. But I really should have had a tiny table next to yours' uncle."

"I'm right here, Baby. You take your time getting into these shoes you'll need to wear for a long time, much longer than I will ever be around."

"Uncle, did you have to say that?"

"Okay, okay. I'm sorry and I pledge to be around forever." Ramalingam spoke with a chuckle. "But right now, I have to run to a meeting. It's that Rolls Royce thing I'd told you about. We could close the deal today. It might be the first deal that you sign on!" Ramalingam had been steadfast in insisting that the authority to represent the company passed directly to Q after Dad. "Do you think she's ready?" "I'm there," Ramalingam had assured Dad.

"I'll tell you more when I return. Till then, feel at home."

"I guess my only contribution to the important meeting will have to be my best wishes."

"Thanks Baby. That'll go a long way!"

Ramalingam closed the door behind him.

Alone, Q looked around. Walking behind the table, she sank into the high backed leather chair. Her mother and she herself looked back at her from a photo frame in front of her. *How on earth does a child get into a father's shoes?*

She looked to her right. There was a corner with two cushioned chairs and a coffee table. On the wall behind, Ramalingam had hung the two paintings. When she had sent them over from London, she didn't exactly think they belonged to her office. But seeing them just then, a warm thought filled her.

Kajal. It seemed just like yesterday.

It was after the Degree Show, a few days before her own final exam. Kajal had returned from clearing out his studio space and had come to her room at the YMCA late in the night.

"I came earlier. You were not in."

"I was in the library at school. My exam starts in two days, Kajal."

"I want you to keep these," Kajal said stiffly, altogether ignoring the issue of her exam.

"What's this?"

"They are for you."

Q tore off the brown paper. "Your paintings!" she exclaimed.

"Just two of them. I'll be happy if you keep them." Kajal helped her with ripping the rest of the cover, and placed the canvases against the wall. "Do you like them?"

"Of course, I love them! But these are valuable, Kajal."

"Not yet. But one day soon you won't be able to afford them!" Kajal grinned naughtily.

Q reached out and lightly touched his face. "I'm sure, painter boy. But don't you dare forget me when you become famous."

"You know Ma insisted that I bring these to you. Every other crap from my studio that I was going to throw away, she's actually getting shipped back home! Can you even believe it?"

Q found herself standing next to the two paintings on the wall of her office room. She stared at them a long time. Yes Kajal was on his way to becoming famous. In his last mail he had written about the prestigious congress in Delhi where he had been invited to run a workshop. Then there was the exhibition in Pune. And come January, he was slated at the Lisson in London. He was working hard. Making new work.

Kajal really sucked at getting a handle on the matter of the time zone. His calls kept finding Q at weird hours in London. "Sorry, were you sleeping?" Q smiled to herself at the thought of his awkward voice.

"What did you expect Kajal? It's like three in the night here. You should know that. How hard is it really to take five hours off your time and work out mine?" Q'd reply back with soft sternness.

"Sorry, sorry, go back to sleep. I'll talk to you in the morning."

"Was there something?" she'd ask him sleepily, knowing completely well that there never was anything.

"No no, nothing at all. Just like that I called. I worked through the night. Guess I myself will get some sleep now. I'll call you in the morning, your time."

"Can you stop talking so much? Just go now." And Q'd hang up. And like she knew he wouldn't, he never called the next day. Or even the next couple of days. But it didn't matter. Nothing made her restless anymore.

Ma. Those three days that she spent with Ma and Baba came back to her. Ma was an absolute doll. Q's face broke into a smile as she remembered what Kajal had told her later, after Ma and Baba had left London. "You know Ma thought you and I were together. You know, like seeing each other. She was so disappointed when I told her no. And then she tried talking me into it. She kept telling me what a great person you are, and what a great match we'd be. She's so childish. She's like she likes someone I'm with and she immediately gets ideas!"

"I'm sure I'm a thousand times better than all your other girlfriends that scared the life out of her!" Q had jeered.

Two days after her exam, Kajal was leaving London. They had met for dinner. Q had brought him to Gordon's in Embankment. It was Steve and her place. It had become sacred, and then she'd grown scared of it. She hated her life to be plagued by such landmarks. Kajal was going to help her move on.

That night Kajal had opened himself like he had never done. "You know there was someone. Nandini." And then he had told her everything. "I don't know what all this means now. But I wanted you to know."

Q walked across to the open window. Outside was a patch of green and the paved parking lot beyond. Three pigeons waddled about. Pigeons in the UK are so fat they have altogether lost the ability to fly! The office cars with the company logo stood in the parking lot. Her life was not purposeless. She belonged to her Dad's dream. She felt happy. That Kajal and she had each other. Uncorrupted. Unnamed. *Special.*

———

Dad continued downhill. With every passing day, he died a little bit more. But not enough. Q found it hard to believe. For she truly trusted that the world had long arrived on a platform where nothing was impossible. Dad had a diagnosis, everyone concerned seemed to understand the very minute details of what was happening to him. And yet there was no help. They could only mutely see him go through the symphony of death unfurling itself upon him. Inch by inch. Minute by minute.

Was he being punished? The questions scalded Q. What was his crime? So many find things other than family more important in their lives – did they all get castigated with such cruelty?

May be it was time for Mama to arrive. But Dad still resisted that like it was the only thing he remained capable of. "Not before I go." He'd made them all vow. He knew he wasn't just going to walk to the end. He understood he'd lose all control days before. But he was assured by the pledge. Why did he insist? Didn't he see there was no coming back? Didn't he need a closure before he left?

It took only a phone call to break her vow. The phone call Q made every day and talked of things that meant nothing. Mama never asked her how Dad was. It was just her pride. What would she do if she only knew?

Q took her morning mug of coffee to Dad's room. Every day. "How are we feeling today?" She'd ask him gaily. "Better." He'd reply with a weak smile. What did it mean? A dying man was getting better?

"How's office?" Those two words seemed to drain his entire daily reserve of energy.

Q rattled off trivial details with great vigor. Was she still that little girl suitable only for the inconsequential? When she finished, Dad would be asleep again. And she'd quietly depart, leaving him to the care of professionals.

And soon as she left, Dad would come alive with the pain. That unbearable pain. He had never slept.

————

Over the next couple of months, Q submerged into the office with passionate piety. She was a quick learner. And of course there was Ramalingam and the entire team. With her Dad struggling to die, the company was riding strong emotional waves of overzealousness. It had become much more than just a job for everyone.

But the market was tricky. There was something lurking. Ramalingam had been long aware. "It's not the time to rest on laurels. There's big bad weather ahead. I can smell it folks."

There's was the automobile sector. But they said the real disease was in housing. Something was going wrong. No one knew exactly what. Not even Ramalingam. "I have a hunch it's all those city workers with their fat bonuses who pop out of the Ivy league with Phds and what have you, and think they know all about the market at twenty five."

————

Early in December, Dad had to be shifted to hospital. When he left home that morning, everyone knew the long funeral procession had started.

"There's this clinic in Switzerland...," someone suggested. It was only the voice of a shared thought.

"I know." Q said sternly. It was the famous euthanasia clinic for the terminally ill. But who was she to decide?

She reached for the phone and dialled.

"Hey Baby." Mama's cheerful voice scared her. "No, just saying hi. I've got a meeting. I'll call you later."

"You've become too busy. You have no time for Mama," Mama complained.

Q hung up. It was too late to break a vow.

———

Five days after the new year.

"But uncle, how can I leave now?"

"It's important Baby. Do you think I don't understand? But it's absolutely vital. We can't let this opportunity slip away. It's just four days and I'm here for the meanwhile. I promise I won't budge an inch." Ramalingam convinced Q.

Dad was on the ventilator. She was told both his kidneys had failed, fluid had collected in his abdomen and lungs, he wasn't breathing on his own and his heart was failing. The end was near.

As she waited for boarding to be announced, she expected her phone to ring any moment and bring her the pronouncement. Then she'd cancel the trip and call up Mama.

'British Airways announces the departure of its flight to Singapore. Passengers are requested...'

* * * * *

23

The bright, cheerful day was such a curse. I never imagined I would be bothered by the sun in London.

Through the coat of cigarette smoke on my tongue, my mouth tasted of grime and unslept alcohol. While the rest of the world was spanking new and freshly laundered. I loathed the world for rotating and revolving nonchalantly while I sat on that bench just like the outcast I had become overnight, wondering what wood it was in those benches that stood up to English rains decade after decade.

At eleven, I went back into the hostel. I pushed my door gently. It was still locked. I knocked. Nothing happened. I banged. And I banged again. A beastly fury rising in me.

And suddenly, Q opened the door. Her face a mix of sleep, shock and confusion.

"What happened?" She asked me anxiously.

I walked in past her. The dark interior, the abundant reek of cigarette smoke, the untidy table and the unmade bed immediately dejected me. How could this be my room?

Q closed the door behind us. "You scared me." Her voice was tentative.

I violently drew the balcony door curtains apart. The harsh sun hurt Q's eyes.

"What's going on?" She was annoyed.

I said nothing. My left hand started to shake. I sat down at the edge of the bed. Cautiously. Taking care not to occupy more space than I needed to. The bed had become untouchable. It shook with my shaking. I did nothing about it.

"I'm sorry, I just slept off. What time is it? You didn't sleep? You missed work." Q rattled off, while tying her hair.

I said nothing and sat there displaying my shaking hand like a weapon to hurt her. Maybe I wanted it to shake even more vigorously. So she could feel even more guilty. *Look what you've done to me.*

Q clutched my left arm. "Can you stop doing that?" *No, I can't stop doing that.* I looked at her face. It was filled with anger. I said nothing and turned to stare out of the balcony.

"Huh…" Q took a deep breath of frustration. Her tone weakened, "What doctor, please say something."

My stubborn selfishness was unrelenting.

"I'm sorry for what I told you last night. Are you reacting like this because of all that?"

I didn't answer. *I want you to be sorry for* what *you told me, and not* because *you told me. I want you to plead, beg and cry. I want you to slash your wrists and then become my slave when I tie one of my socks around your bleeding wrist and save your life.* I was ashamed those thoughts were mine. Ashamed even then, not on hindsight. But I could do nothing to stem the gush. I was conquered.

"But I thought you'd understand. I know my past sucks, but I still needed to tell someone." She sat down next to me.

"Just leave." I had spoken for the first time. Big deal! Royal me!

"Don't say that doctor. Doesn't it mean anything that I told you everything?"

So what did you expect? That I'd dance naked in the corridors. I even remember you telling me that you were in love with me. So? I should paint my face like a clown and jump out of the window screaming that my turn has come? Yaa-hoo! Mera *number* aa gaya!

I said nothing. My left arm kept shaking.

"Why are you doing this? How much worse do you want me to feel?"

And then she got up abruptly, and retrieved her jacket and shoes. I felt like a predator about to lose a prized catch that it was toying with before sinking those big ugly canines into. I didn't want her to leave. I wasn't done with her. I wanted her to tell me again, in greater detail, and this time I was going to intrude with my acidic opinion at every step so I could slice her into tiny strips. And then I'd put those strips together so she could live the remainder of her life being incredibly grateful to me.

I sat there watching her leave. As she reached for the door, she turned back and with a face that I wouldn't forget for the rest of my life, she snapped, "I won't come back to haunt you. I'm so ashamed I ever felt anything for you. You know what – the only person you can ever love is yourself. Take good fucking care of yourself. And just stop that shaking. You're not in a movie. No one's watching you."

That was the last time I ever saw Q. Three weeks later, I left London.

————

I didn't think much of the shakes while in London. I had other holes in the head for that while. It was only after I got back to Guwahati that I gave them their due.

The days started with an extra morning hour in bed. Awake, but struggling, begging for some force to pull me out of the grip of images that I had surrendered to.

Q lingered to grow from strength to strength and cement her place in my head till she became a vice, a blight I couldn't live with. Only I didn't know how to stop her from gallivanting quixotically on the landscape of my brain, causing slapstick commotion in her wake. A flower vase knocked over by her hand, a plaster statue pushed over by the other hand. All inside my head.

Sometimes I understood – the past never offers itself to repair. And the past isn't like a stamp of forever – people change. But it didn't last longer than a moment. I just lay there, ghastly images of sordid, vulgar copulation emanating from my appalling thoughts like smoke from a volcano. Like a blender, Q whipped the grey and white load inside my skull into a fine froth.

Most of all, I believe, it was love that vanquished me. How could I have considered one like her? I was disgusted, with myself as much as with her.

And while my mind got ploughed and fresh, new seeds of poisonous mushroom kept finding nourishment, the shakes continued. It was my left side. The left arm mostly, the left leg rarely. I clutched the leg of a chair but that did not reduce the amplitude. I clasped my thigh and even that did not help. I clutched the bed clothes. The vibrations didn't die. I seized the mattress. They persisted. The shakes came and went at will.

My day at work was a relief. Nothing happened. But as it rushed up to closing, I panicked. Like a leaf about to lose its tethering, I fluttered. Like an insect caught in a candle-flame, I singed. I had Q's disease – I was scared of going back home.

I had always cherished my time alone. I'd look forward to finishing my day at work. I'd lazily drive back to my flat. Turn some music on. Cook a meal. A whisky, a book and my chair by the lamp, with the television turned on for its own sake. Just before leaving for London, I had taken to reading Greek philosophy. Then I'd lay a table for one and eat dinner. Than I'd read in bed till I slept.

But my home had become a bloodcurdling dungeon that wrung the breath out of me like an Iron Maiden.

The pattern didn't take long to set in.

I came to a point where the tremulous left hand impinged upon my work. It started occurring as I consulted patients. Even when I wasn't thinking things and independent of the distasteful images. The shakes became an issue in themselves. I could go on with the nonsense in my head, but not with a trembling hand. It needed to be addressed.

A neurologist was my first stop. But examination and tests there returned nothing. It wasn't physical. There was no muscle weakness or neuronal affliction. I was advised to see a psychiatrist.

Convincing myself to seek psychiatric help was an immense hurdle. I confess I did surprise myself with my clichéd predisposition. I had referred my own patients to psychiatrists when the occasion arose and they had sometimes come back to tell me how much it helped. But this was me! And suddenly, I couldn't let it be known. The popular word was mad. What kind of patient would ever come to me, the mad doctor? I was thinking like a mother trying to pawn off her jobless son into a match. It was a secret I had to protect.

I turned to Dr. Jayesh Senapati. Together we zeroed in. I was somatizing. More specifically, suffering a conversion disorder. Textbooks defined it as a state where a subject developed physical attributes following an outstanding mental trauma. Outstanding mental trauma? How lame was I for one individual's frivolousness, completely disconnected from me, to have become capable of inflicting that upon me? Anyway, anxiolytics and sessions of counseling would sort me out.

I found Jayesh's counseling helpful right away. I must confess once again that I had never thought very highly of an idly-didly monologue coming out of the patient towards a passively listening therapist as a treatment modality. But I was in for a surprise. Every session left me feeling immensely wispy for a good while after and seemed capable of putting thoughts into perspective. Slowly, I began to trust it. It promised to work.

But the shakes remained.

Even as I was getting rid of rubbish from my head. At length, I could say, I was perhaps beginning to understand Q. I was able to exempt my mind from unrest on her account. And also, I sensed love exit me. That was such a relief. It didn't matter anymore where Q was, who she was spending her time with, who she was seeing those days. It would be a lie to say that I approved of her ways, or that I trusted she had changed. She just didn't belong to my scheme of things anymore.

But the shakes remained. The fact was – they worsened. They were more frequent.

Jayesh assured me it was a matter of time. I should be kind to myself. I was coming along fine, but was challenging an acute relapse if I pushed too hard.

"But Jayesh, I'm worried about the surgeries. So far, that's the only thing that seems untouched. I hate to think what it will mean if they start getting affected."

"The more you think about it, the more you offer yourself to it. You know it's a vicious cycle."

"I know Jayesh. But what can I help? Isn't there anything else? Electro-convulsive?"

"No, you don't need ECT. Don't be dumb! All you need is time."

"But I'm really scared."

Then Jayesh presented his suggestion. "Why don't you take some time off from your surgeries?"

It lingered in my head after I left him. Break from surgeries. But how? What would I tell my Director? That I couldn't perform surgeries because of a shaking hand. And then my Director would ask me with surprise – what shakes? And I'd have to explain. Then he'd ask me how long they've been around? Why did I not report it earlier, for all the time that I was jeopardizing unsuspecting patients' eyes and a hospital's reputation? And then the big question – when do I come back? Does Jayesh certify that I'm cured and fit to resume? Would that be credible? It was after all no chicken-pox; it was a non-documentable state of the mind.

No, that wasn't an option. That's how I saw it. I gave up then, and I lost them forever. I kept my ailment under wraps and like a thief, sneaked up to steal my surgeries. I knew it wasn't ethical. I knew I didn't have any business carrying on like that. But it was only for a while.

It was near the end of November that I finally lost my job. Finally – because by then it did seem like a long time coming. Yes, I was offered a chance to hang on – stripped off surgeries for an epidemiological researcher's role, on the back of that skill I picked up in London. But I let it pass.

My Director announced it to me. Guiltily. *Why?*

"You'll understand I had no choice. But these doors are open for you." It broke my heart to hear him talk like that. That man meant so much to me. There was something conclusive about that afternoon – there was no triumphant comeback scripted for me.

"You should have hung on to whatever they were offering you. It's vital for your treatment that you have a job to go to, a schedule to follow. All this idle time will undo the progress we've made so far," Jayesh said in all seriousness after I informed him. "Do you want me to talk to your Director?"

"No, Jayesh, don't. I'll be fine. I couldn't possibly carry me down to the hospital everyday to face pitying, questioning stares and struggle with my own feeling of redundancy despite being on a job. No Jayesh, I'm better off outside of all that. I'll go back when you're done with me."

"Your call. But what do you plan to do with your time?"

"I guess I'll write," I informed him. Not that I had given it any serious thought.

"Okay, but don't go writing about all that rubbish in your head. The last thing I want you doing is re-living the last year." Jayesh paused, and after a thoughtful long breath, he suddenly snapped at me, "I'm serious, okay! You're not going to write any of that."

Calming down, he suggested, "Why don't you write something like Harry Potter? The brand's been around long enough for India to produce its own – smarter, more-efficient and cheaper!"

————

It was my thirty-fifth. I drove to Kamakhya temple through the foggy haze of the early January dawn. I hadn't been there on a birthday in a number of years. In my childhood, it was routine – my parents took me up that hill and we bought a pair of pigeons and set them free into the clear blue sky. The skies of yesteryears always seem clearer and bluer than those of the present.

I spent a calm day at home, writing. Yes, I was flouting Jayesh's firm instruction regarding the content but there seemed no harm.

Around eight in the evening, an uncharacteristic urge for activity befuddled me, and I was left struggling with it for a while. At length, I gave in and followed instinct. It was after all my birthday and there could be nothing wrong with indulging a bit. I even felt upbeat with my newfound energy for the world.

I didn't end up in one of my usual places. While I generally enjoyed with unparallel delight the solitude those places offered through a drink, that evening the proposition was unexciting. I wanted to be someplace youthful, loud and hip. Everything has a beginning.

'Couples Only', a sign at entry read. I looked at the smartly dressed but way-too-bony-for-his-job bouncer. "That's only for weekends," he clarified and let me in.

It was crowded. All tables occupied, there were already people on the dance floor. The music was loud contemporary hip-hop or house or whatever else it was called, just like I had expected. The low lighting was pierced by gay spots and rhythmic strobe lights. There was even smoke from a couple of those machines. I wasn't aware Guwahati had come to offer such facilities. A decade ago, when I wouldn't have been such an outlier on the average age plot of the place that evening, nothing like it had existed.

I sat at the bar. It was well stocked but all it seemed to be selling was beer and fancy looking cocktails. I'm sure beer was all the guys could afford after coughing up for the expensive cocktails their dates drank. I asked for JD.

Feeling quite buoyant, I sipped my drink and turned to face the crowd. I quickly settled into one of my favourite pastimes – scavenging faces. There wasn't much variety though. Loud banter, someone desperately resisting getting mauled onto the dance floor, young Turks hassling the women in the group with juvenile innuendos.

I asked for another drink. The thing with drinking whisky without any mix, especially something as smooth as JD, is that you do end up running through your first three, four really quickly.

As the bar guy put my glass down on the branded coaster, I put a cigarette between my lips.

"Sorry, no smoking indoors, sir," the bar guy interjected politely. I was impressed. Sometimes you do feel great with places sticking to rules, especially in a country where violating regulations for no rhyme or reason is seen as VIP behaviour. "Sorry, I didn't know. Can I leave the drink here?" "Not a problem, sir." I was also impressed with the guy's English. The trend of university students part-timing in a pub in Guwahati somehow brought me joy. "What's your name?" I asked him as I left. "Udit," he replied.

As I stepped outside with the dangling cigarette explaining the purpose, the bouncer at the gate pointed to an enclosure to one side, equipped with a couple of switch-controlled lighters and wall mounted ash-trays.

"Hello!" The sudden voice behind me was female, musical, young and good looking.

I turned around to face her. She was pretty and had taken good care to turn out handsomely. She wore a woolen beret at an angle over her length of straight hair. A long slender neck disappeared into a short, well-fitted, dark dress. Further south, she wore dark leggings and a pair of fluffy, tan camel-leather boots.

"Hi," I answered.

"Can I steal one of your cigarettes?" She asked, confident that I won't refuse.

After a drag, she spoke, "Haven't seen you here before." She was one untidy smoker, exhaling out mushroom clouds.

"I don't usually find the time," I told her.

"So what are you – a busy executive?"

"No, I'm a scientist with the meteorological department." Perhaps being jobless and slightly mad, and finding myself in a strobe-lit joint full of twenty year olds was stroking a feral spirit inside me. I felt loosened from all the discipline that I had let choke my existence for as long as I could remember. It felt wonderful being irresponsible.

"Wow, that's so cool. A scientist in a discotheque! So what's the latest – foresee any meteors crashing into Guwahati shortly?"

"That's classified information," I smiled. But very quickly, an annoying doubt crept in. Beside weather and forecasts and cyclone warnings and all that, was studying meteors also on the meteorologist's agenda? If it wasn't, then it was an unnecessarily conflicting nomenclature the science had chosen for itself.

She tossed more than half the cigarette carelessly aside, and then rubbing her hands vigorously, said, "It's cold. I left my coat inside."

She trudged along as we re-entered and shouted over the bawl of the music, "If you're alone, do you mind me joining you for a drink?"

I showed her the bar with a sweeping arm. "Be my guest!"

As Udit returned my earlier drink, I asked her, "What are you drinking?"

She looked at Udit and replied to me, "He knows." He consented and brought her a dark coloured cocktail.

"So, you don't like your wife." I deciphered her need to prelude everything she said with a 'so'.

"Not at all!" I shrieked. "I love her madly. We've been married over ten years now and still can't get out of honeymoon! We are just so much in love it kills us to be apart for even a day." I was relishing the conversation. It brought me great cheer that I didn't have to devote even a fraction of a thought as lies dropped out of my mouth like targetless warheads.

She seemed neither impressed nor disturbed. "So, is she away tonight?"

"Yes," I said as tragically as I could, "She's gone to present her paper at a conference in San Diego. She's not back for a week. Can you even imagine?" I gulped down the JD and asked for another.

"She's also a scientist?"

"Ya," my drink arrived and I took a large sip while my head searched for a profession to assign to my 'wife'. "She's a vet."

"So, it's some animal husbandry at home, yeah!" she sounded awfully pleased with herself for having come up with her wisest crack in decades.

"Her research is really really interesting. She's managed to get some extract out of lizard footpads – you know those famous vacuum ones – that can actually cure Alzheimer's. You know if she gets good reactions at the conference, she might even be in for the Nobel!" I searched her face for any effect. She looked vague. I sensed she was going to excuse herself to go to the ladies' room and never come back. I felt thrilled.

"What's Alz...whatever?" She hung on.

Downing my fifth whisky, I suddenly hopped off the bar stool and started gyrating and singing aloud with the music. Arms half raised and hips cutting small circles, I was unmistakably quite a sight for the oldest man in the house.

Shot through the heart, and you're to blame,
Darling, you give love a bad name.

She sat there with her legs crossed, beaming bemusedly at me. I grinned back and carried on with my clumsy steps, causing a minor commotion at the crowded bar. No one seemed to mind though. The ambient air of elation was overpowering.

Udit put forth yet another drink for me. "Are you keeping a tab – I'll pay at the end?" I shouted out to him. "No hassles, sir." But I wasn't so sure. I took out one of my bank cards and handed it to him. "Just in case I run away!" I winked. And then grabbing a tissue, scribbled my PIN on it and handed it to Udit. "Between you and me!"

When I turned around, she asked me, laughing and clapping, "You want to hit the floor?"

"Why not?" I shouted back, my body immediately dedicated to the irresistible pulsation of We Will Rock You.

On the dance floor, it soon became only me and my limbs. People happily fell back to make room. She gave up being any kind of a partner as I usurped the dance entirely for myself.

Somewhere inside I did recognize the joker I was making out of myself. But most of me felt enormously blissful and relaxed.

"He's a scientist." I heard someone say.

A number ended. But there wasn't a breather. I ran up to the bar and finished my drink. "Great going, sir. Another JD?"

"Yes ten more." I beamed exaggeratedly at Udit before loudly announcing to the crowd, "It's my birthday!" No one believed me, but they all cheered and clapped. "One round for everyone. On me."

"There's no need for that sir. It's a lot of people." Udit cautioned me.

But I was someplace no one could reach me. I had at long last cut myself free and no one was going to spoil my getaway.

I took my face close to Udit's across the bar counter and locking my eyes into his, spoke like I was handling an errant child, "It doesn't matter what you think, Udit or whatever your name is! I said one round for everyone – how hard is that to understand? Now, will you please do us the honours?" Facing the crowd, I shouted, "The party can't wait forever, can it?" It went mostly unheard. A few people offered an incomprehensible chorus of comments. I turned back to Udit, "Man, did you hear that. Now, will you hurry. And take the bill out of my card. I have loads of money that I have absolutely no use of."

I got back to the dance floor. My movements became wilder. I was sweating all over and my white shirt stuck to me. My glasses flew off my nose and landed somewhere in the crowd. I went momentarily blind before a guy returned them. I thanked him profusely.

I smiled at her. Her head fell back as she laughed. I laughed. The music was hip-hop again. *So low low low...* On my heels and bent knees, I lowered myself down, rhythmically with the words. A random partner joined me briefly. Then another one. *So low low low....* My thighs cringed with the unaccustomed posture and my lower back felt stiff. Then I fell. Bottom down. Generous laughter poured all over me. I made a quick recovery.

I swaggered back to the bar and sat on a stool. "Hey Udit, I'm sorry I screamed at you. But you pissed me off big time, man. It's my birthday, dude." I was slurring.

"It's alright, sir." His job obviously brought him my breed one too many every evening.

"No, I insist on being sorry." And then I turned again to the thinning crowd, "Folks, I want all of you to know that I'm sorry for having shouted at Udit." I grabbed him by the shoulder and sort of hugged him sideways across the counter. The few people that still remained had little interest left in my antics.

"Can I get a drink?" I folded my hands jokingly at Udit.

"Rightaway, sir."

"Cut the sir, man. Just call me doctor. That's what they all call me."

"My my, so you are a doctor now? I thought you were a scientist." She came up from behind and climbed on to the stool in front of me.

"Hey, where have you been? I missed you! Doctor, scientist, plumber, mechanic – what does it matter?" My tongue felt like it had a life of its own that was intensely refusing enjoin.

Udit handed me my drink, and, "Last drink, sir. We are closing," he informed.

"I'm sad now. I was really planning to sleep here!" I laughed wildly at my own idea of a joke. "But but but," harnessing the hilarity, I said, "you have to bring one for the lady."

"No, I'm fine." She said. Udit left us.

One sip from my drink – I had lost count – and my head started swimming. I blinked. When my eyes were open again, the world was fuzzy. I blinked again and tried hard to focus. But the fuzz remained.

I turned to her. "I don't even know your name." I talked slowly – tidying up the slur was primary, but I also wanted to slow down the whole evening.

"Like you said - What does it matter? Let's just call me A, B, C X, Y, Z. How about Q?" She answered, smiling at me.

Q. Her voice reverberated in my head. It was a genre, not any one person. The *nom-de-plume*. It was perfect. Like Om, it was a powerful sound. Q. I pitied Ian Fleming for having wasted it on a minor character. Q deserved more. Q deserved the whole story.

I was going to be sick. I rushed to the bathroom.

At the wash basin, I splashed water on my face and wet my hair. I looked at my face in the mirror. Why was I pretending? I had made a perfect fool of myself through the evening. I was perhaps guilty of even scheming to beat a generation in its act. I splashed some more water. I was drunk and incapable of controlling any situation. *Was this how Myrah had felt when she kissed that guy in a bar in Delhi when Vishesh was away?*

As I emerged from the washroom, I just about escaped crashing straight into her standing at the door. *Who was she?* She was a shadow that was beginning to seem familiar. She was a ghost. She had touched my life with her breath when she herself had still been breathing. When she died, I personally put her six feet under. But the ghost? Who was to guarantee that it won't come back?

"Do you have a car?" *It was Myrah's voice with the entire mischievous texture, warmth and moan.* Like a frightening lightning, everything came back to me! I felt weak. *Yes, I had lived Myrah's life that evening. With Myrah.* She had returned. She had to. For she couldn't have just disappeared like she was walking out of a room.

My left hand started to shake.

"Sure do," I replied energetically.

"Let's go then."

"Let's go then!" I said. *I'd been waiting to go for a long time – drive to the edge of the planet with Myrah so we could both topple over. Then we'd both be ghosts, capable of walking through each other untouched.*

We were in my car. Driving through the night streets of Guwahati was indeed a pretty experience. I lowered the window. The cold air outside was a newborn. I gripped the steering wheel tighter. That calmed the left hand. She lowered the window on her side.

"Where do I drop you?" I asked her.

"What's the hurry? Are you scared?" She stirred me. *Myrah always did!*

"No, I have all the time."

"I love the highway at night. I love the quiet, the loneliness. Come on, you are the romantic kind. We can talk about your wife." She spoke dreamily.

"When did I say no?" My mind had completely disentangled. There could be no harm in exploring. I knew her but she didn't know me and neither did she know that I knew her! *Myrah, I am so going to catch you. Then you can never lie to me.*

Driving on empty streets, past darkened homes, offices, vacant plots of land and under-construction high rises, we were soon out on the highway. We were rushing past street lights and soon there were none left. Only occasional trucks prowled the highway at that hour. The dusty eucalyptus trees on the wide divider that one of the cell phone companies had planted to reduce the burden of its Corporate Social Responsibility. A forgotten poster from last year's election. And next to it – 'Aaraam Highway Dhaba – 5km ahead.' A Call Centre night shift zipped past us on a Qualis.

"Take a left here," she urged me.

I turned onto a service lane and kept driving straight. A stray dog gave us a noisy losing chase.

"Do you want to stop here?" She looked at me. *I looked back at Myrah.*

I hit the brakes. We screeched to a stop. I looked around. There was nothing. Only darkness. *Myrah relished her late night drives with Rishabh on the streets of Guwahati. She had told me.*

"God, I want you so much!" She breathed into my ears and passed her arms across my neck. I felt alive. *I had lost my life to her once. I couldn't lose it again. I was so going to conquer Myrah!*

Pankaj Bhattacharyya

She pushed her seat back. And raising her arms, said, "Just come over!" I did. I was on top of her, my right arm limp to one side, my left arm shaking on the other.

She closed her arms across my back. I felt like I was drowning. Breathless. Claustrophobic. *Myrah was seizing me once again.*

She ran her hand through my hair and rested it on my nape. She looked into my eyes. The car exploded with her lusty laughter. I felt her quaking under me. She was choking on her own laugh. Then she took a long deep noisy breath, like a crepitating asthmatic wheeze. Then the laughter again. "Oh, scientist! I've never had one of your kind before." *Myrah was mocking me, challenging me.* And then she said, the seriousness on her face like a sudden powerful interruption, "This is going to cost you money okay? But we can sort that out after. I'm an expensive birthday treat!"

It was going to cost me money? Who was I with? What was with this world? I looked at her. There was no mistaking. *She was Myrah!*

I passed my hands around her neck.

"Come baby," she gurgled.

My hands squeezed her neck.

"Oh, you like it dirty, don't you? Is this how you treat your wife?" She moaned, satisfactorily amused, stoking my adventurous spirit, and totally in control.

I kept squeezing. Hard, yet smooth.

"Hey, you're hurting me, dude!" She was struggling for breath. There was panic on her face and confusion in her eyes. I kept looking at her. The sight brought me much joy. Everything was falling into place.

Her arms started to flay violently. She slapped the back of my head. She fought to turn me over and free her legs, but under my weight, she only managed inconsequential throbs. She desperately reached to paw my eyes, and as I easily lifted my head beyond her reach, her finger nails scratched my cheek. Releasing one hand, I slapped her hard across her face. She grunted. My hand found her neck urgently again.

I tightened my squeeze.

She was crying. She couldn't make a sound. Her eyes fell wide open, frozen in horror. Finally, I was taking it to its end. I was in control.

I watched her face turn a strange reddish purple. A crowd cheered me abruptly, "Go man, Go!" They screamed. I squeezed harder. Harder. I felt her body convulse in powerful jerks. I smelt urine. Then feaces. *Myrah was disintegrating. Myrah was falling apart.* I was going to win.

I kept squeezing. And suddenly there was no resistance. Only peace. The air in the car came to a standstill. Somewhere in the night, a dog barked. A truck sped away on the highway.

I opened the door and struggled out. She didn't move. Stepping away from the car, I screamed at the sky. A gorgeous full moon was just stepping out from behind heavy clouds. It was the kind of night when one died and found rebirth. I screamed again. There was no one to hear me. I felt sick. Squatting by one side of the road, I threw up in fits. Emptying myself. Leaving myself hollow. Making room within.

I started walking. I was on the highway, walking against the rare oncoming vehicle. My legs carried me surely and strongly. I started running. I indeed ran very fast. Faster than the wind that caressed my face. Faster than any marauding thought that could ever hunt me down.

———

When I reached home, I went straight to my computer. Opening the document I'd been writing, I replaced every Myrah in the text with Q. It didn't take me a minute. Such is the power of technology. Took me a while though to rewrite bits around it.

And then I put in these last couple of pages where Myrah remained. For I could never really kill her. I had to live with her. Unless, of course, I took this tale to its only logical conclusion.

Then I slept peacefully.

* * * * *

By the time I woke up, Jagat's extra-sweet, extra-milky morning tea had long gone cold. It occurred to me to report the hole in the mosquito net to him but the prospect of the next occupant of that room in the Guest House suffering a similar mosquitoed night was too inviting to resist.

Walking to the window, I pulled the drapes apart. The Khonsa morning was just like its night. Grey. The window panes in front of me were sweating. I stretched and yawned. I drew the curtains closed again. I made to reach for my watch on the bedside table but stopped abruptly. No, I didn't want to know the time. Open next to the watch was the diary entry I was writing the previous night. I shut it. There was nothing more to record.

I sat down at one edge of the bed.

It did not seem like an outrageously important moment after all. I had pictured myself shaving, showering and dressing for it. But suddenly, all that seemed quite meaningless. As I laid out the contents of my red toilet bag on the bed, I was quite without emotion. Inspecting my inventory with professional intent, I was pleased. I had prepared well, despite the rush.

Tightening the tourniquet over my left arm made the blood vessels in my forearm swell up. I selected one and slipped the intravenous needle in with my right hand. I started the IV line and watched the Ringers Lactate flow.

With the right hand I picked the first of the three loaded syringes. Piercing the tubing of the IV line with the needle, I pushed the plunger down to deliver its contents into my life. It was the general anaesthetic.

The other syringes contained the neurotoxin and the cardiac poison. If medical science gave you skills to save lives, it also taught you the smoothest way to end your own.

* *